Beach House
Memories

Beach House Memories

Mary Alice Monroe

GALLERY BOOKS

NEW YORK   LONDON   TORONTO   SYDNEY   NEW DELHI

G

Gallery Books
A Division of Simon & Schuster, Inc.
1230 Avenue of the Americas
New York, NY 10020

Excerpt from *Saving Sea Turtles* by James R. Spotila reprinted by permission of The Johns Hopkins University Press.

First Gallery Books hardcover edition May 2012

GALLERY BOOKS and colophon are registered trademarks of Simon & Schuster, Inc.

For information about special discounts for bulk purchases, please contact Simon & Schuster Special Sales at 1-866-506-1949 or business@simonandschuster.com.

The Simon & Schuster Speakers Bureau can bring authors to your live event. For more information or to book an event contact the Simon & Schuster Speakers Bureau at 1-866-248-3049 or visit our website at www.simonspeakers.com.

Designed by Julie Schroeder

Manufactured in the United States of America

1   3   5   7   9   10   8   6   4   2

Library of Congress Cataloging-in-Publication Data
Monroe, Mary Alice.
Beach house memories / Mary Alice Monroe. — 1st Gallery Books hardcover ed.
p.   cm.
1. Self-realization in women—Fiction.   2. Marriage—Fiction.
3. South Carolina—Fiction.   I. Title.
PS3563.O529B44   2012
813'.54—dc23   2012004099

ISBN 978-1-4391-7066-3
ISBN 978-1-4391-7104-2 (ebook)

This book is dedicated to Marguerite,
my dear sister and brilliant muse.

Acknowledgments

I've been infatuated with sea turtles for a very long time. Over the years, many people have acted as my teacher, colleague, and friend. Thank you to all who helped make this book a reality.

First I'd like to thank my editor, Lauren McKenna, for her luminous instincts and guidance. Thank you, Lauren, for believing in this story and my talent 'til the eleventh hour. To Louise Burke for her firm and steady hand of support for each book and who makes me feel like part of the Gallery family, and to Jean Anne Rose and Ayelet Gruenspecht for their faith and for sustaining the PR, Alexandra Lewis, and the entire staff at Gallery Books for their amazing support.

Heartfelt thanks to my glorious agents: Kimberly Whalen, for reading the book and giving her invaluable insights, and especially for her continual support and cheerleading. And to Robert Gottlieb, for always being at my side with his incomparable advice and for memorable meals when I come to New York. Thank you also to Claire Roberts, Jessica Olivio, Adrienne Lombardo, and Alex Slater at Trident Media Group. I'm also grateful to my film agent, Joe Veltre at Gersh.

I'm thankful to everyone at Brilliance Audio for the fabulous audiobooks and for granting me the joy and privilege of narrating my books. A special nod to Sheryl Zajechowski, Laura Grafton, and Mark Pereira. I continue to bask in the joy of my friendship with Eileen and Bob Hutton and rely on their wisdom and smiles.

My love and thanks to Marguerite Martino for her consistent stream of inspiration from the first and for her invaluable critiques. Coffee in the morning with her starts my workday. For editing the manuscript with an eye to accuracy for all things turtles and history, I am indebted—again—to my esteemed friends Sally Murphy and Mary Pringle. A special thank-you to my island neighbor, Mickey Williams, for his stories of growing up on Isle of Palms back in the day, to Leah Greenberg for talking out plots and plans, and to Jennifer Pinsak Penegar, for the gorgeous patchwork shawl that kept me warm while writing and is in the book. And love and thanks to my writer friends Dorothea Benton Frank, Patti Callahan Henry, and Jane Green for their support.

For years of education and camaraderie on the beaches, and for being part of our turtle family, I thank:

My fellow Isle of Palms/Sullivan's Island Turtle Team members: Mary Pringle, Barbara Bergwerf, Tee Johannes, Bev Ballow, Barbara Gobian, Linda Rumph, Grace and Glen Rhodes, Nancy Hauser, Kathey O'Connor; and the support staff: Ben Bergwerf, Peyre Pringle, and Nicholas Johannes. Thanks too, Nicholas, for an education on airplanes. And to all my fellow turtle team volunteers, too many to name. But you know who you are.

My friends at the South Carolina Aquarium. I am especially grateful for the support of Kevin Mills, Jason Crichton, Rachel Kalisperis, Kelly Thorvalson, Shane Boylan, Jack Higgins, Adrian Cain, Kevin Campworth, Josh Kohl, Keisha Legerton, Whit McMillan, Kate Dittloff, and all the staff who contribute daily to support the sea turtles and all marine life in countless ways and with such enthusiasm. I am honored to serve with my fellow board members and grateful for the generous giving of their time and support for our shared mission: Ken Seeger, Sheila Hodges, Kate Jerome, Bruce Hecker, J. Donald Higgins, Bryson Geer, Jonathan Zucker, Todd Abedon, Dixon Woodward, Will Albrecht, Kenneth Bauer, Charles Claus, L. John Clark, John Danahy, Randall Goldman, Erika Harrison, Virginia Hermann, Reba Huge, Wilbur E. Johnson, H. D. Larabee, Laura Davies Mateo, Thompson Penney, David Rivers, H. Del Schutte, Bryan Sherbacow, David L Simmons, John L. Simpkins, Catherine Smith, Stephanie Smith-Phillips, John Swink, Lawrence O. Thompson, Teddy Turner, C. Ray Wrenn, Tomi G. Youngblood, David Tigges. And Emeritus: Pat Conroy, James Ferguson, William Finn, Peatsy Hollings, Hilton C. Smith Jr., Robert R. Macdonald, Layton McCurdy, Robert E. McNair, Richard W. Riley, Victor Samra Jr., Theodore S. Stern, M. William Youngblood, and Jerry Zucker.

My friends at the South Carolina Department of Natural Resources, I thank so many who have walked the beaches with me and provided me with an education on sea turtles, especially DuBose Griffin, Charlotte Hope, Kelly Sloan, and Al Segars.

My fellow board members of the Leatherback Trust in Playa Grande, Costa Rica. Sincere thanks to James Spotila, Frank Paladino, Maggie Kruesi, Harold Avery, Randall Arauz, Robert Raymar, David Wright, George Shillinger, Ray Lowe, Kristin Reed, Tom Elzey, John Spotila, Mario Boza, Pilar Santidrián Tomillo, and the hardworking staff, interns, and volunteers dedicated to preserving the Pacific Leatherback and all sea turtles.

I offer a heartfelt nod of thanks and respect to the memory of Florence Johnston, an original turtle lady in South Carolina, who graced me with numerous interviews before her passing. She was an inspiration. Thank you also to Meg Hoyle at Learning Through Loggerheads, and to another grande dame of the sea turtle world, Jean Beasley and her dedicated staff of volunteers at the Karen Beasley Sea Turtle Hospital in Topsail, North Carolina, and to David Owens at the College of Charleston.

On the home front, I offer thanks and affection to my support staff: Angela May, Buzzy Porter, and Lisa Minnick. As with all my novels, I close with my love and gratitude to those who continually teach me the soul of my story: Markus; Claire, John, Jack, Teddy, and Delancey; Gretta and Zack.

I've taken some liberty in dates in the manuscript for the sake of story. I thank all those who checked the facts of my manuscript. All sins of omission and commission herein are mine.

Finally, I send my sincere thanks to all the people worldwide who have worked tirelessly, volunteered, and made donations— all with great faith and hope for the survival of sea turtles.

Those who come together to walk a turtle beach, to excavate a sea turtle nest to save some hatchlings, to work to stop fishing practices that kill turtles are part of a family. The very act of doing something for the turtles is an expression of faith in something larger than oneself. The reason that I have hope is that there is a large family of people who all do their part to save turtles for one more day.

—JAMES R. SPOTILA,
Saving Sea Turtles

*Beach House
Memories*

One

Lovie Rutledge believed memories were like the tides. Sometimes they rushed in with a pounding roar to topple you
over. At other times they gently washed over you, lulling you to
complacency and then tugging you back to halcyon days that,
with the passing of years, seemed ever sweeter.

She seemed to spend more time with her memories of late,
especially on evenings such as this one when the red sun lazily
descended over the Intracoastal Waterway, and the jeweled tones
of the sky deepened. From the trees, the pensive cries of birds
called all to roost. Lovie sat on the windward porch, still and
silent, attuned to the moody hour. Sunset was her favorite time
of the day, an introspective hour when the sky brought down the
curtain on what she knew were her final days.

Lovie leaned her snowy white head against her chair, gave a
slight push with her foot, and sighed as she rocked rhythmically
back and forth, like the waves slapping against the shore. A small
smile of relief eased across her face.

Peace at last, she thought.

The wailing winds of the hurricane that had blown across
her small island a week earlier had left in their wake the incessant

guttural roar of chain saws. The Isle of Palms had been pummeled, as had most of the South Carolina coast. It would take months to clean up. As though in apology, Mother Nature graced the island with crisp after-storm breezes that spurred the populace to a frenzy of repairs. Lovie was glad for the activity—the bellowing of voices, honking of horns, laughter of children, whoops from the beach, high-pitched calls of greeting as families returned home from evacuation. She heard in the clamor the shared exuberance of hope.

And yet, Lovie longed for the hush and lull of pace that came at the day's end.

Stop your complaining, old woman, she admonished. You should be grateful that you wake up at all! Birdcall or hammering on wood—whichever! The sounds of life around her were welcome—especially now as death hovered like a thief, waiting for its opportunity to snatch away her last breath.

Lovie sank deeper into the cushion and let her tired body ease as she stared out again at a smattering of yellow flowers that had managed to cling to the vines during the storm, and beyond them, the sea. The Atlantic Ocean breathed like a beast snoring serenely in the distance. The gentle rolling water cloaked the secrets it held, while the earth revealed all. Ah, but she wasn't fooled by her old friend.

I thought you were going to take my house with this last storm— and me along with it, she thought with a faint chuckle. *Well, I thank you for leaving us be. At least for a little while longer.* She sighed and kicked off again with her foot. *I've known you too long and too well not to be wise to your mercurial nature. You appear so gentle and peaceful tonight. But Lord help the fool who ignores you.*

Lovie suddenly coiled in a spasm of coughing that racked her frame, so thin now she could be mistaken for a child. When at last the fit subsided, she bent forward, clasping the arms of the chair, gasping for air.

"Mama! Are you okay?"

Lovie turned her head to see Cara's worried face inches from her own. She felt Cara's larger hand tighten over hers in a reassuring squeeze. *Dear, sweet, daughter,* she thought as her pale blue eyes found refuge in Cara's dark brown ones. There were crow's-feet at the corners, adding maturity to the wide-eyed worry. Cara had been dismayed at turning forty, crying that her youth was over and now she was on the downhill slope. Lovie knew better. Cara was still so young! So strong and confident.

Lovie felt the panic that always came with the coughing spells loosen its grip. Gradually her breath came more easily. She nodded weakly.

Cara's eyes narrowed, quickly checking for signs that Lovie needed oxygen or a dose of pain medication. "Mama, it's getting chilly. Let's go inside."

Lovie didn't have the breath to answer, but she weakly shook her head.

Cara hesitated, then with a *tsk* of mild frustration, she didn't force the issue, as she might have just months earlier.

Lovie leaned back again in her chair. Staring at her from the settee across the room was a large calico cat. The cat had mysteriously appeared after the hurricane, lost and mewling piteously. Cara fed her daily, cleaned up after her, and petted her long fur whenever she passed. Cara called the cat the Uninvited Guest and pretended not to care one way or the other about her. But Lovie could tell she was secretly pleased the cat had decided to stay. It was Cara's first pet.

Cara was rather like that cat, Lovie thought with some amusement. The previous May, Lovie had asked her only daughter to come home for a visit. She hadn't thought Cara would come. They'd been estranged for some twenty years. Cara was always too busy, too involved in her career to find time to come back to Charleston. If Lovie was honest with herself—and this late in life, why be anything but honest?—she had to acknowledge that Cara just plain didn't want to return. She preferred the crispness of the North in all its forms. Lovie had prayed that she and her headstrong daughter could patch up their differences before she died. She took a long breath and exhaled slowly, feeling the weariness of her years. How did one reconcile after so long a time? It was in faith that she'd written, and in a twist of fate, Cara had returned.

Cara had been laid off from her high-powered job at an advertising agency in Chicago. She'd arrived at Lovie's door at the onset of summer, feeling lost and restless, uncharacteristically adrift. She'd stayed the summer on Isle of Palms, ostensibly to take care of her mother. And yet, over the past months, Cara, like the lost cat, had been cared for, stroked, needed. The summer had made Cara wiser and more content—not so quick to chase the mouse.

And in the process, she'd rediscovered her mother's love. This had been the answer to Lovie's prayers.

It was autumn now, however, and like the season's end, Lovie's strength was ebbing with the receding tide. She had terminal cancer, and both she and Cara knew that soon the Lord would call her home.

"Okay, Mama," Cara conceded, patting Lovie's hand. "We'll sit out here a little longer. I know you hate to miss a sunset. Would you like a cup of tea? I'll make you one," she went on, not waiting for an answer.

Lovie didn't want tea just now, but Cara needed something to do. Though they didn't say the words often, Lovie knew that Cara expressed her love with action. Cara rose effortlessly from the chair, a move Lovie could hardly recall being able to make.

Cara was strikingly good-looking, tall and slender with glossy dark hair she usually wore pulled back in a carefree ponytail. But tonight was cooler and the humidity low so she let it fall unkempt to her shoulders. It swayed in rhythm with the few long strides it took her to cross the wooden porch.

Lovie's gaze swept across the porch of her beloved beach house that was showing signs of age. Time . . . it passed so quickly! Where did all the years go? How many summers had this dear house survived? How many hurricanes? Two white wooden rocking chairs sat side by side where mother and daughter sat most nights to enjoy the Lowcountry sunset. The recent category one hurricane had destroyed her pergola, and the new screens Cara had just installed hung in tattered shreds, waving uselessly in the offshore breezes. She heard the teasing hum of a mosquito in her ear.

Her little house on Ocean Boulevard had always been a place of refuge for Lovie, a sanctuary through good times and bad, ever since childhood. In the twilight, the quaint and tidy lines of her 1930s beach cottage appeared part of the indigenous landscape beside the tall palms, the raucous wildflowers, and the clumps of sea oats on the dunes. From her seat on the porch, she could see straight out to the Atlantic Ocean without the obstruction of one of those enormous houses that bordered the island's coastline. It was the same view she'd always had, all these many years. When the wind gusted, it rippled across the tall, soft grass like rosy waves and carried her back to happier days when the island was a remote outpost.

Lovie's parents had given the modest prewar cottage to her when she'd married, and she, in turn, would leave it to her daughter. Her house on Tradd Street in Charleston with the heirloom furniture and silver she had already handed down to her son, Palmer. Once upon a time she'd loved that house with a grand passion, yet never as steadfastly as she'd loved Primrose Cottage. She'd created wonderful memories here. The best . . .

But her days were fading as quickly and surely as the sun. In these final precious moments, Lovie sought to divest herself of the encumbrances that held her to the present, tugging at her attention, diverting her from the path her heart wanted to follow.

As the sun lowered in the west and purpling sea met the horizon to blend into one vast vista, Lovie felt the line between the past and the present blur as well. She allowed her thoughts to turn, as they often did at this moody hour, to Russell Bennett.

He was waiting for her. Somewhere out in the vast purpling expanse of water, Russell was biding his time. She sensed this with every fiber in her being. Russell had been the love of her life. She'd lived long enough to say so, though one summer was all they'd had. In retrospect, with the passage of time and grace, Lovie understood that she'd been pulled toward her fate as surely as the tides were pulled by the moon.

She felt it now. She could sense herself slipping again in the insistent undertow of the past, calling her back. There was no use fighting it. It was so easy to simply close her eyes.

And relinquish.

Two

⁓

June 1, 1974

Lovie was thirty-eight years of age. "In her prime," her mother had declared. Her mama liked pat phrases. She spoke them with authority, as though she'd just made up the clever phrases herself. No matter how described, it was true that Lovie's looks had at last blossomed from the sweetness of her youth into a more mature beauty. Or as her mother had pronounced, "From a sweet blossom to a fine example of the flower of Southern womanhood."

Lovie could smile at that description now, but at the time it had filled her with wonder and even pride. She was the wife of a successful Charleston businessman, the mother of two beautiful children, and the mistress of a beautiful house in the golden area of Charleston known to the locals as South of Broad.

Lovie's life circled around her husband, her children, her home, her church, and the endless, myriad responsibilities and obligations each entailed. She didn't complain. Rather, she gave of herself with an open heart and mind, to her fullest. She'd been raised in a proper Southern household and appreciated the importance placed on a well-run home. Her mama had told her again and again that "the woman was at the heart of every home."

Yet, at the onset of every summer, Lovie crossed off the days on the calendar, feeling a growing desperation to shed the demands and expectations of her role in the city and run, feet bare and hair streaming, to her beach house.

And now, at last, she was ready to go. Lovie slammed the hatchback of her Buick station wagon and slapped the dust off her hands with satisfaction. Her final social duty of the season was a dinner party for Stratton's business tonight. Tomorrow she would escape across the Cooper River Bridge on a beeline to the Isle of Palms.

"I'm all packed," she said. "We're off to the beach house first thing tomorrow morning."

"That'd best be everything, Miz Lovie, 'cause I don't think you can squeeze one more thing in," Vivian said. She stood beside Lovie with her arms crossed, shaking her head in doubt as she surveyed the big car with its faux wood siding. "That car look like a suitcase bulgin' at the seams."

Vivian Manigault had been employed as the Rutledge maid since Lovie first set up house in Charleston as a young mother fifteen years earlier. Vivian's primary task was to mind the two Rutledge children, Palmer and Cara, but she also tidied the house, did some laundry, prepared lunch, and, when Lovie was out, started the occasional dinner. For this she was paid a standard wage, had weekends off, and earned an extra fee for working evenings, such as tonight's party. But Lovie felt there was no amount of money that could equal Vivian's worth as a trusted ally.

"How're you gonna squeeze Palmer and Cara in that car?" Vivian continued. "Better not feed 'em too much tonight."

Lovie chuckled. "Every summer I tell myself that I don't need to cram everything in the day I leave. That if I need something I can always just drive back to the city to pick it up from the house. But once I'm at the beach house, it's like I'm a million miles away. I can't bear to leave. So I can't really blame the children for packing everything they own." Her gaze lifted to sweep across the backyard. "Where are those two? They should be home by now for dinner."

"Palmer's back. That boy came saunterin' in an hour ago smelling like one of those boars he's so fond of huntin'.'"

"And Cara?"

"She'll be here."

Lovie caught the quick defense in Vivian's voice. There was a bond between those two that Lovie was sometimes a little jealous of. "Well, she'd better. She knows I have an important dinner party tonight. And I'll be waking her early in the morning."

"Yes'm. But that's *tomorrow*. Tonight you best be watchin' the clock. Your guests will be here 'fore you know it. You don't want to be greetin' them in your work clothes." Vivian reached up to adjust her own pristine starched white collar.

Lovie thought Vivian looked positively regal in her formal gray uniform with the crisp white facing at the collar and cuffs. Tall and as slender as a reed, Vivian liked to say she had the bones of a sparrow and the strength of an eagle. She also had the binocular vision of an eagle, Lovie thought. Nothing happened in the Rutledge household that Vivian didn't know about.

Lovie looked down at her jeans and the frayed white long-sleeved man's shirt rolled up along her slender arms. Both were streaked with dirt from all the packing. She tugged off the cotton scarf from her head and shook out her hair as she mentally switched gears.

"Lord, it *is* getting late. You know how I hate to stop before I finish something. I'm going right up to change. Could you—"

She was interrupted by a short blast from a car horn.

"Yoo-hoo! I'm here at last!"

Turning, she saw her mother's pale blue Cadillac convertible roll into the driveway. Lovie released a short puff of anticipation as she took off across the garden to the car. She arrived as her mother climbed from the white leather seats. Diana Simmons, Dee Dee to most, appeared as she usually did, trim and neatly dressed. Today she wore a pale beige linen dress with a strand of pearls at the neck and beige sling-back pumps. Not a blond hair was out of place, styled in the popular bouffant style, tucked behind pearl-studded ears. Dee Dee was still a pretty woman. Lovie had inherited her large blue eyes and petite Southern belle good looks. The singular difference between them was in expression—Lovie's face was guileless and welcoming, while Dee Dee's appeared strained and her eyes narrowed in perpetual scrutiny.

"I brought the flowers," Dee Dee called out. She opened the back door of her enormous car and began pulling out a cardboard box holding a large silver urn overflowing with freshly cut flowers in an array of spring colors.

Lovie rushed forward to take hold of the box. "Mama, that's too heavy. Let me." Vivian was a step behind her to carry the second box, filled with another silver urn of flowers. "They're beautiful!" she exclaimed.

"They are, aren't they," Dee Dee replied, allowing Lovie to take the box. She reached out to adjust a few blossoms. "It's a vile day. In this heat I waited till the very last minute to cut and arrange them. Let's get them out of this sun. And I want to see your table."

They made their way single file along the narrow brick walkway through the walled garden. Lovie shared her mother's love of gardening and had broken several nails bringing the ancient flower beds back to life. The garden had been in a shambles when she and Stratton had bought the wide-porch Georgian Revival house shortly after they were married. The three women passed neatly bordered beds of spring flowers blooming in full force.

Breathing in, Lovie could smell the freshly mowed green grass and the blooming yellow jessamine vines.

"I hope it cools down enough that I can serve drinks in the garden," Lovie said. "It's so beautiful this time of year. Look, the magnolia is blooming!"

"My dear, it's hotter'n hades! Maybe *after*-dinner drinks . . ."

Lovie imagined guests sweltering in suits and silks. "I suppose so . . ."

"Don't frown, dear. It'll cause lines in your face. I hear it's supposed to cool down after sunset. I should think . . . Lovie!" her mother suddenly exclaimed. "You best stop and see this!"

Lovie stopped abruptly and turned to allow her gaze to follow her mother's outstretched finger. She spotted a child scooting along the top edge of the high garden wall. It was a girl. As she reached their property, she dangerously reached far out to grab hold of a tree branch and then swing down to the ground with the finesse of a circus acrobat, landing squarely on her feet. She nonchalantly swiped the dirt from her hands on her torn blue jeans, then, looking up, her dark eyes rounded at seeing Lovie and Dee Dee staring at her a few feet away.

"Uh, hey, Mama, Grandmama," she called out, wiping the thick shock of dark brown bangs back from her face, leaving a streak of dirt across her forehead in the process. She ambled toward them with her long arms swinging at her sides. Her T-shirt was splattered with dirt and her coltish legs were scraped through the torn knees of her pants.

"Caretta Rutledge!" Lovie called out sharply in surprise. "What are you doing running along the garden walls like that? You could fall and break your neck!"

"Aw, Mama, no I won't. It's a shortcut."

Lovie was astonished. "A *shortcut*? You mean you do this all the time? Vivian, did you know about this?"

Vivian twisted her mouth in a wry smile. "Let's just say I'm not surprised."

"Palmer taught me," Cara added, as though that made everything all right.

"You mean Palmer runs the walls, too?"

"Why, sure. Everybody does it."

Lovie closed her mouth to halt the laugh bubbling in her throat. Though she'd never admit it to her children, running around the neighborhood via garden walls was quite resourceful. Most of the gardens were interconnected by walls. It would, indeed, be a shortcut.

Dee Dee spoke in an admonishing tone. "Now, Cara, you know that's very dangerous. Any one of those old walls could crumble at any time. And you look like a river rat, scuttling the walls like that. It's . . . it's just not ladylike."

"No, ma'am," Cara mumbled.

"When I think of you falling . . ." Dee Dee said, pressing her hand to her heart.

"You're not to do it again, hear?" Lovie said firmly.

Cara looked at her feet. "No, ma'am."

"That's settled, then. Now run along upstairs for your bath. I'll be up later. Vivian's going to bring your dinner on a tray. I have guests tonight." Seeing Cara's slump-shouldered walk, Lovie added, "There's a special treat for dessert."

"What is it?" Cara asked, bobbing her head up. She pressed her dirty palms together as in prayer. "Some of that chocolate cake you made? Please, please, please?"

Lovie saw the sparkle in her daughter's eyes and felt the glow of it in her heart. Then her eyes narrowed. "Cara, where are your glasses?"

Cara's smile dropped as she mulishly kicked a pebble on the slate walkway. "Oh, I took them off. Just for a little while."

"The doctor said you have to wear them all day or you won't get used to them."

"Aw, Mama, they keep getting in my way. Besides, school's over. I'm on vacation. What do I need them for?"

"Maybe to see where you're going when you run along a stone fence?"

"I hate them," Cara blurted. "I look like such a dork."

Lovie's heart lurched for the little girl, and were it not for the box of flowers she was carrying she would have bent to wrap her arms around her daughter. "You look beautiful to me," she said. "Underneath all that dirt. Go on, now. Run along to your bath. And give your hair a good washing. Lord only knows what's tangled in there. And I don't want you sneaking downstairs during my dinner party, hear?"

"Yes, ma'am," Cara called back as she took off toward the house like a gazelle.

"Lord help me, what am I going to do with that child? She's such a tomboy," Lovie said, walking toward the house.

"A firmer hand, perhaps?" Dee Dee suggested. "I've said it before, but you don't pay me mind. You allow that girl to run around like a boy."

From behind, Lovie heard Vivian mutter, "She just a girl that knows her mind."

"For pity's sake, Mama. The child's only ten years old," Lovie said.

"That's plenty old enough for her to learn to mind her manners. Lovie, dear, as your mother, I can tell you that you need to rein her in some, offer her more guidance."

Lovie's cheeks flushed. Her mother was banging the belle drum again, and any insult against Cara felt like an insult against her mothering skills. She rushed to defend her daughter. "You let me play wild when I was a girl."

"Not in town. Only at the beach house. That's the proper place for such behavior. Besides, I could always count on you to be a lady in public. Cara's another thing altogether. Climbing trees and fences . . ."

"She's just high-spirited."

"Headstrong is more like it. *Too* headstrong. It might've been cute back when she was in pigtails, but it's not any longer. It's high time you rein her in."

"What would you suggest?" she asked tersely.

"Cotillion, perhaps?"

Ah, yes, she thought. Legions of young girls and boys from "good" Charleston families endured hours of schooling on manners and protocol. Lessons on how to sit, stand, and greet were drilled into them along with table manners and ballroom dancing. It was expected, if not de rigueur.

"I've already scheduled Cara to begin junior cotillion in the fall."

"Oh? Well, good," she replied, appeased. "That'll teach her some deportment and etiquette. Girls are getting far too opinionated and outspoken these days. I swanny, I don't know what's happening in the world. Women protesting in the streets . . . burning bras . . . Not in Charleston, I can tell you that!"

"Mama, Cara doesn't even wear a bra yet!"

"You know what I mean."

"Don't worry so much. For all her headstrong ways, Cara is a kind, smart, and sensible girl. I have complete faith in her."

"Be that as it may, she *is* growing up. It might help if she stops hanging around the boys all the time this summer."

"Yes, Mother," Lovie replied, swallowing the annoyance bubbling in her chest. Cara was *her* daughter. She didn't care for her mother's opinions, and she didn't have time to listen to them now. Besides, there was no winning. Nothing would change her mother's mind . . . or her own, for that matter.

Lovie knew in her heart that this was Cara's last summer to be wild and carefree, and she was determined to let her have it. Next season she would change schools, enter junior cotillion, and the subtle shift from childhood to adolescence would begin. She loved her daughter's independent spirit, her sense of adventure, and her courage to speak her mind, sometimes with her dukes up. Lovie couldn't remember ever being that strong. Her mother had drummed into her head how a proper lady did not speak out of turn or voice her opinions too strongly, nor should she toot her own horn. Rather, she should allow her home and family to reflect her accomplishments. Likewise, a woman should never seek to overshadow her husband but put her efforts into helping him shine.

Yet as a young girl at the beach house, she was allowed every freedom. She ran wild on the beach, her bare toes digging in the sand and her hair flying behind her. On the waterways, she was Tom Sawyer to her brother's Huck Finn. The beach house had become not only a beloved place but also a symbol of freedom. Only once she reached Cara's age was she firmly, lovingly guided into the responsibilities of her sex. There were days when Lovie longed for that young, outspoken, courageous girl and wondered if she didn't still reside deep within her, waiting for an opportunity to reemerge.

Lovie was determined to give Cara this last summer of childhood.

She led her mother from the walled scented garden into the large, airy kitchen. Old houses could be charming with grand living and dining rooms, but the historic builders gave little thought to the cooks and the maids. The kitchens and third-floor bedrooms, not to mention the back servants' stairs, were cramped and dark. When Lovie and Stratton bought the house in 1960, the kitchen was insignificant and the appliances were antique. Lovie had shocked her mother by ripping out the butler's pantry and a small sitting room to create the open, sunny kitchen that was the heart of her home.

The caterer had taken command of the space and scowled at the intrusion of boxes on *his* counters. The delicious scents of roasting meat and garlic filled the room, and steam was rising from pots on the stove. Lovie and Dee Dee lifted the urns from the boxes and carried the flowers directly to the dining room, setting one on each end of the long stretch of polished mahogany. Dee Dee stepped back, crossed her slender arms, and surveyed the dining table. Lovie swallowed her sudden nervousness. Lovie handled her dinner parties with the efficient calm of a seasoned hostess. Her husband's import-export business often brought important guests to the Holy City, and this year alone she'd hosted six parties, and it was only May. And yet her mother still had the power to make her stomach clench.

"You know I'm a perfectionist," Dee Dee began, circling the table. She reached out, grasping a crystal champagne glass and holding it up to the light with her pink-nailed hand. "Spots."

Lovie paled, mortified.

"They'll all need to be wiped with a linen cloth," Dee Dee added with hauteur.

Lovie caught the cloying scent of the flowers as she signaled to the uniformed waiter in the pantry. He hurried to her side, eyes alert as Lovie gave him instructions. Dee Dee moved from one place setting to the next, reaching out to adjust a fork, rearrange a rose in the vase, straighten a place card.

"It's the details that matter," Dee Dee told her daughter with a hint of scold in her voice.

"I'm well aware of that, Mother. But with the packing, and school finishing up, and Palmer's sports, I've been very busy."

"So has your husband," Dee Dee admonished. "He expects you to show his home at its best at these affairs."

"It's not *his* home, Mama. It's *our* home."

Dee Dee tsked with impatience. "It's no good getting caught up in semantics."

"I'm sorry. I'm just so tired of entertaining. Stratton sets these dates without any idea how much work each party is."

"But Cara, dear, why should he? Isn't that your duty? You are Stratton's wife, the mother of his children. He's the breadwinner, and if you don't mind my saying so, he's provided you with a very nice lifestyle. It's up to you to create a beautiful home and to run it smoothly. To make your dinner parties appear effortless. And," she added pointedly, "to raise your children to be a gentleman and a *lady*."

Lovie pinched her lips tight. Her mother was a social butter-fly. She'd spent most of her adult life in their large historic home in Aiken with beautiful grounds and meticulous gardens. When Michael Simmons died suddenly, Dee Dee surprised everyone by selling her beautiful house at the peak of the market for a terrific profit. She promptly moved herself and her favorite furniture and possessions to an extremely choice condominium on East Bay in Charleston overlooking the harbor. She told all her friends with a sigh of loneliness that she'd needed to be near her daughter, now that she was a widow. Before long, Dee Dee was ensconced in a new group of friends in her ladies' clubs, tennis, theater, and church events. Lovie and the children rarely had visits from her. The truth was, Dee Dee had no idea of all the pressure and strain Stratton's business demanded of Lovie.

Nor, sadly, did her husband. Stratton's lack of appreciation stole the shine from her accomplishments. If the party appeared effortless, he, too, thought it was just that. Effortless.

"Well, it is a beautiful table, my dear," Dee Dee said. "You have outdone yourself."

Lovie caught the glint of envy flash in Dee Dee's eyes. The Simmonses were a proud family whose ancestors wore gray in the Great War, but the family did not hail from Charleston. By contrast, the Rutledges were an old and proud Charleston family. The pedigree opened doors Dee Dee's wealth could never crack. Dee Dee had been thrilled with Lovie's match. The success of her daughter's marriage was her success.

Lovie had come to her marriage with a substantial inheritance, enough for the down payment on their house and to help fund Stratton's import-export company. Still, they had to be frugal. Lovie's gaze swept the room as she recalled the years she'd spent working on the poor, neglected house. She did all her own decorating, sewed by hand the yards of fabric and fringe for curtains, painted and stenciled walls. Room by room, she'd brought this neglected old house back to its former glory. She'd given the task ten years of her life, and it would, she knew, never be finished. These old houses always had some task needing doing.

The waiter finished polishing and stepped back. "Ma'am?" he asked.

Lovie shook away her reverie to step forward and cast a final, proprietary glance over the twelve place settings. The Chippendale dining chairs lined up evenly, the crystal gleamed, the silver shone, and the salt cellars were filled. Tall white candles awaited her signal to be lit.

"Much better," she said. "Thank you."

Dee Dee tapped her lips. "Except, of course, you know Stratton is going to say something about those place mats. He prefers the white damask tablecloth. Well, it's too late to change now. Speaking of late, shouldn't you go upstairs and change?" She leaned closer to deliver a chaste kiss on Lovie's cheek. "I'll be on my way. Good luck tonight. And have a good time at the beach house."

"You won't come by this summer?"

"We'll see," Dee Dee replied with a wave as she strolled from the room.

Lovie doubted her mother would come. She always managed

to create one excuse or another. She'd never enjoyed the beach house. It was her father who had looked forward to their summer vacations at the sea with the same relish she did.

With a last, sweeping look at her table, Lovie hurried up the front stairs.

A short while later, Lovie stepped from her marble bathroom wearing a full slip, hair and makeup in place. She opened the French doors that overlooked her garden. It would be a perfect night for a party, she told herself. The heat would fade with the sun. They'd have drinks in the garden. Closing her eyes, Lovie could smell her beloved magnolia blooms. Their broad, glossy leaves would look striking in the candlelight. She stood for a moment and allowed the sweet-scented breeze to dry her freshly showered, perfumed skin.

"You're letting all the air-conditioning out!" Stratton strode briskly into the room, startling her.

Lovie promptly closed the doors and turned to see that he had already changed into a fresh, crisply ironed shirt.

"When did you get home?"

"While you were in the shower." He scowled, struggling with his gold cuff link. "Damned things, I don't know why I bother."

She came directly to his side and brushed away his hand. He had the fresh soapy scent of his shower, yet she could feel his tension radiate from his body into her own. It was unusual for Stratton to be nervous for a dinner, signaling to her the party's importance. Stratton was a social being. He was a good conversationalist—smart, witty, and quick with that stinging re-tort that could make a group laugh, often at someone's expense. Sometimes she envied his ability to never meet a stranger.

As for Lovie, on a soft night like this, she'd rather sit in her big wicker chair in the garden with a book.

"Stand still, Stratton," she said, clasping the thick gold link that bore the Rutledge family crest.

"You're not dressed yet?"

"I just have to slip into my dress. I didn't want to crease the fabric."

"When are the guests due to arrive?"

"Not until seven. I'm hoping the night will cool a bit before we serve dinner."

"You're going to keep the air-conditioning on, aren't you?"

"Of course, if that old thing will make it. I say a prayer every time I turn it on. One of these nights it's going to fail."

"It's got lots of life still in it," he said, offering his pat answer whenever she wanted to replace an appliance.

"There," she said, finishing the second cuff link. "You're all set." She stood back and surveyed the man who had been her husband for fifteen years.

Stratton Rutledge held his shoulders back with the pride of an illustrious history of ancestors. Though he was a hair less than six feet tall, his carriage combined with his booming voice gave him the semblance of someone *big*. At forty-four, he resembled the portrait of his great-grandfather that hung in the dining room. He had the Rutledge thick dark hair and eyes, the broad forehead, and the proud, even arrogant, nose. Only recently had she seen the beginnings of graying at the temples, which Stratton liked because he thought it made him look older and wiser—good for business. The crisp fabric of his starched shirt rustled as he slipped his arms into his suit jacket. Peering into the mirror over her shoulder, he adjusted his collar and tie.

"You look quite handsome in your linen suit," she told him.

"As long as I look prosperous." He tugged his cuffs. His lips turned downward. "I noticed you used those damn flimsy mats for the table."

"I thought it made the room feel somehow lighter. Cooler. The linen is of the finest quality," she hurried to add, trying to deflect his ill humor. She could smell bourbon on his breath already. "Now please, Stratton, let's not fuss about it," she said, heading for the bed where her dress lay in waiting. "I have to hurry if you want me to greet our guests at the door."

She turned her head away from his frown, wondering why he cared about such things. Thoughts of place mats slipped away as she slid into the spring green silk dress she'd purchased on King Street for the dinner. It was so lovely, an extravagant choice—rare for her and one that crippled her budget. But she just couldn't resist it.

"Zip me?"

Stratton obliged, his large hands struggling with the tiny zipper. So close, the bourbon on his breath made her stomach clench. She didn't trust Stratton when he'd been drinking. She felt the constriction of the dress as the zipper hummed up, the fabric cinching her waist and accentuating her full breasts. Turning, her full skirt flared. She caught the gleam in Stratton's eyes and knew he wouldn't complain when he saw the bill.

"You look lovely," he said with appreciation.

"Thank you," she replied, blushing slightly at the rare compliment.

"But it needs something."

She looked abruptly into the mirror over her bureau, checking her reflection. Her blond hair was sleek in a French twist, her peachy skin shone against the lush silk, and the mabe pearl and emerald earrings Stratton had given her for Christmas gleamed at her ears. She didn't think of herself as a great beauty, yet Stratton had always told her she had a sweetness about her that was fresh and unspoiled. What did he think was missing?

Stratton came to stand behind her and his eyes held a spark of amusement. Lovie tilted her head, curious. He lifted his arms, and as he lowered them she felt his crisp linen sleeve against her cheek, smelled the sandalwood in his aftershave, then—in surprise—the coolness of pearls around her neck.

"Oh, Stratton . . ."

The cultured pearls were so large and lustrous—so extravagant—they took her breath away. Her hand shot up to touch them as her mouth opened in a soft gasp of surprise and a softening in her bones. She'd been wrong. Stratton *did* appreciate her efforts!

He finished clasping the necklace and stepped back to survey her appearance.

"Mikimotos," he said, referring to the pearls. "The best of the best. They cost a small fortune, I can tell you."

"They're so large . . ." She turned, her joy bubbling up as she wrapped her arms around his neck to plant a big, exuberant kiss on her husband's lips.

"One look at those babies and Bob Porter will know we're a solid investment."

Lovie's smile wavered as understanding dawned. The pearls were more for show than a reflection of his appreciation for her. Ah, yes, that would be more typical of him.

"It's an important night, Lovie. Very." He held her gaze. "I need to make this deal. Be sure to talk to Porter's wife, make her feel comfortable. Her name's Ginny or Jeanne . . . I'm told she's shy."

"Of course," she replied, slowly lowering her arms. She felt the pressure of her party's success tighten her chest. "I've never let you down before, have I?"

He lowered to kiss her gently on the cheek. "No, you haven't. I'm a lucky man to have you, Lovie."

She smiled and cupped his cheek. "Thank you for the pearls. They really are lovely."

He stepped back, his smile fading while nodding absentmind-edly. His thoughts were already turned to the business he wanted to conduct that evening.

Lovie spritzed her signature Joy perfume on her neck and

wrists. The scent of jasmine and roses filled the room. "Do you think the party will run late?" she asked.

"It shouldn't. Why? Are you tired?"

"A bit, actually. But that's not why I asked. I'd like an early start for the beach tomorrow morning."

"What, tomorrow?"

"Yes, Stratton," she replied with a slight tone of frustration. "I reminded you every day this week, three times yesterday."

"It slipped my mind."

Lovie opened her mouth to ask how that was possible, but closed it again.

"Do we have to leave tomorrow?"

"We've already put it off until after Memorial Day for this party."

"It couldn't be helped. You know how important this deal is." He frowned and put his hands on his hips in thought. When he looked at her again, his face was as hard with resolution as granite. "Lovie, postpone the beach for a week. The Porters will be staying in town for Spoleto. It's a good opportunity to forge a stronger relationship with them. I was thinking we could meet up with them again later in the week for a performance and din-ner. His wife doesn't know anybody in town."

"She's meeting five other couples tonight!" She saw temper flare in his eyes and her stomach clenched. She didn't want to set him off in a foul temper right before the dinner party. Stratton was quick to rise and slow to cool. He'd blame her for any tension that could mar the evening's mood.

"Stratton, it's just that I practically killed myself today get-ting us all packed. I've all the food prepared. The car is ready. It'd be colossal to postpone now." Seeing frustration in his scowl, she added in a conciliatory tone, "The children are so looking forward to their vacation."

"Hell, summer's just beginning! They can wait a few more

days. You're talking about vacation? This is important for my work. It puts the food on the table. And it's not like *you* need a vacation." He rolled his shoulders and said offhandedly, "You're on vacation every day."

Lovie felt her heart wither in her chest. With that one brief aside, he'd utterly diminished her. She fought the urge to rip the pearls from her neck and throw them back at him.

"Oh, yes," she said icily. "That's right. My life is just one jolly vacation."

She turned away to the mirror and applied rose-colored lipstick. She was so hurt and angry her hand shook. Is that how he measured her? All the hours she spent creating and maintaining his home and family, didn't they matter? True, she didn't have a formal career, didn't bring home a paycheck—no woman she knew did. Her mother had always told her that she shouldn't work after she was married. It was demeaning to her husband, implying that he couldn't provide. Yet did her domestic work, her countless hours of volunteering hold so little value in his eyes?

"I didn't mean it that way," Stratton said, his voice muffled as he put a cigarette in his mouth. He bent to light the tip, inhaled, then shook the flame out. Exhaling, he added, "You know I didn't."

Did she? Lovie glanced in the mirror to watch her husband smoking in a distracted manner. *Who was this man?* she wondered. He stood a few feet behind her, though the distance felt much farther. She didn't know him anymore. Worse, she didn't feel anything for him. Though they shared the children, the house, the business, and a whirlwind of business and social engagements, they didn't share any interests or hobbies. She couldn't remember the last time they'd had a good discussion or even shared a joke. Their dialogue was similar to that of a boss and his secretary—confirming dates on a calendar, gathering information, approving purchases.

Still, he was her husband and she felt sure time together at the beach house where they'd had such happy times would bring them closer together again. The months of summer were a relaxed hiatus for the family, a slower time that allowed for bonding. He'd drive to work from the island and return at night for a swim in the ocean with the children. The summer holiday at the beach house was as etched in tradition as Christmas on Tradd Street.

"You can always bring the Porters to the beach," she suggested. "It would be a nice change for them. I'll make barbeque. Won't that be nice?"

"Maybe . . ."

Lovie kept her silence.

"All right, you go ahead," he said summarily. "I'll manage here for a few days and come out later."

He looked her way. "You know, it's not a bad idea to bring the Porters, too. You'll be leaving Vivian, of course?"

"Well . . . she was going to join us at the beach house next week as usual. Then she takes her vacation."

"She'll have to change plans. I'll need someone to look after me while you're gone. Not only for this week, but later in the summer, too. I've got that trip to Europe in July, remember."

She did remember the trip. Six weeks across the Continent—and he did not invite her to accompany him for any leg of the trip.

"Oh. And I may go to Japan."

"*Japan?*"

He nodded in acknowledgment, his eyes gleaming. "That market is exploding now. There are a lot of opportunities. I want to get in there, and Bob Porter is my key to opening that door."

"Stratton, that's wonderful! Imagine, Japan! I'd love to go there with you someday. Could I? It's so exotic."

"Why, sure, honey. Not this trip, of course. This one is exploratory. Later, though. For sure."

Lovie felt a twinge of disappointment but shook it off. No wonder he was so preoccupied and terse tonight. Business always put him on edge. Perhaps she should postpone her trip to the beach house another week, she thought. If she could just help him a little more, he'd realize how valuable she was.

Her guests were due to arrive soon and she couldn't dwell. She'd discuss it with him later. "I'm going to say good night to the children now." She paused, a hand on the doorknob. "Don't you want to come along?"

"I'll come by later. I've got a few things to tend to before dinner. Oh, that reminds me. I'll be going to the club with the boys after dinner."

Lovie felt her face heat with the sudden flare of suspicion that he would not be going to the club with *the boys* but with one particular woman. Gwendolyn Archer was an overprimped, underappreciated wife of a well-known Charleston lawyer. Charleston was a small town, and gossip flew fast.

"Careful there," she said, eyes on the floor. Then, lifting them, she determinedly sought his gaze. "Don't drink too much."

Stratton's eyes blazed and he growled out, "What are you implying? I'll drink as much as I damn well please."

Lovie tightened her lips, feeling slapped. She turned and, without another word, left the room. She held her shoulders tight as she walked down the hall to her children's rooms. She heard the high note of excitement in their laughter, anticipating their trip in the morning. Their innocent joy brought a smile to her face. Tonight, she would do her duty and play hostess at her husband's business dinner. She would be gracious to Jeanne Porter— for that was her name—tidy the house afterward, and dismiss the hired staff. Tomorrow morning she would rise at dawn, tuck her children into the car, bid farewell to her husband.

Then come hell or high water, she would escape to the beach house.

• • •

The red-and-white Buick station wagon made its unhurried way under cloudless skies out of the city of Charleston toward the sea. It drove low to the ground, loaded down with overpacked suitcases, an odd assortment of dishes, books, and paint supplies, brown paper bags filled with groceries, coolers, and chatting away in the backseat, her two children.

Lovie glanced from time to time in the rearview mirror. Palmer was thirteen but apparently not too old to refrain from mercilessly teasing ten-year-old Cara, who was crouched in the corner, back to her brother, obstinately trying to read. Palmer was complaining how she always had her nose stuck in a book. Lovie sighed and held her tongue, choosing her battles. In the city, her children were always testy with each other, quarreling over insignificant things.

Yet they were different at the beach house. There, they lived their lives not by the dictates of a clock but by the whims of the sultry summer sun. They rose when the bright sun's glare shone like a bugle's call, and once awake, the children were free to explore wherever their hearts led them, needing only to show up at Mama's table for dinner. They fell asleep when the sun lowered, exhausted after a day of swimming, surfing, bicycling, fishing, or boating.

Lovie was a different mother at the beach house, too. She was more relaxed, more at peace without the constant stress of her busy schedule. She smiled more, found she could be more patient, and as the children didn't argue as much, she rarely had to scold. Nor did she tell them to keep their feet off the furniture or to mind that they put a coaster under their glasses. At the beach house, there were no fussy antiques. Only the "not so good" antiques and dishes were at the beach, suitable for damp swimsuits, the ever-present sand, and impromptu visitors. The fridge always held a pitcher of sweet tea and the cookie jar was filled with sugar cookies.

Lovie crossed over the narrow Grace Bridge from Charleston to Mount Pleasant and felt the tension ease from her chest with each mile past the Cooper River. Coleman Boulevard was a quiet road that led to the long, narrow Ben Sawyer Boulevard, which traversed a great, yawning expanse of green marsh. There was something magical about crossing this vast wetland that separated the mainland from Sullivan's Island. She often felt like she was leaving all her problems behind where the earth was rooted and solid. Ahead was the ephemeral sun, sand, and water—so much water! The glistening current of the Intracoastal Waterway raced behind them and just beyond lay the mighty Atlantic Ocean.

She turned off the car's air-conditioning and they all rolled down the windows to breathe deep the salty air. The breeze was warm on her face and immediately she felt the familiar tug of the islands. The tide was low, exposing mudflats spiked with sharp oyster shells, and the cordgrass where white egrets hunted. She sniffed, smiling when she caught the unmistakable, pungent scent of pluff mud. Anyone who didn't like that odor didn't belong here, she thought. Pluff mud and salt air smelled like home to Lovie.

Lovie crossed the Ben Sawyer Bridge to Sullivan's Island and continued past several quaint cottages with hanging baskets of flowers on the porches. In the yards, laundry flapped in the breeze, and in one, a large black dog slept in the sunlight. Her fingers danced on the wheel in anticipation when she reached the third and final bridge she'd cross this morning. The narrow Isle of Palms Bridge stretched over Breach Inlet, where many British soldiers had drowned in the treacherous water during the Revolutionary War. They were trying to attack Fort Moultrie on

Sullivan's Island, crossing the inlet by foot when the unsuspecting force fell victim to the powerful currents.

In no time the station wagon was over the bridge and she was back on the Isle of Palms! Looking in the rearview mirror, she saw her smile reflected on Cara's and Palmer's faces. They were silent now, their eyes eagerly seeking out familiar touchstones. To their left was Hamlin Creek, lined with docks with boats at moor. The current was racing, and she felt her blood match the pace as she turned the car windward down the gently sloping road.

In a breath, she saw Primrose Cottage. She guided the car off the pavement to where the gravel was so sparse the wheels dug into sand as she parked. She turned off the engine, the car rumbled, and she sighed in the resulting silence.

"We're here."

In an explosion of cheers and yelps, the car doors flung open as Palmer and Cara leaped out and ran like wild Indians across the dunes to the beach beyond. Lovie laughed and placed a hand to her heart as memories played in her mind. That was just what she and her older brother, Mickey, used to do. Now, years later, her children loved it here as much as she did. She pulled herself from the car and set her hands on her hips, lifting her face toward her house.

Primrose Cottage was perched high on a dune overlooking the sparkling blue water of the Atlantic. It was the same pale yellow color as the primroses that grew wild on the dunes. With its blue shutters and doors, it looked like another of the wildflowers that surrounded it—purple petunias, sassy Indian blankets, and the lemon yellow primroses for which the cottage had been named. She lifted her hand over her eyes like a visor and searched for signs of wear and tear. The prevailing salt winds and the long winters were harsh on a house. A bit more paint was peeling, sand was thick on the stairs and porches, and there was yard work to be done, but all in all, the little house had survived another winter.

She felt the warmth of the sun as she pulled heavy brown bags of groceries from the car. It was just like the children to run off when she could use their help, she thought with a wry grin. She needed to get the milk, ice cream, and other frozen foods directly into the fridge. Her arms ached as she carried the bags up the precarious gravel path and struggled with the key. Pushing open the wood door, she was met by a wall of blistering heat and stale air in the closed-up house. She made a beeline to the small kitchen and, with a soft grunt, set the heavy bags down on the square pine table. Then with a prayer, she opened the ancient fridge. She smiled in relief hearing the low hum of electricity and feeling the blast of coolness.

Sweat beaded as she hurried to the large patio doors, unlocked them, and pushed them wide open. Next she went around the room and one by one pried open the stubborn windows. The onshore breezes whistled through the little house, smelling of salt and stirring the curtains.

Despite all the changes in her life—growing up, getting married, having children—nothing ever seemed to change at the beach house. It was always here, waiting for her. Constant, fixed, and reassuring. She slapped the dust from her hands, then spread them far out at her sides in a welcoming, open-fingered embrace.

She was home at last! Home on the Isle of Palms.

In a burst of enthusiasm, Lovie felt the young girl hiding deep within her spring to life. Chores could wait. Unpacking the rest of the car could wait. Cleaning and dusting could wait. At this precious moment in time, her children were out on the beach, playing in the sun. This, she knew, could not wait.

Lovie almost skipped to the linen closet to pull out three thick terry cloth towels. She didn't usually use her better towels for the beach, but sometimes one just had to break the rules. She tossed the towels in an empty grocery bag, grabbed her floppy purple hat, and hurried out the door.

Her heels dug deep into the soft sand as she raced along the narrow beach path. This early in the season, the sea oats were low and spring green, not yet the tall gold sentries they'd become as summer waned. She climbed the last dune . . . and suddenly the breadth of the ocean spread out before her. Her heart leaped in her chest. Above, the sky was impossibly blue with white puffs of clouds that matched the fringe of the surf as it rolled to the shore.

Immediately she spotted her children cavorting in the surf like shorebirds—Palmer a shorter, pale-chested sanderling, her dear "peep," running on thin legs, dodging waves. Cara a sleek, slate-black hooded gull, raucously calling and laughing with joy.

Joy . . . It filled Lovie's heart as she sprinted toward her children. She paused only to slip out of her shorts and tug her T-shirt from her body to toss on the sand. Her simple black maillot molded to her woman's body, but she felt ageless as she raced to the waves. With a cry, she leaped into the water, splashing and surprising her children, who whooped in excitement at her arrival. She heard their calls—"Mama! Mama!"—as birdsong before she dove under the oncoming wave. The water was startlingly chilly yet refreshing.

Stroking beneath the water, she felt all the accumulated dust of the city wash away. Lovie kicked her legs, pushed with her arms, and burst to the surface. Gasping for air, tasting salt, she felt the warmth of the sun on her face.

Three

It was a glorious morning on the beach. Lovie pedaled her bike along the shoreline with a grin plastered across her face. She spied a long line of pelicans flying low over the ocean. Her daddy used to call them *bombardiers on patrol.*

She was back on turtle patrol. All fall, winter, and spring she was so busy she hardly had a moment to herself, but in the summer she had only one job—the turtles—and it was the one she cared most about.

She rode her bike along the beach early each morning. Her route began at Breach Inlet at the southern end of the island and ended way beyond the pier to where the maritime forest began. Some days she was able to enlist the help of a friend—usually her neighbors Flo Prescott and Kate Baker. She'd rather be consistent with a smaller patch of beach than inconsistent with the whole island.

The island had changed markedly during the ten years she'd been tending turtles, and it would change much more in the next ten. Yet there was a timeless quality to looking out over the ocean's vastness. For turtle patrol, however, she kept her eye trained for turtle tracks.

Lovie admired the courage of the female loggerhead that, under the cloak of darkness, left her home—the sea—to risk all to lay her nest. She was the brave mother who dragged her three-hundred-plus-pound body in a desperate crawl to the dunes. One by one, she labored to lay more than one hundred eggs, and then, knowing she'd leave her unborn to survive alone, she camouflaged her treasures with thrown sand and returned to the sea.

Lovie had always felt she was the midwife of the nests, taking up for the mother to help the hatchlings survive against the odds. Each dawn, before beachcombers arrived, Lovie sometimes rode her bike, sometimes walked the pristine beach in search of the telltale line of tracks that stretched from the high tide line to the dunes. If she found a nest, she marked it so that she could watch it during the fifty- to sixty-day incubation period and, with luck and God's grace, be there when the nest hatched to help the hatchlings make it safely into the sea.

No one knew this beach better than Lovie Rutledge. Most people didn't look at a beach the same way she did. She knew where the winter storms had created scarps in the dunes, where the lights shone brightest at night, where dogs or raccoons might poach eggs, where the kids liked to spoon—all possible problems for the nesting turtles. Other than Flo and Kate, there were precious few people with whom she could share her passion about the turtles. Or who cared. Mostly they just rolled their eyes and smirked whenever she mentioned the turtles.

She reached up to wipe a line of sweat from her brow. But it was hard work, there was no denying it. The air had been cool when she'd stepped out on the beach, but already the sun was a red fireball rising over the ocean. The rising sun was her signal to head home. She veered away from the hard-packed sand of the shoreline to trudge through the softer, dry sand to the beach path. By the time she reached her house and parked her bike under the porch, sweat streamed down her back. She kicked off her sand-crusted sandals and stepped inside.

"Cara?" she called out. "Palmer?" All was quiet and still.

She set down her backpack and hat and walked down the hall. Cara's bedroom door was wide open. Peeking in, her weary shoulders slumped. It looked like a bomb had exploded in Cara's suitcase, jettisoning all her clothes across the floor and bed. Lovie understood that Cara wasn't consciously messy; she simply didn't care if her shirt was wrinkled, a hem hung low, or there was a button missing. Lovie thought it was her duty to raise her to be neat and tidy and prepared to raise a family of her own. But sometimes, Lovie found it was easier just to pick up after her than nag.

She crossed the hall and opened Palmer's door. She was met with the stale smell of a gym. They'd been here only a day, she thought with a sigh. How could it get that bad that quickly? She'd come in later and clean this room, too. Closing the door, she decided to let her son sleep in.

All the windows were wide open, and offshore breezes wafted through the house. Later today she'd roll up her sleeves and dive into the seasonal shake-up and cleaning of the house. It wasn't mere housework for her. She loved her sweet cottage and the tending of it. In an odd way she couldn't explain, sweeping and washing the floors, shining the windows, plumping pillows gave her a sense of belonging to the house.

But first, she'd rest a spell and have a nice cup of hot coffee. She hummed a nameless tune in the hopelessly out-of-date kitchen and reached up to choose a delicate pink Haviland cup from the collection of leftover china patterns collected by generations. Choosing a pattern was a game she played each morning, one that was pleasurable as much as comforting. The Haviland china had belonged to her beloved Grandmother Simmons, and remembering her brought a smile.

She leisurely poured out a cup, noticing that several of the boxes of sweet cereal were already missing. She poured in thick cream, then carried it outdoors along with a pad of paper and a pen and settled into one of the four white rocking chairs that faced the ocean. Straight ahead, across the long stretch of dunes covered with gnarled greenery and her beloved primroses, rolled the ocean. She closed her eyes and breathed in the heady scents of strong coffee mingled with pluff mud. The marsh mud was especially odiferous today, she thought, before taking a sip.

Lovie enjoyed this peaceful time of morning. Twiddling the pencil between her fingers, leisurely sipping coffee, she jotted a few notes in her sea turtle journal. Of all her summer rituals, this one was the most important to her. Stratton called her strict observance of the nests obsessive, but she knew better. Her sea turtle records faithfully tracked the nests on her side of the island and were, as far as she knew, the only such recorded documents. When she finished this, she began her to-do list. A short while later she was interrupted on *#9 Shake out the rugs* by a cry of anguish from the kitchen.

"Mama!"

Lovie dropped her pencil, rose, and followed the bellowing to the kitchen. She found Palmer standing in front of the open fridge in a T-shirt and baggy boxers. His face had the chalky color of sleep and his blond hair stuck out in odd angles from his head.

"We're out of milk," Palmer said in desperation.

"That's not possible," Lovie replied, relieved that it wasn't blood or fire. "I brought a gallon with us."

Palmer sighed with exaggeration and opened the fridge wider with one hand while with the other he ushered her closer to take a look for herself.

Lovie stepped forward and peered into the fridge, then

opened the cabinet below the sink. In the garbage she spied the empty carton of milk.

"Who drank it all?" she asked, stunned.

Palmer's face clouded, and he slammed the fridge door shut, rattling bottles inside. "Cara did. She finished it off with her cereal and didn't leave a drop for me."

"Palmer, I'm quite certain she didn't drink the whole gallon. How much did you drink last night?"

He scowled, and they both knew it was him.

"Mama, I need some milk," he cried with teen angst, and his voice cracked.

Lovie looked with sympathy at her thirteen-year-old son who was smack in the middle of an awkward growth spurt. His whole body was at odds. The T-shirt was too small under his broadening shoulders, and his skinny legs stuck out from the baggy boxers. He'd read in one of his sports magazines that drinking lots of milk would make him grow bigger and stronger. Palmer was one of the shortest boys in his class, and it galled him that his sister was sprouting up like a weed. Palmer desperately wanted to be *big*—tall and broad so he could compete on the sports teams. So her short, slightly built son was guzzling gallons of milk. It was hard for a mother to witness without a twinge of the heart. Even if a glass of milk did nothing more than grow his confidence, it was a minor inconvenience to keep her fridge full.

"If you mind the house, I'll run to the Red & White." She grabbed her straw summer purse and slipped her hat back onto her head. "Do you think you can survive that long?"

"Yes," he replied, missing the sarcasm.

She chuckled. "So, what are you going to do on your first day?"

He looked at her and his taciturn face sparked with excitement. "I'm heading to McKevlin's. See who's there."

Of course, she thought. McKevlin's was the local surf shop,

and from the first of summer to the last, Palmer hung out there with the boys or was on the ocean riding the waves. She was glad to see her son had a passion, too.

"Want to come along?"

"Nah," he replied, grabbing a sweet cereal box and heading back to his room.

Lovie fired up the station wagon and began backing out when she heard Cara's voice. She looked over her shoulder to see her daughter race toward the car. Like Palmer, Cara was growing fast, too. Not just in height. Growing bangs out was a terrible bother. The thick shock of dark hair was always falling into her eyes. At least they'd grow out fast in the summer, she told herself. This morning the raggedy lock was held firmly against her head with two bobby pins. At least she was wearing her glasses. Poor Cara, she hated them so and cried when she got them, saying how she'd be stuck with the dreadful glasses for life. Cara never forgave her traitorous teacher who had written Lovie a note reporting that Cara was always squinting at the blackboard.

"Mama! Where're you going?"

"To the Red & White. Want to come along?"

"Sure." She hopped into the front seat.

"What have you been up to this morning?" Lovie asked.

"Nothin.' Just walking around." Cara's gaze was checking out the street, ever curious.

Lovie noticed the faint pinkening of Cara's cheeks from the sun. She was glad to have Cara's company. "We're out of milk."

"Yeah," she replied nonchalantly, wiping the sweat from her brow. "Palmer must've guzzled it all last night. Mama, he's crazy about milk. There was hardly any for my cereal. Oh, thanks for getting the sweet cereal, Mama. It was good."

Lovie beamed inside. "Glad you liked it. And let Palmer drink all the milk he wants to. I can always get more."

They drove along Palm Boulevard, the main drag of the

island. There weren't many houses affording her a wide view of Hamlin Creek with its racing current and docks stretched out into the water with boats at moor.

"Mama, stop! There's Emmi!" Cara cried, removing her glasses and stuffing them in her pocket.

Lovie spotted the young girl in pink shorts and top walking along the side of the road, with her arms swinging free as you please. Lovie beeped the horn and pulled to a stop. Emmi froze and her head swung toward the car, eyes wide.

"Emmi!" Cara cried, leaping from the parked car.

Both girls squealed simultaneously. In a flash they had their arms around each other and were doing a happy jig. Lovie couldn't help but smile watching them, remembering the exuberant joy at seeing Flo at the same age. When they pushed back, their eyes hungrily scoured each other in search of any changes time might have wrought over the past school year that they'd been apart. Cara was still taller by inches and Emmi was still heavier by pounds. Emmi was slightly burned from the sun bringing out the smattering of freckles over her nose and cheeks, despite summers of rubbing them with lemon juice.

"We're going to the Red & White. Want to come along?" Lovie called out the window.

"Yes, ma'am," Emmi called back. "I was heading there anyway."

"Well, hop in."

The girls hurried, giggling, into the backseat and commenced chattering like magpies. It was as though Lovie were invisible while she drove. She listened to every word, thrilled for this brief window into their lives.

Cara gasped in shock. "You got braces!"

Lovie looked in the rearview mirror to see Emmi bring her hand up to cover her mouth. Her blush made her freckles darken against her pale skin. She thought Emmi looked a lot like a young Carly Simon, with her enormous smile and red-gold hair. Stratton once said Emmi's smile was a statement. Now that statement had exclamation marks.

"I hate them," Emmi said. "I look awful."

"No you don't!" Cara replied in earnest. "They're cool. Everyone is getting them."

Emmi's hand slipped. "Really?"

"Yeah," Cara replied with authority. "And your hair is so long now!"

"Mama says it makes me look like one of my Scottish ancestors." She ran her tongue over her braces and added sullenly, "I still think I look like a dork."

Cara sighed heavily and dug into her pocket to pull out her wire-rim glasses. She slipped them on.

"You got glasses!" Emmi exclaimed.

Now it was Cara's turn to frown. "Yeah. Lucky me."

Emmi put her hand over her mouth again, this time to hide her giggle.

"I don't need them all the time, though," Cara hastened to add. "Just when I have to see something far away. Like the blackboard, or when I'm riding my bike."

"Now we can both look like dorks."

Lovie held back her chuckle as Cara replied with a hearty, "Yeah."

"You grew some, too," Emmi said.

"Great," Cara said with a groan.

"Mama says girls grow tall faster than boys. Then we stop around thirteen, and it's the boys' turn to grow."

"You think?" Cara said, sounding heartened. "I hope so. I'm almost as tall as Palmer already, and it makes him mad. I can't help it, right? It's not like I want to be tall. The girls at school, they can be mean. Sometimes they call me . . ."

Lovie's attention sharpened as her heart stopped. Immediately she felt a primal urge to let out her claws and protect her child. How could she help her precious daughter understand that she was perfect—smart, beautiful, beloved.

Cara glanced to the front seat, suddenly aware of her mother's presence. When she caught her mother's gaze in the mirror, she delivered a stern *don't look, don't listen, just disappear* message. Then Cara leaned over and whispered into Emmi's ear. Lovie tried to keep her gaze on the road ahead.

"Don't you pay them any mind, Cara Rutledge," Emmi replied to the secret in outrage. "They're just jealous. When you grow up, you can be a model. They have to be tall, you know. They'll be sorry when you're famous, like Twiggy."

Lovie's heart expanded for the girl who defended her daughter. Cara would pay more attention to her friend than her mother on this topic. Lovie tried to cock her head to hear more, but the girls started whispering to each other in the back, interspersed with giggles.

Soon they arrived at the small shopping strip that housed a liquor store, a hardware store, and the Red & White grocery store. This was pretty much the only shopping available on the island and the hub of summer activity. She reached into her pocketbook and pulled out two quarters and gave one to each of the girls.

"You go get a treat while I shop," she told them. The girls took off for the store at a run. Lovie strolled at a slower pace past the public bulletin board. As usual, she stopped to peruse the local island notices and ads. There was a garage sale at Catherine Malloy's next week; someone was selling an old Impala, someone else a dining room table made of oak. An island boy named Brett was willing to do odd jobs. Lovie took down his number since Palmer wasn't reliable. She glanced past a few other announcements when her attention was captured by the words SEA TURTLE STUDY written on 8 × 11 paper. Instantly curious, she removed her sunglasses and bent at the waist to read.

SEA TURTLE STUDY

Looking for volunteers interested in
participating in a study of the
loggerhead sea turtles on
Isle of Palms and Sullivan's Island.
All interested should meet at
the Exchange Club
June 15, 2 p.m.

DR. RUSSELL BENNETT

Lovie straightened slowly as her heartbeat quickened. A sea turtle study here on Isle of Palms? She brought her sunglasses to her mouth and idly chewed at one end. There'd never been a study before, not in the ten years she'd been personally monitoring the island's turtle nests, not even in the thirty years she'd spent summers here. Why would they need a study now? Who was this Dr. Russell Bennett and why was he coming here, to study *her* turtles?

Lovie quickly jotted down the information, then glanced at her watch and hurried into the grocery store. Her mind was no longer on milk but on turtles.

Sea Turtle Journal

June 5, 1974
  The sea turtle swims thousands of miles to reach the beach of her birth to nest. I sometimes feel I've traveled as far just to get to my beach house!

Four

~

L ovie! You're back!"

"Flo!" Looking up from her book, Lovie spotted her friend and rose from the deck chair and waved. Flo came trotting across her scrubby sand-strewn yard, up the stairs to the seaward porch, blue eyes sparkling.

Flo was two years older than Lovie, taller and athletic. Unlike Lovie's sweet freshness, Flo was striking, with her lithe, finely muscled body honed from tennis and long walks on the beach. Her strawberry blond hair was worn short and curled.

The Prescotts had been her summer neighbor since she and Flo were children. The Prescott family owned what Flo's mother, Miranda, claimed was the oldest house on Isle of Palms. It was a Victorian treasure and a rarity on an island largely made up of modest postwar houses built of brick and cinder block. Their main home was in Summerville, but Miranda had moved to the island full-time when her husband passed twenty years earlier. Miranda was the island's beloved eccentric, everybody's Auntie Mame, who traveled to exotic locations, wore long, flowing scarves, and painted brilliantly colored art.

Her daughter, Florence, couldn't be more different. Flo was as grounded as Miranda was ethereal. Miranda had raced through her husband's money, and Florence, by necessity, was frugal. She'd gone to Vanderbilt University, got a master's degree in social work, and worked with troubled teens in Summerville. Lovie, who never finished college, admired her friend's intelligence and dedication to her career. But Lovie couldn't relate to Flo's ideas on how a woman could and should live an independent life.

Even when they were children, Flo didn't want to play the housewife in their games. She wanted to be Amelia Earhart or a female Dr. Livingstone tromping through the marshes. As she grew older, the traditional marriage and family track that most young women subscribed to was not for her. Their friendship was so profound they didn't question each other's choices. They simply understood that Lovie was more of a romantic who desired love in the form of a husband and family, and that Flo wanted her independence. On the evening after Flo had rejected the proposal of Denny Duell, a great guy Lovie and everyone else thought Flo should marry, they'd had too many glasses of wine. Flo had leaned against Lovie's shoulder.

"I've taken care of one child already," she'd told Lovie, referring to her mother. "Why would I want to take on another?"

So at forty-one, Flo remained unmarried and her history of dating was legendary. Yet despite her successful career and diligent, loving care of her mother, Flo also was considered eccentric by locals because she did not marry. "Those Prescotts . . ." people would say with a resigned sigh and a small smile.

Even Miranda had her doubts. Though she might have been a freethinker and exotic in her own life, she continued to hope her daughter would find the right man and marry. It confused Miranda that Flo could date so many men and still not find a husband. When Flo celebrated her fortieth birthday, Miranda had worn black.

Lovie whipped off her sunglasses and sprang to her feet

to meet Flo at the stairs. The two women wrapped their arms around each other and suddenly they were ten-year-old girls again, overjoyed at seeing each other after the long winter.

"Lord, it's good to see you again," Flo said, lowering her sunglasses to peer over them and scour Lovie's face. "Summer doesn't start until Primrose Cottage opens its doors."

"Amen to that. But look at you! So tan already." Lovie twisted her lips in feigned annoyance as she checked out the glow of Flo's early tan that she was showing off in white shorts and T-shirt. "Getting a jump start on me, I see."

Flo couldn't hide her smug smile at the compliment. Tanning had been serious competition between them in their younger days.

"What are you doing here so early?" Lovie asked as she led the way to the chairs in the cooler shade.

"What are *you* doing here so late? Don't you usually come for Memorial Day?"

"Usually." She turned her head to ask, "Do you want some coffee? Water?"

"Just had a cup. I'm fine. Thanks."

Lovie slumped into her chair and moved her book to the table. Flo picked it up to read the title, then sat and lifted her long legs to let her feet rest on another chair.

"You're reading Archie Carr's book on turtles again?"

"Yep. He's the authority." She took the book back from Flo. "Anyway, I'm late in arriving because Stratton had guests come in from out of town," Lovie replied, answering Flo's question. "I had a dinner party for them." She put her hand to her cheek and gently shook her head. "Was it only the other night? It feels like ages ago already."

"You stayed for that?"

"Naturally."

Flo smirked. "He couldn't take them out to dinner at a restaurant, huh?"

"Now, Flo," Lovie said, putting up her hand in an arresting motion to douse the spark before it became a fire. There was no love lost between Florence and Stratton. "It all turned out fine. I'm here now. But I don't usually expect you till sometime in mid-June."

"I've got workers commencing on the roof tomorrow, and I had to be here. They're charging me an arm and a leg, but we couldn't put it off another year. It was getting to the point that every time it rained we set out a fleet of pots to catch the drips. I apologize in advance for the noise and clutter you're going to have to endure for the next few days."

"You've got to do what you've got to do."

"Be sure to tell your two cuties not to run barefoot in the yard until I get a chance to scour the ground for nails. It's gonna be a holy mess. Miranda comes back from Asheville next week, and I surely hope the work's done by then. I couldn't bear to live with her complaining."

"How is Miranda?"

"More cantankerous than ever. Nothing I do to this house seems to be right. She doesn't like to see anything changed from the original. I swear, if I move a chair she takes notice. I do believe she liked it ramshackle and falling down around her ears. Lord knows she lived in it like that for long enough."

Lovie laughed, enjoying the familiar complaints. She knew that Flo adored her mother, and sometimes Lovie envied her, not so much for the devotion but for the teasing and banter between the two opinionated women. She couldn't imagine that kind of relationship with Dee Dee, who was quick to take offense. She leaned back in her chair. "Sort of like my house?"

"Now, I didn't say that." Flo craned her neck to peer out over the house's wood. "Though I've got the name of a good painter, should you need one? I'm just saying . . ."

Lovie chuckled at the not-so-veiled criticism. "Stratton won't spend the money on this place until we've finished the work on the main house."

"You'll never finish that white elephant. No one ever finishes working on those historic houses."

"Like your boat?"

"As a matter of fact, yes. They're money pits. But you can't let this place go for too long. The salt air is hard on these old houses."

"I know, I know." Lovie lifted the to-do list from the table. "I've compiled a list as long as my arm of projects I'd like to begin on this poor little house. But Stratton says not this year."

"Stratton says that every year. Face it, sugar, he just doesn't care for this place. He'd as soon sell it tomorrow."

Lovie frowned, hearing the truth in it. "Well, he can't. Not without my permission. And you know I'll never give it."

"Better not. Your daddy would turn over in his grave. It's a sweet place," she said in a soft tone and letting her gaze sweep the porch. "Keeping your name on the deed to this house was the smartest thing you've ever done."

Lovie didn't comment and instead took a sip of coffee. Her parents had left the modest beach house to her when she married. The rest of her inheritance she'd handed over to Stratton after they were wed, as was expected. But she'd told Stratton that her parents insisted the beach house be kept in her name to be left to their children. It was a little white lie, one that she never felt guilty for. In her heart, she knew that Flo was right. If she gave Stratton any legal leverage over the beach house, he would sell it. And that she could never allow. It'd be like selling her soul.

"Where is that old bird dog, anyway?" Flo asked.

Lovie took another sip, then slowly lowered her cup to the table. "He's at Tradd Street. His business guests are still in town, so he's staying there a little longer to entertain. He wanted me to stay, too, but we decided it was best for me to bring the children out here as planned."

"How long will he be in town?"

"A week or so. Then later in the summer he's going to Europe."

"Europe again?"

"Yes. And Japan . . ."

Flo's brows rose. "Really? Business must be doing well."

"It's booming. Keeping him terribly busy. We hardly see him anymore. He's out late with clients more nights than not."

Flo pursed her lips and looked out at the sea.

Lovie looked at the murky coffee in her cup with shame. She could tell Flo was holding back her words. Had she, too, heard rumors of Stratton's philandering?

Flo swung her head back and smiled. "Hey, that means you'll be alone at the beach house for most of the summer."

"Afraid so."

Flo clapped her hands. "You're free!" she exclaimed. "It'll be like when we were kids. You won't have to play housewife and have dinner on the table when your man comes home. You can eat at my house, and I can eat over at yours! Slumber parties!"

Lovie chuckled at the memories of glorious summers past. "I still have Palmer and Cara, don't forget."

"Bring them along. I love them. It's that old man I can't stand."

"Flo . . ."

"Okay, let's let sleeping dogs lie . . . or go to Europe. Whatever. Well, this is a happy turn of events. It's going to be a wonderful summer." Flo's eyes gleamed as she leaned toward Lovie. "The turtles are out there. I can feel it."

"So can I," Lovie said with shared enthusiasm.

The sea turtles were the glue that bound their friendship, and it had held fast for thirty years. It all started back when they were Cara's age. Every summer since they'd walked shoulder to shoulder along the beach in search of turtle nests. They'd fought back the dreaded ghost crabs, guarded against marauding raccoons, and lay with their ears to the ground by the nests, wondering what those babies were doing deep down in the sand. When they were lucky, they saw nests hatch, and the sight never failed to thrill them.

When they grew older, both girls kept their childhood promise and studied biology at college. Flo later found her passion in psychology and changed majors. Lovie left college after junior year to marry Stratton. But their passion for sea turtles continued to burn.

"Have you by any chance gone out to check on turtle tracks?" Lovie asked. "I went out this morning, but I didn't find any."

Flo leaned forward, eyes gleaming. "As a matter of fact, I *did* see tracks yesterday morning."

"No! Where?"

"By 32nd Avenue."

"I knew I should've been here. Did you mark it?"

"Now don't get your panties tied up in a knot. I didn't see a body pit. Just tracks partly up the beach and a turn around. I figure that mama was just checking things out."

"A false crawl," Lovie said, referring to the tracks left by a sea turtle who didn't attempt to nest. She smiled and wriggled her brows with meaning. "That means she'll likely come back tonight." Lovie felt the familiar rush that always came at the beginning of the sea turtle nesting season. "You in the mood to walk the beach tonight? See what we might see?"

"Could be," Flo replied with a wide grin. "Wouldn't mind seeing me a turtle come ashore to start off the season. Though let's not get our hopes up. You know the chances of catching her are pretty slim. But oh, Lord, I'd love to see one just so I could hold it over Miranda's head. She'll be hootin' and hollerin' that she missed it."

"There'll be plenty more for her to see."

Flo folded her arms. "I don't know. I hope so."

Lovie was alert to Flo's change in tone. "What do you mean?"

"Didn't you hear the big news?"

"News? No. What news?"

From the neighbor's yard they heard the sound of a boat's power motor starting up, gurgling relentlessly.

"They've gone and done it," Flo said dramatically. "Sold the north end of the island to some development company."

"They *sold* it?"

Flo nodded. "To resort developers. Word is they're going to build some kind of country club."

"A *country club*? On Isle of Palms?"

"That's what they say."

"But . . ." Lovie's mind reeled.

"Took the wind out of your sails, didn't it?"

"I'm confused," Lovie replied honestly as she racked her memory banks. "Last I heard, they were offering the land to the county, state, and federal governments for development as a park. What happened there? I had such hopes."

"Well, they did offer. I guess there weren't any takers, or offers they wanted to take."

"Or that could match this one." This would be an old story.

Lovie leaned back in her chair, slump shouldered with defeat. "I really wanted it to be a park. How wonderful would that've been?"

"We all did."

She looked at her coffee cup with a sudden wish it were wine. "Who ended up buying it?"

"I don't know for sure. Some developers from Hilton Head with big plans. There's talk about a marina, condominiums, and plots for houses. As many as a thousand, maybe more."

That news had the power to take Lovie's breath away. "That many? I can't believe it."

"It's going to be a big development. You just know they're thinking of putting in a golf course."

Lovie snorted. "Stratton will be thrilled."

A new voice sounded from the porch stairs. "Who's building a golf course?"

Turning her head, Lovie saw Palmer, his hair wet and caked with sand and his skin glowing from his first day in the summer sun. His shoulders, though slim, had the first hints of manhood in their breadth. She smiled just to see him and felt a familiar gush of love.

"Hi, honey," Lovie called out. "You weren't out long."

"Waves weren't good." He reached the top of the stairs and leaned against the railing.

"Come, give me some sugar," she said, wiggling her fingers in a *come hither.*

Palmer rolled his eyes and pushed off from the railing, walking like a condemned man to deliver a quick kiss on her cheek. She held her hand to his hard cheek and clung to the brief moment. There was a time when Palmer climbed on her lap and told her all about his day, the good and the bad. They had no secrets. Now he was as cagey as a ghost crab, always scuttling around in secret places, popping up unannounced before disappearing again. She was told this was normal for teenage boys. She accepted it. Yet she was always hungrily searching for the sweet boy she occasionally spotted in his quick smile and hasty hug.

"You hungry?" she asked him.

"Yeah. Starved."

"Well, go shower. I'll fix you lunch. Have you seen Cara?"

"No," he replied. Then, "What were you saying about a golf course?"

Flo spoke up. "There's some talk about developers coming in and building a resort on the north end of the island. A marina, houses, condos. Maybe a golf course."

"Really? Cool!" Palmer said, then started heading inside.

Flo grabbed his arm and tugged him toward her. "Hey, you think you can sneak outta here without giving your aunt Flo a kiss?"

Palmer tried not to smile and mocked a grudging kiss on Flo's cheek. She promptly ruffled his hair and sent him on his way. She turned to face Lovie, her eyes speculative. "See what I mean? Everyone thinks it's 'cool' that the forest is being destroyed. It's going to be hard to rally against it."

Lovie heard the truth in it. "Oh, Flo, everything about our sleepy island is going to change. The number of houses will jump by thousands."

"It'll more than double the population."

"When I think of the cars, the roads . . ." Lovie's shoulders stiffened as a thought took root. "The beachfront lots will be the first to go, and think of the lights shining on the beach. What will become of the turtle nests?"

"That issue's already been raised. The developers are going to have to do engineering and environmental impact studies."

"Well, that's something."

"They've got to do it before they can get approval for their development plans."

Lovie thought of the announcement she'd seen posted earlier that day. "Now it all makes sense."

"What does?"

"When I was at the Red & White this morning I saw a sign for a turtle study on the island."

Flo leaned forward in her chair. "No kidding. What did it say?"

"Not much. It was just a notice calling for volunteers for a turtle study that's going to be done here this summer."

"There it is," Flo said with a sharp slap on the knee. "Told you so."

"Hold on a minute." Lovie went into the house and returned a moment later with her purse. Sitting, she dug through it and pulled out a small spiral notepad and flipped through it. "Here. A Dr. Russell Bennett. The meeting is at the Exchange Club on the fifteenth." She looked up. "Bennett. Ever heard of him?"

"No. Is he from around here?"

Lovie shrugged. "I've no idea."

"You're going to the meeting, of course."

Lovie shook her head. "I haven't decided."

Flo's face went still. "Lovie, you've *got* to get involved in that study."

"Why?" she said, feeling the pressure of Flo's expectations. "Don't you remember what happened last year when that land was purchased?"

"They ignored you. So what? You survived to fight another day."

Lovie shuddered, recalling the patronizing attitude toward her years of work with the sea turtles. In retrospect, Lovie felt she'd been naïve to think that she could change the plans of a powerful group of investors. She was left to wonder if her efforts to help the sea turtles were little more than a combination of hubris and hope.

She reached out to lift the book she was reading, *So Excellent a Fishe* by revered sea turtle expert Archie Carr. "The truth is," she said, her fingers tapping the book, "I'm not a professional. They see me as nothing more than some local lady who cares about turtles. And this Dr. Bennett will be no different. To him I'll just be a busybody. A pest he'll have to deal with. Why should I put myself through that? I have some pride left. What I don't have is any authority."

Flo leaned back in her chair and crossed her arms, looking straightforwardly at Lovie. "Because this study will give you a voice. Everyone knows you're the turtle lady of these islands.

Folks will look to you to ask the right questions and expect the right answers. You've been knocking yourself out for the turtles for as long as I've known you. You cared when no one else did. If you don't have the authority, then who does?"

Lovie's face tightened. "Apparently Dr. Bennett does."

"*Him*," Flo muttered. "Don't let the title scare you off. He's probably just some low-level biologist these developers put on the payroll to slant the report in a favorable light. This development is going to be huge. Too much is at stake for them to do otherwise."

"Well, he'll be lucky if two or three people show up. If it weren't for you and Miranda and Kate, I'd be on my own out there. Let him try."

"You're missing the point. It doesn't matter if anyone shows up," Flo replied, gaining steam. "The fix is in. The turtles are out."

Lovie felt a spurt of indignation rise up at hearing the finality in Flo's words. "This is *our* island. We both know there's no way the development won't impact the turtles. Those turtles have every right to nest there. They've been here a lot longer than we have."

"Now there's the Lovie I know."

"What can we do?"

"We can start protesting. Rally the islanders to protect the beaches. At the very least, a controversy will force the study to get done and be given its due. We might not be able to stop the development, but we can try to influence the plans."

The sun was rising and she felt the heat as a renewed fire in her belly. "You're right, of course. But I'm not going to don some hippie clothing and march in front of the Red & White carrying a protest sign. I'll leave that to you."

"Chicken."

Lovie laughed at the old tease they used whenever one of them was afraid to jump. As she rose, the chair scraped loudly against the wood. "It's getting hot out here and I have to make Palmer's lunch."

"He can't make his own lunch? He's thirteen!"

"You know as well as I do a Southern boy can starve in a house filled with uncooked food."

Flo laughed and followed her indoors to the kitchen.

Lovie put her cup in the sink, then opened the fridge to pull out packages of sandwich meat, mustard, hot sauce, and a jar of pickles. "I have my own methods of getting things done," she said to Flo. "I'll go to this meeting and sign on as a volunteer, if only to keep an eye on this Dr. Russell Bennett." Her voice was tinged with contempt at his name. "If he's going to do a research study on our beach, then he damn well better do it well enough to satisfy me. I'll be there every day, dogging his every move. This is *my* beach."

Flo chuckled and opened the jar of pickles. She pulled one out, catching the drips with her tongue. "This time, you won't be considered a busybody." She smirked and put the dill pickle into her mouth. "You're going to be their worst nightmare."

That evening, Lovie walked softly down the hall in bare feet, a night guard peeking in her children's rooms.

Palmer's room was dark, but she could hear his gentle snore, a soft rhythm that blended with the echoing roar of the ocean outside his open window. She quietly closed the door. Across the hall, the light was on in Cara's room. Peering in, she saw that Cara was asleep on her back with a book lying open across her belly. Lovie paused and leaned against the doorframe as her heart softened for the quixotic girl who loved to read as much as she did. In this, at least, they shared a passion. The television at the beach house was ancient, with rabbit ear antennas that were bent from too many frustrated manipulations. She refused to buy a new one, much to the children's complaints. Her pat answer was always, "There are plenty of books you can read." Cara obliged, but Palmer . . .

Lovie crossed the room to her daughter's bedside and carefully lifted the book from her hands. Setting it down, she saw that Cara was reading *A Swiftly Tilting Planet*. Madeleine L'Engle was a favorite author of her adventurous daughter. She stared down at the face that held more of Stratton's dark looks than her own fair ones. She was like her father in other ways, too. She had his stubborn determination, his independent spirit, and, too, his will to win.

Yet unlike Stratton there was softness in her features, fullness in the lips. A sweetness lurking under her scowl that she could see now, as she lay sleeping. Lovie very gently stroked a few strands from Cara's forehead, feeling the moisture of tiny beads of sweat on this humid night. She bent to place a kiss where her fingers had rested. Lingering, she smelled the soap from her shower and an unidentifiable scent that was all Cara. Then she reached to the bedside lamp to pull the chain and extinguish the light.

Careful, she admonished herself. Don't make comparisons. Cara looked like Cara.

Her son and her daughter were as different as night and day. It was a family joke that she'd somehow got the genes mixed up in her two children. Cara had inherited the long, lanky, dark looks of the Rutledge family, while Palmer inherited Lovie's smaller, more delicate blond genes. As the years passed, however, Palmer was bitter that he remained short and Cara agonized that she sprouted tall like a weed. She was not the petite and pretty Southern belle that her mother was. No one laughed at the joke any longer.

They differed in personalities, too. Palmer was lazy. There really wasn't any way to sugarcoat it. He liked to hang around with his friends and play sports. He was well liked, a popular, good-looking boy who rarely rocked the boat. Stratton often frowned and declared he was waiting for something to come along and light a fire under that boy's butt.

In contrast, Cara was curious, competitive, and driven to succeed, whether it was on her report card or on some self-imposed goal. Unlike Palmer, Cara didn't have many friends. With her tall, gangly frame and her brainy reputation, she was not popular. Lovie felt for Cara, but Stratton had little patience with her. When he disciplined the children, Palmer usually caved within himself, muttering, "Yes, sir," and occasionally accepting the stern hand. Cara, however, argued back. Lovie cringed each time Cara went toe-to-toe with him. Lovie's secret fear was that it was only a matter of time before Stratton laid a hand to her.

Glancing at her watch, she realized it was not even ten o'clock and the children were asleep. Lowcountry summer days wore them plumb out. In one day's time their skin was as red as a lobster's from overcooking in the sun, and their lackluster expressions were replaced with the bright-eyed enthusiasm she always imagined Tom Sawyer and Huck Finn wore. The Lowcountry was a vast, idyllic playground for children. She had been right to insist they come to the beach house. Stratton would be fine downtown alone. The thought that he might even prefer it forced its way into her head.

Lovie walked down the narrow hallway lined with black-framed photographs of the Simmons family in the early years of the beach house. Michael Senior and Junior on the Boston Whaler, arm over shoulder. Grandmother Dodie knitting on the back porch. Family gatherings on July Fourth. Dee Dee had removed all the photographs of Mickey after the accident, but Lovie hung them again when she inherited the house, along with new photographs of her children. The house felt empty without Mickey's memories embraced within the walls.

The low ceilings and overstuffed furniture of the living room made the small room cozy in the glow of lamplight. The house seemed to wrap its arms around her, making her feel safe. This quaint cottage had always been her favorite home, where she felt she belonged. Nothing ever seemed to change, certainly not the furniture. It was an eclectic collection of family furniture from both sides. The red cabbage rose chintz-covered chairs and sofa were new when Dee Dee and Michael bought the house in 1945. The rest of the furniture—two Victorian chairs, the piecrust table, Michael's desk, the large navy Oriental rug—had endured years of sandy feet and paws, and the occasional spills. Dee Dee told her that no flooring was as tough as a good Persian rug. Only the collection of local art, many from artists she knew, was her personal addition to the cottage.

Lovie bent to turn on the radio and smiled at the memories that tripped across her mind at hearing the song "Cherish." She poured herself a glass of white wine, then sat at the mahogany desk. The French doors were open to the night's breeze that stirred the sheer curtains. She reached out to flick on the green banker's lamp. In an instant, a pool of yellow light flooded the large notebook lying there. Lovie lightly ran her hand over the muted black leather with the reverence an author might have for her novel. This book held *her* passion. Each entry represented her commitment, as well as her hopes and dreams.

This was her sea turtle journal. The third volume she'd kept on her loggerhead observations since she'd begun her project ten years earlier.

But Lovie's love of sea turtles went farther back. Her father had purchased the beach house soon after he'd returned from World War II. The Beach Company was selling lower-cost houses in the postwar boom. Michael Simmons Sr. never talked about his experiences in the war, but they all knew without asking that his soul needed the solace of the beach to come to terms with whatever happened back in Europe. He spoke of his anguish eloquently through his long, silent walks at sunset and the worn Bible he read every night before sleep. Lovie still remembered the glow of his cigarette piercing the black night and the soft murmur of her parents' voices from the porch.

She and her older brother, Mickey, were best friends. They were, in fact, the *only* friends they had during their stays on the remote island back in the day. Mickey loved the sea turtles, too, but for all the wrong reasons. He thought it was a lark to wait up at night for a big mama loggerhead to come ashore, then hop on her shell to ride the poor creature back out to the sea.

Lovie could trace her memory back to the exact moment she felt her first connection to the turtles. She and Mickey had sneaked out of the house to the beach late one night. The moon was only a ghost in the sky. Mickey was on the prowl for turtles, and before too long they spied a single trail of tracks leading up to a dune.

"Only one track!" Mickey whispered to her excitedly. "That means she's still up there. This is our chance. Now stay low and don't spook her. And keep quiet. Come on."

Lovie had felt a shiver of thrill on that hot, humid night as she hunched over to creep silently behind her brother toward the dunes. They heard the turtle before they saw her. The scratching of her large flippers in the sand rent the night's silence and, drawing closer, Lovie could feel the spray of sand against her face. The loggerhead was a shadowy hulk in the dim light, laboriously moving her shell against the sand, sending sand flying as she camouflaged her nest. They crouched behind a cluster of sea oats nearby and waited, not wanting to disturb her. Lovie felt her heart pounding in awe of her first sight of a mother sea turtle on her nest. When the turtle ceased moving, she could feel Mickey's muscles tighten beside her. Then the turtle began to crawl.

"She's going back out!"

Without warning, he switched on his flashlight and shone the bright white light directly on the turtle. Instantly, the turtle went still. Lovie's mouth slipped open in a gasp at the clear sight of the huge sea turtle within feet of her. So close, the young girl could see the faint outline of the scutes through the sand, their rich mahogany color, and the numerous barnacles that were affixed to her shell. She was magnificent!

Mickey shoved the flashlight into Lovie's hands, almost knocking her over as he leaped to his feet. With a wild war whoop, he raced to the turtle, grabbed hold, and jumped onto the turtle's shell.

"Giddyup!" he cried like a wild cowboy.

The sea turtle lifted her head, and Lovie heard a strange guttural hissing noise through the open beak. But Mickey wasn't warned off. Instead he just laughed louder and shouted, "Giddyup!" again and again.

"Mickey, get off! That's so mean. Get off her!"

"Don't be such a baby!"

The sea turtle began moving again, flipper after flipper, dragging herself back to the ocean. The poor thing. It broke Lovie's heart to see how hard it was for that turtle to get back to the sea, especially with a wild boy on her back. Every few steps, the turtle stopped to rest. Lovie could hear the heavy, labored breaths. Enraged at the insult to such a beautiful beast, she begged Mickey to get off, but her cries fell on deaf ears. He thought it was fun and was determined to ride that poor turtle into the surf.

Then it happened. To this day Lovie wasn't sure she hadn't imagined it. The big sea turtle had stopped again. Mickey clucked and patted her shell, obnoxiously trying to get her to move. Lovie bent close to the loggerhead's enormous head. There were tiny barnacles by her eye from which flowed a trail of tears.

"I'm sorry," she said softly.

The turtle's large almond-shaped eye met hers. In that singular moment, Lovie felt a bond with the mother turtle, an unspoken connection that transcended species. Her child's heart responded.

The sea turtle began crawling again, huffing heavily with the burden of Mickey. Watching her flippers dig deep into the sand to claw her way back to the sea sparked a fire of indignation in Lovie. She stomped closer to her brother, then with all her might shoved him, knocking him clear off the turtle's shell. He landed in a graceless thump in the sand. The startled turtle lurched forward, picking up speed.

"Hey," Mickey shouted. "What'd you do that for?"

Lovie was angrier at her brother than she'd ever been before. She raised her fists in the air and screamed, "You stay off that turtle, hear? It's wrong! Wrong, wrong, wrong!" Tears were flowing down her own cheeks and she began to cry, great heaving, hiccupping sobs that did more to stop her brother than anything she might have said.

The turtle made quick her escape, plowing toward the sea. Mickey didn't chase after it this time. He stood with his arms limp at his side, at a loss for how to console his sister.

"I'm . . . I'm sorry, Lovie. I didn't mean nothin' by it."

Lovie wanted to stop crying, but she couldn't. The night sky suddenly seemed too big and she felt alone and frightened and tired. Mickey came closer and stood helplessly at her side, his hands clenching and unclenching.

"Quit crying, Lovie. I didn't know it got you so upset. I was just having a little fun."

"I *told* you to stop."

"Well, I stopped, didn't I?"

Lovie sniffed and swiped her nose with her arm. "But only 'cause I knocked you off."

"Yeah, you sure did," he said with a soft laugh. He rubbed his shoulder, then playfully, gently shoved hers. "You're pretty strong when you want to be."

This brought a small, reluctant laugh to her lips.

Mickey pointed toward the ocean. "Look, Lovie. The turtle's almost at the ocean now. Let's watch her."

She clutched his arm tight in desperation. "You promise not to jump on her again?"

"Nah, I won't," Mickey replied, a little shamefaced. "Come on!"

Mickey and Lovie sprinted the ten yards to where the waves rolled onto the shore. The sea turtle paused at the shoreline to lift her head, as though catching the scent that would guide her home. The stars shone softly from above. Side by side, brother and sister stood, united this time, and watched as the great sea mother crawled into the sea. Now that she'd reached water, she moved gracefully. Lovie and Mickey scrambled to remove their shoes and followed her in. The water was cold and murky, but they stayed with her into deeper water, clear up to their waists. The waves washed the sand from the turtle's shell, revealing for a glorious instant the rich, glossy mahogany color before she took one strong push with her flippers and disappeared into the depths.

Lovie looked into her brother's eyes, and they both smiled.

Mickey never rode the turtles again after that night. The following summer his interest shifted to girls, and things were never the same between Lovie and her brother after that.

Lovie's fascination for sea turtles continued to grow as she did. Every passing summer she couldn't wait to get to the beach house and the turtles. From the first day till the last, she searched for turtle tracks and, later, nests.

She went to stand at the screened porch door. Her arms were wrapped around herself as she thought back again to the young girl who had made a commitment to that valiant sea turtle so many years ago. Did she want to get involved with the study? Wrestle with authorities? If the controversy became heated, her name could end up in the newspapers. Stratton wouldn't like that; he'd made that clear the last time she was in the paper, and it was only the neighborhood news. Naturally, her mother would be horrified. She could hear Dee Dee admonishing that it just wasn't something a well-brought-up lady would do.

Lovie stared out at the darkness that masked the vast sea beyond, but she could hear the powerful waves rolling in to crash against the sand. Somewhere out in the swells, her beloved loggerheads were biding their time, waiting for some signal from deeply stored instinct that it was time to brave the unknown and lay their nests. Each nest, each egg, was precious to her. No one knew this beach better than she did. This was a critical moment for the island.

As she listened to the waves, the roar drowned out the voices of her mother and Stratton and the naysayers. In their place she heard the voice of her father and her brother calling out to her from the sea, echoing Flo's words.

If not you, then who?

Sea Turtle Journal

June 8, 1974

Against great odds, the sea turtle crawls across the long stretch of beach to lay her nest high on a dune. She will lay over a hundred eggs in each nest and she will nest four or more times each season. Each nest she digs is a selfless act. Each egg is a triumph of hope.

Five

～

Island time is a state of mind. For some it means a slowing of
pace from the hurried, punctual grind of the city, the aban-
donment of routines, schedules, appointments. For others it is
the acceptance that from sunup to sundown, what gets done gets
done, and what doesn't will get done soon enough. It's finding
pleasure in and appreciation for the fleeting moments.

Slipping into island time doesn't happen overnight. Once
someone arrives on the island, the transition can take from three
to five days, longer for some ragged souls. For Lovie, this summer it took a full week.

During her first week, Lovie had too much to do to reach
that easy island pace. Stratton telephoned to tell her he'd decided
to bring the Porters to the beach house for a barbeque after all.
Primrose Cottage was a classic island cottage of the kind that
well-to-do Charlestonians had brought their families to, to escape
the summer heat. They were the soul of charm and simplicity rep-
resenting a gentler time in history, but not grand. Stratton would
want the house shown in its best possible light for this event. She'd
spent the week slaving over her house and garden, knocking items
off from her to-do list with a methodical determination.

By Friday afternoon, the pine floors were lustrous from a washing with Murphy Oil soap, the paned windows were sparkling, the clunky old appliances were scrubbed, and the ancient claw-footed bathtubs gleamed. The cupboards were bursting with food, and the sweetgrass baskets on the counter were overflowing with fresh vegetables and fruits from the market. Pots of cheery flowers and hanging ferns decorated the porches, and in the shade, more flats of flowers waited to be planted. She was racing against the clock and had just finished putting the chicken in Aunt Leah's marinade when Stratton called.

"Stratton, don't forget to bring the wine," she said, a little breathless from running for the hall phone. "And did you find out what drinks the Porters like? The bar is dreadfully low here. We need almost everything. Could you take care of that? Oh, and I especially need brandy for the trifle. I'm making Mama's recipe. We always get so many compliments, I'm sure they'll like it. I thought we'd have dessert on the screened porch. Though if Jeanne is wearing perfume, she might attract mosquitoes."

"Well, Lovie . . ." Stratton cleared his throat. "That's what I wanted to talk with you about."

Lovie was wiping her brow and caught the tone in Stratton's voice. She let her hand drop from her hair. "What's that?"

There was a brief pause. "The Porters aren't coming, after all. They've decided to go north to their farm. They have a hunting lodge there—ducks, boar, deer, birds. I hear it's quite the place."

Lovie felt awash with irritation. "Well, that's very thoughtless of them, thank you very much. I don't know what constitutes good manners up north, but in Charleston it's hardly proper to cancel at the last minute without thought to all the preparations I've made. I mean, really, Stratton! If it was an emergency, of course I'd understand. But to change their mind to go hunting?"

"I'm sure Jeanne Porter didn't mean to insult."

"I should've known that a woman who wore so much makeup didn't have good breeding."

Stratton sighed low over the phone but didn't reply.

She thought of all the stress Stratton must have been under the past week and how he must be disappointed to have lost the opportunity to extend his friendship to a man he hoped to enter business dealings with. "I'm sorry. That wasn't kind. And I'm sorry they canceled. I know this was important to you. I hope you're not too disappointed. You can always invite them to come another time. Come home. The children and I miss you." She laughed lightly. "I've cooked and cleaned for days. We'll feast."

He skipped a beat. "Well, here's the thing, Lovie. The Porters have invited me to join them at their lodge. They have a private plane and the plan is to fly out first thing in the morning."

Lovie took a moment to get this straight in her mind. She twisted the phone cord in her fingers. "I see. So you're going."

"I'd like to." He was being polite, seemingly asking her permission. Yet she heard in his tone that he'd already made up his mind.

"How long will you be gone? This time?" she asked, not bothering to disguise her pique.

He responded in kind, his voice gruff with irritation. "A week at the most."

"A week," she repeated, glancing at the calendar hanging on the wall. It showed a beach scene and the words THE BEACH COMPANY, the company that had sold the island's northern end. Stratton was leaving for Europe after the Fourth of July and wouldn't be back until the end of summer. "What about your time with us? You've already got so much scheduled you'll be away most of the summer as it is. You have responsibilities to more than your business, you know. You have a family, too."

"I'm well aware of my responsibilities," he said in a low voice that dared her to challenge him.

She did not.

"Why do you think I'm working so damn hard? Sure, I wish I could come out to the beach, to hang out with you and the kids. But some of us have to work for a living."

She wanted to ask him what he meant by that, to let him know how much that comment he'd tossed out so thoughtlessly had hurt her. But in truth she already knew exactly what he'd meant. She also knew she was pushing his buttons hard and back-pedaled. There was no point in arguing over the phone like this. It solved nothing, and at that moment the only word she wanted to hear was "good-bye."

"Look," he said in a conciliatory tone, "you know this is important or I wouldn't do it. Porter can open doors for me in Japan. That's the future. It could mean a lot for us. For our family. I need your support now—without the third degree."

Lovie laughed, a short, bitter sound that had nothing to do with thinking the situation was amusing but because it was what she'd come to expect. Lovie clearly remembered the many times he'd said those exact words to her over the years, and how many times she'd rallied. Weekends, weekdays, when she was pregnant, tired, last minute—it didn't matter. She was his wife and that's what wives did. They stood by their husbands through thick and thin, for better or for worse.

Yet this had been a particularly long and cold winter, and his many evening absences had been noted and counted. Lovie wondered if her desperate craving for the feel of the sun's warmth on her skin was because her husband had grown so cold.

"It seems you've made up your mind." Her voice was lifeless. "Have a good time."

There was silence on the other end, as though he were thinking of what to say. Apparently he didn't have much to add because he said only, "I'll call you when I get back. Give my love to the children."

She hung up the phone feeling empty, vacant—like he'd already left.

June 15 came slowly for Lovie. She rose early as was her custom, swallowed a quick cup of coffee, and went off to ride her bike along the shoreline. Thunder rumbled faintly, and dark clouds hovered low over the Atlantic Ocean. Lovie hoped for a little rain to water her newly transplanted flowers, but she wanted to make it back to the house before the first drops fell. Glancing at her watch, she figured if she hurried she'd have enough time to do a little research at the library before the two o'clock meeting.

There were no tracks found this morning, so she made it back in good time. She went to her room to iron a favorite village print blouse. A short while later she emerged, the crisp blouse tucked into bell-bottom jeans. Her hair was neatly plaited into a braid that fell down her back like a skein of flaxen-colored wool.

"Cara!" she called out, walking out of her room.

"Kitchen!"

She found Cara sitting at the kitchen table with Emmi, their long thin legs roped around the chair legs. They were slathering thick layers of peanut butter on Wonder bread. The smell made her mouth water.

"Girls, I'm going to the library, then there's the meeting at the Exchange Club. Do you want to come along? You can pick out some new books. Maybe you'd like to volunteer for the project. If you write a paper on what you did for the study, I'll bet you'd get extra credit at school." She tried to make her voice upbeat and encouraging.

"Nooo way," Cara replied, rudely shoving her palm out. "You're not roping *us* into turtle duty."

"It's not turtle duty," she replied, firmly lowering Cara's hand from in front of her face.

Emmi tried to refuse politely. "We already have a lot of reading on our list this summer, Mrs. Rutledge."

Lovie didn't miss the commiserating glance the girls shared. She gave up. She'd tried for years to get the girls interested in helping the turtles, and it was like pulling eyeteeth. Summer after summer she met countless children thrilled at the prospect of seeing a hatchling. She loved teaching children about the turtles and the nesting cycle. But Cara and Emmi, and Palmer as well, not only had no interest in the sea turtles but shared a disdain for them.

"Fine," she said on a sigh. "Suit yourselves. I won't be gone long. I'll just be a few blocks away at the Exchange Club. Now remember, girls. You're to stay in the house till I get back, hear?"

"Yes, ma'am," the girls replied in unison, then looked at each other and giggled.

"Oh, no, don't you two get any ideas," she said with suspicion.

"We won't, Mama," Cara replied.

Lovie looked at the two girls. Their blue eyes were the very picture of innocence. She didn't believe them for a moment.

"We're ten years old," Cara said. "We're not babies, you know."

Lovie leaned forward to kiss Cara's cheek. "Of course you're not."

The Exchange Club was a little wood-frame building that sat on a prime piece of real estate alongside Hamlin Creek. Sitting on Palm Boulevard, the clubhouse was a favorite spot for locals to gather for small weddings, birthday parties, garden club workshops, oyster roasts, and about any other meeting on the island. Lovie looked at the sky, considering. It was a short walk from Primrose Cottage, but she didn't want to get caught in the rain. She grabbed an umbrella from the basket by the door and headed out.

The winding gravel road was bordered by sandy lots that were overrun by wild indigenous palms, shrubs, and wildflowers. She walked the three blocks to the Exchange Club at a clip, swinging her green-and-white umbrella. A black-and-white cat sunning in the middle of the road didn't appear the least bothered by her passing. As she approached the parking lot, she was surprised to see at least ten cars, and stepping out from one was Kate Baker. Her red ponytail fell over her shoulder when she bent to pull something from the car, offering full view of her generously filled-out flowered Bermuda shorts. When she stood, she was carrying a tray covered in aluminum foil.

"Hi, Kate. What've you brought?" Lovie asked her, taking hold of Kate's purse to lighten her load.

"Oh, hi, Lovie. Cupcakes," she replied, her blue eyes sparkling with pleasure at seeing Lovie. "The mayor asked me to bring something for the meeting."

"He didn't ask me to bring anything."

"He probably has other plans for you, Miss Turtle Lady. Are the girls being good?" asked Kate.

"Oh, sure. So far," Lovie replied with a chuckle.

"They'd better. I told Emmi I'd tan her hide if she stepped one foot out of your house. When those girls get together, mischief isn't far away. Bless their hearts."

"Oh, look. There's Flo waiting for us by the door." She raised her voice and called, "Flo!"

Flo stood at the double doors, talking with animation to Lois McLeod. She looked long and lean in her white pedal pushers and gingham blouse. Lois stood erect, her brown hair straight to her shoulders, her arms crossed, and a serious expression on her face. They'd called her "Beanpole" as a girl, and she'd never filled out. Her owlish eyeglass frames accentuated her pointed features. When Flo heard her name called, she turned her head, smiled, and waved them over.

These were Lovie's best friends on the island, women she'd known for years and the only ones who, when they could, offered to help her patrol the beach in the morning in search of turtle tracks.

"What took you so long?" Flo asked Lovie. "I thought *you'd* be the first one here."

"I was at the library. I did some research on this Dr. Bennett."

Flo stepped closer, alert. "What did you learn?"

"He's a bona fide biologist and researcher, and a teacher at the University of Florida. So much for your theory, Flo. In fact, he's authored or coauthored an impressive number of papers, and I was surprised that I'd actually read some of them." She looked at Flo. "He's no flunky, that's for sure."

"We don't know his personal life," Flo argued. "I can't imagine an assistant professor makes a big salary."

"Come on, Flo." Sometimes Flo wouldn't give up on an idea, like a terrier with a bone. "I don't know that a corporation *can* hire someone biased for a study like this," Lovie continued. "I mean, otherwise the study would be biased."

Flo rolled her eyes. "Don't be naïve. This is the seventies. Watergate, Nixon, corruption of judges, the CIA activities in Chile. Want more examples?"

Lovie glanced at her watch. "We're all here. Why don't we just listen to what he has to say?"

The meeting room was one large open space, like an auditorium. Simple but functional with linoleum floors, a bar on one side, and a fireplace on the other. Windows were open on this humid afternoon, tall floor fans were whirring, and already a cluster of eight women stood around a folding table that held a large crystal bowl of punch. Lovie recognized them all and felt a stiffening of her spine to see them here. Over the years she'd called each of them to ask her to join the turtle project, but all had been too busy or too disinterested to get involved. But here they were, suddenly interested when a biologist from the University of Florida—a man—summoned. Lovie couldn't help but feel the insult personally.

The front door opened, and George Clarke, the mayor of the island, rushed in, flustered and red faced. George was a portly man with thick gray hair and a rounded belly that spoke of his love for Southern fried food and beer. As he walked their way, he paused to wipe his brow with his handkerchief and adjust the narrow dark tie in the collar of his short-sleeved white shirt. His hands free, he clapped them together and came before them like a man relishing the sight of them.

"Well, well, ladies! Don't you all look lovely today? I'm assuming you're all here to talk turtles this afternoon?"

"Of course that's why we're here," Flo muttered to Lovie with a twinge of disgust. She couldn't abide being patronized.

"Ah, Lovie," the mayor said, reaching out to clasp her hand in greeting. "I'm especially glad you're here. We couldn't have a meeting without our resident Turtle Lady, could we? How are the turtles this year?"

"It's early yet, but we've got four nests that I know of. A good start."

"Splendid," he replied, patting her hand as his gaze searched the room. He nodded in acknowledgment of a wave.

Lovie's lips tightened in annoyance at his disinterest, and she slipped her hand back.

"Is Dr. Bennett coming?" Lois asked.

The mayor was quick to dispel any worry. "Dr. Bennett will be here in just a few more minutes. He flew in today all the way from Virginia, but the storm caused delays. He flies his own plane, you know. He took me up in it last week to fly over the island. I tell you, it gave me a whole new perspective to tour the island from the sky. Yes, sir, a whole new way of looking at things. This development is going to be such a boon."

Lois leaned in. "The rumors have been flying, but nobody knows anything for sure. *Is* there going to be a golf club?"

"Nothing is finalized, of course," Mayor Clarke began with caution. But his enthusiasm caught up with him. "But I think I can safely say that there are hopes for a golf club. And a tennis club."

Flo perked up and jabbed Lovie in the side.

A murmur of excitement followed, with someone saying, "A golf club, right here on Isle of Palms!"

"That will bring in the right kind of people," one of the women added. "The kind that will build nice houses."

"Exactly. And that will bring in a good, strong tax base," concluded the mayor. "We'll be able to build more roads, a better fire department, and increase our police force. Yes, ma'am, it will mean great things for our island." He clasped his hands together.

"It will also mean the destruction of the maritime forest," Lovie added soberly. "I, for one, am sorry to see it go. Once it's gone, it's gone forever."

"There's always a price to pay for progress, my dear," Mayor Clarke said in a sage tone.

There followed several minutes of discussion on the flaws and merits of the potential country club and golf course. Lovie refrained from speaking, choosing to listen to the opinions, most of which, to her surprise, seemed to favor the construction of the country club. Was she the only one sorry that a park wasn't going in? Frustration bloomed in her chest and she glanced at her watch. It was two twenty. How much longer did Dr. Bennett expect them to wait?

Minutes later the door opened and two men stepped into the

room. They both appeared to be somewhere in their early forties and were dressed in khaki pants and the kind of pale brown, multipocketed shirt that was ubiquitous among men involved in wildlife. Theirs bore the emblem of the University of Florida. The first man to enter was shorter, wiry, with neatly trimmed brown hair. His arms were burdened with papers and what looked like a poster. The second, taller man walked past him and proceeded directly to the group. The mayor strode toward him with his hand outstretched and a broad smile on his face. They met in the center of the room, shaking hands and exchanging a few words.

Lovie studied the man who clearly was Dr. Russell Bennett. He was over six feet tall with the rangy, athletic fitness of a man who spent most of his time out of doors. Echoing this, his skin was darkly tanned and his blond hair was so bleached by the sun it looked almost white. He had a long, angular face, but his eyes were hidden behind dark Ray-Bans. Despite his common, uniformlike clothing there was an elegance about him. He moved with the restraint that she recognized as breeding and privilege.

Eager to begin, Mayor Clarke asked everyone to take a seat. A few dozen folding chairs had been set up, and Lovie wondered if Dr. Bennett was disappointed at the low turnout. She, frankly, was surprised that eight showed up.

She took a seat between Flo and Kate in the front row and clasped her hands over her pocketbook in her lap. Looking up again, she saw Dr. Bennett standing behind the table while, behind him, the other man was setting up a color poster that showed the basic anatomy of the loggerhead sea turtle. Dr. Bennett removed his sunglasses and surveyed the crowd. Lovie was surprised by the brilliant blue of his eyes. What made them truly remarkable, she decided, was the sharp contrast of the whites of his eyes against his dark tan. It made the blue all the more astonishing.

Lovie shifted her gaze back to her lap, thinking it had been a long while since she'd been so struck by a man's appearance. Certainly not the response a married woman should have for another man.

Kate leaned over to whisper, "Now I know why so many women showed up."

Lovie responded with a wry grin, as much at her own ridiculousness as the others'. The front door opened and two women she didn't recognize walked in.

"Take a seat, ladies," the mayor told them, obviously pleased to see two more join the group. "We're just about to begin."

They hurried to find seats, bringing the number of women to an even dozen.

The humidity was rising and the room was stuffy. Outside, the storm was about to let loose. Mayor Clarke wiped his brow, cleared his throat, and began.

"I guess we're all here. We best get a move on. Don't want to get caught in the storm, do we? Thank you all for coming. I know you're here to listen to Dr. Bennett, not me, so I'll make my introduction short. As you all know, the city, the Beach Company, and the Sea Pines Company are conducting environmental and engineering studies of the northern end of Isle of Palms for the purpose of providing vital information to determine just what that land might be used for and how the environment would be impacted by the development. After an exhaustive search, we were fortunate to find the very best man for the job."

Clarke turned and offered a polite bow of acknowledgment to Russell Bennett. He then lifted a sheet of paper, cleared his throat, and began to read his prepared statement.

"Dr. Bennett is a leading expert on sea turtles. He has a degree from Harvard University and did his graduate work at the University of Florida. Dr. Bennett's studied sea turtles all over the world. He's traveled to the Caribbean, South America,

Central America, Mexico, and Costa Rica, and of course did exhaustive work with the sea turtles in Florida." He looked up from his papers and smiled. "Now he's right here on the Isle of Palms and we're mighty pleased to have him head up this important study. So without further ado, I present to y'all Dr. Russell Bennett."

There followed a polite applause. Lovie watched as he calmly looked out at the audience. Then he smiled, and it transformed his scholarly, even diffident expression into one of surprising warmth.

"Thank you for taking time out of your busy lives to come here on this humid day to listen to me speak about the research project I am about to begin for the Isle of Palms," he began.

He had a melodious voice, pleasant to the ear with its gentle Virginian accent. "The purpose of the study is to determine what impact a development the size and scope of the proposed resort would have on the local wildlife, in particular nesting loggerhead sea turtles. On this island, as in most of South Carolina, loggerheads are the only species of sea turtles that nest regularly. Not the green or Kemp's, and certainly not the leatherback. Still, the loggerheads are a species on the decline, so every nest is critical."

Lovie glanced around the room to see puzzled expressions on the women's faces. He was talking over their heads. No one else in this room beside herself and Flo even knew the difference among the sea turtles.

He took a breath and began pacing, using his hands as he spoke. "I see several components to the project: management, monitoring, research. We'll form teams to walk the island to locate nests and accumulate data crucial in monitoring populations, formulating protective regulations, and help support those making management decisions, and maximizing reproduction for recovery."

Strike one, Lovie thought. Even she was having a hard time following.

A hand went up and he paused. "Yes? Do you have a question?"

It was Debbie Underwood, a part-timer from Ohio. "Uh, you say we got loggerheads. How many kinds of turtles are there?"

A faint smile crossed Dr. Bennett's face, a dawning of understanding. He bent his head in thought, then leaned back against the table in the manner of someone about to begin a long story.

"I should begin with a little background information first," he said with a smile.

Lovie hid her smile in her palm. *Strike two*. Dr. Bennett had just realized that he wasn't speaking to a group of graduate students but to a handful of housewives, most of whom knew little about sea turtles. She waited, curious to see how he'd handle the situation. Or if he even could.

To her surprise, Dr. Bennett had the gift of a natural storyteller. He launched into a fascinating history of the sea turtles, beginning with mythology, including her favorite that Earth was borne by three elephants carried on the back of a turtle. He then moved on to a brief lesson in anatomy, blending dry statistics with amusing anecdotes. He seamlessly led into why sea turtles needed our protection. Lovie knew all these basics, but she enjoyed hearing someone talk so comfortably and with such authority on a topic she held close to her heart. His love for the turtles was obvious, as was his passion to preserve and protect them. Kate and Flo exchanged a look of astonishment with Lovie when he spoke of his studies with Archie Carr, the father of sea turtle study and conservation. For sea turtle enthusiasts, whether lay or professional, an association with Carr was the gold standard.

The hour flew by as Dr. Bennett outlined a basic sea turtle monitoring project. To Lovie's surprise, it was not significantly different from what she'd been doing for ten years on her own. They were to form teams that divided up the beach into smaller sections. Every morning they were to walk the beach in search of turtle tracks. If they found tracks, they were expected to report to Dr. Bennett so that he could go to the site and confirm the nest. As the season progressed, they would also monitor the hatching of the nests.

In the end, Dr. Bennett hit a home run. A dozen volunteers clustered around the table to sign up for the project and shake his hand.

"Look at them," Flo said with resigned humor. "This project is no different than what you've been doing for years, and now they can't wait to sign on the dotted line."

"I know," was all she could say, but in her mind she felt further diminished. She wanted to leave as soon as she'd signed her name to the list. "Flo, let's duck out before we get caught by the rain. I need to get back to the girls."

"Wait just a minute more," Flo pleaded. "I'd like to meet him. I thought he was fabulous, didn't you?"

"Your opinion of Dr. Bennett has certainly risen. Now you're all smiles and hearty handshakes." She leaned closer. "Are you sure it's not his blue eyes?"

"Actually it's his friend, the one with the brown hair, I've got my eye on." Flo turned her head quickly as her turn in line came up.

"Delighted to meet you, Dr. Bennett," she said in a loud voice. "That's an impressive résumé of work you've got there. It'll be an honor to work with someone of your caliber."

"Thank you," he replied with an urbane smile. "I'm glad you approve."

Standing behind Flo, Lovie's smile stiffened, catching the hint of sarcasm.

"You know," Flo added, stepping aside and glancing at Lovie, "she might not have all your credentials, but we have our own turtle expert here on Isle of Palms."

Lovie cringed. How *could* Flo introduce her as an expert? Anything she said now would only appear ridiculous to someone with the degrees and accomplishments of Dr. Bennett.

"Really?" Russell Bennett replied with polite interest. "I hadn't heard that. I'd love to meet her."

Flo turned to indicate Lovie standing beside her. "She's right here. Dr. Bennett, meet Olivia Rutledge. She's been studying our loggerheads for over ten years. All her life, really. She's always taking notes and roping us into walking the beaches looking for tracks. We call her the Turtle Lady. If anyone knows about our loggerheads, it's this lady right here."

Russell Bennett turned his head and fixed his gaze on Lovie. She felt the air sucked out of the room as their gazes met and his blue eyes bored into hers with the heat of a blowtorch. The attraction felt profound. Important. Unwelcome.

He seemed to skip a beat before tilting his head and saying courteously, "Mrs. Rutledge."

Lovie was tongue-tied. She pulled her wits together enough to offer, "It's a pleasure to meet you, Dr. Bennett."

"So, I understand that you're a . . . turtle lady?"

Lovie frowned and saw the faint amusement in his eyes at the term, and her blush deepened. She was accustomed to Stratton, the mayor, and other men belittling her work, and stiffened her shoulders, determined not to allow this Ph.D. to diminish her status on the island.

"Yes," she replied, looking directly into his eyes. "That's a term of affection. I've been interested in the sea turtles that nest on our island, but I don't claim to be an expert. Amateur naturalist might sum it up better."

He seemed to note that. "What work have you done?"

"I patrol the beaches in the morning, and if I see a nest I place a marker by it." She was deliberately vague.

"Then you must know how many nests you've had. You've kept a tally, I suppose?"

"Of course. For the nests, and the hatches, too, of course."

He appeared astonished. "Mrs. Rutledge, that could be extremely helpful."

"Nothing to what you're used to, I'm sure," she said with sarcasm. By the way he studied her, she felt sure it didn't go unnoticed.

"She's just being modest," Kate added, stepping closer. She smiled at Lovie with affection. Lovie wished she could, for once, just reach out and put her hand over Kate's mouth. "She's out there every morning, and when she's not, she ropes one of us to go out there looking for tracks. Never misses a day. And she's always scribbling in her notebook about this or that."

"You write your observations, too?" he asked, taking interest.

"Honestly, Dr. Bennett, they're making way too much of it," Lovie replied.

"I'd appreciate the chance to see them. Your records could really jump-start my project. *Our* project now," he added, glancing up at the few women who had lagged behind to listen to the conversation. They enthusiastically agreed and urged Lovie to comply.

"Some of my observations are personal," she hedged.

"I assure you, I'm only interested in the turtle data. Mrs. Rutledge, if it's not too inconvenient, could we set up a time to look over these records? I'm sure you have more information than you realize."

Lovie took a deep breath, trying to think of a reasonable reason to refuse. The silence grew awkward.

"If there's one thing Archie Carr pounded in our heads," he

added to persuade her, "it was to listen to anecdotal stories of the natives."

Anecdotal stories? she thought, drawing herself back. *Natives?* Could he be more insulting? "I'm sorry, Dr. Bennett," she said curtly. "I'm sure the simple markings of a local native could have no interest for you. I really must go now. The storm is about to break."

As though on cue, thunder clapped loudly, seemingly overhead. Everyone moved to rush out the door, giving Lovie the perfect opportunity to slip away. She hurried to the door and saw that she was too late. The clouds opened up and it was a deluge. These torrents were not uncommon on the island as a strong storm front moved quickly from the mainland out to sea. The pounding rain was deafening and difficult to see through. Lovie paused at the door, feeling trapped.

"Mrs. Rutledge . . ."

She heard Dr. Bennett coming after her, calling her name. She cringed, realizing she'd left her umbrella inside. Looking over her shoulder, she saw through the open doors that he'd been momentarily detained by two women. He looked her way, marked her departure, then tried to excuse himself from the ladies.

Seizing the moment for her escape, Lovie stepped into the storm.

Six

〜

The rain was cold and biting, drenching her clothes within seconds. Lovie had her head bent and kept walking forward, fast, her hands clenched as they pumped the air. It wasn't the first time she'd found herself stuck when a storm broke. It'd happened many times while walking the beach. Sometimes a storm front approached like a wall of gray rain and she could literally step *into* a storm. But today she was upset because she was ruining a perfectly good pair of shoes.

"Mrs. Rutledge!"

Lovie couldn't believe it. She looked over her shoulder to see a vague image of a man trotting through the misty downpour after her. What kind of an idiot would pursue her in this tempest? she thought, but she didn't stop. Maybe he'd take her obvious hint. She was only a block from home and picked up her pace.

"Mrs. Rutledge!"

A moment later he was at her side. She glanced over to see Dr. Bennett, his face scrunched in a grimace as he was pelted by the rain. He, too, was drenched, and she could see the color of skin beneath his soaked shirt.

She kept walking but asked, shouting to be heard over the rain, "What could be so important that you'd follow me in this storm?"

"I couldn't let you leave without apologizing," he shouted back at her, keeping up with her pace. "I didn't mean what I said back there. Well, I did, but it came out all wrong."

They were approaching her house, and Lovie was left to wonder if she could, in good conscience, leave him in the storm. Drat, she thought, mentally kicking herself, she wouldn't leave a dog out in this rain.

"I can barely hear a word you're saying," she shouted. "Please, come inside out of the rain."

He hesitated. "Are you sure?"

"You can't stay out here. Come in."

She led him up the stairs to the porch where, mercifully, they were protected from the pummeling of the cold rain. Water dripped down her face and she mopped it with her hands. Looking down, she was horrified to see her drenched blouse left little to the imagination. Lovie plucked at her blouse as she slipped out of her shoes and, opening the door, hurried inside. While Dr. Bennett unlaced his shoes, she scurried through the living room to her bedroom, trailing water and calling, "Cara? Emmi?" There was no answer. She grabbed two towels from her bathroom, wondering where the girls had sneaked off to and realizing she was alone in the house with Dr. Bennett.

She returned to the living room to find Dr. Bennett standing by the front door looking like a drowned rat with his hair plastered against his face and his clothing clinging to his well-muscled body. He seemed embarrassed.

"I'm terribly sorry to be dripping all over your floor."

"Can't be helped," she replied, handing him one of the towels. "And these old floors have been dripped on for years."

He accepted the towel gratefully and began mopping his face and hair, but it was obvious that he'd never get those clothes dry. "I should make a run back to the Exchange Club. It was idiotic of me to chase after you, but when I realized how what I'd said to you could be misunderstood, I couldn't let you leave like that."

Lovie's stern expression softened somewhat with her mood. "This rain won't last too long. They'll likely wait it out indoors and you'd be stuck dripping in those wet clothes, catching your death of cold. Might as well wait here where it's warm and dry."

"Can I call them? To let them know where I am."

"There isn't a phone in the club, I'm afraid."

He thought for a moment. "Then it appears I'm stranded and at your mercy." He shrugged with exaggeration.

She smiled. "If you go into the bathroom at the end of the hall"—she pointed—"I'll get you a robe and dry your clothes."

"I don't want to put you to any trouble," he said again.

"I'm not going to launder and iron them. I'm just going to toss them in the dryer. They *can* go in the dryer, can't they?"

He chuckled. "Sure. They've been through a lot worse."

"Well, then. If it's all the same to you, I'd rather you didn't continue to drip on my floor. I'll get that robe."

A short while later the dryer was humming and Dr. Bennett emerged sheepishly from the bathroom, tightening the belt around Stratton's white terry cloth robe. Lovie peeked through the kitchen door to see his long, tanned legs poking out from the robe. It seemed oddly intimate to have him walking around in a robe, with the children gone and the two of them alone in the house. She was glad she'd turned on lamps in the living room. He was walking around the room, looking at the art. He stopped to admire Lovie's collection of seashells and peered closely at the silver-framed photographs of her family on the mantel. She smiled when he lifted the primitive clay sea turtle that her father had created one summer. It was her prized possession.

Lovie had changed into the first dry clothes she grabbed from her bureau—white shorts and a navy T-shirt. She was measuring coffee into the percolator when Dr. Bennett entered the kitchen.

He continued his perusal around the cramped room—the scrubbed wood table with the lazy Susan that held the turtle salt and pepper shakers and hot sauce, the small clay plates on the walls with art of turtles. He tucked his hands in his pockets. "You have a lot of turtle art," he said.

She chuckled. "Oh, yes. I get a lot of turtle things as gifts. I have quite the collection."

The wind gusted, shaking the windows. "Storm still raging," he said, stating the obvious. "Seems like you have quick, fierce storms in the afternoon here, too. They're common in Florida."

"They move fast coming in from over the mainland on their way out to sea." She plugged the percolator into the socket. "We should have hot coffee in a minute."

"It's a nice cottage. Very warm and welcoming."

"Thank you. It belonged to my parents, and now me. Someday it will go to Cara and Palmer."

"I assume they are your children?"

"Yes," she replied, reaching up for two cups.

"Ah, Meissen," he remarked, noticing the Blue Onion pattern. He picked up a coffee cup and turned it over to look at the underside. "Crossed swords," he said, acknowledging the mark of the blue-glazed porcelain that protected it from forgery. "My grandmother collected Meissen ware. It was her passion." A slight smile of remembrance crossed his face. "She had a lot, too."

Sensitive to the awkwardness of the two of them in the confined space, Lovie kept busy. She went to the fridge for milk and, noting that Palmer had already drunk half the gallon, poured some into a white creamer. She placed that and the sugar bowl on a tray with two spoons and napkins. Paper would have to do, she thought, as she carried the tray into the living room. Pools of light spilled out from the lamps, making the room feel cozy. Thunder rumbled, softer now, and the rain sounded on the roof with a consistent, but less insistent patter. It was a good afternoon to stay indoors.

"You know, Mrs. Rutledge, since I'm here," he began, following her into the living room, "I might as well take a look at your sea turtle records. No time like the present. That is, if you've forgiven me enough to let me see them." He laughed, defusing the tension. "I really would appreciate taking a look. They could jump-start the whole project, especially since the nesting season has already begun."

Lovie knew this was coming and considered it as she set the tray on the coffee table. She enjoyed for the moment holding some power over him.

"Cream or sugar?" she asked him.

"No, thank you. Black is fine."

Lovie poured and offered him the cup and saucer. She poured herself a cup but didn't drink. Setting the coffeepot on the tray, she thought his apology seemed sincere and he'd lost the arrogance she'd found so distasteful at the club. Lovie cast a discreet glance at Dr. Bennett standing across the table. He was, in fact, looking anything but arrogant in his bare legs and feet.

She said, "Yes, Dr. Bennett. You can look at my journals, records, observations, whatever you prefer to call them. I'm a little embarrassed to show them. They represent a great deal of time and effort, and have served my needs, such as they are. But they also include some comments of, well, a more personal nature. Nothing I can't show you, but . . ." She shrugged and let her arguments go. "There are quite a lot of notes, I warn you."

"The more the better. Where should I sit?"

Lovie walked to her father's desk and pulled out the chair. "Why don't you sit here? You'll want to spread out the maps and there's good light."

"Maps, too?"

Her lips lifted in a smug smile. "A few. We natives do what we can. I'll fetch the journals."

While he settled himself in the chair, Lovie went to the cabinet below the bookshelf and pulled out the three journals. She ran her hand tentatively over the soft leather.

After she'd married and inherited the beach house, she'd discovered a manila folder in this same cabinet where her parents kept old papers and photographs. Curious, she'd opened it and discovered an old composition notebook, the kind she'd used to write essays in at school. It was filled with her father's observations of the loggerhead sea turtle nests he'd discovered and those he'd witnessed hatching. In the folder there was also an assortment of rough sketches of the island's beach with an X marking the location of every nest he'd discovered, season after season. The maps were spotted and wrinkled; he'd obviously carried them with him on the beach, perhaps folded in his pocket. That he'd never told her about this file had stunned Lovie.

The following winter, Michael Simmons passed away. Her father had been her inspiration to begin recording the turtle nests on the Isle of Palms. In the beginning, she'd found comfort in continuing her father's efforts. On mornings she was tired, ill, or just not in the mood, she remembered her father and forced herself to get up and walk the beach. No day was missed. No details were omitted.

Yet, how would her record of "native observations" measure up to the scientific work of Dr. Bennett, a professional biologist with a Ph.D.? She blew out a plume of air and patted the journals. She would soon find out.

She carried the three journals to Dr. Bennett along with two manila folders, one filled with her maps, the second her father's original file.

Dr. Bennett moved aside papers cluttering the desk, making space for the journals. He looked at them, rubbing his hands like a man before a feast. "I'll just get started, then."

Lovie scooped up the miscellaneous papers and stood motionless, watching with her breath held, as Dr. Bennett opened the first volume. She didn't realize her hands were tightening on the papers, crushing them.

"There's a system," she said, self-consciously. "At least, one develops as the years pass." She paused. "I made changes as I figured out what I needed." She realized she was already making excuses and tightened her lips, willing herself to stop babbling.

"I'm sure I'll make it out," he replied absently, head bent over the journal. "It goes back more than ten years," he exclaimed, surprised.

"Farther, actually. If you include my father's data." Something compelled her to add, "But Daddy only recorded what he'd found on the days he walked. It wasn't every day so his reports aren't consistent."

Dr. Bennett looked up from the journals, his gaze speculative. "And yours are?"

Lovie lifted her chin, not appreciating his tone. "Yes. At least in the later years they are. The first year or two I might have missed a few days. If the children were sick, or whatever. As time passed, I began to see I couldn't miss a day, so I enlisted the help of friends to cover for me when I couldn't make it out. There weren't many volunteers, but somehow we made it work."

"And you've been walking the beach, recording your findings, for ten years." He spoke with a sense of wonder, as though he couldn't quite believe it.

"That's right."

"That's a long time. What prompted you to begin?"

"What prompted *you*?" she asked. She was beginning to get annoyed by his questioning of her motives.

He smiled good-naturedly. "Fair question. Where do I begin?" He leaned back in the chair, relaxed and at ease. She had the feeling he could be equally comfortable in a grand estate, as the Bennett home likely was in Virginia, or in some hut in South America.

"My father taught me to hunt and fish at a young age, but I was more interested in the turtles, lizards, snakes, and other reptiles I found. My mother was a good sport about all the strange pets I had. We spent summers at our home on Virginia Beach and winter vacations in Bermuda. I guess you could say I spent a lot of time outdoors, especially on the beach. I was always fascinated by wildlife and landscape. It was only natural that I'd study it as a grown-up." He tilted his head and studied her face with another of his teasing grins. "I'm going to hazard a wild guess and say you loved critters as a child, too."

Lovie chuckled and thought to herself that this gentle teasing was part of his personality. Part of his boyish charm.

"At last! I've cajoled a smile from Mrs. Rutledge."

"All right, yes," she conceded. "I've always collected a weird assortment of critters and shells. But turtles . . . There's something about them. They're so charismatic. I only really got to know them when I was ten years old. That's when my parents bought this house. We lived farther north in Aiken but spent summers here. My father loved the loggerheads and I loved him, so . . ." Lovie felt a sudden pang of longing for her father. She missed him, even after all these years.

Lovie didn't want to talk more about herself. It didn't seem fair, given how forthcoming he'd been, but she'd already shared more than she'd intended. She stepped back from the desk. "I won't delay you any longer, Dr. Bennett. The rain will stop and your clothes will be dry before you know it. I'll leave you to read, and if you'll excuse me, I've got to make a few phone calls and track down my runaway daughter."

An hour later, Lovie sat straight in the side chair, her legs crossed, her foot tapping, and clutching a glass of ice water. The humidity from the storm made the room feel like a steam bath. A bead of sweat formed at her upper lip and her T-shirt clung to damp spots in all the wrong places. She glanced up at the ceiling fan that whirled noisily at high speed but offered only minimal relief. She was glad Cara and Emmi had gone over to Miranda's house. It would have been intolerable if those two were here, snooping around with their big eyes and ears trained on the handsome man in Stratton's bathrobe. No, she wouldn't want that tidbit of information floating around the island.

Across the room, Russell Bennett sat hunched over a notebook, elbows on the table and his long legs bent. He hadn't accepted her offer of a cold drink and didn't appear the least uncomfortable on this steamy day. Not a drop of sweat trickled down his brow, even though she felt like a lawn sprinkler. Not to sweat in that terry robe—he couldn't be human, she thought.

Lovie heard the high *ding* of the dryer and sprang to her feet, glad to have something to do. The laundry room in the cottage was little more than a large pantry closet that opened to the kitchen. She pulled out Dr. Bennett's brown shirt and trousers, feeling the act was somehow intimate, at the very least strange, to be handling another man's laundry. She noticed that the quality of the cotton was very good and that though the cuffs were slightly frayed, likely from his fieldwork, they bore the initials RDB in subtle dark brown thread. Even his socks were a cashmere blend. Someone dressed him well, she thought, and credited his wife. If they were Stratton's clothes, she wouldn't think of not ironing them. She'd be shamed to send her husband out in public wearing wrinkled clothes or missing buttons. But

Dr. Bennett was not her husband and he could very well iron his own clothes. Besides, unlike Stratton, who found a loose thread distracting, Dr. Bennett struck her as the type who wouldn't even notice that the shirt and trousers were terribly wrinkled.

But at least they were dry, Lovie thought as she hung them on hangers. She'd volunteered to help with the turtle project, not be his personal maid. She carried the clothes to the living room.

"Your clothes are dry," she told him, holding the hangers in the air.

Dr. Bennett looked up, distracted. "What? Oh, good. Good. Just set them anywhere. I'll get to them in a minute." With that, he went back to his work.

Spoken like a man accustomed to being taken care of, Lovie thought, irked by the subservient role he'd just placed her in. Glancing over her shoulder, she saw that he was engrossed with her sketch of the beach erosion that occurred on the island the previous year. He was comparing it against sketches of the dunes made earlier. If he'd bother to ask her questions, she could talk at length about the serious erosion of the beach and the patterns of accretion.

Rubbing her hands together, Lovie's gaze aimlessly swept the room, the clock. To anyone walking it at that moment, it looked like a peaceful, companionable scene. It was four o'clock on a rainy afternoon, the room was cozy, softly lighted, a man worked at the desk, a woman was doing laundry, and ceiling fans whirled. In reality it was anything but peaceful.

Lovie felt her impatience rising up in her throat, choking her. She couldn't sit in the stifling room just waiting for him to finish for one moment longer. She felt as though she were waiting for the results of an exam or, worse, her thesis. Those pages held more than a record of events. She'd given this project her all—her best ideas, her best efforts, her best years. In her heart of hearts, she felt if her work didn't measure up, then somehow *she* didn't measure up. She didn't sign up for this.

She walked swiftly across the room to the porch. The rain was little more than a drizzle now, so she pushed open the doors and stepped out into the fresh breezes that blew in from the ocean. She held on to the railing and inhaled gulps of the moist air while gazing on the low-lying clouds that moved farther out to sea like an armada.

A short while later, Dr. Bennett joined her on the windward porch. "That breeze is welcome," he said, coming to stand beside her.

She turned her head to see that he was now properly dressed again in his wrinkled shirt and trousers. Oddly, they suited him. He looked all the more the naturalist in his element.

"I thought I was the only one feeling the heat," she said with sarcasm.

"If I did, I didn't notice. I was too engrossed in your records."

Lovie closed her eyes a second, bolstering her resolve, then turned to lean against the railing. She crossed her arms, wary. "And . . . ?"

"Mrs. Rutledge, what you have there is a wonder. Absolutely astonishing. I didn't know what to expect, but I certainly didn't expect this."

Lovie released the breath she'd been holding in a soft laugh. A small smile eased across her face, and she felt a flood of satisfaction. She had to hear more. "How do you mean?"

"I mean I am truly amazed at the level of thoroughness and perspicacity you've shown in your records. You clearly show a grasp of the nesting habits of the loggerhead on Isle of Palms, and also of anthropogenic activities. I've never stumbled on anything like these before."

"I never thought . . ." she stammered. "They were just . . ."

She laughed lightly, flustered by the praise. "I don't know what to say. I'm so glad," she said, meaning it. Her relief made her giddy. "I wish my father could hear you say this."

"Ah, yes, well . . . To be honest, your father's notes are not, as you said yourself, consistent. I'm afraid they won't be of much help."

"He only did it for his own curiosity and pleasure," she replied, feeling the need to defend her father.

"No criticism meant. Just that, in terms of methodology, Mrs. Rutledge, your observations provide a remarkably consistent record of the sea turtle population on this island for the past ten years. Through your system of patrolling the island's beaches, you've established, conclusively, that on the Isle of Palms the loggerhead sea turtles are in decline. That's astounding. Well done, Mrs. Rutledge!"

"Not the whole island," she corrected. "Just the southern end, from Breach Inlet up to the maritime forest."

"True, but it's actually better that you were consistent in one area than willy-nilly all over the island."

Lovie's lips twitched. Hearing the word *willy-nilly* from this scientist's lips was amusing. Still, hearing her work described as following scientific methodology and that her findings were astounding made her stand straighter with pride.

"First, let's get out of the way that you should publish your findings."

"*Publish?*"

"Of course. Your data is important information on the regularity of nesting on this island. Second, you've just single-handedly shot this project into high gear," he continued. "I'll wager no one knows this island or the turtles here as well as you do."

"I'd accept that wager," she replied, confident in that knowledge.

His blue eyes narrowed as his lips twisted in a wry grin. "I can see why they call you the Turtle Lady."

Lovie held back her smile, amused. "I'm going to assume you mean that as a compliment."

He smiled openly then, and his sincerity surprised her. "I do. I really do."

In his wrinkled shirt, under the brightening sky, with his tan making his eyes seem to shine, Lovie felt a frisson of physical attraction that flustered her. She wondered if he felt it, too, because they both looked away and stepped back a pace.

"Thank you, Dr. Bennett," she replied with a curt nod of her head. "I appreciate that."

"I'm still wondering why," he said.

"Why what?"

"You didn't answer me earlier. Why do you do it? What compelled you to keep these records, all on your own, so consistently—I dare say obsessively—all these years?"

Lovie's mind flashed back to that single turtle whose gaze she'd met so many years before, and all the turtles she'd encountered since. One female after another. One hatchling after another. She'd responded not as merely an observer but also as a woman. How could she explain the depth of her emotions, something as ephemeral as having felt a bond with a wild animal, to this scientist? She decided she wouldn't. It was too personal.

"Hard to say," she replied vaguely. "I'll never really know if I chose this project, or if the project chose me."

His eyes glimmered with appreciation at her answer. He moved a step closer, speaking in earnest. "You know, Archie Carr always says that naturalists were born, not made. Unlike other areas of science, like chemistry and physics, where a scientist chooses to pursue a subject that interests him. Or as Archie put it, the heart follows the mind. For naturalists, it's the reverse.

The mind follows the heart. You, Mrs. Rutledge, are a true naturalist. You're rare."

Lovie felt his words intensely. There was no teasing now, no slanted comments about her being a turtle lady, no condescension for a well-meaning woman who loved turtles. He'd called her a naturalist. He viewed her as an equal. He couldn't know what that meant to her.

"Mrs. Rutledge, I wonder . . . Would you consider being my assistant in this project? Well, not assistant. More a partner. A colleague?"

"A colleague?"

"Yes. Your knowledge of the island, the nesting sites, your records, are invaluable. I'll have to burn the midnight oil to get this project under way as soon as possible."

Lovie wanted to jump on board and say yes, but an unpleasant thought that had been niggling in the nether regions of her mind all afternoon surfaced again. One planted by Flo. She hesitated, rubbing her palms together.

"Dr. Bennett, before I agree to the project, I have a question for you."

"Fire away."

"You've been hired by the development company, haven't you?"

"That's right."

"And they need this impact study in order to move forward with their plans."

"Yes," he replied in a tone that told he was wondering where her questions were heading.

"Once you gather all the information, what will happen to it? Will they seriously consider the findings, or just file and ignore them? They have a lot invested in this property, and from what I understand, the plans for the development are on a grand scale. What's to stop them from doing whatever they like and ignoring the needs of the turtles? Building groins, docks, walls along the beach like they did in Florida?" She looked briefly at her hands. "How can we be sure the report won't be in any way . . . biased?"

Glancing up, she saw that his face had tightened, barely perceptibly. He crossed his arms and considered her question, his gaze fixed on Lovie. "You're questioning my motives?"

She hadn't expected him to respond so bluntly. He continued to stare at her, barely blinking.

"I'm just asking what others are thinking."

"I see." Dr. Bennett hesitated. "You think perhaps I'm getting a little cash under the table? Maybe a new lot in the new development, something to sweeten the report?"

"I'd like to believe you aren't," she replied honestly. "But I don't know you at all." She saw the surprise on his face and ran her hand through her hair. "This is our island. This isn't academic for us." She spoke quickly now, wanting him to understand her position.

"I've been up against guys like these many times before, trying to get them to turn off the lights shining on the beach, reduce noise, stop people from riding the backs of the turtles, poaching. The list goes on and on. And you know what I get? A pat on the head and someone telling me to keep up the good work. That kind of condescension is infuriating, not to mention insulting. No one wants to see my records or hear my opinions. I'm dismissed. So I've gone it alone. I've walked the island every day for years, knowing all along there was a possibility that no one would ever see my work. And I didn't care. Because I know at the very least I'm making a difference in the sea turtle population on this island, hatchling by hatchling. Even if it's small. I've earned the right to be suspicious of anyone who comes in and takes over *my* project. So I'm asking you, Dr. Bennett, if we succeed in getting more volunteers and we all put our backs into the project, what's going to come of it?"

His smile was rueful, even a little sad. "What's going to come of it?" he repeated. "Do you want an honest answer?"

She nodded.

"I don't know. Nobody does. There are no guarantees."

Now Lovie's lips tightened in frustration. It seemed too easy an answer.

Dr. Bennett sighed and put his hands on his hips. He suddenly looked very tired.

"I'm a lot of things," he began. "I'm a biologist, a student of natural history, a field researcher. But I'm not a politician. I'm here to study the nesting cycle of the loggerheads on this island and to offer an opinion on the impact the development's plans will have on them. Period. What happens after that is not up to me."

"So you just come in, do your job, and leave?"

He shifted his weight and pursed his lips in thought. "I leave your island, yes. But I'll continue the good fight. My work with sea turtles is more global. I don't confine myself to one beach. This is a migratory species, Mrs. Rutledge."

"I'm aware of that," she snapped back. "But this isn't just any beach to me. It's *my* beach."

"You refer to the beach, even the turtles, as yours. That kind of territorialism can be dangerous in research."

She felt slapped. "There you go again, Dr. Bennett. Taking the imperial stand of one who knows so much more, has so many degrees, has traveled the world. Well, good for you! You're a man. You had that choice." She pointed to herself, feeling her heat rise. "I took another path. I never had that freedom."

"It's not an issue of male or female. I have several female colleagues," he argued.

She walked farther away from him, turning her back. "I realize that. Of course. Yet, from where I stand, I see things differently. Perhaps it's because I *am* a woman, I stayed in one place. I tended the beaches as an animal might tend her nest."

She turned to face him. "I doubt you'll understand what I'm about to say, but any woman would get it immediately." Lovie began pacing across the porch, searching for words for something that she'd never had to explain before. What she did was so instinctual. She didn't have words on the tip of her tongue.

"It's rather like housework," she began. "No, that's not quite right. I mean . . . How can I explain it? When a woman is in her home, she's always looking, or more, scanning, wondering if the pot's boiling, if she's out of milk, if the children are in view, if the doors are locked." She was talking as much to herself as to him.

"We women walk around our houses every day, day after day, picking things up, patting things down, observing patterns, changes. We tend our nest by being fully present. We pay attention to the details, over and over. Our motions are circular. Nonlinear." Lovie looked at him, earnestly hoping he'd follow her drift.

"It was like that for me on the beach. I'm sorry if my use of the possessive offends you, but that's how I felt. I was tending my nests. This is my home. Each hatchling was a baby. Each one mattered."

"You were making it personal."

"And that's not professional?"

"Frankly, no."

"Well, then, so be it! Of course it was personal. Caring *is* personal. It's what kept me out there, day after day, year after year. I know that you would die before you called a hatchling a baby, but my calling it a baby doesn't diminish the work I did—and continue to do. Or that my friends do. I promise you, it's what the volunteers will feel, no matter what you tell them."

He didn't reply.

"You said so yourself. My results are . . . what did you call them? Astonishing."

"They are."

"I know they are," she said boldly. "I'm excited about my findings. Once I got results, new questions arose in my head, and sometimes those questions changed. My father, bless his heart, pointed to those questions because he was curious. I simply tried to answer those questions."

"I never meant to insult . . ."

"But you did." Lovie paused, feeling the tension rise. "The power of tending does not require a degree from a university, Dr. Bennett. It requires persistence, careful observation, and most of all, *caring*. I don't do this to become famous. It *is* personal. So don't question my motives or my integrity."

"But you can question mine? Do you think because I have a degree, because I use methodology, because I take the larger view, that I love the individual turtle less? That I could take a bribe and sell them all down the river?"

Lovie felt heat rise to her cheeks. "No. I'm sorry. I should never have insulted you like that."

He was silent a moment, then said, "Nor I, you." He took a step closer. "Mrs. Rutledge, I assure you I'm not taking a bribe or getting rich doing this study. Frankly, I'm already rich enough. I don't need any more money. But even if I did, I wouldn't."

She crossed her arms, listening.

"To be honest, I don't blame you for checking me out. You're about to hand over ten years of work and you want to be sure I'm not some mouthpiece for the developers. But I hope you'll trust me. And if you don't trust me, trust my credentials. Make a few phone calls. I'll let my reputation speak for me."

She felt a bit ashamed for reacting so strongly. She'd never had an outburst like that before in her life, at least not to a guest. This mattered so much to her, and there was something about

Dr. Bennett—his stature in the field, his breadth of knowledge, his respect for her work—that made her rise to the occasion to be his equal. Indeed, she felt his equal. This made his apology mean the world.

"Thank you, Dr. Bennett. That won't be necessary." Her lips twitched. "Besides, I already did my homework. Your résumé is impressive. I mean, Lord almighty, you list Archie Carr as a reference."

"Why am I not surprised?" he replied with a chuckle. He turned and leaned against the railing, his shoulders slightly slumped forward in a more companionable position. "You know, no one goes into the business of ecology or championing sea turtles, or any other species, to make money. It's damn hard work, but"—he looked at her and offered a conciliatory smile—"like you, I love it. I couldn't give it up. It's a bitch out there sometimes. I work long hours under the burning sun, in humidity that makes this seem like a cakewalk. I'm half eaten alive by mosquitoes, I face poachers with machetes . . ."

Lovie laughed. "Heavens!"

He shrugged. "And for what? Nothing less than to preserve a noble species for our children, and our children's children, and beyond." He looked at her, and their eyes met. "I'm not that different from you, Mrs. Rutledge. We both do it because we love it."

"Yes," she said with passion. "It's not just about the knowledge, is it, Dr. Bennett? It's about the wisdom. That layer of intelligence working beneath it all."

"That's it exactly," he said in a voice tinged with wonder.

"But we're losing the battle," she exclaimed. "The number of turtles, at least on this island, is on the decline. If this research project can't protect them, what will? Sometimes I feel so . . . helpless."

"It's a battle that's not going away, believe me. Developers are in the business of making money. I can tell you already that there will be those who will read my report and feel it presents unjust restrictions on their plans for a hotel, or a house, or a golf course. They'll be up in arms. They'll go to the local people and remind them of the jobs the construction will bring, the tax dollars, how the development will increase the value of their homes. Money is a powerful motivation. But," he said with a lift of his shoulders, "there's always compromise. That's what we have to fight for."

"I'm not a very good general," she said with a short laugh. "I'm more the good foot soldier."

"Don't sell yourself short, Mrs. Rutledge."

The doorbell rang. To Lovie's mind, it sounded like the bell in a boxing ring. The rising tension had been broken. Lovie turned, but Dr. Bennett laid a hand on her arm, stalling her. She swung her head around, surprised at the touch, and looked up into his startlingly blue eyes, close to her own.

He said, "What happens after we finish the project depends more on you and the people who live on this island. Do the turtles matter? What do you want this island to look like in ten years? In the year 2000? What part of this island, if any, will be preserved? One thing's for certain. There are going to be a lot more people moving onto this island in the coming decades. There's only so much island property out there. Developers will continue to develop, that's a given. True, this is only one beach in the world. But as you so aptly put it, it's *your* beach. But I'm here to help in any way I can."

The doorbell rang again, followed by an insistent knocking. Lovie turned and hurried to the front door, wishing she had just five more uninterrupted minutes with Dr. Bennett. Earlier, the hours seemed to move slower than molasses, but this last half hour had sped by.

She opened the door and there Flo stood with her hair mildly damp and frizzing in the drizzle. Beside her was the man who had accompanied Dr. Bennett to the meeting. He was a congenial-looking man, at five seven nearly as tall as Flo, wiry, with close-cropped dark hair.

Flo was the first to speak. "The storm finally let up and here we are. Is Dr. Bennett here? We saw him run after you and just assumed . . ." Then, looking over Lovie's shoulder, her mouth spread to a cat's grin. "Ah, I see he is."

Dr. Bennett came to the front door, towering over Lovie, and the two men smiled as old friends. "Bing!" he cried out. "Sorry if I made you wait and worry. I got stuck in the downpour and decided to stick it out. Mrs. Rutledge was a saint. She let me drip all over her carpet. Oh, Mrs. Olivia Rutledge, please meet my colleague, Dr. Bingham Wolitzer."

"My pleasure, Dr. Wolitzer. Won't you come in?"

"No, thank you, I can't stay. Uh, Russ, we really should be going. We have to get the keys to the rental house before they shut down."

"Right." Dr. Bennett turned to Lovie. "Thank you again for the towel, the robe, the sanctuary from the storm. Most especially, thank you for the chance to read your journals. I would very much like to study them again." His gaze was open, without recrimination or judgment. "But that's up to you."

"I've made up my mind," she replied. "I'd very much like to take the long view and be part of the project." She smiled with meaning. "As your partner or colleague. Wait here a minute." Lovie walked quickly to the desk, swept up the journals and her maps, and carried them back to Dr. Bennett, letting her hands linger a moment as she handed them over. "Here you go. Oh, wait, I'll keep this one," she said, taking this summer's journal. "I'll still need it. Even if you have different forms, and I'm guessing you will, I'll keep my journals." She patted the leather, then gave him a warning glare. "Guard them with your life."

"Thank you. I'll get them back to you safely."

"You'd better!"

Lovie heard a cough and, looking up, she saw Flo with her eyes wide with wonder. She tilted her head and her gaze bored into her as if to say, *What are you doing?*

Bing spoke up again. "We'd better get going."

Dr. Bennett said to Lovie in the manner of a colleague, "I'll start getting the beach divided up into sections. Could you help me assign the slots?"

"Yes. And I'll walk the beach tomorrow morning so we don't lose a day."

"Don't bother. Tomorrow morning I'll do a flyover."

"A what?"

"I'll fly my plane over the island to look for tracks."

Lovie thought of her provincial rusty bicycle. "Really? You can see them from that high up?"

"Sure. The tracks are readily seen when you fly low."

"That'd sure save a lot of time each morning. What do you need us for?"

"They can't afford for me to do a flyover every morning. And there's the weather. Good ol' footwork is still required. But tomorrow I'll get a good base for the project, especially in the northern section that's not been done yet."

"Must be something to see the whole picture from the sky."

"Have you ever been up in a small plane?"

Lovie's stomach tightened at the thought. She'd heard tales of crashes in fields and the sea. "Me? Heavens, no."

"Well, come on, then. Join me."

Lovie didn't want to admit to him that she was afraid of even the idea of going up in a small plane. "Oh, no," she stalled, physically taking a step back. "That's okay. I'll just ride my trusty bike on terra firma."

"You *should* come," he replied urgently. "Since you're going to be in charge of the volunteers, it'll give you a sense of the whole island like nothing else can. The bird's-eye view."

She hesitated, wringing her hands, as her mind scrambled for an excuse.

"I thought you were my partner?" he goaded.

Lovie looked over to Flo for support. She was mouthing the word *chicken*.

"Thanks. I'd love to," Lovie told him.

Dr. Bennett's face brightened. He actually seemed pleased she was coming. "Great. I'll pick you up at six tomorrow morning. On the dot. We have to get in the sky early. Oh, and wear something cool. It can be hotter than hades up there in the summer." He hesitated, as though unwilling to leave. "Till tomorrow, then."

He turned to leave, and Flo, who was blocking his path, stepped back, giving him room to pass.

Bing stole the moment to step nearer to Flo. "See ya, Red," he said close to her ear. "I'll pick you up at six, too."

Flo's smile was seductive as she waved good-bye. She stepped into the house and stood by Lovie as they watched the two good-looking men walk to the large green Jeep and climb inside. The engine started with a roar, and after a quick wave of hands, they pulled away.

Lovie looked at Flo with confusion. "Are you going up in the plane tomorrow with Bing?"

"No. Why do you ask?"

"He said he was picking you up at six."

Flo laughed and shook her head. "He's picking me up for dinner at six! You weren't the only one getting friendly with someone this afternoon."

• • •

The summer night was fresh and clear. The storm had passed and the strong breezes swept away the humidity and mosquitoes. Lovie sat on her favorite dune at the farthest edge of her property, overlooking the ocean. It was higher than the surrounding dunes, and behind it dipped a lower plateau that was hidden by walls of sand and sea oats. At this spot Lovie could choose to either sit at the height of the dune and look out over the beach or nestle unseen in her hidden space to read or write.

She lifted her face to the breeze as she sat high on her dune and listened to the roar of the incoming tide. It was reaching ever higher up the beach, stretching its watery fingers close to her dune. Around her she heard the young sea oats shaking in the strong wind that rustled the pages of her journal. She smoothed the pages with her palm, feeling that her thoughts were as buffeted by the wind. What could she possibly write tonight that could express the exhilaration she felt? Looking at her notebook, she thought of the myriad details that filled it—location of nests, dates, condition. But there was so much more that she felt and sensed than these figures could represent.

Like today. What a glorious day! She hadn't felt such excitement since . . . she couldn't remember when. Lovie stared out at the ocean and felt the wind rustle through her hair. Dr. Bennett couldn't know what his comments meant to her. Her turtle journals represented the most significant effort of her life. She'd initiated her journals and maintained them for knowledge's own sake. It was a private devotion. Something she might someday pass down to her children.

Over the years, this devotion had been the source of ridicule. She felt sure those who said the words didn't know that their comments had hammered at her self-esteem as strongly as the waves pounding the shore. She'd endured the patronizing gratitude of officials: *"Keep up the good work"*; the gentle teasing with a gentle head shake: *"Bless her heart, Lovie and her turtles"*;

the derision of Stratton: *"You waste too much time on those damn turtles"*; and even the groans of her children: *"Aw, Mama, not the turtles again!"*

In contrast, Dr. Bennett's words this afternoon were the first that gave her work praise, even validation. She replayed his words in her mind over and over all evening: "What you have there is a wonder. Absolutely astonishing." They made her feel she could burst with pride and a heady joy that had her sitting in the wind, grinning wildly.

Bending over the journal, she eagerly began to write.

Sea Turtle Journal

June 15, 1974

Pride of one's work is not improper, unladylike, or vain. Low self-esteem is not modesty. We can all take a lesson from the sea turtle. She does not travel thousands of miles or risk all for her ego. She has an instinct for greatness—one that I believe is found in all living creatures.

Seven

⮜⮜

The following morning, Lovie was standing eagerly at the front door by six on the button. She'd carefully chosen blue jeans and a cotton shirt, having read somewhere that one should wear only natural fibers on a plane in case of a crash because man-made materials were flammable.

She couldn't eat breakfast; her stomach was tied up in knots at the prospect of flying. And because she was prone to motion sickness, the thought of being sick in Dr. Bennett's plane made her stomach tighten even more. While she waited, she thought about how she was hardly a seasoned traveler.

Her expeditions were usually by car to Southern cities a day or two away. The Rutledges had family in Chattanooga, Tennessee, and she and Stratton both loved visiting them in the mountains. Atlanta was always a draw, and she drove there often with friends. Once they had taken the children to the Outer Banks of North Carolina for vacation. Of course, there was the family farm in North Carolina, but Lovie rarely went there since it was used exclusively for hunting. Stratton brought Palmer out with him on occasion for male bonding. Lovie had never felt the need for travel. The beauty of the Lowcountry with the marshes, the ocean, the winding creeks, and all its wildlife kept her spellbound. And the city had a charm like no other.

In fact, the only time she'd ever flown in a commercial airliner was on her honeymoon. Stratton had taken her on an extensive first-class trip to Europe, showing her in high style his favorite cities: Paris, Rome, Munich, and Gstaad. They rode a lot of trains, took a wild ride on the Autobahn, and hustled in a flurry of cabs. They traveled somewhere most every day of their two-week excursion. Stratton knew Europe well and was eager to share with her his favorite haunts in cities he'd been to countless times in his life. She couldn't remember ever being so glad to return home.

But a small plane was entirely new to her, and she wasn't sure she wanted to experience it. She peeked out the window and then glanced at her watch: six fifteen. Could Dr. Bennett have forgotten his invitation? she wondered. Finally, at six twenty, she heard the roar of his Jeep coming up the drive. The big engine rumbled as she rushed out the door with her backpack.

Dr. Bennett didn't get out of the car, but he pushed open her door as she approached.

"I was afraid you'd forgotten about me," Lovie said as she climbed in.

"I got held up," he replied, looking over his shoulder at the driveway.

She'd barely buckled her seat belt when he rammed the gear into reverse and shot out of the driveway like a bat out of hell. Lovie held on to her seat during the hair-raising trip to the small airport on Isle of Palms. He pushed the Jeep hard, rushing the yellow lights and then slamming the brakes at stop signs. Looking over, she saw that his angular face was tight with tension and, though she couldn't see his eyes behind his sunglasses, his forehead was lined with focused attention. He shifted gears to come to a stop and clenched and unclenched his hand as he waited.

"Are you all right?" she asked, genuinely concerned.

"I'm fine," he replied curtly. Then he took a breath. "Sorry I was late. I had a phone call from home I had to take."

Not a pleasant one, she thought, and wondered for the first time about his home life. He didn't wear a wedding ring. She realized that though she'd thoroughly checked out his professional credentials, she knew virtually nothing about his personal life. "I hope everything's okay."

The light turned green. Dr. Bennett pushed the gear into first and hit the gas. "As well as can be expected," he muttered as he took off again.

Lovie decided to let the conversation drop. She wouldn't pry—they were hardly friends. Besides, she wanted him to concentrate on his driving. At any moment she expected to hear a police siren for his speeding. She made a mental note that punctuality was obviously important to Dr. Bennett.

The airport was little more than a grass runway and a single large hangar. A few planes were parked beside it. It was early, and though the air was still cool, the rising sun promised a warm day. Dr. Bennett took off in long strides toward a small white propeller plane with a dashing red-and-navy stripe painted across its middle. The plane had two wheels that looked ridiculously small under the body and another one under the nose. Lovie walked at her own pace, watching with interest as he immediately began checking the outside of the plane. He ran his hands along the wings, checking the flaps, the propeller. She assumed it was the equivalent of looking under the hood of a car and kicking the tires. He looked lean and fit in his khaki pants and white cotton shirt, she thought, then flushed slightly for checking him out.

He saw her approach and waved her closer.

Lovie slowed her steps as she drew near the small plane, suddenly filled again with an inner voice saying *no, no, no.*

Dr. Bennett turned to open her door, then called out, "Come on, let's go!"

Lovie stopped six feet away and shook her head. "I'm sorry."

"Is there a problem?"

"I, uh . . ." She swallowed hard.

He removed his sunglasses and squinted as he studied her face. "You're afraid."

"No!" she blurted. She didn't want him to perceive her as weak. She wanted to be his equal. A professional. "I'm apprehensive," she replied. "I've heard that flying in a small airplane like this is dangerous. That there are more accidents in small planes than in cars on the road."

"I wouldn't fly in one if that were true," he replied. "There are accidents, true, and it's always a tragedy. But the number one cause of accidents is pilot error. Not the plane's error. Don't underestimate this baby," he said, indicating his plane. "This is what we call a high-wing model so I can see below while I fly. It's easier to land, and it can, in an emergency, be landed on the beach, if the pilot knows what he's doing. And I assure you, Mrs. Rutledge, I know what I'm doing."

"After the way you drove, I'm not so sure."

Dr. Bennett put his hands on his hips and looked away, considering her statement. When he turned back toward her, he took a few steps closer and spoke without the earlier terseness.

"Forgive me, Mrs. Rutledge. I started the morning off on the wrong foot. I have to remember I'm not in some jungle, barking orders at Bing, but in Charleston—with a lady. If I promise to mind my manners, will you come? What you'll see from the sky will amaze you. You don't want to miss it." He held out his hand in invitation.

That he was suddenly so chivalrous won her over. Lovie took a breath and stepped forward. He led her to the plane and handed her up into the small cockpit. It was a tight fit, and she wondered how two more people could ever ride comfortably squeezed into that backseat. He rounded the plane, and as he climbed in beside her she could see the muscles of his forearms knot and flex. They sat almost shoulder to shoulder in the compact space that smelled of leather and oil. It was her nervousness that made her suddenly queasy, and she hoped again she wouldn't get sick. Her hands shook slightly as she followed his instructions to buckle her seat belt. Next he handed her a set of headphones.

"It gets pretty darn noisy up there," he told her. "Deafening, actually. You'll want these. I've set it to internal conversation on the radio so we can talk to each other."

Lovie put on the headset and Dr. Bennett bent close to adjust the fit. Inches from his face, she couldn't help but notice that his lower lip was fuller than his upper and that he'd missed a small spot on his chin when he'd shaved. She could smell his soapy shaving cream in the small space between them. No cologne. It was subtle . . . nice.

For the next several minutes, Lovie sat quietly while Dr. Bennett focused on his instruments. There was a spread of gauges with red and green lights. He flipped switches with confidence and checked monitors and other things that only a pilot would understand, but it was impressive to watch. Once again, she had the time to wonder about the life he led outside work. Or even if he had much of a personal life. He seemed a candidate for the all-work-and-no-play type.

At last he looked over, smiled, and gave her a thumbs-up.

Lovie forced a grin and faced the runway. She took a deep, calming breath, and they began to move forward. They taxied to the end of the runway and slowly made the turn. All at once the engine began revving loudly. She clutched the seat as they gained speed and said a quick prayer.

Suddenly the plane was off the ground, and in another instant they were airborne, high above trees that looked like broccoli. She released her breath, saying, "Wow . . ."

Dr. Bennett laughed under his breath and she remembered that she was on the radio. She turned to face him, flushing slightly, but he seemed pleased that she was enjoying herself.

Lovie never knew she could feel such freedom. They soared into the sky like a large bird and, unlike in a commercial airplane, she felt she was part of the sky, not simply a passenger traveling through it. It was akin to riding on a small boat in the Intracoastal, skimming close to the water, racing against the current. Or what she imagined riding on a motorcycle might be, rather than in a car. It was noisy, to be sure, but more intimate. More thrilling.

Dr. Bennett banked and in a burst of color and light, the sparkling blue ocean spread out before her. She looked down through her window at the long line of white beaches. The rolling surf cut a ruffled edge on the sand that was bordered on the opposite side with green foliage. The beach looked like the fringe of lace sticking out from a green velvet coat.

"Do you like it?" he asked.

"Oh, yes," she replied, grinning. "It's exciting. And I can see so much! I had no idea. There's the maritime forest," she exclaimed. Then, as they drew nearer, she startled and pointed excitedly. "Look, Dr. Bennett. Tracks! I see a set right there . . . wait, there's another. Two sets of tracks!"

He nodded, pleased. "They must be fresh this morning. The rain yesterday would have wiped out any from the day before. Hold on. I'm going lower. It might get a little bumpy."

Lovie peered out the window as he lowered the plane to what couldn't have been much more than two hundred feet over the sand. The plane did, indeed, bump.

"How low do you plan on going?" she asked, slightly alarmed.

"I have a rule not to get the engine wet with salt water," he replied, then chuckled.

Lower, it felt to her like they were going much faster, racing along the coast.

"I can see everything!" she exclaimed.

"Yep," he replied. "I can identify turtles from up here. I've seen turtles mating. There's usually another male stalking the mating pair. It can get pretty tempestuous. We can do surveys of breeding grounds up here, which is important to assess populations." He reached out, pointing to the beach. "There's another track."

Lovie's gaze darted to the beach, excited. "And look!" She laughed in delight. "There's Flo! She's waving. She doesn't know it's us." Lovie began wildly waving back, laughing when she saw Flo's shocked expression of recognition as Dr. Bennett tipped the wing.

Lovie sat back in the seat, grinning. "It's not often I catch that expression on Flo's face."

"Have you been friends long?"

"Since childhood. We're two peas in a pod."

"Really? I would have said you were quite different."

Lovie raised her brows. She knew this was true but was curious what he picked up on. "How so?"

"I don't know either of you very well, so take anything I say with a grain of salt. But Flo is very direct. Outspoken. You know right away where you stand with her."

"And me?"

"You're harder to figure out. One minute you're a soft-spoken lady and the next you're a firebrand ready and willing to take my head off."

Lovie chuckled. "I am not . . ."

He nodded, smiling. "You're passionate. At least about turtles. I like that."

Lovie sighed and said ruefully, "I wish my husband did."

Dr. Bennett swung his head to look at her and said with a crooked smile, "I wish my wife did."

Their gazes met and they both laughed again, enjoying the discovery of common ground.

Dr. Bennett turned to look over his shoulder. "Okay, let's take a look at Sullivan's Island."

As the plane banked, Lovie felt a bit woozy. She swallowed hard and tried to focus on the beach, not her flipping stomach. As he brought the plane a few hundred feet higher, the ride was smoother. From where she was perched in the sky she could see Sullivan's Island spread out before her and in a flash understood Mayor Clarke's enthusiasm. They spotted only one set of turtle tracks on this island, then turned and made the round-trip, circling the Isle of Palms on the back side where several docks jutted out into the racing water of Hamlin Creek.

"I might know this island like the back of my hand when I'm on foot, but it's another world up here," she told him. "A completely different perspective. You're right. I needed to see it. Have you always flown?"

He nodded. "I caught the bug young. My father loved to fly. He'd take us to places from Richmond regularly."

"Ah, so you're one of the Richmond Bennetts?"

"Guilty as charged. But I spend precious little time there. My base is in Florida where I teach, and my research work with sea turtles takes me all over the world. The Caribbean, Honduras, South America, Africa."

"You don't fly in this plane, I hope!"

He laughed. "Well, I fly this Cessna everywhere I can. I'll be flying back and forth from here to Florida all summer so I can keep up with my project there. You'd be surprised how far I can go in this baby. I bought her three years ago. She's a good machine," he added, patting the wheel. "But no, I take commercial internationally and hire a small plane when I'm there. Well, that's not entirely true," he caught himself. "I fly to the islands all the time. My family has a place in Bermuda."

"I've never been."

"It's a beautiful place. Pink-shelled beaches. Pristine. Very British. My wife loves it there."

Aha. "What's her name?"

"Eleanor. She flies, too. Or at least she can. I think she originally thought if she wanted to be with me while I traveled on research, she might as well be my copilot. So she took lessons. We used to travel together quite a lot." He shrugged. "We were younger. But now, it's difficult with Pippi in school and her boards and committees."

She wondered at the slight change in tone. "I can sympathize. My husband travels a lot, too. He's in the import-export business. I used to want to go with him on his trips, but . . . well, I suppose someone has to be the rock at home, and it's usually the woman, right?"

Ahead, she saw the runway and felt a twinge of regret that her first flight was coming to an end.

"Thank you, Dr. Bennett," she said with sincerity, "for insisting I come."

"I thought for a minute you were going to bail."

"You thought right."

"I'd be delighted to take you up again."

"Maybe," she replied. "My stomach might not agree, however."

He looked stricken. "You get sick? I wish you'd told me. That happens sometimes when we fly low. We hit some convection."

"That's okay. It's me. I'm not good on boats, either. It's all that rocking. I'm best with my feet on terra firma. But I thank you for the offer. I really enjoyed today. It was glorious, more so than I'd expected. And it gives me a much better sense of how to divvy up the island."

"Exactly," he said, excited at the prospect. "The way I see it, we'll need to carve up the island into sectors, then send out volunteers to walk them in the morning."

"That's a lot of beach," she told him. She was calm, accustomed to the challenge of getting the turtle nests patrolled on the island. "To cover all that distance and mark the nests, we'll need a bigger group of volunteers than the dozen we have now."

"Double. Maybe triple," he agreed.

"I hate to tell you this, but I was surprised to see you got a dozen volunteers. I've been trying for years to get a group started, with little luck. How do you propose getting . . ." She paused, doing the math. "Thirty-six?"

"I don't know. I was hoping you'd tell me. We both know the likelihood of volunteers skipping a day or dropping out entirely will be high if we don't. What kept you going?"

"It was the unknown. The curiosity of wondering did she come last night? Will I find a nest? Seeing the data compile over the months. I think once the volunteers catch the spirit of the hunt, they won't skip."

"Not all people are like you, Mrs. Rutledge. Let's just make that a given. Still, I'd like to make it as easy and pleasant for the volunteers as possible. With more volunteers, we can have smaller stretches of beach marked off and fewer days for the volunteers to walk. That would limit the probability of missing a day of survey."

Lovie was enjoying the discussion, the possibilities, of a project she held dear. "We could ask each woman who signed up to try and get two or more friends to sign up. We're a close-knit group on the island. Why don't you let me take over this part? I know the island and I know the women."

"Great. The volunteers are all yours. Here's the thing. We'll need to move fast. I want those teams on the beach this week. According to your records, you already have four nests. Plus the two below." He rubbed his jaw in consternation. "I should've been here weeks ago."

"Me, too."

They shared a commiserating glance, smiling. They both were enjoying the straightforward talk and the shared eagerness to get to work. She felt she could work with him and learn a great deal in the process.

Then she was ignored as his attention returned entirely to his instruments. He appeared completely at ease at the wheel, confident and efficient. Lovie no longer felt afraid. As they approached the runway, he began flipping switches and talking on his radio. Lovie remained silent at his side. As smoothly as they'd taken off, they landed.

She stretched her legs, feeling the movement in her blood and hearing a soft buzzing in her ears as she stood on the mowed, grassy airfield. Dr. Bennett spent awhile with his plane while she stood by and watched another plane taxi into position, rev the power, and gracefully take off into the sky. She raised her hand like a visor to watch.

"All done. Ready to go?" he asked, coming at last beside her.

They walked at a more leisurely pace back to the Jeep. He was true to his word and minded his manners, opening the car door and helping her to her seat. When they were driving down Palm Boulevard, he was all business once again.

"I'd like to go ahead and start partitioning the sections of the beach. Call me an optimist. When do you think we'll get more volunteers?"

"The phone tree is in action. I'm hoping for more today. Flo's fielding the calls."

"Good. Let's table that for later today. We'd better get right to the beach. Time's a-wastin' and we need to check out those tracks we spotted. And while we're at it, I want to see how you mark the nests."

"What? You think I'm not doing it right?"

He smirked. "If I say yes, do I get my head chopped off?"

"Perhaps," she replied, but she had to smile. "You just wait and see. I'm pretty proud of my system. It's worked for me, anyway."

"Well, let's go."

"I need to check on my kids first. They were sleeping when I left."

He looked at his watch. "Okay. But quickly, okay? We really need to check those nests before it gets hot out there. There's a small window of opportunity to move the nest."

She swung her head to look at him, stunned. *"Move a nest?"*

"Right," he replied, eyes on the road.

"You can move a nest?" she repeated, trying to get it straight in her head. She'd never even considered moving a nest. To her mind, nests were to be observed only.

"Under specific circumstances," he said. "I take it you've never done this?"

"No, of course not. I wouldn't presume."

"That's fair. Good answer, actually," he said, glancing from the road. He smiled in a tease. "So it looks like I might have a few things to teach you after all."

She smirked, enjoying the banter, and looked at the road ahead. "Perhaps a very few things."

"Mama, you're back!"

"Yes, but just for a minute," she said, setting her backpack on the kitchen table. Cara was slouched in her Wonder Woman pajamas, one long leg bent at the knee with her foot resting on the chair, eating a bowl of cereal while reading a book. "Cara, you're not dressed yet!"

Cara only shrugged and craned her neck to peer around her mother. "Who's that?" she asked, still chewing.

Lovie turned to see Dr. Bennett following her, his steps measured as he entered the kitchen. The moment he spotted Cara, he smiled and his blue eyes kindled with warmth. "Hi."

"Cara, this is Dr. Russell Bennett, the man in charge of the summer's sea turtle project. Remember, I told you about that? And this is my daughter, Cara, still, sadly, in her pajamas."

"A pleasure to meet you, Cara."

Cara was chewing her cereal but her dark eyes were fixed on Dr. Bennett. It was clear she needed time to make up her mind about him.

"Where's your brother?" Lovie asked Cara, drawing her attention. Lovie was embarrassed for her daughter's rude staring.

"Still in his room." She scooped another spoonful of cereal into her mouth.

"Lord, what am I going to do with you two?" Lovie muttered, putting one hand on her forehead as she thought. She'd only be gone a short while and the children were old enough to leave alone for an hour or so. "Listen, Cara, I'm going to the north beach with Dr. Bennett to mark the two nests we saw in the plane."

"You went up in a *plane*?"

"I did. A small propeller plane. I'll tell you all about it later. I'm in a hurry now. Should be back in an hour or so. Are you okay until then?"

"I guess," she replied, her gaze returning to Dr. Bennett.

"I'll just grab the supplies," she told Dr. Bennett, and hurried to the back porch. Her supplies were neatly organized and stashed in a red plastic bucket. She grabbed that and made a beeline back to the kitchen, only to find Palmer staggering from his room, scratching his head and yawning. He was naked except for his boxer shorts. Lovie rolled her eyes and wondered if her children could have planned a worse impression.

"Who's that?" Palmer asked sleepily. He pointed to Dr. Bennett in the kitchen.

Lovie reached out to lower his hand from midair. "Don't point," she admonished him. "That's Dr. Bennett of the turtle project. We'll be back in an hour. I'll introduce you then. And I hope by then you'll have some clothes on."

"I won't be here," he told her, eyes on the strange man in khaki pants talking to Cara in the kitchen. "Where are you going with *him*?"

"To check a nest, what do you think?" she replied, rustling his hair. He ducked from her hand, obstinately. Lovie walked past him into the living room, wondering whether Palmer's frown was from the mussed hair or the fact that she was going off with a man he didn't know.

"All set!" Lovie called out.

Dr. Bennett said good-bye to Cara and promptly joined Lovie in the living room, pursing his lips and delivering to her a quick roll of the eyes. He took the bucket from her arm and held open the front door for her. Lovie turned to call out good-bye to the kids. Her voice was caught with surprise to find both Palmer and Cara, standing beside one another, watching her leave with scrutiny.

Back in the Jeep, Lovie felt compelled to say, "I apologize for my children's manners. They've been taught better."

"No matter," he replied.

"But it does matter. At least to me."

He didn't respond. She studied his face as he fired up the engine, then her gaze shifted to his hand as he jerked the gear into first. It was tanned and long fingered with a few scratches crisscrossed against the skin. He hit the gas and they took off once again. Her floppy hat flew from her head to land in the backseat. She laughed and climbed over the seat to fetch it. As she held her hat with one hand and the doorframe with the other, they bumped along Palm Boulevard. She loved the way the wind washed over her in the open car and how she felt more connected to the landscape. So different from the elegant smoothness of Stratton's Mercedes. And the rugged truck made her feel young again. Palmer would love this big ol' Jeep. He'd probably call it "cool." She saw again in her mind his suspicious scowl and thought with a giggle, *If he could see me now.*

Thinking of the children, she turned to ask him, "So, what did she say to you?"

"Who?" he asked.

"Cara, of course."

"She gave me the third degree," he replied with a light laugh.

"The third degree?"

"Ah, yes. Let's see . . . She wanted to know what kind of a doctor I was." He turned to look at her with a sly grin. "I told her I was a turtle doctor."

Lovie laughed. "She won't be impressed by that," she chided him.

"She wasn't. Said something about how I wasn't a *real* doctor."

"Oh, no . . ." Lovie suppressed her laugh.

"Oh, yes." He nodded, chuckling. "Then she proceeded to ask what the inside of a turtle looked like, where did I live when I wasn't on the Isle of Palms, if I was married, how many children I had, and, oh, yes, she wanted to know if I'd take her up in the plane, too."

Lovie shook her head, thinking that Cara already had more information on the elusive Dr. Bennett than she did. "She *is* inquisitive."

"I liked her. I'm not sure I can say the same for her."

"I don't think she can figure you out. I don't usually bring strange men into the house."

His brows rose. "I shouldn't think so."

The plane ride seemed to have brought back his humor. She was relieved he wasn't driving like a madman any longer, though he did still push the speed limits.

"So you have two children?" he asked. "No more hiding in the rafters? Off at boarding school? Half brothers, half sisters . . ."

"No, just the two." She glanced at him, glad for the opening. "And you?"

His face tightened slightly, and for a moment she wasn't sure he would answer.

"A daughter," he replied. Then quickly, "How old are yours?"

"Palmer is thirteen and Caretta is ten."

He turned to look at her, one brow up in surprise. "*Caretta?*"

She chuckled and nodded feebly. "Yes, I admit it. I named my daughter after the loggerhead species—*Caretta caretta.*"

"Don't tell me her middle name is Caretta, too?"

Lovie laughed and shook her head. "No, but I thought about it."

"You *are* a fanatic, aren't you?"

"I suppose I am. But honestly, I simply liked the sound of the name. I had a hard time talking my husband into agreeing to it. And my mother." She paused, remembering Dee Dee's hysterics when Lovie could not be dissuaded from the name. Her expression softened. "I'd thought . . . hoped . . . that she would come to love the turtles for which she'd been named. I had dreams that we'd be walking the beaches together, that she'd take over for me when I was old and doddering. But," she added matter-of-factly to avoid slipping into the maudlin, "she's not the least interested in sea turtles. Neither is Palmer. And," she said with chagrin, "she hates her name."

"Just wait. She'll change her mind someday. Kids like to be the same, you know. Especially at her age. My daughter's name is Philippa. It's an old family name. But she hated it. Insisted everyone call her by her nickname, Pippi."

"Like Pippi Longstocking?"

"Exactly. She lived for those books. Collected them all."

"Cara likes them, too. Please tell me your little girl doesn't have those crazy red braids."

"No, thank God. She's blond, blue eyed . . . a real beauty. Just like her mother." His voice sounded tight and his hand clenched and unclenched again on the gearshift, as it had that morning.

Lovie looked out the window and wondered about the tension that suddenly spiked his voice. She'd thought he'd finished talking about family, but he spoke again, his voice having resumed its pleasant tone.

"Pippi is thirteen now and suddenly she likes having a unique name. Young girls can be quixotic. So give Cara time to grow into her name. Though I, for one, am a fan of the name Caretta. I only wish I'd thought of it."

They'd come to the end of the paved road where the maritime forest began. Dr. Bennett slowed to a stop in front of a wide makeshift metal gate. Likewise, conversation ended.

"I'll get the gate," he said, leaping out with effortless grace and trotting to the gate. He opened the combination lock and swung wide the gate. After he drove through, Lovie didn't wait to be asked and jumped from the Jeep to close the gate.

They drove a short distance. Lovie looked at the woods, or what was left of it, shocked and devastated by the changes already carved by the developers.

"Oh, Dr. Bennett," she said, remorse ringing her voice. "Look at what they've done."

Eight

～

It looked like a hurricane had ripped through the maritime forest. Tall palmettos and huge branches of ancient live oaks littered the earth like matchsticks along a wide swath of roads that crisscrossed the property.

But the wildlife endured. She saw deer tracks along the muddy road, and birds called from the trees. Here and there great shafts of light broke through the intense foliage to shimmer on drops of water on leaves.

"This used to be a wild jungle," Lovie said. "So magnificent. There was only a single gutted dirt road that led to the Sand Dollar Campground. Now look at it. It's really changing, isn't it?" she said, envisioning what the sale of the forest truly meant.

"I've seen this kind of thing happen all over the world. Coastal property has become hot real estate. Did you come here often?"

"No, sadly. Not as an adult, anyway. When we were children it was always the big challenge to hike through it. The oaks, palms, and brush being so thick, you could get lost in here. But the real scare was the ghosts."

"Ghosts?"

She gave a short laugh. "Oh, yes. Ghosts, haints, ghouls . . . This is the Lowcountry. There are ghost stories everywhere. Didn't you know?"

"I knew Poe lived here for a while."

"On Sullivan's Island as a young man. There's also Black-beard's Ghost and Osceola, the great Indian chief who died in Fort Moultrie. But before them were the spirits of the slaves whose bodies washed ashore after being unceremoniously dumped from the ships as they made their way into the har-bor. The Gullah claim the spirits roam these islands. But these woods . . . these woods are haunted by ol' Nicodemus."

Dr. Bennett chuckled. "Okay, tell me. I'm a sucker for a good ghost story."

Lovie warmed to the task. "Legend has it that Nicodemus was a root doctor who knew the voodoo. While he was alive, he used to hold secret ceremonies in this forest. When he died, he was buried at the foot of the great old live oak where he used to hold meetings. His ghost is said to roam the forest to capture children who dared to come into his woods after nightfall. He cuts off their fingers and toes and sends them to their parents as a warning."

"I bet the kids love that story."

"They do, in a love-hate kind of way. Generations of Low-country kids have earned their badge of courage here."

"Including you?"

"Of course, including me. I'm one of the few girls who signed the book. The challenge was to hike through the woods to the Point at the northern tip of the island."

He smiled again. "Dare, double dare kind of thing?"

"Exactly."

He looked at her face. "I can just imagine you, all pigtails and scraped knees, hiking fearlessly through the forest." He shifted in his seat and faced forward. "Well, if you're game, let's try our luck and see if we make it."

"You're on."

Dr. Bennett pushed the Jeep into gear. "Hold on, it's going to be a bumpy ride," he said, and once again the big wheels spun in the dirt. He wore an expression of intense concentration as they began the arduous trek across the rough sandy, wooded terrain.

Dr. Bennett was skilled at maneuvering the growling, rumbling big Jeep through the rutted path. Lovie held on to the door, yelping when they hit a big bump and she went tumbling, all the while sporting a wide grin. Once again her hat went flying. This time she was lucky and caught it midair.

"You okay?" he shouted over the roar of the engine.

"Yeah," she called back. "It's like riding a motorboat in a choppy current."

She loved the adventure of it all. Missed it. Her daddy used to have a beat-up truck he called *Mighty Moe*. Lord, he loved that ol' truck, and he'd take her and Mickey all over on what he called an "island crawl." He'd ride on the beach, along the forest's rutted road, anywhere. Once they camped out at the Sand Dollar Campground. Those were the best times.

Lovie felt a sense of wonder that she hadn't thought about that in so long. Both her daddy and Mickey were gone now, and this adventure today brought back that part of her that loved things wild. She glanced over at Dr. Bennett, his muscles straining as he guided the Jeep like a bucking bronco. Her daddy would have liked him, she thought.

She inhaled the pungent scent of the earth mingled with a hint of honeysuckle and cedar. She was surrounded by green—giant loblolly pines, tall and straight palmettos, and the thick tangles of vines. She truly could be in a jungle, she thought. Certainly, it was hot enough. Insects hummed near her ear. In shafts of light she saw hazes of winged bugs, countless. She swatted a mosquito at her neck, then wiped her brow with her sleeve. At last the road opened up, and they lurched from the deep shade into the sunshine of the dune field. A welcoming breeze cooled the sweat along her brow.

Dr. Bennett stopped the Jeep and wiped his brow. "This is as far as the Jeep can go. We can take the rest of the way on foot." He put on a battered brown baseball cap with Univ. of Florida embroidered in dark brown. Then he went to the back to pull out his backpack and gear.

Lovie couldn't wait to get out on the beach. Having seen the turtle tracks on the northern beach from the sky, she wondered how many nests she'd missed over the years. And she was eager to explore this area of the island. She grabbed her backpack, put her hat on her head, and followed Dr. Bennett. The red bucket filled with small wooden stakes batted against his thigh as he walked. Their feet dug into the soft, dry sand.

"There." Dr. Bennett pointed to a set of tracks barely visible across the sand.

Lovie's practiced eye saw them, too. Her gaze followed the double tracks to a circular disturbance. It was just below the tide line, marked by wrack and shells.

"Looks like a body pit," she said, feeling excitement as they drew near. "She laid eggs, I'd bet on it."

"What makes you so sure?"

"Look at the difference in the length of the incoming and outgoing tracks. She was up here for a long time. She had to have laid eggs."

"Good observation," he said. They reached the body pit and set down their backpacks and gear.

Lovie studied the circle of disturbed sand and smiled. "Yep, there are eggs here . . . somewhere."

"Yeah, I think so, too. What would you normally do now?" he asked her.

"Well, after I'd located the egg chamber, I'd place a stick at the nest to mark it. I measure two feet from the center, so I don't hit any eggs. Then I'd record the location in my journal. Later, I'd check on the nest as I made my rounds, to look for any changes."

"You'd leave the nest there?" he asked her.

"Of course."

"Doesn't it concern you that the nest is below the tide line?"

"It's only just below," she replied hesitantly. She knew a lesson was coming and that he was baiting her. "And no, it doesn't bother me. It's where she laid it."

"How many nests have you witnessed hatching below the tide line?"

The question surprised her, and she paused, resting her hand on the backpack to think about it. "Hatching? It's hard to say. I don't see all the nests hatch, of course. And usually the nests are laid above the high tide line, along the dunes." She shook her head. "I'd guess very few."

"I'd guess none."

She was rattled by his certainty. "Why do you say that?"

"Simple. Because if the nest is left here, below the tide line, then at high tide, the seawater will wash over the nest. Repeatedly. That kills the eggs."

"What else could I do?"

"When I discover a nest below the tide line, I move it to a safe location higher on a dune."

"Won't that hurt the eggs?"

"Not if it's done within hours of being laid. After twelve hours in the sand, the embryo within the egg becomes increasingly susceptible to damage. That's why I rushed to get here.

I never move a nest after nine a.m." He looked at his watch. "We have to hustle. Come close. I'll show you how it's done."

Lovie licked her dry lips, feeling like a novice. She'd never dared to disturb a nest, much less move it. She'd never had the authority.

Dr. Bennett walked around the nest, chin in his palm, studying it. "First you study the field signs. Look there," he said, pointing. "See the sprayed sand? That's what she does when she's covering her nest. A sure sign."

Lovie bent to one knee and plucked up broken vines and uprooted sea oats. "Here's broken vegetation," she called out. "I've always seen this as a sign she dug a nest."

"Right. Good," he said, obviously pleased with his student. "Then check out the mounds. The nest is often in the biggest one and nearest to the end of the incoming track. I usually use a canvas bag, but if you'll bring over that bucket of yours, I think it'll be perfect for this job."

Pleased, she went for the bucket while he knelt at the mound. Lovie knelt beside him, hawking his every move.

"This is where I *think* the eggs are," he began. "Sometimes those turtles are good at fooling you, and you can be stuck out here for a long time hunting for eggs. Now, before I begin," he said, and his voice became more insistent, "this is *not* something we want all the volunteers to be doing. Is that clear?"

"Yes."

"Probably best not to talk much about this either. The fewer people who know we move nests, the better."

"What about Flo? She's experienced. We might need more help."

"Maybe. We can talk about that later. For now, though. It's just you and me. Okay?"

Being singled out made her feel that she really was sharing the responsibility of the project with Dr. Bennett. Always a good student, Lovie watched carefully as he dug with his hands deep into the sand, scooping out one handful after another. A foot deep, she caught a pungent, fishy scent and knew he was near. Dr. Bennett stopped digging and, instead, used his fingers to probe cautiously deeper into the sand.

He turned his head and his blue eyes sparkled with discovery, inches from her own. "I've found eggs!" he exclaimed. "Look." He moved back.

Lovie bent closer and peered in the nest, then gasped at her first sight of the pearly white tops of two turtle eggs. It felt like Christmas. In all the years she'd done this, she'd never dug into a nest, never saw an egg unless it had been ravaged by a raccoon or a dog. Dr. Bennett covered the bottom of the bucket with some of the sand from the nest.

"We'll place one egg at a time and carefully move it to the bottom of the bucket, careful not to rotate it. Ready?"

"I'm a little nervous," she confessed.

"No worries. If you drop one, we'll eat it for breakfast." He laughed at her expression. "Of course, I'm kidding. Watch me do a few, and when you're ready, just start. We'll count them as we go."

She watched Dr. Bennett retrieve the Ping-Pong-ball-size eggs one after the other from the nest and carefully place them in the moist nest sand inside the bucket.

"Are you going to help or just watch?" he chided her.

Lovie reached down some two feet to wrap her fingers around a first egg. It was still warm from the sand and leathery and so soft it indented with pressure from her fingers. She held it like it was spun glass, careful not to jostle, and gingerly laid it on the pile of eggs in the bucket.

Egg by egg, one hundred and thirteen were retrieved. They lay nestled securely in the bucket and, lifting the weight of it, Lovie marveled at how the turtle had managed to carry them all inside her, plus the weight of her shell. She remembered the female loggerheads she'd watched painstakingly crawl over the sand, pausing to rest and then pushing off again, determined to fulfill their destiny on the dark beach.

They moved the eggs to a spot Dr. Bennett selected higher up along a pristine dune where the eggs would be safe from salt-water flooding.

"How many nests have you dug?" she asked.

He was digging steadily, using a large cockleshell to round out the bottom of the chamber. Lovie's view of the new nest site was blocked by his broad back. The fabric clung to his body in spots where sweat pooled. How long had it been since she'd been so attentive to the shape of a man's body? she chided herself. But he was beautiful to watch, like a dancer. His lean body was fine-tuned for the labor.

When he was done, he sat back on his heels and took off his hat, wiping his brow with his sleeve. "Would you like to do the honors?" he asked.

She nodded, feeling her heart leap in her chest. With reverence, Lovie reached into the bucket, retrieved an egg, and then cautiously set it an arm's length deep into the new egg chamber. Russell sat beside her, watching and keeping count.

"That's number one," he said. "Careful not to rotate them. Two. Three . . ."

She lowered egg after egg into the deep nest. When at last she'd finished, Dr. Bennett covered the settled eggs with the original moist sand. Lovie firmly patted the sand down on the top, feeling a profound sense of accomplishment.

"I've seen the mama turtle pound the sand with the bottom of her shell like a drum," she said.

Dr. Bennett cast a sidelong glance. "Don't let me stop you. Is that part of your routine, too?"

She laughed, overjoyed at the experience of moving the nest. "Not yet, but if you said it was, I'd do that, too."

"You really love this, don't you?"

"No more than you."

He didn't reply. He didn't have to. Their mutual grins said it all.

"What's next?" he asked her.

"Well, I mark the nest with one of these small wooden stakes." She picked up a stake and the measuring tape. "Then I record the data in the journal. I suppose we'll need a new data form, now that we're moving nests."

They measured and placed the stake into the sand, then sat on the beach and talked awhile about what additional data he wanted included and why. He showed her how to measure the tracks and how to fine-tune the placement of the nest marker and what information to put on it. Lovie felt like a sponge, soaking up all the knowledge, and likewise making suggestions based on her experience in a fair give-and-take. Then, their first nest of the project finished, they moved on.

The sun was rising, as was the heat. The ocean sparkled beyond, tantalizingly cool. Lovie took her hat off and allowed the light breeze to cool the moisture building along her scalp. A few more people were on the beach now. They glanced at the two of them, wondering what they were doing. Lovie knew that time was of the essence. They walked without speaking to the northern tip of Isle of Palms where Dewees Island lay a short distance across a small inlet. Lovie was the first to spot the long stretch of turtle tracks.

When she approached, she saw that something was very wrong. Telltale flies buzzed over a hole in the sand, and circling it were dozens of broken eggs crawling with ants.

"Raccoons," Dr. Bennett said, surveying the ravaged nest. "I saw it from the plane."

"What a shame. I rarely have problems with raccoons on the south end."

"It's no wonder up here, with that forest. Feral dogs, boars, not to mention crabs all like to feast on turtle eggs, but those damn raccoons are a serious problem. Eggs are like manna from heaven for them. What I wouldn't give for a good coon dog." He reached into his backpack and pulled out a pair of plastic gloves and handed them to Lovie. "Another lesson," he said with a crooked smile. "Not as pleasant."

She groaned. "One I'm sorry I have to learn."

"This can get nasty," he said. The nest smelled of sulfur, and ants roamed the broken eggs. She followed him to the nest and watched as he opened it wide to assess the damage. "That rascal did a good job," he said, pulling out broken eggs.

Lovie slapped biting ants as she counted forty-eight eggs destroyed out of the possible hundred or more eggs in the nest. They filled the nest back with sand and buried the broken shells close to the shoreline where the scent wouldn't draw predators.

They stood in the ocean, washing off their hands and cooling the bites that went clear through the plastic gloves. When Lovie returned home, she'd rinse her hands with lemon juice. It was the only thing she'd found that took the smell away.

"I've got some chicken wire under the porch," she said. "We can make a covering for the nest so that varmint won't get any more of the eggs. Maybe we should put wire mesh over the other nest, too."

"No, we have to leave it to document the hatching success in nature."

Lovie drew upright, indignant. "What? You mean just leave it unprotected?"

"I know it sounds harsh, but we need to evaluate what happens without intervention."

"But there *is* intervention. Me!"

"See, this is what I mean about getting personal. I know it's frustrating to just watch while raccoons and crabs take so many nests. But we have to let nature take its course for now. I'm sorry."

"No. *I'm* sorry, because I can't go along with this. You say you're here to monitor what goes on here on this island. Well, this island has *me*," she said, pointing to herself. "And I'm going to put mesh over that nest to protect it from raccoons. Whether you like it or not, whether you help me or not, I'm still going to do it."

She was angry, at him for being so inflexible and at herself for losing her temper. Her feet splashed as she walked determinedly from the ocean, eager to get to her things and get out of the sun. A sudden wind kicked up and sent her hat sailing. This time it flew far back and landed in the waves. She ground her teeth as she turned to fetch the now despised hat.

Dr. Bennett was already going after it. He plucked it from the ocean and came back to her carrying the sodden straw hat. He held it out to her as he would a peace offering.

"Thank you," she said, taking it.

"I think you'll need a new one."

She smirked. "It's put in a lot of years."

"Mrs. Rutledge, I didn't mean to bully you. I realize you've been doing things your way on this island for a long time, but I have to change things up a bit now for the study."

"I've been a good sport," she argued back, feeling heat. "But you told me I was your partner in this project. If that's true, then you'll try to understand that my continuing to protect the nests on this island will not disrupt your findings because I am part of this island. Whether they build that resort or not, I'm still here. I'm a constant, so you have to factor that in. Right? I am going to protect that nest. And any other nest that needs my help. It's what I do."

He listened, studying her.

"I appreciate all you taught me today," she said in a softer voice. "I realize I have a lot to learn." She looked back at him. "But I can teach you a few things, too. Isn't that what a partner-ship is all about?"

He slowly nodded. "Very well, Mrs. Rutledge . . . Partner," he amended with a smile. "We've got a lot of work to do. If we're going to build a project—and that mesh net—we'd better get started."

She looked into those impossibly blue eyes and saw ac-ceptance, and something more she couldn't name—validation? "Since we're partners, please call me Olivia. Or rather, Lovie. That's what everyone calls me."

"Everyone calls you Lovie when you have such a beautiful name? If you don't mind, I'll call you Olivia. If you'll call me Russell."

"Not Russ?"

He laughed and shook his head. "Only Bing calls me Russ, to rile me."

"Okay, Russell." She smiled, almost shyly.

"Okay, then, Olivia."

Lovie sat in the Jeep and looked straight ahead, sipping cool water from her thermos. She and Russell didn't speak on the ride home, but there was none of the awkward tension one often felt in silence. Rather, it was comfortable riding beside one another. Something had changed between them this morning. Their earlier friction had altered to something deeper, certainly friend-lier. Definitely positive. She didn't dare glance at him for fear he might be looking at her with the same wonder she felt sure was on her face.

She glanced at Russell as they pulled into her drive. He'd taken off his brown baseball cap, and his short blond hair had curled slightly in the humidity. He turned and smiled when he put the car into park. "Good-bye," she said, climbing from the Jeep as gracefully as she could carrying a bucket full of sticks and a backpack. She clumsily slammed the heavy, creaky door and rounded the Jeep's enormous hood with the bucket banging against her leg.

"So, I'll see you later this afternoon?" he called out from his window.

She turned to face him. "Uh, yes, of course. Around two okay?"

"Perfect." He smiled again, and she wondered if he had any clue of its power. "See you then. Olivia."

She waved, unable at that moment to call him Russell.

She staggered up the stairs to the porch and unloaded her gear in a pile to be dealt with later. She was sweaty, plastered with sand, and smelled of rotten eggs, but inside she was glowing.

"I'm home!" she called out, closing the door and walking straight to her bathroom. She stripped off her damp clothes, casting sand like a sea turtle, and stepped directly into the luxuriously cool shower. She sighed as the water cascaded down on her. It felt like half of the beach washed from her skin and hair.

Soaping up, her mind circled around the conversations of the morning. There had been so many powerful moments. Especially at the end . . . Lovie could tell that it was hard for Dr. Bennett—Russell—to give in on the issue of the raccoons. She smiled. Once again, she was being that pushy, pesky turtle lady. But he'd borne it well, with kindness, dignity, even respect. He didn't yell at her or say that she didn't know what she was talking about or tell her not to get involved in things she didn't understand, as Stratton would. She thought that was what mattered most to her. Russell had listened to her. He considered her his equal. It was his respect for her that swung the argument in the end. She squeezed the water from her hair and paused. It had been a very long time since she'd experienced that.

When she returned to the living room, she felt cooler, more herself. It was after ten o'clock and she hadn't had breakfast. She went first to the kitchen to pour herself a cup of stale coffee, craning her head for sign of the children. She found them out on the porch with Emmi Baker, eating enormous wedges of watermelon. Juice dripped down their chins as they took turns spitting seeds over the railing in an age-old game. She paused at the window to drink in the sight of them, tanned, relaxed, talking—and not fighting. This mood, she thought, was what summer was all about. She cocked her ear to overhear their conversation.

Palmer spit a seed and landed a good one. He chuckled smugly and leaned against the porch railing. "Beat that," he said, wiping the juice from his chin with his arm.

Lovie knew Cara wouldn't back down from a challenge. She watched as Cara slurped up a big bite of melon, singled out one seed, and fired. It fell short. Her face flamed as Palmer guffawed. While the girls spit round after round to beat him, Palmer ate his fruit with an eye open for any cheating. He knew better than to turn his back on Cara during a competition.

"Hey, what do you girls think about a game of hide-and-seek, over at Fort Moultrie?" Palmer asked.

"Not today," Cara said. "It's too hot."

"Maybe it'll cool down later. It's breezy up there on top of the fort."

"Maybe," Cara replied, then spit again. "How about the mud-hole?"

Palmer snorted. "Not with you."

"Why not?"

"'Cause you're a girl. Duh."

"Who says a girl can't go to the mudhole?"

"Nobody." He scowled. "But it's weird. You've gotta stop tagging along everywhere I go."

"I'm not," Cara shot back. "I like to go to the same places you do. That's all. Right, Em?"

Emmi nodded.

Lovie moved closer, listening to every word. Stratton had told her that Palmer had complained that Cara was hanging around the boys too much, and now she wondered if it was true.

Cara asked, "You gonna try hiking to the Point this summer?"

"I guess," Palmer replied. "I do that every summer."

"Me, too," Cara said.

"But you never make it . . . every summer."

Cara stood straighter, indignant. "I'm going to make it this year. You just watch me."

"You say that every year, too."

"I almost made it last year."

"Oh, yeah? Well, close is no cigar. You got to make it all the way to the Point and sign the book. Or it don't count." Palmer lowered his voice and attempted a scary drawl, "Nicodemus is waiting for yoooooou."

Cara angrily spit out a seed. It was a sad attempt that landed on the railing.

Lovie felt for her little girl who wanted to compete with the boys. She was faster, smarter, even taller than most of them. How could she help her daughter see that she could be all those things and more—as a girl. And yet, Stratton and her mother urged Lovie to mold her into the kind of young lady who wouldn't want to make it to the Point or swim with the boys in the mudhole.

"You'll see. This summer, I'll do it," Cara said, squeezing her melon so tight her fingers dug into the fruit. "Won't we, Em?"

Emmi bit into her melon and nodded unenthusiastically.

Palmer gave a smug laugh. "You're a girl. You won't make it."

A spark of pique rose in Lovie, and she opened the porch door. The children's faces showed surprise that she was home.

"I'm glad you cut yourself some watermelon," she said to them in a cheery voice. "How is it?"

"It's a good 'un," Palmer muttered as he took another bite.

Lovie went to the table to cut herself a piece of the melon. "You know, Palmer, girls make it to the Point, too." She picked up her wedge and walked over to join the children at the porch railing. She could tell by their shifting glances that they were uncomfortable that she'd overheard them.

"Oh, yeah?" Cara asked, eyes bright. "Who?"

"Yeah, who?" Palmer asked it as a challenge.

Lovie heard a hint of Stratton's smug superiority in Palmer's voice and she didn't like it. "*Me*," she replied.

She thought it was time her little boy was taken down a peg or two. She looked out over the sandy grass for the seeds that lay farthest away. Taking a bite of the watermelon, she saved a seed in her mouth. Then leaning over the railing, she gathered her air and spit out the seed. It sailed far beyond Palmer's best shot.

Cara and Emmi cheered and clapped.

Lovie laughed and looked at her scowling son. "Not only did I sign the book, but your uncle Mickey and I were some of the first ones. We were part of the gang that started the challenge. Go check the book if you don't believe me." She wiggled her brows. "If you dare go back."

She glanced at Cara and Emmi. Their eyes were wide with astonishment and awe.

"Now, if you'll excuse me," Lovie said, dabbing her mouth with a paper napkin. "I'll make lunch."

"You actually moved an entire nest? You *touched* eggs?"

Flo's eyes were agog as she sat forward, chin in her palm,

across the teak table from Lovie. There was an unspoken agreement that every evening the three women—Lovie, Flo, and Miranda—gathered during the season on Lovie's porch to toast the sunset with a glass of wine. The sky was darkening, and the children were inside. Peace was restored at Primrose Cottage.

Lovie launched into a colorful description of the morning's experiences, embellishing details, knowing she had an appreciative audience. When she was done, Flo sat back in her wicker chair, swirled her wine, and scrunched up her face in a frown.

"Now I'm mad."

"Why?" Lovie asked, feigning innocence.

"I want to switch jobs with you. While I'm out there hoofing it in the heat, you're up in the sky getting a personal tour of the island with Mr. Blue Eyes. Then he gives you private tutoring on how to move a nest. Which, by the way, I'm not sure we should do. Really, Lovie, where does he get his authority?"

"From the U.S. Fish and Wildlife Service," she replied dryly.

"Oh, well." Flo swallowed her wine. "It's still not fair."

Miranda swirled her wine in her glass. "You sound just like you did when you were ten."

Flo jokingly stuck out her tongue at her mother. "I feel like I'm ten. Lovie gets to do all the fun stuff."

Lovie giggled at Flo's excellent imitation of their fights as children. "I know it's not fair. But hey, it's my job." She lifted her chin in mock superiority. "And the boss likes me. Or my work, anyway."

Flo wagged a finger at her. "You know, kiddo, if word gets out to the other ladies on the team who get hot and flustered at the mere thought of spending an hour alone with the dashing Dr. Bennett that you're going out with him solo every morning, there'll be mutiny."

Lovie sipped her wine and leaned far back in her chair. "Don't worry, Flo. He'll teach you, too. I'll make sure of it."

"You will, huh? You sound like you're walking in high cotton all of a sudden."

Lovie laughed into her wineglass. "Maybe I am. And maybe I'm just happy."

Flo smiled but looked at her suspiciously. "Are we still talking turtles here?"

Lovie only shook her head to throw off the comment, but when she looked back at them over her wineglass, her eyes glimmered.

Sea Turtle Journal

June 16, 1974

What a day of firsts! First plane ride. First moving of eggs. There are several nests on the north end of the island. And seeing the vista of so many miles of pristine white beaches fills me with hope. My idea of what I can do to help turtles has expanded, like seeing the coast from the sky instead of simply on foot.

The bummer was the old problem of raccoons. We returned with wire mesh and secured it over the nest to prevent further invasion. Archie Carr predicted that the biggest threats to the loggerhead population were raccoons and real estate development. Since I'm now faced with both, I have to ramp up our defense. I may not make a big difference, I may not make headlines, but I will take a stand on my island. Someday we're all going to have to make a decision—do we want to save the sea turtles?

Nine

～

So it began. By the following week, the Sea Turtle Project was officially under way. Lovie and Russell had met at Russell's house several times over the first few days, poring over her notes and a large map of the island he'd put up on his wall. They walked the beaches to check out the conditions of the dunes and the accessibility of the beach by foot, especially on the northern end where the forest grew thick. For three days she'd returned from hours on the beach sweaty, with sand stuck to her like a second skin, and scratches from briars on her arms and legs. Russell looked as bad, but he seemed indefatigable.

For her part, Lovie's phone tree had yielded a rich crop of volunteers. The project was the talk of the island, as was the dashing Dr. Bennett. Twenty-one additional women and five men—husbands roped in by their wives—signed up, to bring the total number of volunteers to thirty-eight. Forty if Russell Bennett and Lovie were included. To Lovie, that number was a boon, more than she'd ever thought possible.

At a hastily assembled meeting at the Exchange Club, Russell and Lovie presented the details of the project to the volunteers and assigned specific days and locations they were to walk early in the morning to search for turtle tracks. It was a simple plan. Lovie and Russell were the core team of the project. When the volunteers found tracks, they were to call Russell, who in turn called Lovie. Then the two of them would investigate the nests. At the end of the meeting, Russell handed out brown cotton T-shirts emblazoned on the left side with ISLE OF PALMS SEA TURTLE PROJECT encircling a green turtle. All the volunteers were delighted, and Lovie thought it was a great unifying tool. For her, Russell also ordered a matching brown baseball cap with the same emblem, to make up for the hat that had been destroyed by its dunk in the sea. Lovie was ridiculously pleased to wear it.

The next morning, the full cadre of volunteers was on patrol. By the second week, Lovie had grown accustomed to her new schedule of sitting by the black rotary phone on her desk, dressed and ready and waiting for the call to action. The volunteers had to cover their stretch of beach by six thirty so they could get back home and call in any found tracks no later than seven.

As she sat by the phone sipping coffee and waiting, Lovie couldn't help but wonder if she liked this new, regimented routine. She was accustomed to being independent in her mornings. When it was only her, she could wake up early, grab a cup of coffee at leisure, and stroll out on the beach. Her fingers tapped the desk and her foot wagged impatiently. Suddenly the phone rang and she lurched for it.

"Hello?"

"Good morning. You up yet?" It was Russell.

"Very funny."

"Then come on over, partner. I've got today's list of nests to check out. Meet me at 26th Avenue."

"I'll be right there."

She always felt like a fireman at a drill. With adrenaline and caffeine racing in her veins, Lovie grabbed her blue backpack, already prepacked with her notebook, pen, a towel, her thermos, and a small garden trowel, picked up the bucket, and dashed out the door.

It was after seven and already the sun was shining. The summer solstice was around the corner. There would be long days and sunlit evenings that stretched to nine o'clock. As she stepped into the sunshine, she could feel the day's promise of heat and humidity. Her station wagon was already steaming. She cranked down the windows and turned the ignition. The engine strained but didn't fire. "Darn rust bucket," she muttered, and tried again. It wouldn't start.

She hit the steering wheel, cursing. She'd been having this problem with the ignition on and off for the past year and learned the hard way not to flood it. It took all her patience to let the engine sit a moment. The last thing she wanted was to be late on her first day out as a team leader. She said a quick prayer, and this time when she tried the ignition, it fired. She hit the gas, a little too eagerly. Her wheels dug into the sand, spitting gravel as she tore out of the driveway. She thought that she was driving almost as recklessly as Russell as she sped to the 26th Avenue beach access path.

The weekend tourists didn't start arriving on the island until later in the morning, so the narrow road was almost free of traffic. She made it to 26th Avenue in good time and parked off the curb. She huffed and puffed as she trotted along the winding beach path with her backpack and bucket, the soft sand making it feel like she was running through quicksand. Birds called, and from somewhere she caught the scent of bacon cooking. Sweat began to form, but she pushed herself harder. She refused to be late to her first call, especially knowing how important punctuality was to Russell. The moment she reached the end of the path and stepped out onto the beach, she felt the welcoming light summer breeze from the ocean and stood a moment to let it cool her skin.

To her surprise, there wasn't a soul on the beach, save for a yellow Labrador retriever trotting along free as you please. Sanderlings ran back and forth along the jagged shoreline, expertly playing tag with the waves while seeking food in the sand as the water receded. Above, seagulls called out their laughing cry. She had just turned to the left, then the right, when it dawned on her that she'd beat Russell to the site. A sly grin of victory eased across her face and, with renewed vigor, she began searching for the reported tracks.

Except there weren't turtle tracks anywhere. She walked in either direction, then stopped short, staring at the only thing she could find that remotely resembled turtle tracks.

"Olivia!"

Lovie startled at the sound of her name and looked up to see Russell walking swiftly toward her. He was dressed in khaki shorts and a beige shirt with the long sleeves rolled up to the elbow. He was looking at something in his hands, picking at it. She waved him over.

When he reached her side, he looked at the marks on the beach and shook his head in disbelief. "*That's* what was reported?"

Lovie nodded and began laughing. "Tire tracks! These have to be from Donnie's garbage cart. See how the tracks go up to the trash bin?"

Russell frowned and muttered something under his breath. "Rookie mistake. We showed them pictures . . . Who was the volunteer this morning?"

"Ida Walters. Don't be too upset, Russell. It's to be expected at the beginning. She's a novice and it's her first day out. She probably wasn't sure so she called it in. Once they see real turtle tracks, they won't make this mistake again. Better she call it in and let me check it out than make that decision herself."

His face relaxed, mollified. "Sounds like you have experience with novice volunteers."

"Oh, yeah," she replied in a tone that said it was more than occasional. "Don't you?"

"In my work, I train graduate students who already have experience." He took off his cap and ran his hand through his hair. "Though," he added, "from time to time, I come across a person who, for one reason or another, has taken it upon herself to try to protect the sea turtles. She's usually called the Turtle Lady."

"Oh, Lord help me." Lovie groaned with exaggeration. "I suppose I should've seen that coming."

"Don't get me wrong," he hastened to add. "They do a great service. And no one can doubt their integrity."

"But . . ." Lovie added warily.

"But for the most part they don't have any training. Granted, we're just learning a lot about turtles ourselves, but a few individuals are mavericks without any supervision. Every once in a while you meet one who, shall we say, is a tad aggressive. The lines between serving and self-serving start to cross, and she may cause more problems than she prevents. And it's hard to convince her otherwise," he added dryly.

"Aren't you being a little hard on us?"

He put his hand up in a pledge. "Just a few, but I swear, the stories I could tell."

"Do tell," she egged him on.

He rubbed his jaw, chortling. "There was one case we refer to as 'the nutcase,' a woman who, when she was in her cups, went out on the beach at night with a pistol and ran everyone off, hollering, because she thought they were disturbing the turtles."

"No," Lovie said, shocked. "Not in Charleston!"

"No, not in Charleston," he conceded. "Of course, this wasn't a turtle problem but a law enforcement problem. The local police came and, well, had a good talk with her. Few days later, the captain returned my call and told me, 'I didn't get to talk to the perp in person, but I know I found the right house because of all the turtle eggs in buckets in the garage.'"

"*What?*" Lovie said, hand to her cheek. She was horrified yet couldn't help laughing. "You're kidding. In buckets?"

Russell nodded, laughing now, too, remembering it. "In the garage. Which is why when I heard you were the local Turtle Lady, I thought I might be in for a battle."

Lovie could only shake her head in chagrin.

"Well, just to show I don't think all turtle ladies are trouble, I brought you a little present."

She looked at him with mock distrust. "What?"

He handed her a large cockleshell, beautifully formed with a large center, perfect for scooping sand. "I thought you might need one. For the nests."

She was touched by his thoughtfulness and would toss back on the beach the one she'd already found for herself. "It's perfect. Thank you, Russell. I almost forgive you."

"That's the best I was hoping for. Okay, let's get on back to the car. We have a few more to check on."

The following day, Russell picked her up at the beach house since they knew her station wagon wouldn't make it through the rough terrain at the Point. They found the nest, then, moving on, they discovered that the tracks at 7th Avenue were a false crawl. It was getting late by the time they headed to the last nest at Breach Inlet.

The small inlet between Isle of Palms and Sullivan's Island was notoriously dangerous because of its wild currents, and it had claimed the lives of several people over the years. Because of its current, the fish gathered and the sharks and dolphins hunted in these waters. A lone fisherman was checking his poles dug into the sand. In the distance, Lovie spotted a mother dolphin and her young one arcing through the smooth water. She stopped and pointed. The sight never failed to take her breath away.

Russell stood beside her, savoring the moment. "I always enjoy watching the female of a species teaching her young," he said in a far-off tone. "There are few things in nature more moving."

"But the turtles don't have a mama around to teach them, do they?"

"Nope. Different scheme. The turtle is a reptile. She lays a whole mess of eggs and then heads off, figuring a few of them will make it. Not any different from those fish out there, dolphin not included, of course. She's a mammal. She has just one calf at a time, sometimes two, and nurses them for a year or longer. Both biological formulas have worked pretty well for millions of years." He paused to look around. "Carr used to say about sea turtles that the whole race and destiny of the creature are probably balanced at the edge of limbo by the delicate weight and that magic number of one hundred eggs."

"I wonder how the turtles would have fared if, millions of years back, they chose the other formula, had fewer offspring and tended them in the sea, like the dolphin. Not leave the eggs in the sand."

"I suppose they would have survived that model, too. They're a resilient species. It's not their reproduction scheme that worries me. I'm more worried about their survival. Humans are their biggest threat. And the changing landscape. They're a migrating species. It's not parochial. It's global. That's the challenge they face now."

"I feel the same."

He looked away from the dolphins to her. "Does your husband share your interest in turtles?"

"Stratton? Heavens, no. He'd as soon eat a turtle egg as relocate one. In fact, he's told me how they used to collect turtle eggs to bring to his nanny to use for baking cakes. It was said to make the cakes moist because the white of the eggs don't ever cook hard like the yellow." She laughed shortly. "It still makes me mad."

"I've heard that. I don't know that it's true. Probably an old wives' tale. But I don't intend to test it out, either." He moved forward again. "We'd better get finished. It's getting hot out here, and your husband will wonder what's happened to you."

"No worry there. He's not here. He's staying at our house in Charleston."

"Really?" He sounded surprised.

They began walking across the beach, cutting footprints in the untrammeled sand. "He's working," she explained. "He used to join us here for the summers. But in the past few years, business and travel have been keeping him incredibly busy. He comes out whenever he can."

She was making excuses for him. The need to preserve the appearance of a solid and happy family came naturally to her.

"Is that a hardship for you?" Russell asked.

She thought about the past few weeks. Other than her disappointment at having been stood up for her barbeque, she hadn't given him much thought at all.

"Not anymore. It took a little getting accustomed to at first," she replied, feeling the need to put up a good front. "I have the children, of course. And Flo and Miranda next door. Friends stop by." She raised her arm carrying the bucket. "And, thanks to you and this project, my plate is full."

"It *has* been a busy start."

She turned her head, thinking the question about her husband was rather personal. "Why do you ask?"

"I didn't mean to pry," he replied in a more serious tone. "I was just wondering. You see, throughout most of my marriage I've been gone a lot, too. Probably far too much. It wasn't easy for Eleanor." He paused and swung his gaze back out to the sea. "I suppose I was curious to hear your side of the story."

Lovie walked a few paces, wondering what she could say to that admission.

"Every marriage is unique," she replied vaguely. She walked a few steps more across the sand and decided to venture honesty. "But I think a lot depends on how long you were away, how independent each of you were, whether what you had could withstand the strain of separation. I don't know . . . so many different things."

"You seem to manage it well."

She wanted to tell him looks could be deceiving, but she held her tongue. She didn't know him well enough for that much honesty. And her mama had taught her never to hang her dirty laundry out in public.

"Do you see your daughter much?" she asked, deflecting the spotlight from herself.

"Pippi?" He smiled at the thought of her. "As much as I can. She's spending most of the summer at a camp in Maine. Eleanor is taking a tour of Europe with her mother and sister."

"Eleanor's going to Europe? Maybe she'll run into Stratton."

They laughed congenially before he spotted the nest, and the conversation ended. This nest, too, was in a good location on the dune and, being the last, they finished marking it at leisure, while Russell told anecdotal stories of different species he'd worked with around the world. The heat was building with the rising sun, and Lovie's clothes were sticking to her damp body. When they were back in the Jeep, she thirstily sipped cold water from her thermos as he drove her home.

The Fourth of July holiday was the busiest week on the Isle of Palms. Tourists were already pouring in from points north, their cars jam full of suitcases, coolers, and families eager for a celebration at the beach. American flags were flapping along Palm Boulevard as they slowly crawled home. At a stop sign, she spotted a vintage gold VW bug with red, white, and blue streamers and covered with flags.

"Oh, look at that cute car," she said, pointing. "I used to have one like that in college, only mine was white. Gosh, I loved that car."

"We all knew someone who had one of those," he joked.

"Well, what did you drive?"

"A Triumph." He glanced at her from the wheel with a smug smile.

"I should have known," she replied, picturing him in the sporty British car that was the passion of all but owned by few. "And I'll just bet it was red."

The light turned green and he shifted into first. "It was."

It was well after nine by the time they reached her beach house. Lovie was stunned to find Stratton's black Mercedes parked there. It was like déjà vu in that they'd just been talking about him.

"Looks like company," Russell said, peering through the windshield.

"My husband's back."

"Oh. I should stop by to meet him."

"No, not now. It's hot and we're both full of sand. Why don't you come by on the Fourth for barbeque? I was going to ask you. I imagine it'd be nice to have a home-cooked meal."

"I wish I could, but I won't be here for the holiday."

"Oh. Of course," she stammered. "You want to go home for the holiday."

"To Maine, anyway. To see Pippi. And don't worry. You won't be left alone with the project. Bing is returning today to cover for me while I'm gone."

"That'll be good news for Flo."

Russell's face went serious. "I don't think it's a good idea for them to get too friendly."

"No fraternization with the natives?" she teased.

He didn't laugh. "It complicates things. They're working to-gether and all."

"They're both consenting adults," she said, surprised by his attitude.

"It's not that," he replied. "I don't want to see Flo get hurt. Bing is, well, gregarious."

"He's not married, is he? Engaged?"

"No."

"Then don't worry. Flo can take care of herself. In fact, it's Bing you should be worried about."

She'd thought he would smile, but his face was still serious. Perhaps this was a subtle warning to her and she should be a little less friendly herself?

He said, "I'll fly out the day after tomorrow, but I'll only be gone a few days."

"We'll manage," Lovie replied, "but I do have a favor to ask. Could you take the time to teach Flo how to move a nest before you go? It means so much to her, and we can use the help when you're gone."

He nodded. "I'll give her a call. I'll take her out with us to-morrow."

Lovie got out of the Jeep, and her thoughts shifted to Strat-ton's return. Rather than feel elated, she felt an odd dread that stemmed, she suspected, from her guilt at feeling an attraction for Russell Bennett. She'd done nothing wrong, she reminded herself. There was nothing to hide.

Stratton hadn't been due until tomorrow. Of course he didn't have to call if he'd decided last minute to come early, but it might have been nice if he had. Now she'd have to wait to call Flo about meeting with Russell tomorrow, and with Stratton home, the girls wouldn't have their usual wine gathering tonight. She felt the niggling of annoyance.

At the door, she paused to set down her backpack, kick off her sandals, and shake some of the sand from her clothes. She was just smoothing strands of hair from her face when the door swung open.

"There you are!" Stratton was in his tan pants and a clean white polo shirt. He pulled her into his muscled arms and kissed her soundly.

"Stratton, I'm all sweaty," she said, stepping back from his arms.

"You are a tad rank," he said with a teasing grin. "Where've you been?"

"The beach. Where else? What a surprise! Why didn't you call and let me know you were coming early? I'd have prepared something special."

"I don't need anything special. Just you. I'm just glad to see you. I missed you," he added with a hint of ardor, pulling her closer. Instinctively, she shrank away.

Stratton held her close. "And the kids," he added jovially.

Lovie looked over his shoulder into the living room to see Cara and Palmer standing near, grins stretched across their faces. She smiled and patted his shoulder. She should be happy to see him, she told herself. They were a family again. They needed this time together. It was time to rally.

"How long are you here? Don't you leave for Europe soon?"

"After the Fourth. I thought I'd come here early and spend some quality time with the family, what with me being gone so long. So let's start the party. How about a cool drink?" he asked her, heading for the kitchen.

"Sounds wonderful. I'm just going to run and get cleaned up," she said, making an excuse to dart to the shower. "Y'all just help yourself and relax. I'll be out in a minute."

The shower felt blissfully cool as it washed away the morning's sweat and bits of sand from her body. She closed her eyes, smelling the pine in the soap, and tried to recapture the conversation with Russell on the beach, something about instinct and change. She'd never met anyone like him before.

The water turned off with a loud *clunk* and she stepped into a thick, thirsty towel. Dabbing her face with a corner, she stepped into the bedroom, relishing how cool her skin felt now, all clean and rosy. The white bedroom with its lace at the windows, the crystal bowl filled with seashells, the whitewashed furniture had always felt like her room. It surprised her to find Stratton standing by the dresser, emptying his pockets. He turned to face her.

"You look cooler."

"I am," she said on a sigh. "I feel so much better."

He finished emptying his pockets and put his hands on his hips. He lowered his head in thought, then swinging it back up, he asked, "Why were you out so late this morning?"

She glanced at the clock. It was nearly ten o'clock. Lord help her, it was late. "I had no idea. The time flew by!"

He came closer and handed her an iced drink with a wedge of lime. "What were you doing out there so long?"

"Thank you," she said, taking the glass. "It's the new project I mentioned. For the turtles. We cover the whole island now, not just our end. We had four nests to check out just this morning. And we move the nests now." She sighed. "I'm learning so much."

Looking up, she noticed his eyes glaze over at the mention of turtles.

"Learning so much?" he repeated. "What the hell do you have to learn? You make it sound like you're doing some serious research out there. Damn, Lovie, you didn't even graduate from college or have a serious job. Don't blow this up out of proportion. And you left the children all that time? Alone?"

She took a sip. Gin and tonic so early? she thought. But she was so thirsty she sipped the drink, feeling its tart coolness quench the burning in her throat from all the words she wanted to say right now.

"They're not that young anymore," she replied carefully. "Palmer is thirteen. I babysat other people's children at that age. And Cara is ten going on forty."

"Sometimes I think you care more about those damn turtles than you do your own children."

"Stratton!" she said, simmering. "That's not fair. And uncalled for. What would you know, anyway? You're not here."

"Let's not get into that . . ."

"Besides, Flo is always on call next door."

"Her," he said with a grunt. "I wouldn't trust her with a cat."

Lovie didn't comment, didn't want to fan another fire.

"Speaking of Cara . . ." He moved to close the bedroom door. Then, stepping back, he knitted his brows and said in a lower voice, "This summer, you ought to spend more time with Cara. Teach her to be the young lady she's expected to be."

Lovie reached for the drink and took a swallow. "You've been talking to my mother, haven't you?"

"She may have mentioned something about this. But the concern is all my own. She's always hanging around the boys. When I came home she was telling me about how she spent the afternoon at the mudhole."

"What's wrong with that?"

He gazed at her with eyes simmering with incredulity. "Hell, Lovie, do you even know what or where the mudhole is?"

Lovie didn't, so she didn't respond, but her rounded eyes gave her away. She'd assumed it was one of many mudbanks that appeared when the tide was out.

He snorted. "Figured you wouldn't, and you want to know why? Because you're a girl, that's why. The mudhole is out on the back of the island where they've been dredging the waterway.

It's this gray mud, like silt. On hot days, the guys jump into the mud because it's cool." He began chuckling, using his hands as he spoke. "Palmer was telling me they like to coat themselves up real good and play ding dong ditch."

"What's ding dong ditch?"

"It's when they run around the neighborhood, ring the doorbells, and when someone comes to answer the door they scatter like palmetto bugs when the light goes on. The neighbors are starting to complain, by the way."

"Palmer told you all this?" She couldn't believe her son would confide anything in Stratton.

"Sure he did. I used to do stuff like that when I was his age. And here's the thing," he added, his humor fading from his voice and his face. "Them boys are half naked in that mudhole. And Cara's been hanging out there, too."

"She isn't . . ." She stopped, remembering the conversation she'd overheard.

"She *is*. Palmer doesn't want her hanging around him and his buddies all the time."

"Why didn't he say something to me?"

"Why don't you ask him that? He probably doesn't want to rat out his sister. But hell, Lovie, we all know she runs around the island like some wild Indian." His face clouded and he lifted his hands in frustration. "I love her, she's my little girl—and she's not a great beauty." He shook his head, seemingly at a loss. "But hell, Mama, she needs a woman's firm hand to bring out her feminine side. Her birthday's coming up. When Vivian comes out, maybe you can go into the city, take her to Elza's on King Street. Spoil her a bit. Get her some proper fancy dresses and shoes. And white gloves. She might like that. Don't all girls?"

Lovie knew Cara would hate it. And so would she. Shopping with Cara was a nightmare. She was in a stage that Lovie could only hope she'd outgrow. Nearly ten, Cara was a mulish shopper, not liking anything, especially anything her mother picked out, braying complaints, shooting daggers with her eyes, and shrugging her shoulders at every dress. Lovie looked at her husband's tight-faced expression and thought Stratton and his daughter were cut from the same cloth but neither of them recognized it.

Yet her heart ached for her daughter as she thought of her trying to hang out at a boys' mudhole. "Yes, all right. I'll take her to Elza's and a few other stores. We'll make a day of it. Palmer will need some new clothes for high school, too. I guess they're both growing up, aren't they?"

"My point exactly." He seemed relieved that Lovie got the message and this sensitive discussion had come to an end. He glanced at his watch. "Where's this day going to? I've been here all morning, waiting to see you. I've missed you, Lovie."

His tone was seductive, and his gaze slid to her breasts. Lovie tightened the towel around her and walked over to the bathroom, farther from him, to turn off the light.

"Did you know that the northern end of the island, where the forest is, has been sold?" she asked, distracting him.

"Really?" he said, his interest piqued. "No. I thought they were going to field offers."

"Apparently they got an offer they couldn't refuse," she quipped, quoting from the popular new film *The Godfather.*

"Who from?"

"The Finch Corporation. They intend to build a tennis club and sell lots for hundreds of houses. I've heard as many as five to eight hundred. There's talk of a marina, too. Maybe even a golf course."

"No kidding?" He grinned. "That's great. A deal like that will increase our land value. It's about time somebody brought a high-class resort out here. That choice real estate was just sitting there, waiting to be grabbed. I wish it could've been me."

"I'd hoped it would become a park. All that beautiful forest . . ."

"I wonder," he said, ignoring her comment. "Maybe we should buy a lot or two when they come up. Get in early."

"For an investment, you mean?"

"Of course."

"I imagine they'll go for a lot of money."

"We could sell this place."

"You're joking, of course."

"I don't mean leave the Isle of Palms. We'd just sell this dump, then use the money to buy a lot or two." His eyes gleamed with the scent of a new project. "We could build ourselves a brand-new home on the water, or maybe overlooking a golf course. Both, if we play our cards right. We could build that fancy new kitchen you've been wanting. And a room for Vivian. We wouldn't have to squeeze in this place like sardines."

Lovie felt a sudden cold and wrapped her arms tightly around herself. "I'll *never* sell this house."

He frowned at her tone and waved his hand dismissively. "You're just being emotional. You'd love the new house, too. It'd be bigger and better. And we'd be part of the golf club. You know it'll be first-rate."

"I don't golf."

"I do! You could learn. It's something we could do together. Hey, aren't you always complaining that we have nothing in common? That we don't do anything together? Well . . ." He spread out his palms, letting his silence speak the obvious.

She shook her head sadly and turned away.

"Now what's the matter with you?"

"Nothing."

"Lovie . . ." His tone was exasperated.

She turned, her eyes on the ground, feeling sadness well up in her. "You didn't even ask what I was excited about."

He sighed heavily, with exaggeration. "Let me guess. The turtles."

She felt her enthusiasm die in her veins. "Yes."

"What else? Lovie, it's always the turtles."

She lifted her gaze and saw her husband standing in front of her, impatience, perhaps even derision, shining in his eyes. With a sudden clarity that pierced her heart like a shard of ice, she realized that he didn't want to hear about the Sea Turtle Project, nor did he care one whit that she'd moved a nest or carried in her palms her first sea turtle egg. These things just didn't matter to him. Or, to be fair, they mattered to him as much as golf mattered to her.

Once they'd shared their interest in the great house on Tradd Street. Those had been some of the happiest days of her marriage. What a thrill it was to search for their first house together. Shoulder to shoulder, they went from house to house, room to room comparing notes. Once the purchase was made, however, the hunt was over for Stratton. He'd killed that project and was on to the next. It was up to her, the wife, to do the "fixings."

"I'm getting cold," she told him honestly. "Give me a minute to get dressed and I'll make you some lunch."

He cast a crooked smile, one she knew so well and that made her muscles stiffen. "Well, since you're taking off that towel . . ."

She stepped back, putting out her hands, not wanting at that moment to be touched. "Stratton, the children are right outside."

"We'll be quiet."

"I'm tired," she said, trying to step out of his grasp. "And the porch doors are open."

"I'll close them." He plucked at the corner of her towel to let it fall from her body to the floor. His cool hands slid along her naked skin from her waist, up her arms, then down her back as his lips found her neck.

"Wait, wait," she said, pushing him back. She went to the

porch French doors and, reaching past the lace, closed them. Then she went to her bureau to retrieve her gin and tonic. She took a few good sips, feeling the coolness slide down her parched throat. A moment later, she welcomed the gin swimming in her veins.

Stratton was in his underwear and socks, having removed his pants. He was unbuttoning his shirt as he walked toward her.

Lovie closed her eyes and in a flash saw a tall, lean man in khaki pants, sandals, with his shirtsleeves rolled up over tan arms. She shook the image from her head just as she felt Stratton's heavy weight against her and they tumbled back upon the mattress.

Ten

≈

Lovie rallied at the home front. After lunch, she packed a cooler and they all went to the beach for a family swim. She lay on her back, resting on her elbows under a big hat, and watched Stratton bodysurf with Palmer and Cara. Her husband lost his stiff town civility and became a fun-lovin' Lowcountry boy out on the beach, the boy she'd fallen in love with. He needed to be here as much as the family needed him.

As the afternoon waned, Palmer headed north to the pier to see his surfing buddies and Stratton returned to the house to make a few phone calls. Lovie and Cara spent the remaining hours spread out on colorful towels and read novels, contented as cats.

When the girls returned to the beach house, Stratton had fired up the barbeque and was standing in front of it, nursing a beer and regaling Palmer with a speech about the art of barbeque being man's work. Lovie enjoyed listening to the male voice out on the porch as she made potato salad, cold bean salad, and banana pudding. Cara, conveniently, had ducked out to Emmi's house with a kiss and a promise to be back in an hour.

It was a relaxed evening, like old times. Without the pressures of Stratton's job or the children's school schedule, they sat around the table and talked about their favorite television shows—Palmer liked *Hawaii Five-O*, Cara preferred *The Waltons*; their favorite movies—Palmer and Cara both loved *Blazing Saddles*, Stratton preferred *The Godfather*, and Lovie claimed no movie would ever beat *Gone with the Wind*. She glanced at Stratton across the table, leaning back in his seat, slightly flushed from beer. He seemed so pleased to have the family together again and said so, many times.

Later that night, they made love again, with more tenderness than that morning. As she fell asleep, Lovie listened to the cicadas singing outside her window and prayed that they'd get through this rough patch they'd been stuck in and find their way back to love again.

The following morning, she rose as the first pink rays of dawn broke the darkness, dressed quietly in her shorts and team T-shirt, and went to the kitchen to make coffee. Even though it was Sunday, it was nonetheless a beach patrol morning. Turtles didn't know what day of the week it was. She was luxuriating in sipping coffee and reading the Sunday newspaper in peace when the phone rang. She lurched to grab it at the first ring so no one would be awakened. She heard Russell's familiar voice and, as luck would have it, there were no nests reported.

"The turtles are all in church this morning," he joked.

She'd laughed, feeling unusually happy to hear his voice but also glad, for once, that she had the morning free. She wrapped an apron around her waist and took stock of her kitchen. It had been a long time since she'd made corn cakes and bacon, but this morning she had the time and the fresh berries, and her mama always told her there was nothing a Southern man loved more than a hearty breakfast. Stratton, bless his heart, could make mistakes, but he was here and he was trying. So would she.

The days sped by quickly. By the time the fireworks exploded in the sky on the Fourth, Lovie thought that Stratton had slowed down to island time. He was relaxed, easier to be with, even cheerful. The children enjoyed spending time with him when he was in this gentler mood and not the martinet seeking out their flaws. Lovie felt such hope that when the time came for him to go abroad, she actually regretted his leaving and worried how their marriage would survive these long absences.

When Stratton was gathering his papers from the desk, Lovie sat on the bed folding his clothes and putting them into his suitcase. She'd given him the expensive travel bag for his fortieth birthday and loved the smell of the fine brown leather. She wrapped his shoes in tissue paper and set them beside his toilet bag. Then she laid his folded shirts and underwear neatly on top of those.

"What date will you be back?" she called out.

"Uh, I can't remember offhand. September something. I'll call when I check my itinerary," Stratton called back from the living room.

"September's a long way away. The children will miss you."

"Uh-huh," he replied.

Lovie smoothed his blue silk tie with her palm. She began placing it into the slim zipper pouch on the side of the suitcase when her fingers ran against papers. Taking them out, she saw that they were Pan American plane tickets. Here was his itinerary, she thought, and opened the long journey agenda. He was going to five cities in as many countries. A busy schedule, she thought. She opened the second ticket, assuming it was for Japan. She was curious to see what cities he was going to. Tokyo? Kyoto?

She paused, confused. The cities listed weren't in Japan. They were the same European cities and the same dates. Was it a duplicate? She looked up at the name on the ticket. *Ashley Cole.* Lovie went cold and slowly opened her fingers. The tickets fell open into the suitcase.

She felt numb, like they say one feels after being hit with a bullet. A sting and then nothing. Then erupted a sudden fury and a hurt so scorching that her throat burned from holding in her tears as she stood there, immobile, staring with disbelief at the tickets splayed open in his suitcase.

She heard a noise beside her and saw through the blur of tears Stratton's hand reach into the suitcase and grab the tickets. She heard his heavy sigh and waited.

"You're reading too much into this . . ." he began.

She didn't respond, refused to look at him.

"It's not what you think. It's strictly business. That's all." When she didn't say anything, didn't move, he tried anger. "Hell, Lovie, stop playing the role of the wounded wife. It's ridiculous and beneath you. Ashley is my secretary. Nothing more. This is a big trip with a lot of business. I need her to *work* for me, hear? *Work*."

Lovie turned and looked at him blankly. "Then why didn't you tell me she was coming? Why didn't you ask me to join you?"

"What? And leave your precious turtles for the summer?"

"Don't you try and twist this around on me! This has nothing to do with turtles," she shouted at him, losing control. "We both know what this is about."

"It's business!" he shouted back at her.

"Then go do your dirty business," she cried. "Go on. Go!" She threw his tie at him. It landed gracelessly on the floor. "And don't come back here. We were fine without you. Why did you have to come back?"

Stratton grabbed her shoulders and shook her so hard her head wobbled like an infant's. He held her so tight his fingers felt like iron probes digging into her shoulders. They stared at each other, and for one moment, there was such anger in his eyes, Lovie feared he might strike her. He pushed her furiously away and turned and went to the closet to pull out his suit. "I can't talk to you when you're like this," he told her.

Lovie walked from the room, rubbing her shoulders, and went to her refuge in the kitchen. She felt unsteady on her feet, so she bent and clutched the counter like her life depended on it. She felt if she let go, she'd either scream or go running back into the bedroom and start fighting with him again, demanding answers to all her other suspicions. But she couldn't. He'd been drinking and his anger could be frightening.

She remembered the one time he'd struck her. Was it two years earlier? She couldn't even remember what the fight was about. But she'd never forget the shock of the sharp sting of his palm across her face, or the shame. He'd apologized, bought her a gift, and took her to dinner. Later, he'd blamed it all on her for getting him so mad. He swore he'd never hit her again, and he hadn't. But she knew the anger was there, simmering like a pot on the stove. She had to mind the heat.

He did not meet her gaze when he left. He stepped close and kissed her in a perfunctory manner, told her he loved her and that he'd buy her something very special in Japan. She listened to his hearty good-byes to the children and held herself rigid until she heard the roar of his powerful Mercedes engine disappear down the road.

After he'd left, she felt an inflamed jealousy and might have hurled dishes to the floor like she'd seen in movies, except that her children were home. She fed them a picnic dinner of left-overs and allowed them all the ice cream they could eat while she stared out the window, clutching her arms so tight her fingers left bruises. It wasn't only because Stratton was traveling with an-other woman, a rather young but plain and common woman, she thought bitterly. She felt hurt and envy because he wasn't going with *her*. His wife. She'd asked to go.

Finally, as the sun began to set, the children skulked off to their rooms, casting worried glances at her over their shoulders and whispering to each other. They knew something was wrong, but she didn't have it in her to reassure them, as she usually did after a family upset. She didn't trust herself to open her mouth other than to say a shaken, "Good night, my darlings."

Only when the house was quiet and the sky darkened did she feel the relief of the familiar steel wall of indifference begin to drop. She was quite skilled at this form of self-protection by now. She could shut and lock this imaginary door of apathy quickly. This wasn't the first time she'd been suspicious that her husband was fooling around. She wouldn't be the first wife of a successful man to suspect her husband was chasing skirts. After all, Stratton's father was well known to have had a roving eye.

Lovie recalled something Stratton's mother, Linnea, had told her one evening over sherry. They'd been talking about husbands in general, sharing congenial, even humorous gossip. Eventually the conversations had drifted to their own husbands, and along this vein, the mood had darkened.

"Successful men can have large egos," Linnea Rutledge told her daughter-in-law. She was a slight, graceful woman with graying hair that floated like a nimbus around her head. Her voice, too, was breathless. She spoke slowly, enunciated each vowel and consonant. Lovie knew her to be kind, even otherworldly. Nothing seemed to fluster her. Largely, Lovie suspected, because she didn't care about anything as much as she did the birds she studied and painted. She identified and painted birds with a passion that consumed her.

"I suppose they need this to succeed. Sometimes, however, a man's ego demands more than any one woman can satisfy. It's not love, my dear," she hastened to add when Lovie had stiffened in protest. "Oh, no. Love is something quite different. Love and marriage are sacred. What I'm referring to is more . . ." Linnea had sighed, frustrated at finding the correct word. "More an easing of stress. A conquest, perhaps. Men are still such boys in this way. I'm sure there are many different reasons, but never love. So sometimes, with husbands such as ours, it's wise to look the other way if they have a . . ." Linnea lifted her chin a tad. "An indiscretion. It's a passing thing. Inconsequential. *We*," she said with emphasis, "are their wives."

Linnea continued, "It is in our nature as women to be strong and yet yielding, like the palm tree in a storm. It bends but it does not break. This is our strength. Why we endure, and have for centuries through unspoken hardships. Southern women should never be brittle. And," she said brightly, "we have so much, don't we? Our children, our home, our full lives. And we have each other. We are the foundation of our family. Remember this, Lovie, and"—she sighed—"should suspicions arise, let them remain only that. Look the other way, toward your blessings." She'd patted Lovie's hand and said softly, "It's easier. Trust me, my dear."

Lovie had followed her mother-in-law's advice. When she'd first married, she didn't believe she could have contemplated such an arrangement. Her father had been kind, honest, and true. Lovie couldn't imagine him ever having an extramarital fling. Or, for that matter, having the energy for one. He'd always worked so hard. But she also knew it was against his nature. Her mother used to joke how she could leave Michael in a room full of naked women and he'd not cheat. Dee Dee, for all her love of being social, was equally chaste. When she dressed up at night, she did so for other women, not men.

So it was hard for Lovie to accept that Stratton could be unfaithful. He made her believe there was something wrong with *her*—she wasn't pretty enough, sexy enough, or good enough in bed. Especially as she grew older, had children, and her muscles softened. He'd never said so in words, but he was disappointed that she didn't want to try certain positions or use erotic toys that embarrassed her to even talk about, much less bring into her bed. She wished she had someone she could talk to about such things, but it was hardly like discussing a new recipe, was it?

For fifteen years, Lovie had looked the other way so as not to see what she didn't want to see. Was this what some called turning the blind eye? Yes, most likely. Was it cowardly? Perhaps. Yet some days she felt that it took far more strength and courage to do just that, to keep the family going, than to raise a fuss.

So now, hours after Stratton had left, all Lovie mustered was a chilling, apathetic blend of anger and regret.

Later that night, the song of the insects swelled in chorus, a sweet, steady breeze blew in from the ocean, and the wine was chilled. It was a perfect evening for a heart-to-heart with her best friends. Yet Lovie found it hard to concentrate on Miranda's difficulties with her current painting or Flo's upcoming plans with Dr. Bingham Wolitzer. Eventually, the table grew quiet while Flo and Miranda exchanged worried glances.

"Okay, kiddo, spill the beans," Flo told her. "What's bothering you? Or are you going to make us get you drunk first?"

Lovie wanted to laugh but didn't have the heart. With these two women, she could be honest and know that her words wouldn't be broadcast around the island the following morning.

"You know that Stratton is going to Europe," Lovie began, staring at her wine.

"Yeah. And Japan. He travels all the time now," Flo said slowly.

"With his secretary."

Flo's eyes widened. "No, he is not!"

"Oh, yes he is. I found the tickets in his suitcase. I don't think he meant to tell me, but there they were. So he blustered right through, going on and on about how he needed to bring her because he was forging new business and he had so many meetings to conduct, new people to meet, follow-ups, et cetera, et cetera. It all sounded plausible enough. Perfectly innocent."

"But you don't believe him." This came from Miranda.

Lovie paused, considering her words. It was all still so fresh. And yet not. These suspicions were hardly new. How could she explain all the doubts and feelings of shame that had whirled in her these past few hours?

"I've thought about it at length and . . ." She paused. "I choose to believe him," she replied.

"You *choose* to believe him?" Flo shook her head in disbelief. "What the hell does that mean? How do you choose to believe or not? Mama, explain it to me, because I don't get it."

Miranda reached out and patted her daughter's hand. "You've never been married."

"As if that'd make a difference," Flo sputtered. "And I can tell you right now if that's what marriage is about, I don't ever want to get married. Girl, if a man did that to me, I'd kick the old coot in the balls so hard he'd be singing soprano."

"Flo!" Lovie exclaimed with a shocked chuckle.

"I mean it. Hell, Lovie, where's your gumption? Your self-respect?"

"What choice do I have?" she cried, stung. "He's my husband. The father of my children. I'm not going to leave him, so I might as well choose to believe him. I don't want to know the truth."

"So you can sugarcoat it."

"He'd never do anything to embarrass me or the family. He cares for me too much."

"He cares for his own reputation too much," Flo fired back.

"Yes," she admitted. "And his family. And his family name. And, I like to think, my reputation, too." She sighed. "Oh, Flo, it is what it is. What choice do I have? Please, don't badger me. Not tonight. I'm trying to hold on to what little self-respect he's left me. To make the best of it." She closed her eyes and took a long swallow from her wineglass, emptying it.

Miranda bided her time as the candle flickered between them. "You mean," she said in a more even tone, "you won't even talk to him about it?"

"Oh, I'll talk to him," Lovie said. "Of course I will. But not now. Not this summer. He's off to Europe." She felt her eyes fill with tears and took a moment to tamp down the quick spurt of emotion. She looked out toward her old ally, the sea. The inky sky shadowed the vast ocean, but from the velvety blackness she heard the steady roll of the surf as a friend whispering *there, there* in a comforting rhythm.

"Do you want to know the truth?" Lovie said at length, turning her head to face Flo. Flo's face and torso were barely visible in the light of the candle. The darkness made the talking easier. "At some level, I was glad to hear he'd decided to go to Japan. Because that meant he'd be gone longer. That sounds awful, doesn't it? But it's true. That was my first thought. I wouldn't have to deal with him snipping at my heels all summer, complaining about my being gone so much, especially when I started going out to the nests at night, too. I can hear him now. 'You're going out *again*?'"

Flo chortled in the darkness.

"You know I'm right."

Flo lifted her glass and sipped. "Yeah."

"You said it first. I'm really free this summer. This project might mean nothing to him, but it means everything to me. And I'm going to do whatever it takes to do it right. Russell Bennett is a great teacher."

"Even if he is a jerk," Flo interjected.

Lovie huffed but ignored that comment. Flo was still angry that he hadn't taught her how to move a nest yet. "Try to understand, Flo," she said. "For me, it's like being in graduate school and an internship all rolled into one. I'll never have this chance again. And what's more, Dr. Bennett respects my records, my work, and my ideas. This is more than a hobby to me. It's a vocation. I'm proud of my work. I'm proud of *me*! Not because I'm Mrs. Stratton Rutledge, or Palmer and Cara's mother, or Michael Simmons's daughter. But because I'm Olivia Rutledge." She laughed. "The Turtle Lady. This work is mine."

Flo was silent a moment. Then she reached out to fill Lovie's wineglass and handed it to her. She picked up her own glass.

"I have to say, I've never heard you talk like this before. I've never heard such conviction. Well, good for you. I'm proud of you, too, sugar." She raised her glass. "Here's to you. And the best summer ever."

Later that evening, as Lovie lay in her bed, she felt restless. The breeze stirred the curtains at the window, its salty scent luring her thoughts to the sea—and Russell. He had only been gone for a few days but she was surprised at the emptiness his absence had left in her life.

True, he was a taskmaster. Keeping records had become demanding. Russell wanted more information than she'd ever collected before—the measurement of tracks and description of any similarities like the scraping trail of a barnacle or the lopsided evidence of a missing flipper. He wanted a description of all the field signs, the moving of nests, recording the number of eggs, the success rate, and predation by ants, raccoons, crabs, and more. Yet even with all his demands, his occasional ornery comments, and his indefatigable energy—she missed him.

She reached over to the bedside stand for her sea turtle journal. Opening it, she began to write.

Sea Turtle Journal

July 10, 1974

Dr. Bennett demands that I act the expert I am. He expects the best out of me and pushes me to set higher goals and to believe in my ability to achieve them. This kind of mentorship is, I know, rare. So in the end, with all these records, the turtles have taught me to observe closely, to trust my instincts, and to pay attention to the smallest of details.

• • •

A few days later, Flo was beaming. She'd just moved her first nest, and her feet were barely touching the sand.

Lovie let Flo carry the bright red plastic bucket, which had somehow morphed into an honor. Last summer, Lovie had spotted the bucket on her porch. She'd figured that the light weight would make the bucket the handiest carry-all for the sticks, plastic tape, and other paraphernalia she needed for nests. Little did she know it would also be the official transportation for eggs.

Flo found the second set of turtle tracks, and this time mama turtle had laid her nest in a proper spot higher along the dunes. Flo was disappointed, but Lovie was glad they wouldn't have to move this one. She preferred to let nature rule out whenever possible.

Once Lovie located the eggs, Flo marked the nest with Russell's wire plastic flag. He preferred his own system for nest marking rather than the wooden stakes Lovie had used. They were color-coded for the month: blue flags for nests in June, yellow for July, and green for August. False crawls had red flags. As the summer progressed, they could walk the beach and know at a glance which nests were due using the color code. It was only early July, and already they'd marked twenty-eight nests. The rainbow of flags was cheery as they flapped in the wind.

Lovie measured the tracks, then sat on the dune to record everything in her journal. While she was bent over her notebook writing, she heard the faint roar of a plane's engine. Her gaze shot up and she spied a small plane coming closer, flying low. Recognizing it, her heart leaped to her chest and she sprang to her feet.

"Russell's back!" she cried in surprised delight as she spotted the familiar white Cessna approaching in the blue sky. She ran closer to the shoreline, waving her arms in a wide arc, splashing in the waves as she grinned wildly. She felt like her heart was soaring, too. "Russell!"

Flo ran up beside her, waving as well, joining her laughter, as the two cried out cheers of welcome. The plane flew low along the beach, then Russell tipped the wing in acknowledgment before the plane regained altitude and continued along the coast.

"He's back!" Lovie exclaimed, catching her breath. She was totally caught up in the moment. She hadn't allowed herself to think how much she'd missed him, but her joy had erupted without bidding. She stood watching the sky with her hand over her eyes like a visor until the plane was out of sight. Dropping her hand, she turned to see Flo eyeing her with a puzzled expression. "Why are you looking at me like that?"

"You seem pretty excited to see Russell come back," she replied.

"Why, sure I am. Why wouldn't I be?"

"Are you getting involved? In a nonprofessional way, I mean?"

Lovie's heart skipped a beat. She hadn't expected that question this morning . . . or ever. "No," she replied. "I didn't even like him at first. You know that. But since then we've become good friends."

"Friends, huh? Bing and I are friends, too. But I'd be lying if I said that's all we are. I've seen the way you look at him."

"You're letting your lovesick imagination get away from you," she replied. Then, "But what if I were?"

"That's dangerous ground you're treading there, missy. It's one thing to work closely with someone, to admire him. To even be infatuated with him. But that's where you need to leave it. Need I remind you he's a married man?"

"No," she said in a huff. "Need I remind you that I'm a married woman?"

Flo hesitated, deflating the tension. "No. I don't want to see you get hurt, that's all."

Neither spoke for a moment. "It's funny," Lovie said, "but

Russell said the same thing about you. He didn't want you and Bing to get romantically involved."

"Tell him to mind his own business," Flo retorted.

"As a matter of fact, I did," she said to Flo. "But you should take your own advice."

"What?" Flo asked, aghast. "Are you having an affair?"

Lovie put her hand on her friend's arm. "Oh, Flo, no! But I'm attracted to him, I can't deny it. What's wrong with that?"

"Nothing at all. There isn't a woman on the team who doesn't dream about Dr. Bennett."

"Exactly."

"It's just I don't think Dr. Bennett is dreaming about any of them. He's dreaming about *you*."

"Stop being ridiculous. We're just friends. We spend a lot of time together."

"Bing even noticed the way he looks at you." She chortled. "Bing said Russell talks about you like you're Rachel Carson and Emily Post combined."

"Really?" Lovie felt a rush of mixed feelings heat her face.

Flo raised two fingers. "Girl Scout's honor."

"You were never a Girl Scout."

"No," Flo admitted, "but I'm your best friend. All joking aside, I remember we made that pinkie promise." She raised her baby finger between them. "I'm here for you, forever."

Lovie hooked her finger to Flo's. "Forever."

Eleven

July brought the intense heat of the Southern summer. The ceiling fans at the beach house were whirring around the clock. The house was steamy by midday, so Lovie closed the shutters and blinds during the peak hours and served cold drinks in the shade of the covered porch. After a swim in the ocean, the ninety-degree heat didn't feel too oppressive.

July also meant that the first sea turtle nest on Isle of Palms was due to hatch. A volunteer reported seeing a concave drop on the 6th Avenue nest, a good sign the nest would hatch sometime that night. So Russell and Lovie were starting out the evening rotations as well.

Lovie was always excited for the first nest to hatch. After dinner, she changed into her turtle team T-shirt and plaited her blond hair into a long braid that fell down her back like a rope. The humidity was high and she hoped the mosquitoes wouldn't be too bad while they sat at the nest. She leaned over the sink, closer to the mirror, to apply a coat of ChapStick.

"Why are you getting all dolled up?" Palmer was standing in the hall staring at her, his head tilted in scrutiny.

"I'm not getting dolled up," Lovie exclaimed. "I'm just getting ready to go out on beach patrol."

"You're putting on lipstick."

"Oh, for heaven's sake, it's not lipstick. It's ChapStick! And what difference would it make if it was?" she blustered, but inside she felt a faint cringe that her son, like his father, was a natural-born hunter. Stratton could catch the scent of prey when no one else could.

For the truth was, it wasn't just the nests tonight that she was looking forward to—but also seeing Russell. It was only natural she'd like to be presentable for once, she told herself as she set down the ChapStick and turned off the light, not meeting Palmer's gaze. In her heart, she knew she *had* taken extra care with her appearance. She'd even ironed her shorts in the dreadful heat—something she never did when she went out by herself.

"You meeting up with that Dr. Bennett guy?" Palmer asked, tossing a ball in the air with his hands.

"As a matter of fact, I am. We're the team coordinators. Is that all right with you?"

Palmer didn't answer. He just kept tossing the ball.

Cara, who was sitting like a kitten on the large easy chair in the living room, looked up from her book and yawned. "Have a nice time, Mama."

"Thanks, sweetheart." Then she had a thought. "You know, kids, I think we're going to see a hatch tonight. Why don't you both come with me?"

Palmer leaned against the doorframe. "You just sit there and wait for the sand to move?"

"Pretty much."

He snorted and tossed the ball. "The guys are having a pickup game of basketball tonight. Besides, I've already seen a turtle nest hatch."

"It never gets old," Lovie replied.

"Nah," he replied. Then, remembering his manners, "Thanks anyway."

Lovie was glad to see the suspicion dim in his eyes.

"Cara? How about you?"

"No, thanks, anyway," Cara mechanically replied, returning to her book.

"Please? I'd really like to share this with you. Just once." She heard a soft rapping on the front door. "Please?" she asked again as she went to the door.

She hadn't seen Russell since he'd returned from Maine. He was dressed in dark green fishing pants and an olive shirt with the sleeves rolled up. In the light at the front porch, his eyes seemed to sparkle at seeing her. She paused, lost for a moment in the sight of him.

"Ready?" he asked.

"In a minute. Come on in," she said, stepping aside. She felt awkward, as though he were a gentleman caller picking her up at her house. "Did you have a good trip?"

"It was a long flight but worth it," he said, entering the house. "I just got back a little while ago."

"I'm glad," she replied, catching a scent of his soap. He must have just showered, she realized. "I'll just get the bucket and a flashlight."

Cara had set aside her book, and Palmer walked back into the room, his eyes trained on the tall, fair-haired man.

"Russell, you remember my son, Palmer."

She was glad to see Palmer step forward to shake Russell's hand, but he only mumbled his hello.

Russell took it in stride. He turned his attention to Cara, who sat with her long legs curled up. "So, Caretta," he said, using her full name, "did I tell you I think you have a beautiful name?"

Lovie held her breath.

Cara's dark eyes narrowed as if trying to decide if this man was sincere or teasing her. "I'm glad someone likes it," she said grudgingly.

Lovie felt her face blush as she went directly to the porch to grab her backpack. "We're off to the beach," she told the children in a perfunctory tone.

"Cara," Russell said, this time using her preferred diminutive, "why don't you join us? I think we'll have some luck tonight."

Lovie was about to say that Cara didn't want to go, when her daughter set her book on the table, unfolded her legs, and replied, "Sure."

It felt good to get back in the Jeep. Her old station wagon just didn't have the same panache. On the way, Lovie told Russell about Flo's progress and updated him on nests. Cara sat in the backseat, listening. Reaching the beach, Lovie was disappointed to feel only a whisper of breeze, barely enough to rustle the fronds of the sea oats. She knew that when the sun lowered, the mosquitoes and no-see-ums would come out in merciless force. Lovie spread out beach towels for her and Cara while Russell settled on the dune and stretched out his legs, leaning back on his arms.

"What was I thinking, wearing shorts tonight?" she said. "My legs are bare for the bugs to feast." She dug into her backpack for bug spray and began applying it to her legs and arms, then moved to do the same for Cara. Even Cara knew enough to wear long pants, she thought.

The moon had not risen yet, but the night was clear, and looking up she could tell the stars would be bright.

Cara crawled over to peer at the nest. "You sure it's going to hatch tonight?"

"No," Lovie replied with a light laugh.

"But you said . . ."

"We're never sure, honey," she said. "But we think so."

"When will they come out?" Cara asked.

Lovie and Russell exchanged amused glances. This was the question most visitors asked, over and over.

Russell answered, "If I were a betting man, I'd say in the next hour or so. And if all goes well, they'll all come out like an eruption. We've only recently learned that the hatchlings work together under the sand as a team to get the job done. Imagine, Cara. They've been digging in there for days in fits and starts."

"You mean they're already hatched out of the shells?"

"Yes, a few days ago. It's crowded in there. When one gets tired, another one stirs him up again. So flailing and digging, they rise to the top as a group. Kind of like an elevator." He pointed to the concave circle atop the nest. "This tells us they're resting near the top now, breathing the air, and waiting for the trigger."

Lovie watched her daughter grow intrigued. "What's the trigger?"

Russell leaned closer. "The cooling sand. That's why the turtles emerge at night, under the cloak of darkness."

Lovie could tell Russell was enjoying teaching Cara about the turtles. "I wish Palmer was here," she said. "He should be learning all this, too."

"He's a teenage boy. This doesn't interest him," Russell said.

"I have to admit, I do not understand teenage boys."

"It's a tough time. It was the age my father began expecting me to be a man. He took me on outings with him." He chuckled. "Not to see turtles. We did manly stuff like hunting and fishing and flying."

"Daddy takes Palmer hunting," Cara said.

"And my mother was like yours, pressing me to be a gentle-man." He chuckled. "It was her life's work."

"I feel for her," Lovie said. "It's pulling teeth to get him to cotillion."

"No wonder!" Russell replied. "Cotillion is torture for young boys. Especially on a beautiful day. We'd rather be out playing ball, doing almost anything rather than eating tiny finger sandwiches and dancing a waltz in a stifling suit, holding some girl's hands with sweaty palms. I shudder to think of it, even now."

"Me, too," Cara agreed, swatting a mosquito.

Lovie laughed again, thinking of Palmer scowling and cursing in the car all the way to cotillion. "It's a necessary evil."

"Maybe," said Russell, "but I have a theory that's the reason young boys get so angry at their parents. We feel our rights are being abused." He shook his head and chuckled lightly at some private memory. "It wasn't until much later that I spent more time trying to figure out who I was and why I was here, that kind of thing."

"I don't know if we ever completely figure out the *who*," said Lovie, wrapping her arms around her knees. "I like to think we keep evolving."

"I found out the *what* at an early age. I've always been a loner. Parties and small talk continue to be the same torture for me now as they were when I was a boy. My parents had hopes I'd go into finance or politics or law." He snorted. "Wasn't going to happen. I took a year off from college to sail, dive, travel. I was always drawn to water. The more I grew interested in the animals that lived in the sea, the more I wanted to study them. Marine biology soon emerged as my passion. I could see myself as a science teacher. But I also loved being outdoors, doing fieldwork. That led me to research." He spread out his palms. "And here I am."

Lovie wondered what it would be like to be a man with that kind of freedom to make choices. To follow your passions like bread crumbs till they led you home. She couldn't even imagine.

Russell swatted a mosquito and shifted in the sand to sit cross-legged. He peered up at the sky. "Here we are, struggling with our little lives. But when you look up into the sky, it puts everything into perspective. Take a look, Cara," he said, pointing to the sky. "See that pretty milky swath? That's Via Lactea. It has another name. Do you know it?"

"Duh," Cara said. "The Milky Way."

"Right. It contains two hundred to four hundred billion stars and maybe some fifty billion planets," Russell continued. "Makes you feel somewhat insignificant, doesn't it?"

Lovie could see that Cara was eating this up, as was she.

"In the big picture, yes," Lovie replied. "In my own little world, I'm still the star," she said as a joke.

"I think, Olivia Rutledge, that in any galaxy you'd be a star."

Lovie was glad the darkness hid her smile. She glanced at Cara, who was leaning back on her elbows, staring up at the sky. Lovie looked up at the stars, too, and basked in the glow of that compliment.

"I can't think of anywhere I'd rather be than right here, under a bright moon and stars, listening to the roar of the ocean . . ." Russell said. "What could be better than this?"

"Nothing," she replied. "I feel exactly the same. That's why I'm always out here. I'm drawn to the ocean, too. It's in my blood."

"Mine, too."

Another bond, she thought. Lovie reached out to slap a mosquito from her ankle. "I'm getting eaten alive," she said.

"I'll check the nest." He rose to walk to the dune. A moment later he called out, "You two better come over here. I think it's starting."

Cara scrambled to the nest with Lovie right behind her, her heart pounding with excitement and scooping up the towels to get them out of the way. She arrived just as there was a cave-in, and seconds later, the sand seemed to boil over with tiny hatch-lings, one after the other scrambling out from the hole, flippers waving comically, rushing down the dune's slope to the sea. Rus-sell and Cara walked with the vulnerable hatchlings to the shore, guarding against attacking ghost crabs. Lovie remained at the mouth of the nest to count the hatchlings as they emerged.

The light of the moon brightened the beach so that from the dune Lovie could see the hatchlings as tiny dark shadows, dozens of them, fanning out across the beach. Beside them, she watched Cara, pointing to something with excitement, bending low to study a hatchling. She rose to ask Russell a question, then they went together to the water's edge. Russell leaned over to talk to Cara, his arm outstretched to the hatchlings entering the sea. Lovie smiled, knowing he'd be explaining the hatchlings' dive instinct to her.

Lovie could see that her daughter was swept up in the emo-tions of the evening. She'd always hoped for this, and here it was unfolding before her on this moonlit night. Rising to a stand, Lovie wrapped her arms around herself and felt her own emo-tions soar. She watched her daughter and Russell at the shoreline, waiting until the last hatchling made it successfully into the sea before they began their trek back. Lovie felt she was the moon, glowing, guiding them toward her. She tucked the memory of the night into her heart, knowing she'd remember it always.

The two shadowy figures walked toward her across the moon-drenched beach. Cara broke rank and ran the final few feet to her mother to fall against her, arms tight around her waist.

"Mama, you were right. It was cool! I called one of the babies Dumbo because he kept going the wrong way. But he made it."

Lovie reached down and hugged her daughter, incredulous and grateful. "I knew you'd love it."

"You're not going to make me walk the beaches every morn-ing now, are you?" she asked, worried.

"No," she replied with a light laugh. "We're covered. You're off the hook. This summer."

"Whew, good," she said with an exaggerated drawl.

Russell came closer and picked up his backpack. "Let's hit the road. These mosquitoes are relentless." He slapped his neck.

"Meet you at the Jeep!" Cara grabbed her towel and a flashlight and took off for the beach path.

Alone, Russell spoke softly. "She's really a great kid. I wish I could get Pippi down here."

"Why don't you invite her? I'm sure she'd love to come."

He shook his head grimly. "She wouldn't come. She's angry at me at the moment."

"I'm sorry."

"So am I." He paused, then said, "You're a good mother. But I'm sure you know that."

"Does any mother know that?" she replied. "We try. I think that's the best we can do."

"Is it? You put your children as a priority. I respect that. Admire you for it."

"Russell," she said, sensing his pensive mood, "what's troubling you?"

"You don't want to hear my troubles."

"I do. If you think it will help."

He sighed, reluctant to speak. Lovie waited, not pushing him, hoping that he'd trust her enough to confide in her. He seemed to need a friend now.

"My daughter told me she didn't want to see me. That she hates me. And that neither her mother nor I made her a priority, especially when she was little. So she's decided we are no longer her priority. She hates me. She actually told me to go home."

Even in the dim light, where she couldn't see his face, she could tell it was hard for him to say.

"Oh, Russell. She's thirteen and her hormones are racing. You told me about teenage boys. Let me share with you something about teenage girls. They fight with words, and they say *I hate you* far too often, not having a clue what daggers those words are."

"Perhaps, but, sadly, I have to admit she's right. I was always gone, traveling somewhere, far too much when she was little. I was making a name for myself. And when I was home, I was working all the time."

Lovie understood that scenario all too well. He could have been describing Stratton. "And Eleanor?"

He began walking toward the beach access path. Lovie walked slowly beside him.

"She wasn't there, mentally." He stopped walking and looked off at the sea. "Eleanor and I lost a child," he said at length. "It took her a long time to get over that."

"I'm so sorry," Lovie said in a rush. She put her hand on his arm in a gesture of sympathy. She couldn't imagine the unspeakable pain of losing a child.

"You never really get past it. Poor Pippi got caught in the crosswinds of her parents' grief."

Lovie tried to see his expression, but it was too dark. The sadness in his voice hinted at the depth of despair he must have endured.

"Is that when you began to travel?"

"I wish I could say yes. But I'd always traveled for my work. Our son was only two years old when he died." He shook his head and made a sound of disgust. "I wasn't even home. I don't think Eleanor has ever forgiven me for that."

She squeezed his arm. "Russell, you can't blame yourself for that. You couldn't know."

"I wasn't there," he said sharply.

Lovie began to withdraw her hand, but he reached up to

place his hand over hers, keeping her palm on his arm. "I'm sorry. I get, well . . . it's tough to talk about Charley," he said, seemingly embarrassed for going on. He held her hand in one of his and reached for her other.

"I do understand," she said. "I lost my brother and I still miss him."

"How old were you when he died?"

"Not much older than Cara. His name was Michael Jr. but we called him Mickey. I wish you could've known him. You'd have liked him. We were close coming up. He was your basic good kid. By no means an angel, mind you, but a good-hearted rascal of a good ol' boy—with dimples, to boot. He was respectful and polite when called upon to be so. My mama would have nothing else. But in the summer?" She chuckled. "He was a wild hooligan, like all the other boys."

She paused, remembering. "One night when he was seventeen he was coming home from a party. He was out on Hamlin Creek in Daddy's Boston Whaler. It was late. Dark. He was going too fast for that narrow strip up by the marina."

She looked at Russell. His eyes never left hers.

"He drove the boat straight into a dock. He didn't see it sticking out in the waterway. He was thrown from the boat and drowned." She swallowed and looked up at the sky. "It was just a tragic accident." She sighed. "They said he'd been drinking."

"Even if he hadn't been drinking, he could've run into an unlit dock at night."

"Maybe," she said, thinking that in either case, Mickey was still gone.

"He was my brother and I loved him with all my heart. But I'd think losing your child would be worse. I wanted to tell you so you knew that, at least to some degree, I might understand what you and Eleanor must have gone through."

Russell sighed and looked at his hands. "We didn't survive it," he said bluntly. "Not as a couple."

Lovie thought his hands felt warm and very dry from his work in the sand. He squeezed her hands lightly. "Hey, I didn't mean to unload. I guess I needed to talk to someone tonight, and somehow, I knew you'd understand. Not judge. I don't have many people I can talk like this to."

She felt that something more might be said when Cara shouted from the beach path. "Hey, what's taking you two so long?"

They both abruptly dropped their hands and turned toward the voice.

"Coming!" Lovie called back.

Russell turned to pick up the bucket and flicked on his flashlight. Together they walked silently to the beach path. She followed his broad shoulders and the white beam of light that snaked along the narrow, sandy path, one foot after the other, as his words replayed in her mind, as she knew they would for the long night ahead.

Sea Turtle Journal

July 15, 1974

Saw hatchlings emerge from the nest tonight. The hatchlings scrape with their flippers, plowing through broken shells and compact sand, working as a team. This causes the floor of the nest to rise slowly to the surface, like an elevator.

This was Cara's first time witnessing a hatching. I was delighted and surprised by how enraptured she was, and how curious. My own sweet hatchling. I stood back and simply watched the magnificent spectacle of dozens of hatchlings, using that teamwork again to keep the team motivated, rush to the sea.

They followed the golden moonlight, but once in the sea, they swim off independently for three days to reach the safety of the sargassum floats in the Gulf. I watched and thought how, when I feel lonely in the darkness, I'll remember this night and the astonishing light of the moon and know that I am not alone in this beautiful world of synchronicity.

Twelve

From the first of July until the end of August when schools called children back home, the cottages were occupied, the campgrounds were full, and the island's only motel was booked. On any given Saturday or Sunday afternoon, cars crept along Palm Boulevard. No one was in a hurry. It was a Southern summer in full swing on the Isle of Palms.

The turtles kept coming, too, and the turtle team was hopping. So far the team had lost only one volunteer, someone's husband who never really wanted to join the project in the first place. All the other volunteers were thrilled at being part of the sea turtle summer. With so many nests this year, most of the volunteers had found a set of tracks, which gave them a tangible connection to the project. Lovie always put the name of the volunteer who found the nest on the stick in permanent marker, designating it as *his* or *her* nest.

The first time he saw her writing down the name, Russell had asked her why she did this.

"It seems a small gesture, but it means the world to the volunteer," she replied. "It gives her a sense of ownership of the nest, and because of that, she'll be emotionally invested in its welfare and check on it more often."

"Nice," he replied sincerely. "I'd never have thought of that on my own."

It was true. The volunteers were like proud parents of the nests. The phone tree lit up whenever a nest was discovered. So when Russell conducted the first inventory, three days after that breathtaking emergence of the first nest, thirty people showed up to watch.

Lovie had never done a nest inventory. She'd never had the authority to open a nest after the emergence—or at any time, for that matter. She was as excited as all the others when she reached the beach at seven a.m. As was Cara, who had woken early to come to the inventory of what she now considered *her* nest.

Russell wasn't happy to see so many people clustered in a semicircle around the nest in a hushed excitement. "So many people here this morning. Aren't they supposed to be patrolling the beach?"

"All done and no new tracks this morning. You should be happy they're here."

"Any time I open a nest, I'm afraid it will be misconstrued and set precedence in the mind of the public that nests are fair game to being touched."

"I'm sure they wouldn't dream of doing that."

"Are you? And what about the people who are not volunteers? I shudder to think of what could happen. Besides, Olivia, we're not conducting the inventory for the entertainment of the volunteers."

"Stop being so stingy," she replied.

He stopped, looking at her, affronted. "Stingy?"

"Yes. You're a regular Scrooge. Bah, humbug."

"I don't think I'm a Scrooge," he replied, hurt.

"You are . . . a little bit." She tried not to chuckle. "Volunteers are the backbone of the program. They're out there every morning because they care. We owe them every kindness."

His face grew thoughtful. "You're right, of course."

"I know. That's why you need me," Lovie replied, and began walking.

Despite his initial concerns, Russell couldn't help the teacher in him from coming out. And Lovie knew how much he sincerely appreciated the volunteers' support.

Russell put on latex gloves and began digging into the opening of the nest. Lovie knelt beside him, helping. Cara stood beside her, clasping her hands together in excitement.

"As you can see," she told the crowd that had clustered so close around them it was getting too warm, "we're opening the nest. We only do this several days after the hatchlings emerge. We want to give the babies a chance to come out naturally."

"Babies?" Russell asked wryly, turning his head.

Lovie rolled her eyes. "Just dig," she prodded him.

"We do this to determine the success of the nests," she told the crowd. "Of course, a live nest should never, ever be opened, not even touched."

Slowly and with great care, Russell dug with his right hand through the soft sand. She watched his face as his arm disappeared deep into the hole, a study in concentration. Then he paused, and his face lit into a boyish grin. Slowly his hand emerged, and there was a collective gasp. Lovie heard Cara's squeal beside her. In his hand was a three-inch hatchling. Its tiny shell was coated with sand, and the little flippers were batting in the air eager to take off. The crowd pressed closer with cries of, "I can't see it" and "Can I hold it?"

"Can y'all back off some? We can't breathe in here," Russell said as he handed Lovie the hatchling. Flo and Kate jumped to action, moving the crowd back a few paces. Lovie felt the air cool immediately. She held the hatchling in her hand, so small, so vulnerable. It was hard to believe that in thirty-some years this turtle might return to the Isle of Palms three feet in length and over 350 pounds.

"Here's another," Russell called, and handed it to her.

Lovie looked around for what to put the hatchlings in. They were scrambling wildly in her palm, eager to escape.

"Flo!" she called out. "Could you hand me the bucket, please?"

In a flash, Flo dumped the contents of the bucket and, maneuvering her way to Lovie's side, set the bright red bucket beside her. Lovie placed the hatchlings in and immediately they commenced scampering around, eager to get to the sea. The crowd sighed, "Awww," and surged closer.

Russell came over, carrying two more that had been trapped in the roots of nearby sea oats. He paused to look at the hatchlings in the bucket, then up at Lovie with a quizzical expression. She held her breath, wondering what he'd think of her bucket idea.

"Good call," he said, and his smile was approving. He handed her two more hatchlings.

"Hey, back up a bit, please," Flo called out, waving her hands to push back the group that was crowding closer for a better look. "Give them some air. You'll all get a chance to see the babies. I promise."

Lovie glanced at Russell for his reaction to the word *babies*. He only smirked and shook his head.

Russell had fished five healthy hatchlings from the nest. Five that likely wouldn't have made it out on their own. While he and Lovie counted the hatched and unhatched eggs for their records, Flo took ownership of the bucket and carried it around the circle, giving each of the people a chance to get a close look. "Don't touch," she said to the children eagerly reaching in to pet the turtles.

Lovie and Russell finished with the nest and led the group to the sea. Flo carried the bucket to Russell. The volunteers clustered in a tight group, along with a few tourists who were fortunately in the right place at the right time.

"We're going to let these hatchlings walk to the water," he explained. "The trek across the sand is what helps them orient correctly so that once they are in the ocean with no landmarks, they swim in a straight course, usually into the waves. After these little guys enter the ocean, they'll have some fifty miles to swim to get to the Gulf Stream. We don't know exactly. Some say only one in a thousand turtles makes it. So let's wish these turtles Godspeed."

Flo stepped forward to guide the group back, her voice booming. "They need to see and smell the ocean. So I'm going to ask y'all to please fan out in a large semicircle. That's right."

The group willingly obliged.

"We couldn't do this without the whole team," Russell said to the group. "Each and every one of you is important to the project. But I think you'll agree with me that no one deserves to release the first batch of hatchlings more than Olivia Rutledge."

Everyone smiled in approval, and their applause was heartfelt. Flo released a piercing whistle.

Lovie felt the emotion rise up to blur her vision. She blushed, always a little shy at being called out in a group.

Russell handed her the bucket. "Madam, would you do the honors?"

Through her tears, Lovie could see the five dark hatchlings scurrying at the bottom of the bucket and hear the raucous scratch-scratching of their sandy flippers against plastic. Their brown-black coloring was a sharp contrast to the bright red of the bucket.

"Cara?" she called. "Will you help me?"

Cara bolted forward to put her hands on the bucket.

"Good luck," Lovie murmured to the hatchlings, then she and Cara lowered the bucket, letting the hatchlings scramble free to the sand.

They were comical, like Keystone Kops, as they bumped and crawled over each other to escape. Endearing little tracks, miniatures of those left behind by their mothers, trailed along the moist sand as the turtles fanned out, determinedly following the age-old call of the sea.

Lovie rose to her feet and her gaze swept the group of volunteers gathered around the hatchlings. Some of them had brought their children, hoping they'd learn from the experience. Lovie saw how they were all children in this experience, with eyes as large as saucers. A few had cameras and clicked madly, free to photograph in the daylight. This was the first sea turtle hatchling most of them had ever seen.

Cara diligently followed a lone straggler as it made its way to the surf. The hatchling paused for a fraction of a second, lifted its head as if to sniff the sea for direction, then took off again. The ingoing tide reached higher with each wave, finally sweeping over the hatchling, washing off the sand and revealing the gleaming reddish-brown color of its shell. Tasting its first salt water, the hatchling surged eagerly forward with renewed vigor. A second, larger wave captured the hatchling, and in that miraculous, tumbling instant Lovie saw the hatchling dive. She reached out to grab Russell's hand, so awed by the power of this ancient instinct. Immediately this last of the turtles began swimming furiously, gracefully, with the skill of 180 million years of training.

As the wave receded, carrying its passenger along into the vast sea, Lovie again felt her eyes fill. She wasn't sure if she cried for the hatchling or for Russell's words. But everyone was getting teary eyed, hugging each other and patting friends on the back.

People came up to congratulate them and to thank Russell for allowing them to be part of the project. For so many years she'd hoped to enlist the help of islanders for the sea turtles, and this summer it was actually happening.

The group began disbanding, calling out farewells and walking off toward different paths to their homes and their lives. Flo was far ahead, talking with Miranda as they exited the beach. Cara was walking home along the shoreline, playing tag with the waves. In all the excitement, it wasn't until Lovie began walking back that she realized Russell was still holding her hand.

Russell drove Lovie to his house, where she'd parked her car, and she climbed into her old station wagon. It was an oven inside, so hot it hurt to sit and her thighs stuck to the fabric. The engine whined but didn't turn over. "Not again," she muttered. After a third effort, the engine was wheezing, fainter and weaker. She put her forehead in her palm and groaned. She cursed her folly for not getting the car checked out when it had happened earlier. She'd been so busy, but that excuse seemed lame. Now she was stuck. This could take hours . . . She looked out the window, but Russell had already gone into his house.

Lovie slammed her car door, hating the old rust bucket that had failed her. She felt her cheeks flame with each step as she walked toward Russell's two-story cinder-block house, painted a color somewhere between salmon and peach. It was the second home of a friend of the mayor's and made available to Russell for the summer. It was a choice piece of property, ocean side with long, rolling dunes to the beach. But the front yard was a scrubby patch of sand, weeds, and wild grasses.

She made her way along the narrow cement walkway that went straight as an arrow to the front porch, which was, in kind, a dreary slab of cement. No potted plant, no hanging fern, no decorative front mat broke the dry monotony of the neglected entryway. Sand piled up under the doorframe where Russell's sandals were left. Even the door was dusty, with spiderwebs at the corner. Lovie rang the doorbell and waited, but there was no answer. She tried again and waited, peeking in the window, but the curtains prevented her view. When no one came, she wondered if the doorbell was broken. She knocked twice, harder each time.

At last, there was a shuffling of feet behind the door and then it swung open. Russell was wrapped in a towel, dripping wet and obviously just stepping out from the shower. "Olivia!" he exclaimed. His face reflected his surprise at seeing her, then quickly changed to pleasure.

Olivia flushed to see his broad bare chest and his wearing only a towel. "Oh, I'm sorry to bother you," she stammered, trying to avoid looking directly at him.

His smile slipped to reveal concern. "No bother at all. What seems to be the matter?"

"It's so embarrassing, but my car won't start. I meant to take it in to the garage. Looks like I shouldn't have waited."

He tightened his hold on his towel, gave it a quick hoist up. "I'll just get dressed and we'll take a look. Come on in."

Lovie followed him in, appreciating the immediate coolness and the relief of being out of the glaring sun. For all that she complained about Stratton's need for air-conditioning, on this blisteringly hot morning she appreciated the closed shades and blissful artificial chill.

"I apologize for the mess," Russell said, quickly picking up a pair of trousers from the back of the chair and a pillow from the floor. "I've got about three projects I'm working on simultaneously."

"I'll just make a call and get out of your way." She was embarrassed to catch him unawares.

"No hurry. Use the phone. It's right there on the desk. I think there's a phone book there, too, somewhere under that mess. I'll be down in a flash." He raced up the stairs.

She'd been in his house back in June when she'd helped set up the program. Other than more books and more mess, the place looked pretty much the same. The rental house was typically furnished with moderately priced furniture meant to look beachy: rattan sofas, palm-printed fabrics, bad art of beach scenes and sailboats. The walls were white and the floors were a neutral brown tile, pleasant but boring. She thought she'd find it hard to stay for the whole summer without adding personal touches and color.

Russell Bennett, it appeared, couldn't care less about style or color. Only work seemed to matter. Every spare flat surface was covered with books, tilting piles of overflowing manila folders, science magazines, and dirty dishes and coffee cups. The dining room had been changed into a makeshift office. An enormous poster of the island hung on the wall. It was marked with colored flags that indicated the nests. Cheap metal file cabinets had been added, as well as movable bookshelves. Someone smoked, too, she thought, noticing the filled ashtrays, and wondered if it was Russell or Bing.

She used the phone to call home. Palmer answered and she explained why she was held up. She was looking in the phone book for the number of the local garage when Russell returned downstairs.

"Can I get you some water?" he asked.

"Yes, please. And an aspirin? I've got a headache blooming."

Noises of cabinets opening and closing and water running came from the kitchen.

"Here it is," he said, coming up behind her carrying a glass of water. He handed her two aspirin and she accepted them gratefully. "You're probably dehydrated. You'll have to be careful to bring enough water in your backpack, especially on these hot days."

Lovie nodded, swallowing down the aspirin. "Thank you." She drank the water thirstily.

"Did you eat today?"

She shook her head. "I try to grab something before I leave, but I stayed in bed a few extra minutes this morning."

"You should eat. You're getting thin."

She was surprised that he'd noticed. She had been losing weight, but it wasn't intentional. She was simply running around so much she sometimes forgot to eat. She pulled the elastic from her hair and released her braid, removing the constriction from her aching head.

"You also look exhausted."

"I am a little tired."

He took her glass and refilled it. Then he gave her a banana from a selection of fruit on the kitchen counter. "A little potassium would do you good, too. And here's a salt shaker. Sprinkle some on your palm and lick it. It'll help restore your balance. You eat while I go out and take a look."

She ate the banana with her eyes closed and rubbed her temples. A short while later Russell returned, shaking dust from his pants with one hand and studying a green liquid on his other.

"Bad news, I'm afraid. There's an enormous puddle of coolant under there. It's bad. If it was just leaking a bit, I'd fill it with coolant and follow you to the nearest station. But this car's not going anywhere. You'll have to get it towed."

"Towed? Oh, Lord. That could take hours."

"Prepare yourself. It's the water pump. I just hope you haven't damaged your engine. You might have quite a job on your hands. It could be awhile till you get your car back."

"But I have to have a car. I'm alone here."

"You could rent one."

She nodded, bringing her fingertips to her temples.

Russell grabbed the phone. "What's the name of the station on the island?"

"The Isle of Palms filling station." She handed him the scrap of paper she'd written the number on.

Russell smirked. "Of course."

"They're good," Lovie replied, scrunching up her lips from the salt. "Ask for Pop."

The tow was arranged in short order. "He'll be here in fifteen minutes."

"I feel like such an idiot," she said.

"Why? Because your car broke down? It happens to the best of us."

"Perhaps it's a sign. The car has over a hundred thousand miles on it. I've been thinking about getting a new one, but Stratton says it's still got a lot of life left in it."

"I notice he's not driving it," he replied. "How do *you* feel about it?"

"It's been a good car."

"But do you like it enough to keep it?"

"No, I hate it!" Then a reluctant smile eased across her face. "But it does have a lot of life in it, at least as far as memories go. I've driven everywhere in that old beast—car pool, to church, back and forth from the beach house to the city, to the children's recitals, graduations, games. And countless turtle nests over the years. That car has been true blue. It's just getting old. And it did try to warn me . . ."

"So you'll fix her up and keep her?"

"To be totally honest, I've been longing for a smaller car,

something sporty and easier to park for the island. I admit I've been a little jealous of your Jeep. Maybe it's time for me to look around a bit."

Russell rubbed his jaw, then reached out his hand to her. "Come with me."

"Where?" she asked, surprised.

"Are you up to going back out for a little while? How's your headache?"

"Better. But . . ."

"Can the kids spare you for a bit longer?"

"I already called them. They're fine. Cara's at Emmi's and by now Palmer's at McKevlin's surf shop."

"So we're good to go." Grabbing his keys, Russell opened the door, and Lovie stepped out into the piercing wall of sun and heat. Suddenly, she heard a high-pitched voice.

"Hello! Lovie!"

She turned to see a tall, broad-beamed woman in a bright orange flowered Hawaiian muumuu and matching orange floppy hat walking toward them. Beside her was a short, wiry man with a leathery tan and fisherman's cap. He walked with a rolling gait like he was still on a boat.

"Hello, Ada," Lovie replied, cringing inside. Ada would stop you in the street and chat forever.

"Why, you're the last person I expected to see here," said Ada, drawing near. Her large blue eyes slunk from Lovie to Russell in scrutiny.

Lovie plastered her hostess smile on her face. "Ada and Wally Blair, allow me to introduce you to Dr. Bennett. He's come to conduct the turtle research project here on the island. Surely you've heard about it?"

"No, no I haven't," she replied, eyes still on Russell. She looked like she was going to gobble him up for breakfast. "But we've only just got here. We're a little late this year." She looked at Russell and asked pointedly, "You're staying in Hank Harrison's house, Dr. uh, Bennett, was it?"

Russell stood with his hands behind his back. "It is, and I am."

"Then we're neighbors. Isn't that nice? Wally, we won't have a house of screaming kids or drunks next door to us this summer." She smiled sweetly, then asked, "I don't imagine you'll have too many wild parties?"

"No, ma'am. I'm the quiet type."

Lovie thought the old harridan almost looked disappointed.

"So, you say you're working on a project for sea turtles?" she asked. "Which one is that? I swear, I've never heard of a turtle project on Isle of Palms. Lovie, don't you just walk the beach all on your lonesome? What do they call you? Oh, yes." She smiled sweet as sugar. "The Turtle Lady."

Russell's lips tightened and he didn't reply. Lovie could tell he wasn't about to, either. She sighed inwardly and launched into a quick description of the project, then had to bring Ada up to speed on the potential sale of the northern portion of the island. Her husband, Wally, stood as still as a bird dog with his eyes fixed on the ocean. Beside her, Russell wore the polite expression of attentive boredom.

"Mercy, that's a lot of news. I suppose that's why you two had so much to catch up on—off the beach, that is." Ada waved her hand in front of her face. "Isn't it hot?"

"Exactly," Russell interrupted. "Mrs. Rutledge is expecting a tow truck. Her car broke down in this heat after the turtle patrol. I'm sure you don't want to stand in this sun any longer than you have to. You'll excuse us. A pleasure to meet you both."

Without waiting for their response, Russell took hold of Lovie's elbow and guided her away from the Blairs.

"Thank you for that," Lovie said sotto voce. "We could've been stuck there all morning."

"She's insufferable," Russell said. "Her innuendos were about as subtle as a sledgehammer."

Lovie hoped that Ada would be peeking from her window to witness the tow truck. Surely that gave her an excuse for being seen coming out of Russell's house midday. Mercifully, the tow truck arrived a few minutes later and, after a quick discussion, towed the station wagon off to the garage.

"Okay, hop in. I'll take you home. But first, I want to show you something," Russell said, guiding her toward the Jeep.

Lovie looked over her shoulder at Ada's house. As she suspected, she saw a hand holding back the curtain at the front window. "It won't take long, will it?" she asked, buckling up.

"Depends," Russell replied with a wink.

They drove only a few blocks to the town's shopping strip. Instead of turning in, Russell crossed the street and parked the Jeep beside the big PALMS MOTEL sign.

"Here we are."

"Russell," she began, and cleared her throat. "What are we doing here?"

"I want to show you something. It's right over there. Really, how long can it take to look? Come on."

Lovie puffed out a plume of air and pushed open the door. She walked around the Jeep and spotted a small, gold VW bug with a red store-bought FOR SALE sign in the windshield.

"It's the car we saw in the street," she exclaimed. "The one with all the flags."

"Right. I saw it again the other day with the FOR SALE sign, so I followed it."

Up close, she saw with some alarm that the gold paint contained a faint glitter that sparkled in the sun. But the cream-colored canvas convertible ragtop was adorable. Inside, the car had a matching cream-colored leather and snazzy black trim. It was old but in surprisingly good shape.

"I already checked it out. It's in amazingly good condition with very low mileage. It's hard to believe, but it's actually owned by the proverbial little old lady who only drove it on occasion. She bought it on a whim and had this custom paint job done. She kept it in the garage most of the time."

"With that glittery paint job, I can see why. How much does she want for it?"

"Take a look at the sign."

Lovie walked closer and bent over the hood to peer at the price. She raised her head, incredulous. "You're kidding?"

"I know! It's a steal. I don't even need a car and I thought about buying it for Pippi."

"Oh," she said, slightly disappointed. "Then *you* should buy it."

"No, you should. Pippi probably wouldn't accept a car from me right now. Besides, you desperately need a car and you just said you had in mind something small and sporty. I admit, the paint job is a little, well, over the top, but mechanically it's sound. One of us should buy it. And soon. She just put it out last night and it'll go fast at that price."

Lovie stood back and looked at the car through the eyes of possibility. It might be a tad embarrassing to drive a sparkly gold car, but on the other hand, it had a certain je ne sais quoi that was appealing. It was small, it would be easy to park by the beach access paths, and with the ragtop down she'd be opened to the outdoors. It wasn't a Jeep, true, but it was decidedly more feminine. Easier to handle. And the price was right.

"Stratton might get angry at me for making an impulsive purchase," she worried aloud.

"Don't you have pin money, or mad money, or whatever you call it tucked away somewhere?"

Lovie drew back her shoulders, feeling a prick of pride. "I have my own money."

"Well, then?" He leaned against the front hood and crossed his arms. "It seems to me it's your decision, then, isn't it?"

Lovie swallowed. She realized she'd never considered the money she'd brought to the marriage as *her* money. Stratton had always taken charge of their finances. He was very good with money, and it was the way it had always been done in her family. He'd put her on a budget and went over the bills carefully. In fact, she thought of the money as *his* money. But at the very least, it was *their* money. And he was off to Europe, she thought, feeling the old anger rise up once again. He didn't consider her opinion when he bought something, like that big black Mercedes he'd brought home from Germany last year.

"Yes," she replied, "it is my decision."

"Well, this car has personality. If you take it, you'll need to give it a unique name."

"You mean something to make all that glitter pretend to have a purpose?"

"Exactly," he said with a chuckle. "How about Lucille?"

"As much as I love Chuck Berry, that's not what I was going for. It'll come to me."

"Then you want it?"

She felt a bubble of excitement and nodded. "Yes."

"Good decision. Let's call the number and settle the deal right away, before someone scoops it up from under us. And then," he added, "I think we need a night off. No nest is imminent and we're both tired."

She walked around the car, letting her fingertips slide along the golden steel, grinning, feeling a little of its gold sparkle sprinkle on her.

Sea Turtle Journal

July 22, 1974

The 300-plus-pound loggerhead has a powerful shell over 3 feet in length. Although sea turtles cannot withdraw their heads into their shells, the adults are somewhat protected from predators by these great shells.

There is always the worry of gossip, especially in a small community. But the turtles have taught me to develop a hard shell against gossips, naysayers, or those who want me to fail.

Thirteen

L ovie couldn't remember the last time she'd slept past six or got to bed before eleven with sand still in her eyes that no shower ever seemed to wash away. There was enough sand at the bottom of her shower stall for a sandbox. Turtle duty for July was round-the-clock; the turtles were kicking butt.

And Lovie couldn't have been happier.

She and Russell spent so many hours together. They were comrades more than colleagues. He'd seen her sweaty and coated with sand with her arm shoulder-deep in a nest, scratched and bloodied by brush, her hair a tangled mess, even her teeth unbrushed.

She rolled out of her gravel driveway in her sporty new car and drove along Palm Boulevard, enjoying the soft growl of the engine, the breeze in her hair with the top down, and the easy pace of the morning. Her gaze wandered to check the ospreys' nest on the platform that her pal Clay Cable had set up on Goat Island, just for her. Last year the nest had been marauded by a hungry great horned owl. It destroyed any eggs that were there, and the bereft parents flew off. For Lovie, it was hard to accept that nature was survival of the fittest. Or, as Clay had said,

"Honey, the owl has to eat, too." Ospreys were site loyal, however, and Lovie was relieved when the lovebirds returned in February to try again. Clay and Lovie were hopeful that the young osprey couple would have better luck this year. The two small heads she'd spied in the spring peeping over the rim of the nest were now as large as their parents'.

Cheered, she started to hum as she made her way down the boulevard. A young man was jogging along the creek, and farther on she passed an elderly couple on bicycles. She reached the beach to see that Russell had already arrived.

"Olivia!" he called out, raising his hand.

She smiled at his usual greeting and waved back. She never tired of him calling her name—Olivia. He was the only one who called her by her full name, and she loved the sound of it on his lips.

It was a textbook case. The tracks led high up to the dune where Lovie quickly found the broken vegetation, the thrown sand, and the push-off ridge the turtle made with her flippers. Russell was making her find the eggs more often now, and she was getting good at it.

"This brings the total nests for the island to sixty-six," Russell said, wiping his hands on the small towel he carried in his backpack.

Lovie entered the information in the record book, brushing away the ubiquitous sand from the page. "Do you think we'll make it to eighty?" It was thrilling to think they could really get that many nests this summer. "When I was just doing my end of the island, I think the highest number of nests we ever hit was forty-four."

"We'll make it to seventy-five, maybe more. But I hate to burst your bubble," Russell said with a wry grin. "I won't even tell you how many turtle nests we get along the Atlantic coast of Florida."

She closed the journal and put it into her backpack. "Well, I know Florida is the mecca for nesting turtles," Lovie replied defensively. Then curious, she had to ask, "But how many would you say? Three hundred? Five hundred? A thousand?"

"Thousands," he replied.

"That many . . ." she said, rising with a sigh. It was almost enough to make her want to move to Florida. Almost.

"But every nest counts," he reminded her.

She smiled, thinking how typical it was for him to bolster her confidence.

Two days later, tracks were reported at the Point. Lovie parked at Russell's and they drove together in the rugged Jeep across the rough terrain to the far northern tip of the island. The beach was deserted and the ocean was as smooth as glass.

"It's anyone's guess where it is. The volunteer just said it was high up in the north. Let's walk that way," he said, pointing. "See what we find."

Lovie wiped her forehead and regretted that she'd forgotten her thermos in the car. The bucket banged her thigh as she walked alongside him. It was a beastly hot day and it felt like the sun was trying to ignite her brown cotton shirt. Even the sand seemed to burn her toes.

"I call this dedication," she said.

"Or obsessive-compulsive," he chided.

"You're the one who's making the rules," she said with a teasing bump of her shoulder against his. Then she felt a sudden worry that the gesture was too forward.

"I know, I know," he replied, seeming not to notice. "Just remember this is a short-term study. Once I'm gone, you can sigh in relief and not keep doing the northern end. You can go back to covering just your end of the island."

There it was again, she thought, almost wincing. Talk of his leaving. She knew the day was coming, understood that he was here for the duration of the study only, and then he would go back to his job, his life, far from here. Far from her. She smiled, determined not to be maudlin.

"You don't think I'll stop doing the whole island, do you? After this?" she said in a blustery manner, forcing the cheer in her voice. "Not likely." She walked a few more steps. "By the way, I *can* continue what you taught me? Moving nests? Inventories?"

"Oh, God," he mock groaned, "I've opened Pandora's box."

"Russell!"

"Believe me, Olivia, if ever I trusted anyone to do the job right, it'd be you. I'll see what I can do to get you a permit. You'll need some kind of authority."

"Authority." She rolled the word on her tongue, liking the sound of it. "At last. Even if I'll never get paid."

"Don't feel too bad. I get paid very little."

"I wondered about that," she replied. "How do you afford planes and your family trips to Europe, houses in Maine, Bermuda?"

He smirked. "The old-fashioned way. I inherited it."

"Ah, yes," she said. "I thought I caught the whiff of a patrician about you."

"Oh, really?" he replied. "And what about you, Mrs. Rutledge. I assume of *the* Rutledge family, signers of the Declaration of Independence?"

"My husband's family . . ."

A brief smile of concession flickered across his face. "I'm fortunate to have my trust fund, I admit it. It allows me to do the work I love and still be able to fund my research."

"You can be proud of that."

"A fate of birth."

"True, but you could be gallivanting, sailing around the world, gambling. A wastrel."

"Ah, you've met my brother?"

She laughed and bumped his shoulder again, enjoying the banter and the sound of his laughter beside her.

They walked at a leisurely pace under the scorching sun. Lovie looked longingly at the ocean. Water, water, everywhere, nor any drop to drink, she thought. The inlet between Dewees Island and Isle of Palms reflected the blue sky and sparkled in the sunlight, luring her. Along the shoreline, shells littered the beach. She spotted several unbroken angel's wings, pristine whelks, and skate's purses. Cara would love it here, Lovie thought idly.

"It's so isolated here," Russell said, as though reading her mind. "So idyllic. We could be on a deserted island far, far from Isle of Palms."

Lovie spotted in the distance a particularly attractive cedar. It was ancient and had spent countless years yielding to the relentless storms and wind. Something triggered in her memory. The tree was unique. Its trunk was bent far landward by the wind, like a bonsai. The twisted boughs and greenery were shaped by the hand of God to create an arc of shade over the sand.

"I know that tree," she said with wonder. "Of course, it has to be!" Despite the blistering heat, Lovie took off at a clip toward the tree. Russell was close at her heels. When they reached the tree she stopped, her face glowing with joy and perspiration.

"I can't believe it. This is it, the umbrella tree. I remember it from my childhood. Why, Russell, we've walked all the way to the Point."

"The Point?"

"Yes!" she exclaimed, delighted. "I told you, don't you remember? This is *the* Point of the challenge. Nicodemus. Ring a bell?"

"Oh, right," he said, keeping up. "Ghosts and voodoo. The ultimate test."

"Yes, that's right. And this," she said, coming at last to the bent cypress, "this is the spot." At the base of the tree was a roughly hewn wooden cross. "Look!" Her voice was ringing with the excitement she felt racing in her veins. "My brother made this cross! We all searched for just the right driftwood on the beach. What a day that was. I painted it," she said, surprised that, though chipped, bits of the blue color remained on the wood. "It's haint blue."

"What's haint blue?"

"Remember how I was telling you about all the spiritualism and voodoo stories that grow as thick as kudzu around these parts? Well, haint blue is a vivid, dark blue color that the Gullah paint on the trim of doors and windows to keep out evil spirits and demons. I've heard it's also good to ward off spiders. The Gullah also believe that souls may be trapped in the world between here and there. So they paint their ceilings a lighter blue to signify to the lost souls where to go to get to their final resting place."

Lovie dropped to her knees. She let her backpack fall to the sand beside her and searched for her cockleshell, then began to dig in the sand under the arch.

"I can't believe I've found it again, after all these years."

"Found what?" Russell asked, going to his knees beside her, curious now.

Lovie's shell struck metal. "Just wait," she said excitedly, and dug more quickly. A short while later, she pulled up a dented metal box and set it down on the beach between them.

"Good God, Lovie," Russell said in mock surprise. "You've found Blackbeard's treasure!"

"I've found something worth far more," she said, her eyes

kindling with delight. Opening the box, she sucked in her breath. "It's still there," she said, exhaling with wonder.

Inside the box were a brown Moleskine notebook, a classic #2 pencil, and a brown spider that scurried out of the box to disappear. Lovie wiped her sandy hands on her shirt, then reverentially lifted the book out of the box. The leather was warm and bits of sand encrusted the edges. She wiped away the top layer of dirt and sand, and could read the letters, written in capital letters in a child's script. A smile filled with tender memories flitted across her face as she traced her finger across the letters.

THE SECRET OF THE POINT

Opening it, she found the pages dirty but still in decent condition. She read aloud the oath that, many years before, she'd watched evolve as Mickey and his friends huddled together to create the myth.

> I solemnly swear
> that I hiked through the deep woods,
> I survived the fearful ghost of Nicodemus,
> to reach this sacred spot. If I'm lying,
> may Nicodemus cut off my toes and fingers
> and feed them to the fishes.

"Nice touch," Russell said, "that bit about the cutting off toes and fingers."

"We thought so."

"We?"

She nodded. "My brother Mickey and his friends. But I tagged along. Mickey and I were great pals when we were young. Like Mutt and Jeff." She ran her finger down the first page of names, all written in pencil. With age, the writing had faded, but they were still legible. All of them were boys' names, except for one: Olivia Simmons.

"Look! There's my name."

"Well, now I know where Cara gets it from," Russell said.

"Gets what?"

"Her bravery, curiosity, independence."

"Hardly. Cara is much braver than I am. And far more independent. I love that about her."

Lovie flipped through the twenty or more pages filled with children's names, smiling when she saw Palmer's name. "Almost all boys. They've all shared in this brotherhood," she said, looking around at the uniquely bent tree in a remote tip of the island. "And now the era is ending. It's all so sad. What should I do, Russell? Should I keep the journal? I don't want it destroyed."

"No! Absolutely not. It's not yours to keep. It belongs here."

"But it will get dug up when they build the resort. It'll be destroyed."

"You don't know that. How long has it been since you signed this book?"

"I don't know exactly. Over twenty-five years."

"So it's survived here for a quarter of a century. Trust that it will survive here for another. Maybe more. After all, Cara hasn't signed it yet. Nor have her children. They deserve that chance."

Lovie thought of Cara finding her way to this point, unearthing the box, and signing her name with a great sense of triumph. That alone would be worth leaving the book in place. "To think, my grandchild might sign this book." She chuckled softly, remembering that hot summer's day, not unlike today, when four boys and two girls put the journal into the metal box and covered it with sand, marking it so that in the years to come, other children would find their way to it.

"Little did we know on that fateful day that this challenge would endure for decades."

"That's the magic of youth. They have complete and utter faith. They believe. Isn't that the real challenge of the Point? To keep believing, against all odds? Life is all an act of faith. What are we without that?"

Lovie looked at his eyes, so bright with that faith he talked about. Sweat beaded on his brow and over his lip, sand clung to his clothes, and his hair was windblown. All at once she saw Russell Bennett in a new light. He was unlike anyone she'd met before, yet in a sense, he reminded her of her father. Not in looks or even personality, but in qualities. Strong and determined, yet also kind and wise. Even noble.

She closed the book and moved to put it back in the box when he held her elbow, stopping her.

"Excuse me, Mrs. Rutledge, but I believe I've earned the right to sign that book."

She raised her brows and handed him the book and the pencil. Lovie wondered about the man who signed the book with his tight script, then closed it with a sigh of satisfaction.

"You're a Peter Pan, do you know that? All pirate hunts, good deeds, and sailing about."

Russell chuckled at that. "We've all got a little pixie dust on us," he replied. "Or I hope we do. Life would be very dull without it." He handed her the journal. "Time to bury the treasure."

"Hmmm, maybe I got that wrong. Perhaps you're Hook."

"Who does that make you? Wendy or Tinker Bell?"

"Wendy," she replied, opening the box. "Definitely Wendy."

"The mother. It fits," he replied.

"The storyteller," she said.

Laughing, they closed the metal box and lowered it into the hole. After they covered it back up with sand, Lovie scratched an X on the sand with her finger.

"Just in case Cara gets here," she said, patting the sand.

Sea Turtle Journal

July 24, 1974

Russell talked about faith today. How believing something is possible against all odds is what gives us the strength to persevere. Isn't that what we're doing with every hatchling we release? We have to have faith that this hatchling will escape the jaws of predators, avoid the tangle of dangerous nets, and find its way home. We have to believe the beach will still be here, waiting to welcome her, as it was for her mother, and her mother before her.

Fourteen

≈

August's first week brought a heat wave with no end in sight. It was just after nine and the morning sun was already brutal. Russell and Lovie answered a report of tracks and had been walking toward the northern tip of the Point from their access path for thirty minutes. Russell stopped and whipped off his hat, then wiped his brow with his sleeve and said irritably, "This was a wild-goose chase. There aren't any tracks up here."

Lovie's lips were dry as she scanned the beach. It stretched out like a desert, and the air was heavy with humidity. "I feel like I'm Lawrence of Arabia. Where's my camel?"

Russell dug into his backpack and pulled out a thermos. He put it near his ear and shook it. "I have a sip of water left. Maybe. Here, you take it."

He was being gallant, and she let him. She took a careful sip, just enough to moisten her mouth. It felt like drops of rain on an arid desert. She handed it back to him. "There's enough left for you."

Grateful, he tilted his head back and swallowed the last of the water. "We should head back and get out of this sun. It's a scorcher."

They picked up their gear and began walking toward the Jeep at a determined pace.

"Speaking of heading back," Lovie said, broaching the subject that had been plaguing her thoughts at night since he'd mentioned leaving the other day. "When do you think you'll actually be leaving here?"

"When the turtles do. Sometime late this month."

So soon. Lovie knew that he was leaving at the end of summer, but that had always seemed so far away. As August began, the end loomed close. She kept walking, one foot ahead of the other deep in the soft sand, but her heart felt like it was dragging. In contrast, he'd sounded like it was just another date, just another job to finish. Of course her feelings were one-sided.

"But," she began, "we'll be having hatchlings until late in September. I thought you'd be here till then."

"I wish I could, but classes start at the university." He took a few steps and then said with some pride, "They've made me a full professor."

Lovie stopped short. "Congratulations!"

"Thanks. It's a pretty big deal for me. I'll have to fly back and forth a few times starting next week to prepare for the semester," Russell continued. "But this team is a well-oiled machine now. With you at the head, you'll all do fine."

Lovie felt a sudden regret for her efficiency.

"I apologize that I'll have to leave you to finish up the data for the season," he told her. "I'll have enough information to render an opinion to the resort in an official report. We both know that there are significant numbers of nests up here at the northern end, and the builders will have to take precautions to protect the nesting beaches. So at the end of the month, officially my job will be done." He turned to face her, smiling gently. "But if I know you, you'll want to dot every i and cross every t on this report."

Lovie felt a sudden sadness rush over her with the force of a wave, tumbling her emotions. "I didn't realize you'd be leaving that soon."

"I'm afraid so."

She didn't reply. Of course he was leaving soon. That had been clearly understood from the day she met him. He had a job to do here that lasted for the summer. He'd render his opinion with the report and fly back to his life, one that did not include her. She had to keep that in the forefront of her mind and get past these clearly inappropriate feelings she was developing for Russell Bennett. They were immature, unrealistic, and dangerous.

"Olivia," he said gently, bending closer to look at her face, "are you all right?"

She quickly wiped the sweat from her brow, disguising her emotions. "Yes, I'm just hot. And a little off-kilter. Nixon is resigning from office today. I don't regret his leaving office, but it's still oddly upsetting."

"Yes, it is," he agreed. "The whole nation is holding its breath. I have an idea. Let's go for a swim and cool off. I mean, we're here at the ocean, right? Isn't that what people do to cool off?"

"But I haven't got a swimsuit."

"So?"

She looked at him askance. "I'm a little too old for skinny-dipping."

"No you're not. If you're game . . . But I was going to suggest we just swim in our clothes. They'll get wet. Who cares?"

"You're kidding."

"Nope," he said with a glimmer of mischief in his eyes. "Come on, Olivia. Where's the girl who signed that book?" He wagged his brows, egging her on. "I'd bet Wendy would." He kicked off his sandals, dropped his backpack, and tore off his shirt.

Lovie couldn't help but stare at his lithe, muscled body, so smooth and tanned, more like a young man's than that of someone in his forties. Stratton's muscles were already softer, and though he wasn't fat, his belly was rounded and hung slightly over his belt from too much drinking and not enough exercise.

"Well, come on!" he said. "The ocean's over yonder, waiting."

Lovie jerked her gaze away, embarrassed to be caught looking at him. She hastily set down the bucket, dropped her backpack, and stepped from her sandals. Then, remembering, she took off her watch and hat and slipped them in the bucket. When she looked up, he was holding out his hand to her and his blue eyes were as shining and inviting as the ocean. Giggling, she took his hand.

They ran together toward the ocean that glistened in welcome, not slowing when they reached the water, and plowed into the waves. Dropping hands, they began swimming. Lovie laughed and squealed, releasing the young girl inside her, splashing and enjoying the novelty of swimming midday in her clothes.

It'd been years since she bodysurfed, but Russell gave her pointers—how to spot the right wave, when to kick off. He was always there to lend his hand and help her back up, and she relished his lavish praise. While they waited for the waves, he told her stories of waves he'd surfed around the world, and she could imagine him, young and tanned with long blond hair, riding the big ones.

"Here comes one," he called out.

Lovie glanced over her shoulder to see a wave building behind her. She pointed her arms out in front of her.

"Go!" he called.

Lovie began stroking the water, pushing hard when the wave caught her, and she felt herself lifted forward, sailing on the crest. She stopped stroking and rode the wave, flying again, free.

But it was short-lived. When the wave reached the shoreline, it gracelessly sent her skidding along the scratchy sand. Laughing, she swallowed some seawater and began coughing. Russell was there in a flash, taking hold of her waist and helping her to stand.

"I'm all right," she choked out. "Swallowed water."

Russell patted her back while she coughed again. His smile was tender. "Better?"

She nodded and took a few clear breaths. She realized his hands were still at her waist and her palms lay flat against his bare chest. She became aware of the few inches between them as she stared at his wet skin, watching his chest rise and fall beneath her fingertips.

He pressed her closer. She let her hands slide around his back even as his slid around hers. She laid her cheek on his chest and felt him kiss the top of her head. Her breasts pressed against him and her lips tasted salt on his skin. She closed her eyes and knew this was a point of decision. Like the wave, she could step back in retreat, or roll forward and ride the wave.

His head lowered and she knew in that moment that this was a force of nature. She didn't want to stop. She wanted to feel his lips on hers. *Just a kiss*, she told herself. *He's leaving soon. Who could it hurt? Just one kiss* . . . Lovie tilted her head back, so slowly it felt like seconds passed with each degree, and looking up she saw his eyes, those startling blue eyes, looking into hers with a hunger and desire that ignited her own.

His mouth sought hers, and she felt the coolness of his lips, trembling, seeking. At the touch of his tongue, her breath caught in her throat and she felt a rush of her blood. She lifted her arms around his neck and pressed her breasts against him as his hands roamed under her shirt to her skin and held her tight. The waves crashed against their legs, rocking them, as the kiss deepened. All thoughts vanished in white light save for the reality that she was kissing Russell and it felt so good, so right.

They separated slowly, both still caught up in the tempest of emotions that had spilled over in that kiss. They pressed their foreheads together, breathing hard. Lovie took a step back, feeling his hands slowly, reluctantly slide from her arms.

She hated to pull away, but an inner alarm had gone off and she obediently heeded it. She didn't know she could feel suddenly so cold under the beating sun, but outside his arms she began to shiver.

"Let's get you dry," Russell said, taking her hand. He led her out from the water to the sand where their backpacks lay. He rummaged through them both, pulling out the small hand towels and handing one to her. He used his palms to flatten back his hair against his head and the towel to rub his arms, belly, and legs, while keeping his gaze on her. Lovie dried what she could with her shorts and T-shirt clinging to her body like a second skin. She reached up to tug out the elastic from her braid, and using her fingers as a comb, she undid the braid and smoothed her hair under the sun.

They both were silent as they made the trip back through the forest. Over the past month they'd traversed the same trail so many times the road was easier to cross, but it was still bumpy and full of ruts. The Jeep broke through the shade into the sun once they reached Palm Boulevard, and the heat of the late morning sun bore down on them in the open-topped vehicle.

The gold bug was waiting for her in Russell's driveway. Russell put the Jeep into park and left it running as they sat a moment, each waiting for the other to speak.

"I better get changed," she said, and moved to open the door.

Russell shot out his hand and held it over hers. "Olivia," he began.

She couldn't meet his gaze. "Yes?"

"I don't want you to think that the kiss . . . that it didn't mean anything."

Her cheeks burned as she wondered what that kiss could possibly mean to him. Or more, if he could imagine what it had meant to her. She wasn't like Flo, unattached and free to kiss or make love when she chose. Even if she was, she had always been a one-man woman. She'd kissed many boys, of course. She wasn't a prude. But Stratton had been her only lover. Yet this kiss was so much more than making out on a date or the good-night kiss one received at the door. This kiss had felt to her as though it had reached back through the ages, to former lives, to reunite them. She had felt she belonged in his arms. After years of feeling alone, Russell's kiss had made her feel she belonged to someone again. To him.

"I don't," she replied, then lifted her gaze. He was looking at her with an expectant expression. "It's just that we've crossed some line. I don't know if we can go back."

"I don't want to go back," he replied, squeezing her hand. "If you only knew how many nights I've been tortured, wanting to kiss you, not daring to cross that line. What happened today . . . I'll never regret it."

She didn't know how she was supposed to react. "I don't know what we're supposed to do next."

As if sensing her unease, he let go of her hand and turned off the engine. "I think we're supposed to get out of these wet clothes," he said. "Do you want to come in? I can lend you a T-shirt."

She shook her head and turned to the door. She didn't trust herself to go inside his house, to his room. "No. I really need to get home and check on the kids. And get out of these clothes. I'm sure I look a mess."

"Olivia . . . You look beautiful."

She laughed shortly and smoothed her damp hair from her face with her palms. "I'm sure."

His smile contradicted her. "We don't need to check the nests tonight. Nothing is due to happen for a couple of days. I have an idea. Would you like to have dinner?"

Lovie looked out the window, wrestling with her answer. Was it proper for her to go out to dinner with him? Could they act as colleagues, after what happened today? Or was this a step toward a new relationship, something deeper and more personal? She looked up into his eyes and suddenly realized that she wanted to go that step farther, to know him better. And she wanted him to know her.

"Yes," she replied. "I'd like that very much."

Lovie strolled through the living room, took a sip of her wine, and listened to the sultry voice of Carole King fill the room. She hummed, going over in her mind the conversations with Russell, the sensations, the kiss. She ambled back to her room, sipping wine, feeling it flow through her veins, making her feel like she was floating. *What a week it has been.* And tonight she and Russell were going to dinner.

That's all it was, she reminded herself. She told herself it was just two friends sharing a meal, though her body believed it was so much more. Her senses were working overtime.

It was just after six, and both Palmer and Cara were spending the night at friends' houses. All afternoon she'd thought of little but tonight. She'd leisurely soaked in a perfumed tub, shaved her legs, and even painted her toenails. Now she had to choose something to wear, pulling out from her closet dress after dress. The green silk was too formal. Her favorite little black dress was too sexy. She wanted something casual, not too datelike, but pretty. She pulled out a long black-and-white paisley peasant skirt and, smiling with inspiration, went to her bureau for a white tank top festooned with delicate colored ribbons. It slid over her body like water.

She looked in the mirror and stared at her reflection. Her skin was glowing and her blue eyes appeared brighter with anticipation. She reached up her arms to plait her hair in her usual French braid, then thought again. With a faint, indulgent smile, she let her hair fall from her fingers to spread across her shoulders. Then she picked up her brush and stroked it till it gleamed like polished gold. Humming to the music, she took a small pink tea rose from the vase of flowers and slipped it behind her ear. Who says I can't be a hippie, she thought with a coquettish swish of her hips.

She spritzed lightly with Joy and put aquamarine studs in her ears. As she did so, the large diamond on her hand caught the light like a prism. It was a magnificent, classic six-prong Tiffany diamond that had belonged to Marietta Rutledge, Stratton's grandmother. She remembered the night Stratton had put the ring on her finger.

Lovie had met Stratton through a mutual friend while she was at the all-women's college and he was at the nearby all-male college. A common joke at the time was that the girls went to Converse but majored in Wofford. Stratton was a few years older, handsome with his dark looks, well connected, and considered a good catch by the women who were working hard for their Mrs. degree.

Stratton and Lovie dated for two years while her mother wrung her hands, placing his photograph in a prominent place in the house. The summer after Stratton graduated, he drove north to Aiken to have dinner with Lovie and her parents. Dee Dee's eyes had been especially bright that evening as she welcomed Stratton into their historic home on Park Avenue. Lovie was proud of the ten-bedroom home on five acres in town and knew that Stratton had taken in each attribute, the quality of the furniture, and the signatures on the paintings. For her own part, Lovie was considered a good catch as well.

That weekend she'd felt like an actress playing a role in a well-rehearsed play. Everyone knew his or her part. Her father was making an unusual effort for Stratton, walking him through the home, pointing out the personal photographs of Lovie growing up with a tenderness that bordered on nostalgic. Dee Dee had set the table with their best china and silver, insisted that Lovie get her hair done at the beauty parlor and that she buy a new dress. When Stratton led Lovie out on the veranda and pulled a small black box from the pocket of his blue blazer, she wasn't surprised. His proposal was expected. As was her answer.

That was fifteen years ago. Was she happy that night? she asked herself. She did say yes. She turned off the bathroom light and walked slowly through the hall past the black-framed photos of her family. She stopped before her wedding photograph and looked at their faces. Who were those young people? She no longer knew the naïve, smiling bride in that photograph.

Feeling the weight of memories, Lovie tugged the rose from her hair and tossed it away before closing up the house.

Her new VW sat in the driveway where the old Buick had been parked. It had all happened so fast she could hardly believe the car was really hers. Russell had driven her to the bank for a cashier's check, then they'd driven back to meet the owner in the parking lot, and the deal was done. It was the first car she'd bought entirely on her own, with her own money.

She'd decided to name her car the Gold Bug after the story by Edgar Allan Poe. The snazzy ragtop took up a fraction of the space the station wagon had. Her high heels tapped the wood steps as she hurried down to her new car. She had to fuss for a while to finally get the convertible top down, but at last she managed. She felt moist by the time she fired the engine. The darling little car started right up and made an amusing diesel-like *blump-blump* noise rather than the Buick's low growl or the purr of Stratton's Mercedes. She patted the dash with affection and pulled out of the driveway.

When she arrived at Russell's house, she hit the horn. The

nasal *beep* made her laugh. The front door opened promptly, and she smiled, knowing that he'd been waiting.

"Olivia!" he said, smiling as he stepped out. He waved and locked the door.

It was the first time Lovie had seen him wearing anything other than beach wear. Tonight he wore beige trousers and a crisp white shirt that appeared to gleam against his dark tan. Over his arm he carried a navy blazer. When he turned to face her again, his face lit up with a smile. Her heart skipped and she felt again the girlish rush she'd scolded herself not to feel and worried that all her good intentions were in jeopardy.

Russell slid into the car, tucking his long legs into the small space. He was still wearing his sandals, she noted. He turned, and she could almost feel his gaze as it lingered over her dress, her earrings, her face.

"So this is how a Turtle Lady dresses off the beach, huh? You look beautiful."

Lovie sensed a new tension in the air between them. "Why, thank you, sir. I was thinking the same about you. But I suppose our praise has to be qualified by the fact that we always see each other in sweaty, sandy clothes."

He chuckled as he buckled up. "Then let me say that you look especially cute tonight in your glittering new car."

"I do, don't I?" she replied with a tilt of her chin. "Russell, meet the Gold Bug."

Understanding dawned and he laughed with appreciation. "Olivia, that's perfect. Poe wrote 'The Gold-Bug' while he was living on Sullivan's Island, didn't he?"

Lovie nodded. "I pulled the book from my shelf last night and read the story again. I don't think I'd read it since high school. Typical Poe, creepy, dire, and pure genius. The description of the bug was perfect. Shiny gold, heavy, two black eyes, antennae." She laughed again. "That's my car."

"I thought perhaps we could head to the city?" Russell suggested. "I hardly ever get there. Someone recommended the Colony House."

Lovie paused, awash in anxiety. This was a favorite restaurant that friends of Stratton would likely be dining at. In fact, there were not many restaurants in Charleston where she wouldn't be recognized by a friend of hers or some crony of Stratton's. Like the Isle of Palms, Charleston was really one small town. Everyone knew each other and their extended family members as well. When it came to a local married woman having dinner out with a man not her husband, was any town different?

"Let's not go there," she said. "It can be so stuffy."

"Where do you recommend? Anyplace is fine, as long as it's not on the Isle of Palms. I've eaten at every restaurant here, more than once. And there are only two."

"We could go to the Lorelei. It's a quaint little place in Mount Pleasant, right on the water," she said. "Nothing fancy."

"The Lorelei it is, then. I actually prefer smaller, local restaurants. As long as the fish is fresh and the company good, I'm happy."

"You'll like this place, then. It overlooks the docks at Shem Creek where the local shrimp boats bring in their hauls. The shrimp will be so fresh you'll have to beat it before you eat it. The scenery is a bonus."

They arrived at the restaurant before seven, while the sun was just beginning to lose its hold on the day. The Lorelei was little more than a cottage on the deep-water marsh. A row of stately shrimp boats with their bright green nets up were docked along Shem Creek. On the docks, men in white boots were still stooped over their catch, shouting and cursing at the pelicans and seagulls waiting for any tidbits tossed overboard.

Lovie was keenly aware of Russell's hand politely against the small of her back as they walked into the restaurant. As the waitress led them into the formal front section of the restaurant, which had soft glowing candles and linen tablecloths, Lovie furtively scanned the tables of couples, seeking any familiar face. She was relieved when they were led to the back room, a more casual, airy space. A mural dominated the wall. It told the story of Lorelei, the great beauty who sat on a cliff overlooking the Rhine, singing and combing her long golden hair. Her beauty and her song distracted seamen, causing them to crash to their death on the rocks below.

"She looks a little like you," Russell murmured by her ear as they walked to a table by the window. She caught the faint scent of his aftershave and felt an immediate rush. She wondered how she was going to manage a whole evening with him, talking, sharing stories, feeling her body respond and not so much as touch.

Once settled at their table, they ordered beers. Outside the large window, the sun was beginning to set over a vista of shrimp boats docked along the darkening marsh.

"I've been all around the world," Russell said, looking out, "but I've never seen a sunset as beautiful as those in the Lowcountry. Everything about this place is mysterious and seductive."

"The Lowcountry gets into your blood and binds all of us who live here. Rich or poor, we all live like kings. We never stray too far or want to live anywhere else."

"It's that unique combination of nature and history," Russell said. "Richmond has that, too. Though when I'm in Charleston walking down the narrow cobblestone streets, I have to remind myself it's 1974, not 1774."

"Right out there," Lovie said, pointing to the ocean, "not too far away, is the Confederate submarine, the *Hunley*, sunk during the War Between the States. Folks are still looking for it."

"Like the *Titanic*," he said ruefully. "I doubt they'll ever find either one."

The waitress interrupted them for their order. Caught off guard, Lovie glanced at the menu and quickly decided on her favorite, grilled flounder with collards and sweet-potato fries. Russell went for the classic shrimp and grits. Then, because he'd never tasted it before, they both ordered a cup of she-crab soup.

They began talking in generalities, finding their way through the awkward beginnings of a dinner date. They steered their way through what schools they went to, jobs held, people they knew. When the dinner came at last, their beers were finished and Russell filled both their glasses with chilled white wine.

"What's it like living in Virginia?" she asked him. "You must feel the same sense of history in Virginia that we do here in Charleston. Especially with your family heritage."

He set the wine bottle on the table and traced the edge of the label with his finger. "Oh, yes," he replied without humor, "there's that. My family history is always present, like a shadow."

"Do you have any brothers or sisters?"

"I have one brother, John. He's younger and likes to joke that he's an only child. He says that because he's involved in the family banking business, lives in Richmond, and has two sons. As far as my father is concerned, my purpose for being born is to continue the family business—and the family name. I have a wonderful daughter. But he wasn't happy until I produced a son . . ." Russell's face went still as he stared at the flickering candle.

"I'm sorry."

Russell shrugged. "That's my father," he continued, his tone bitter. "It's always about competition for him. About winning. Especially for me as his elder son. Throughout my childhood he thought sports were a testing ground of my mettle. I had to try out for all the teams. For holidays he invited the cousins over for pickup games of football. I have this one cousin, Leopold." He snorted. "Leo. He's two years older than me and a real bruiser. Twice my size. He'd come after me with no holds barred. Thank God I could run fast, but when he caught me I got bloodied. Dad thought that it'd make a man of me."

Lovie listened intently, moving the flounder on her plate. "He doesn't sound so different from Stratton. Palmer is his only son but, sadly for him, he's built more like me than his father. So it's soccer and baseball and hunting. Palmer is not, shall we say, a scholar. But Stratton has a lot of expectations for him. I worry for my son and what that pressure does to him. Your mother must have worried for you."

"Mother . . ." Russell thought for a moment. "If my father wanted me to carry on the family name, my mother wanted me to maintain the family honor. The Bennett name is her life's vocation."

"What did she think of your career choice?"

Russell raised his brows as he considered the question. "As long as I went to good schools, married the right girl, and maintained an honorable career, she's content. To her mind there's a certain prestige to being an academic. My father, of course, was furious that I didn't follow in the family business or go into politics. He simply refused to accept that I found biology more interesting than banking." Russell changed his voice to a gruff imitation of his father. "There's no money in that, son." He shook his head. "Every year, usually around my birthday, I can expect him to put his arm around my shoulder, offer me a good cigar, a glass of aged scotch, and discuss man-to-man whether or not I'm done with all this foolishness and ready to begin a real career."

"A *real* career? Does he have any idea of how many articles you've written? In important journals, too."

He lifted his brow. "You know all that?"

"Of course I do. You know, I should be put out that you're surprised."

"I'm only flattered. I wish I could say the same thing about my father."

"I'd always thought you were so fortunate to have had so many choices—your wealth, family connections, intelligence, just being a male. I never considered how those same benefits could also be obstacles. Even still," she said, cutting into her fish, "forgive me if I don't cry a river. Those hurdles are small cotton compared to what a woman in the South has to contend with."

Russell looked around the room, pretending to search. "Excuse me, but is that Flo I hear?"

Lovie laughed, enjoying the break of humor. "Flo's not the only woman who feels this way, Dr. Bennett. At least as a man, you're encouraged to pursue a career. Women are encouraged to pursue a husband. A woman who wants a career is looked upon as an odd egg. Look at Flo. She loves her career and she's good at it. But she never married. Do you know what people think when they see her?"

Russell shook his head, eyes sparkling with amusement.

"They think it's either"—she raised a finger—"such a pity that a good-looking woman like her couldn't catch a husband, or"—she raised a second finger—"she's a lesbian."

Russell barked out a laugh.

"I'm serious! Any woman who wants to achieve outside the home has a lot of hurdles. Unless, of course, she wants to be a teacher, or a nurse, or a secretary. And even then, she often quits when she gets married or has children."

Russell leaned far back in his chair. "I can understand that. Women I've worked with have told me stories of the battles they've had to get their degrees and how clever they had to be to break down barriers just to get jobs in the field. For the most part, they've given up a personal life to make it happen. Call me an optimist, they tell me it's changing."

Lovie was doubtful. "We both know that change moves as slow as molasses in January here in the South."

He chuckled and lifted his hands in concession.

"It's one thing to worry about myself," Lovie continued in a more serious tone. "But I know my Cara won't want a traditional lifestyle. I fear for the challenges she'll face. And the disappointments. I'd hate to see her dreams squashed."

"Have a little faith. We put a man on the moon, after all."

"Exactly," she said wryly. "A man. The women are still firmly rooted to the earth."

"It doesn't have to be that way for her. She's young yet, like Pippi. Look at the barriers already being broken down today. The women's liberation movement is making strides. She can be whoever and whatever she wants to be."

"Is that so?" she said in a soft voice, thinking of Stratton's directive to her that she take Cara to buy dresses—and white gloves!—to learn to be a lady, to take her place in society. "Maybe in California and New York. What concerns me most are not only the external obstacles like jobs, education, salaries. I think more insidious are the internal obstacles." She paused, thinking of these obstacles she knew too well. "Things like lack of confidence, not speaking up, low self-esteem." She looked at him. "And simple validation."

Russell set his fork down and asked, "What about you? Did you ever want a career?"

"Me? No. I fell into line at an early age. The truth is, I never questioned that I'd get married and have a family. It's what I wanted. I never really expected that I'd do anything other than be a wife and mother. I'm from a traditional Southern family, and when I met a man from a background not unlike my own and from a similar family, I more or less assumed my life would continue in the same way it always had. I moved from Aiken to Charleston, but nothing was really very different. Like my mother, I'm involved in my children's schools, my church, Junior League, and fund-raising." She smiled wanly. "Not even the house I live in is all that different, with its high ceilings, plastered walls, piazzas, and garden."

Lovie sipped her wine, thinking of the photographs she'd perused on her wall earlier. She slowly lowered her glass. "Honestly, I was so young and so naïve when I got married. I could write a book about what I didn't know back then. What I do regret is not finishing college. I left after junior year to get married, so I never graduated. So, no, I never pursued a career per se. But I love to learn. I always have. And I loved sea turtles. I'd majored in biology in college, so I got a good foundation. Since then, I've pored over books and journals, just about anything I could get my hands on concerning turtles. That's how I knew about your papers. And I can quote Carr chapter and verse. I might not have a career that pays me a salary, but I do have a vocation," she said with a hint of pride in her voice.

"I've had graduate assistants who aren't as knowledgeable as you are at fieldwork. Olivia, you are an amazing woman."

She released a self-deprecating laugh. "Far from it. I'm just a Southern woman with a good mind, no fear of hard work, and a passion."

The waitress came to take away their plates. There was a moment's awkwardness as they waited. Russell poured more wine and they ordered coffee.

"What about Eleanor?" Lovie asked. "Did she graduate, have a career?"

He looked at his wineglass, swirling the wine, seemingly disinclined to discuss his wife.

"I'm sorry," Lovie said. "I don't mean to pry."

"You're not prying. Yes, she did. Like you, however, she wanted to stay home and raise the family. She's very active in her community."

"*Her* community? Not the same as yours?"

He cleared his throat. "Eleanor lives in Richmond with Pippi. I have a place in Florida near the university. Eleanor believes the schools are better, and then there's family. It just seemed easier if I fly back and forth."

The waitress brought the coffee and set down the sugar bowl and creamer.

"I didn't realize you lived in different states," Lovie said, after the waitress had left.

Russell picked up his cup of black coffee. "It's the best solution we could come up with. She wants me to leave the university and return to Richmond. Eleanor was never as content as my mother with my career choice," he said, and took a sip. Setting the cup on the saucer, he added, "She never adjusted to living on the salary of an assistant professor, and I didn't want to depend on my family. I felt as my wife, she shouldn't either." He laughed shortly. "We argued about that, too."

Lovie didn't respond.

"Eventually," Russell continued, "she began to take my father's side. Eleanor felt—still feels—that it's time for me to stop playing with turtles."

Lovie was appalled on so many levels. "Your research, teaching—Russell, that's who you are. It's your life."

Russell reached out to place his hand over hers. "I appreciate hearing that. I really do. But that life gets lonely sometimes. Work is only a part of my life."

Dusk was setting in, and as the room darkened, the candles flickered brightly. Lovie was intensely aware of their hands together on the table. Her skin was electrified where it touched his.

At the same time, she was very aware that they were in a public place and worried lest someone might see them. She couldn't allow a scandal or, at her age, to make a fool of herself. She gently let her hand slide back into her lap and saw the disappointment flash in his eyes.

He looked at his hand and tapped his fingers on the table. "In retrospect, it's too easy to blame my career or my travel entirely for the problems in my marriage. Or my son's death. I was unhappy before we lost Charley. Perhaps I never loved Eleanor the way she deserved to be loved. I didn't put her first. I take the blame for that. Now I'm quite certain that she's not in love with me. Or she could never ask me to give up what makes me feel significant as a man. Or as an individual."

They continued to talk or, rather, Russell talked and Lovie listened, about how he and his wife had become increasingly distant and separated from each other's lives, how he didn't know if the marriage could be saved. The candles flickered lower and the coffee cooled. Other diners had paid their bills and left. The room was quiet and intimate. Lovie felt he was looking to her for some response, and she struggled with her words.

"I know what it's like to have your work—your passion—go unappreciated. You can deal with strangers feeling that way, but when it's your loved ones, the hurt goes much deeper. It somehow diminishes you."

He was quiet a moment, then said, "So Stratton doesn't support your commitment to the sea turtles?"

"Hardly." She didn't dare to go on, to tell him how her husband didn't respect her work in their home, either. She dabbed her mouth with her napkin and set it on the table between them. "Goodness, it's getting late. We're closing the place."

Russell raised his hand for the check, and the waitress hurried over, eager to clock out. Lovie looked around at the few people left at the bar and realized they must've been talking for hours. As they rose, she glanced at a clock on the wall, stunned to see it was already nine thirty.

"I had no idea how late it was," she said as they left the restaurant.

"I didn't either. I was lost in the conversation," he said, gently holding her elbow. She stopped and looked at him. His face was all angles and shadows. "I really had a good time tonight."

She looked in his eyes, saw the emotion flickering like the candles, and sensed he was going to kiss her again.

"Olivia," he whispered, and reached out for her.

Lovie stepped back, flustered. "I had a lovely time," she murmured, and turned and walked away toward the car. With each step she wondered what might have happened if she'd held on to his hand and not let it go. If she'd waited one moment longer before stepping away. And how one small gesture could alter one's course for happiness.

Fifteen

The vast expanse of marsh shimmered in the flattering colors of twilight. Lovie and Russell were silent as the Gold Bug buzzed over the Ben Sawyer Bridge. Lovie relished the feel of her hair blowing freely in the convertible. The breeze was soft and salty, and the scent of the marsh permeated the air. She turned her head to glance at Russell beside her. His elbow was on the open window and the hair around his collar curled in the humidity. His profile appeared outlined in the deepening sky—strong cheekbones, a straight nose, and full lips. As if he'd sensed her looking at him, he turned and their eyes met. Her colored cheeks gave her away, and they both smiled. Eyes back on the road, Lovie was lured into a mellow mood, sated with good food and conversation.

So when she pulled in front of Primrose Cottage, she was shocked to see Flo and Miranda swing open the front door, and she felt again that chill of apprehension.

Lovie climbed from the car as the women raced down the steps to meet her halfway to the house. Russell came more slowly behind her, keeping a respectful distance.

"Where were you?" Flo cried in accusation.

Lovie's throat constricted and she paled. "I . . . I just went to dinner. At Shem Creek."

"You didn't tell anyone where you were going," Flo said, eyes blazing.

"No . . ." Lovie stammered. "What's happened? The children . . ."

Miranda stepped forward and put an arresting hand on Flo's arm. "Everything's fine, child." She looked at Flo. "Don't need to scare everyone all over again."

"Miranda," Lovie said, panic racing in her veins, "is it the children?"

"We had a little excitement earlier, that's all," Miranda said. "The children are fine."

Lovie swallowed and took a breath. "What happened?"

"Kate called us around seven looking for you," Flo said. "She was all in a panic. The girls hadn't come home for dinner. No one knew where you were, and we called just about everyone. Including him," she said, indicating Russell.

Lovie glanced over her shoulder. Russell stood quietly a few feet behind her, dressed in his blue jacket and pressed pants. Lovie realized that their clothing was evidence that their dinner was more than project business. Still, Lovie didn't appreciate the tone of accusation in Flo's voice. "What happened then?" she said curtly.

"We all went looking for them," Flo said, stating the obvious. "We were out for over an hour, and I gotta tell you, Lovie, we were scared. You know how those kids take off—the woods, boats. They could've been anywhere. Charley Baker took his boat to explore the creeks, thinking maybe they got lost in there or stuck at low tide. I was most scared that I couldn't reach *you*. It was after eight and the sun was setting . . . I was about to call the police when those two girls came walking into Kate's house."

Lovie's hand flew to her heart. "Where were they?"

Despite her anger, Flo's lips reluctantly twisted into a grin. "Those two . . . They got it into their heads to make it to the Point."

"No!" Lovie said in a burst, and then laughed shortly. "I'll tan her hide!"

"No you won't," Miranda said gently. "She's already shaken and tired. And I seem to recall a time when two other girls hiked that trip."

Lovie looked again at Russell. His face had relaxed to relief and mild amusement, and when their eyes met, their day at the Point flashed in her mind.

"How are they?" Lovie asked.

"Oh, they're fine," Miranda answered. "Under the circumstances, Kate thought it best to have Cara come home. She's in her bed now. I think she needs her mama."

Lovie nodded, feeling the need to be with Cara, too. "Thank you all so much. I had no idea you'd need to reach me."

"Course you didn't," Miranda said. "We were just flustered, is all. Emotions ran high. Isn't that right, Flo?"

Flo nodded. "Sorry I jumped on you like that. I was wound up like a clock, counting the minutes. I started worrying about you, too," she added, laughing with embarrassment.

Lovie stepped forward to hug her friend, then Miranda. "Good night. I'm going in." She turned to Russell, aware that Flo and Miranda were hawking every move, every nuance. "Oh," she said, suddenly remembering she'd driven. "You'll need a ride."

"No problem. It's not far. You stay here. You've got things to tend to. I'll walk."

Lovie smiled gratefully. "If you're sure. See you tomorrow," she said without a hint of the intimacy they'd shared earlier. "Thanks again for dinner."

Russell nodded with equal indifference. He lifted a hand in silent farewell, then turned and walked quickly away.

• • •

Lovie stepped into her quiet house, noticing that someone had turned on the lamps. She set her purse on the front table and went directly to Cara's room. She found her lying on her back in bed, idly playing with the hair of an old doll she hadn't touched in years. Cara looked up when Lovie entered the room, her dark eyes conflicted. Lovie could see she was both relieved to see her and afraid she was going to be in trouble.

Lovie stopped at the foot of the bed, soaking in the sight of her. She crossed her arms and said in mock displeasure, "So, I heard you had quite an adventure tonight."

Cara pursed her lips and ran her fingers through her doll's hair. "You heard."

"Of course I heard. You had the whole town up in arms."

"I'm sorry, Mama," she said, but didn't take her eyes from the doll. "I didn't mean to. I reckon Emmi and I just got lost." She raised her eyes, dark with worry. "It was all the roads they cut up in there. We kept following one, then the other. I couldn't figure out which way was which!"

Lovie saw the fear creep back into Cara's eyes and remembered just how young her brave little girl was. She came to sit on the side of the bed and gently brushed back the long bangs from her forehead, damp with moisture. "That had to be scary."

Cara nodded, pouting. Then she suddenly looked up, and a spark of light flashed in them. "But Mama, I made it to the Point!"

"So you made it!" Lovie exclaimed. "I thought you were lost before you got to the Point. Oh, Cara, you finally did it."

Cara's dark eyes danced with excitement as she nodded. "And Emmi did, too. It's just like I imagined it," she raced on. "We found the old tree and the cross, and then we started digging.

Mama, the metal box is in there! I couldn't believe it was really true. We opened it and you'll never guess what we found."

"The book."

"Yes!" she said with awe. "Just like you told us. And I saw your name!" she added in a rush. "And Aunt Flo's!"

A smile flittered across Lovie's face. Seeing the thrill in her daughter's eyes reminded her of that exact feeling in her own heart, so many years ago. "Did you sign it?"

"You bet," she said, wiping her nose. "And so did Emmi."

"And you buried it back in the sand?"

"Of course," Cara said, eyes wide. "I don't want the ghost of Nicodemus after me."

Lovie chuckled. That part was new, and she wondered what imaginative child came up with that clever twist. "You said you got lost. How did you find your way home?"

"The beach! I remembered you telling me that if I ever got lost, I just had to remember we lived on an island. That the beach would lead me home. And it's true! Though," she said, frowning, "it sure was a long walk."

Lovie laughed and kissed her daughter's forehead, breathing in the scent of soap. Russell's son flashed through her mind and she let her lips linger on her daughter's face, wondering how she'd ever be able to continue on if anything happened to Cara. "Yes, it is." She pulled back and looked in her daughter's eyes. "But you know what? I'm proud of you."

"You are?" Cara asked, incredulous.

"I am. You didn't panic. You thought your situation through, and in the end you figured out what to do. Grace under pressure. Not every child can do that."

"Who's Grace?"

Lovie laughed again. "Never mind, my darling girl. Just remember two lessons learned today. The first is to trust your instincts. The second is to never go off without telling some-one where you're going." A lesson I learned tonight as well, she thought.

"Yes'm," Cara replied, yawning.

She could see her daughter's anxiety ease from her face to be replaced by sleepiness. Lovie was humbled by the power a mother held over her young. "Good night, my darling," Lovie said, and reached to turn off the light.

"Don't turn it off," Cara said sleepily. "Please?"

"Of course, if you want it on."

"Mama? Can you sit with me awhile?"

Lovie's heart lurched at the request, one she hadn't heard in a long time. Cara was hell-bent on being a big girl. She didn't like kisses and hugs and bedtime rituals. Lovie had missed them desperately. She lay on the bed beside Cara and breathed deep the scent of lavender on her skin. With her free hand she stroked the damp hair on Cara's forehead and hummed a nameless tune, as she did when Cara was very young. Cara didn't chase her off or tell her to stop treating her like a baby. She reached up to hold Lovie's hand and bring it closer to her chest.

"I love you, Mama." Her voice was muffled and sleepy.

Lovie held Cara tighter. Her gangly daughter felt smaller, more fragile. Still a little girl, despite her big-girl attitude.

"I love you, too, my own sweet Caretta."

Lovie sat on the porch with her legs curled close to her chest and her arms wrapped around them. She rested her chin on her knees and looked out over the sea, listening to the sound of the surf as the comforting voice of a friend. She had always felt akin to the sea, as though she were a twin, sensitive to its moods. Tonight she could feel the turbulence of the surf inside her body.

Then she heard a new sound, the gravel crunching under

tires and an engine. She didn't move, listening closely. She heard a car door slam, then a shuffling in the sand and gravel. She counted the footsteps with her breaths. She uncoiled her legs and rose to peer over the railing. Her breath caught in her throat.

Russell stood at the bottom of the porch steps with his hands in his pants pockets and one foot on the stairs, looking up at her expectantly. "I wanted to come back, after things settled down, to see how Cara was. I thought it was better I left when I did, under the circumstances. But I was worried. Are *you* okay?"

Lovie felt her heart expand. "I'm glad you came. I was thinking about you, too."

He began walking up the stairs toward her.

"Wait," she said abruptly, and hurried to the stairs. She looked over at Flo's house to see lights still on. "I don't want to wake anyone. Let's take a walk. Wait here a minute. I'll get my sandals."

She was still in her long skirt and he was still in his dinner clothes. She ran to her bedroom and grabbed a shawl from her closet, then to the screened porch and stepped into her sandals. Her heart was beating as fast as a small bird making good its escape. She was careful not to let the doors slam as she hurried across the porch and down the stairs to where Russell was waiting. He smiled again at seeing her and held out his hand.

They spoke little as they walked in single file along the narrow path, Lovie in the lead. She knew where she would take him. Step after step in the cool sand, she followed the call of the surf, past rolling sand dunes to where the path opened up to the beach. As always, she felt the rush of air. It slid over her body like silk.

"Come this way," she said when he came up behind her. "I want to take you to my favorite dune." She led him several feet along the dunes to its highest point, where the sand flattened to form a kind of perch. The beach was deserted, save for the ubiquitous peeps still skittering along the shore at this late hour. Russell came to stand at her side. She glanced at him and saw that he was looking out at the sea. She wondered where such a vista took a man like him who had seen many oceans.

"This is my dune," she told him, feeling possessive. "Ever since I was little, it's where I come to think or to just stare out at my old friend. We've had many conversations, the sea and I. And over there." She pointed behind them to the small plateau nestled behind the dune. It was a circular haven, surrounded by tall sea oats. "I used to pretend that was my castle. I've often slept there, under the stars."

"So this is another of your secret spots?" he asked her.

She laughed lightly. "Yes. Everyone who grew up on the island has their share of secret spots. But I only share this one with special friends," she said, gently teasing him.

"I'm glad you consider me your friend," he told her, and he sounded sincere.

So much more than a friend, she thought, looking up at a sky that was alive with brilliant stars sparkling. She felt their shimmering light reflected inside her. "When I was little, there were so few houses here," she said. "I rarely saw lights shining at night by Breach Inlet, except for the Prescott house, of course. The nights are always so black out here and the stars shine so bright."

"I love that about the islands," he agreed. "The more remote, the more visible the stars."

"Let's sit," she said, and spread out her shawl. Lovie sat on the dune and felt him beside her, his shoulder against hers, his legs next to hers. He was so near she sensed every breath he took and tried to match hers to his. The ocean stretched its watery fingers higher up the shore, toward her.

"How is Cara?" he asked.

"Oh, she's fine. She had a few lessons on growing up tonight, but I'm proud of her." She turned and said with a secretive smile, "You'll never guess where she went."

"The Point."

"You guessed," she said with a chuckle.

"It wasn't hard. Not with her. So she joined the ranks with her mother, uncle, and brother and signed the book?"

Lovie nodded. "It's official." She patted his arm. "And you, too. You signed the book."

"Yep," he said proudly. "A high point in my career."

They sat looking out at the sea, lost in their own thoughts. After a while, Russell said, "Lovie, earlier this evening . . . I didn't like the way our evening ended. It all felt so rushed. Flo was making accusations and I could feel my temper rise. I didn't think putting in my two cents at that moment would help, so I left feeling like some teenager who brought his date home late."

"Flo . . . She wasn't so bad."

"Are we talking about the same woman?" he said teasingly.

"She means well. She's my best friend, and she loves my kids like they're her own. She was just wound up pretty tight when Cara was lost and she couldn't reach me. When she saw me come home with you, well, she jumped to conclusions."

Russell leaned closer to her. "What conclusions were those?"

Lovie smelled again the lingering aftershave and closed her eyes against the onslaught of sensations, squeezing the sand in her fingers. "Well . . . that you and I . . . are a couple," she ventured.

"Ah," he said, letting his fingers brush lightly against hers. He leaned closer so that his breath stirred the air against the tender follicles of her ear. "And that would be a terrible thing?"

She closed her eyes and her heart beat faster. Yes, she wanted to say. It would. I know what that implies—intimacy. An affair. That was unthinkable. Nothing she'd ever contemplated, at least not seriously. All her life she'd been careful to construct boundaries that she never crossed, never even approached.

Until now. She couldn't deny her feelings for Russell Bennett. She hadn't felt such desire, had not trembled like this, for any man before. And she read that desire in his eyes as well. But to cross that line—to make love—there was no going back from that. She'd made love to only one man in her life, and that was her husband. She was not as experienced as Flo in these matters, or as cavalier. Making love was, to her, the ultimate act of intimacy. It wasn't merely sex, but a giving of herself—heart, body, mind, and soul. Her body knew what it wanted—him! But her mind warred against it. All she was and ever had been, all she thought was right, told her to run away. Yet all she was at this moment, the woman who was alive and breathing now, cried for the feel of his lips on hers once again.

Lovie felt her breath quicken and looked with despair out to the sea, for a clue, some answer. But tonight the ocean merely breathed in and out, brooding, as though it, too, were watching, waiting.

"Olivia?"

Reluctantly, she turned to face him again, drawn to the light in his eyes like any other moth to a flame driven by instinct. She recognized the same soul-stirring sensation she'd felt the first moment she'd looked into his eyes, and the unfathomable certainty that she was bound to him in a way she'd never been connected to any other man, not even her husband.

He read her answer in her eyes and moved slowly toward her, letting his lips, his cheek, gently skim hers, inhaling her scent. Lovie felt each cell in her body respond to his slightest touch, sending her blood racing. When at last his lips found hers, he took his time, tentatively tasting her reaction. Lovie lifted her hand and let her trembling fingers trace his jawline and the stubble grazing her tender fingertips, then curl around his ears to the soft hairs behind them. Then she let them slide behind his neck, holding him there, drawing him closer.

Their kiss surged and deepened, and she felt the pressure of his body against hers, holding her tighter. Pushing her slowly back against the cool sand, their weight crushed the small primroses beneath them. She closed her eyes as his full weight stretched out over her. They fit together perfectly, and as they clung together her woman's body felt that at last it had found the man's bones from which she'd been created, and she was overcome with desire to become one flesh.

She opened her eyes then and, trembling, she slowly pulled her head back. For a moment, their breathing shared a small space. He raised himself slightly above her as he looked into her eyes, questioning. Lovie moved to rise, and immediately he shifted his weight, allowing her room. She climbed to her feet and he rose beside her, looking unwaveringly at her for her signal. Lovie reached down for her shawl with one hand and for his hand with the other. Turning her back to the ocean, she gently tugged Russell to follow her down to the small plateau in the dunes, to her secret spot where they could lie surrounded by tall sea oats, lost in the moon shadows, muffled by the pulsing beat of the sea.

Sixteen

~

Russell had been gone for three days at the University of Florida. He'd called Lovie the night before to tell her that he hoped to be back on the Isle of Palms sometime today and, if he was, he would meet her at their dune.

Their dune . . . Just the sound of that one personal pronoun had the power to curl her toes. One small word that said so much.

Lovie felt she'd been living in a dreamworld the past week. They'd met several times at the dune late at night, after they'd made their rounds on the beach checking for nests. As they walked, they talked about everything and nothing, the past and the present; they had no secrets between them. The only subject they did not broach was the future. It was as though they had an unspoken pact not to mention what would happen at the month's end. Lovie knew that there could be no future for them. That this one summer was all she had, and it had to be enough to last a lifetime.

"What's got you so quiet this morning?" Flo asked her.

They were walking the beach at 28th, checking a report on dozens of tiny turtle tracks coming from a nest. The island turtle nests were hatching frequently this late in the season, and

Lovie was getting fewer reports of large female turtle tracks and more reports of tiny tracks—*tracklings*, Flo called the adorable, miniature turtle tracks left by the three-inch hatchlings as they emerged from the nest. As long as they headed to the sea, Lovie considered the emergence a success.

"Just thinking," Lovie replied, swinging the red bucket at her side. It clanged noisily.

"Let me guess. About a certain biologist who's been MIA the past few days?"

Lovie's lips twisted in mirth. "Maybe."

"Oh, get real, Lovie. I don't know whether you're just blind to your own feelings, or you're blind to his. Or if you're deliberately fooling yourself. But it's written all over both of your faces."

"What's written?" she asked with a sinking feeling.

"You're infatuated with him. In lust with him. God forbid, in love with him. You're in one of those things with him!"

"Don't say that."

"Why not?" Flo asked, more gently now. "If it's the truth."

"People will gossip, that's why not. So, no, I'm not in love with him, okay?"

"You've always been a terrible liar," Flo said.

Lovie stopped and her shoulders drooped.

"So which is it?" Flo asked, rounding to face her. "Are you in lust or what?"

Lovie sighed and said with difficulty, "I think I'm falling in love with him."

Flo exhaled loudly. "Wow."

Lovie looked away. "Yeah. Wow." They began walking again, ignoring the few early beachcombers—mothers with kids in tow carrying shovels and buckets, and the ubiquitous joggers—the smattering of surfers out in the ocean waiting for a wave, the black Lab and the mutt sniffing and barking at the remnants of a horseshoe crab by the shoreline.

"It snuck up on me," Lovie told Flo, feeling relieved to talk to someone about her feelings at last. "I didn't wake up one day and think, *I'm in love with him*. Just the opposite. I fought it. At first I thought I was just attracted to him."

Flo snorted. "Who isn't? He's insanely good-looking."

"It would've been easier if it was just his looks," Lovie said. "But from the very first time I met him, when Russell turned his head and his eyes met mine for the first time, I felt my stomach drop. Not with joy, but with such dread. My first thought was, *Oh no. Please God, not now.*"

"Really?"

"It was such a strong feeling, and I fought it. Really, I did. I told myself that I was being ridiculous, a schoolgirl." She looked over to see her friend's darkly tanned face looking straight ahead, listening carefully. "I may be married, but I'm not immune to good-looking men."

"I didn't say you were." They walked a few more steps. "Okay, so you're not in love. You're in lust."

Lovie shook her head, rejecting that argument. "I wish. That I could deal with." She wondered if she'd be able to explain to Flo the evolution of her feelings for Russell. "From the first, it was immediately obvious that we shared interests. We were passionate about the sea turtles, the research, and the project. From the first, he treated me as an equal—it was *our* project.

"Even then I told myself I was attracted to his intelligence, his experience, and all that he could teach me. That what I felt for him was nothing more or less than a student's crush on her teacher. I could deal with that. But over the months, as we've spent more and more time together, my feelings—and his— matured into something much deeper. We were in contact with each other all the time. Mornings, evenings on the beach, and if we weren't together we called each other on the phone.

Whenever we had an idea." She shrugged and looked off, her thought trailing. "Whenever."

Flo studied her face. "Have you slept with him?"

"What? No!" Lovie replied as a knee-jerk response. She took a few steps, then glanced up. "You think I shouldn't?"

"I'm the last person to tell you that." Flo shook her head in frustration. "If you were single, I'd be the happiest woman in the world for you. I truly would. But you're not. You're married. It complicates things."

"I know."

"Sugar, I just want you to be happy. You deserve it. You deserve a real love, one that's reciprocated, that makes your toes tingle. We both know you're not getting that from your husband. I have this theory."

"I can't wait to hear that," Lovie said with sarcasm.

Flo put out her hand. "Wait, wait. Just listen. I have this theory that women try to block out their unhappiness with work. Take yourself, for an example. You keep yourself busy from the moment you wake up till you collapse at night. You give to the turtles, to the children, to your marriage, to your church, to the schools, the list goes on. All to keep busy, because something fundamental inside of you remains unfulfilled. Unfortunately, that is a bottomless hole that can't be filled. Girl, you've been giving to everyone but yourself for so long now, when the prospect comes up, you feel guilty."

"I don't know what you're talking about," Lovie said, and took a step.

Flo reached out to grab her arm and stop her. "Lovie, open your eyes and see what's going on in the world. You're not trapped. Women like Gloria Steinem and Bella Abzug and the National Organization for Women—they're fighting for our rights. Burning their bras as a statement of being unshackled.

I even saw one woman give the finger to a newsman on national television!"

"And that's supposed to impress me? Well let me tell you, Florence Prescott. They're not burning bras here in Charleston," Lovie replied angrily. "Everyone I know is shocked at the public displays we're seeing on television. Those Yankee women—they're certainly not Southern *ladies*—just want to be poor imitations of men."

Flo's mouth dropped open. "Listen to yourself! You sound like Stratton."

Lovie paled and tightened her lips. "I do *not*." She started walking toward the nest, feeling the heat of the accusation scorch the back of her neck.

"Look, I didn't mean that," Flo said, catching up with her.

"Yes you did. And you were right. I'm sorry. I didn't mean it."

"All I'm trying to say is that I want you to be happy. I've been watching you all summer, and there's something simmering between you and Dr. Russell Bennett, no matter how much you tell me—and yourself—that it isn't. Lovie, I'm your best friend. I'm on your side. If what you say is true, and this guy is your soul mate—then go for it."

"Are you telling me to have an affair?" she asked, stunned.

Flo shrugged. "It wouldn't be the end of the world."

Lovie stared at her with eyes wide, feeling like a fish on a hook.

Flo looked back at her and narrowed her eyes. "Lovie . . ."

From overhead, Lovie heard the distinct sound of a small plane's engine. Her attention immediately shifted and her gaze darted to the sky. "Listen!"

She stood rigid, eyes on the sky. A moment later she saw the plane, flying low, approaching from the north. "It's Russell!" she cried out, and her heart rate doubled. She dropped the bucket and ran closer to the shoreline, waving her arms wildly in an arc over her head. "Russell!" she shouted.

The Cessna flew low over the beach, and she spotted the dashing red-and-blue stripe. When it neared, the plane tipped its wing and flew on.

Lovie let her arms drop to her sides and stood watching, her heart beating wildly, until the sound of the engine faded and the small speck in the sky disappeared down the coast.

Flo walked up to join her at the shoreline. "He's back."

"Yes," Lovie said, slightly breathless from the excitement. She turned her head to see Flo frowning and her blazing blue eyes studying hers from under the brim of her pink cap.

"You *did* sleep with him," Flo said.

Lovie swallowed uncomfortably and nodded once.

"And you didn't tell me?"

Lovie put her hands to her face. "Oh, Flo, I couldn't tell you. I couldn't tell anyone."

"But I'm not anyone," Flo replied gently. "I'm me. Flo. You tell me everything."

Lovie dropped her hands and looked into the trusting eyes of her friend. "I wanted to but I knew we'd start talking, and honestly, I don't know what to say. I'm happy, I'm confused, I'm feeling guilty."

"You're a mess."

"No, that's the point. I'm not. I'm deliriously happy."

Flo chuckled, her eyes warming. "Good. I'm really glad, Lovie. You deserve some happiness."

"But this way? Flo, I'm having . . ."—she swallowed again, having difficulty even saying the word—"an affair." Hearing the word aloud suddenly booted her from her dreamlike trance into the chill of reality.

"Shit," Flo said. "Gotta tell you. I never thought I'd hear those words coming from your mouth."

Lovie nodded. "I know. Do you think I'm a terrible person?"

"No, of course not. I just don't want to see you get hurt."

"I'm more worried about hurting others. Stratton, the children—"

"Stratton's an ass," Flo interrupted. "Do you think he's losing sleep that he's hurting three people I happen to love? I'm not worried about *him*."

"But you *are* worried about the children."

Flo sighed and nodded. "And you. You're vulnerable. And you hold yourself to a pretty high standard. You always have. It's one of the things I most admire about you."

Lovie laughed forlornly. "Oh, Flo, please don't put me on that pedestal. It's awfully lonely up there." In the distance she saw the small flag marking the nest. "I know I took the vows—to love, honor, and obey. I got the honor and obey parts. What happened to love? I was promised love, too."

"Oddly enough, I think Stratton loves you . . . in his own self-centered, controlling way."

"Are you defending him? You don't even like him."

"No, I don't. And I'm not defending him. His kind of love is self-serving. He's not a good husband and he's a rotten father. He's gone all the time, and when he's home, he drinks like a fish. But you married the insufferable boor."

"So you're saying I'm trapped."

"I'm not saying that, either," Flo said, stopping. Her voice rose in frustration. "That's what I was trying to say earlier." She leaned close and kissed Lovie's forehead, then drew back and pointed her finger in Lovie's face. "I'm saying get a goddamned divorce!"

That night on the beach, the sky was filled with gloomy purples, pale pinks, and insipid blues. Lovie felt the moody colors seep into her spirit and the weight of the humidity settle on her. The sea was gray and roiled in agitation of the impending storm. On such a night the beach was deserted, save for the ubiquitous peeps still skittering along the shore at this late hour. She spread out the old red-and-black checked blanket on the dune and sat waiting, staring out at the dark sea as the last remnants of the twilight dissipated.

Lord help me, she thought as she looked out over the ocean. She longed for Russell to be here. It was like a sickness she couldn't shake. Especially when she sat here alone on this dune— *their* dune—where they'd secretly met for several nights.

As though he'd heard her silent plea, she spotted his tall, lanky figure walking onto the beach from the access path. Her breath hitched and she turned on her red flashlight and waved it in front of her, signaling her location. She saw him wave in an arc over his head and continue toward her. She climbed to her feet, smiling.

"Olivia!" Russell called, approaching. He wrapped his arms around her and hugged her tight against his chest. "I missed you," he said against her ear. Then, pulling back, he held her head in his hands and seemed to memorize her face. "I couldn't wait to get back."

"I've missed you, too. I saw your plane this morning!"

He chuckled. "I almost parachuted, I was so happy to see you." He glanced at the sky. "Glad I made it in early. Wouldn't want to get caught in that sky."

"Did it go well in Florida?"

"Well enough. There's never enough time. I'm going to have to go back again next week."

"Again? You have so little time left here."

He slipped his arms around her shoulders. "How are you? The kids are well?"

"Everyone's fine. The project has been busy. Thank God for Flo. She and Bing make a good team. He's a nice fellow, by the way. No matter how tired he gets, he's always cheerful. And he has a wonderful way with children at the inventories. They love him." She chuckled. "I think Flo does, too."

Russell didn't comment.

Lovie looked over at his face. "Does their relationship bother you now that we've begun . . ." She hesitated, not knowing what to call what they shared. Affair? Relationship?

"Even if it did, I can't say anything about it now, can I?"

Lovie frowned, not liking his frustrated tone. She stepped out from his arms and felt the space between them.

"My concern was always for Flo after the project was over and Bing left," he said.

"And now we're in the same situation," she finished for him.

"Yes, only ours is much more complicated."

"Yes," she agreed.

She heard him exhale and she sat. When he moved to join her, she scooted a few inches, giving him room on the blanket. As he stretched his long legs, she was acutely aware of his every movement, the inches that lay between them, and the heat from his body. He rolled up the sleeves of his shirt, then stretched out his arms, leaning back. Lovie stole a glance to see his tanned face staring out at the sea. He'd told her once that he felt more at home by the sea than anywhere else on the earth. How our DNA harkened back to those ancient times when we were all fish, before we had the audacity to crawl on land.

They began talking about what had happened in the project while he was away, what nests were imminent. He told her what he was designing for his curriculum at the university. Clouds were moving in from the north, their wispy forerunners blanketing the few stars before moving on again. The air was cooling in gusts from the sea.

"The tide will be high around ten thirty," he said. "If the clouds stay back, the moon should be high by then, too. It'd be a good time for the turtles to come out. They'll have an easy time of it. But tonight the clouds will cover the moon and stars. It'll be dark."

"Does the full moon trigger the turtles to come out?" she asked.

He shook his head. "No. That's an old wives' tale. The female adults come ashore when they need to nest, whether the moon is full or it's pitch-black. Same for the hatchlings. They come out when the sand is cool no matter how bright the sky or where the tide is. No matter what the dangers. It'd be nice if it all worked out that way. In nature, things don't always happen at opportune moments in time." He sighed heavily and looked out again at the sea. "Sometimes, timing gets all screwed up."

Suddenly the darkness over the ocean was rent by quick bursts of light, one after another. The split-second flickering revealed an enormous armada of black clouds.

"Heat lightning," Lovie exclaimed, looking out over the sea.

"Look at those clouds," he said. "That's a big storm far out there somewhere."

Lovie looked at the wall of deep blackness over the ocean, so much darker than the night sky overhead. "It's moving this way."

"Possibly," he replied as another flash lit up the sky over the ocean. "The light could be from an intense thunderstorm some hundred miles away. That's what's so deceiving about heat lightning. You don't hear the warning of thunder. Suddenly, there is the flash of light, and it's startling. On a humid night like tonight, the light can be reflected off a layer of haze."

As he spoke, several more flashes illuminated the sky, bursts that disappeared as fast as they came.

"It's so eerie," she said in a soft voice.

"What is?"

"How the clouds are all a façade. Looking out over the ocean, everything appears so quiet. The dark is broken by only a few faint stars. Then suddenly, out of nowhere, the sky explodes, and for this brief moment—a fraction of that—you see that behind that dark curtain there are these seething, tumultuous storm clouds. It's like nature is a grand magician. The truth is hidden behind the veil."

She turned to face him. Only the outline of his features was visible. "Russell, isn't that what we're doing? I'm afraid of the façade we're creating. We meet under the pretense of checking the turtle nests."

"But we *are* checking the nests. Anything else we do is no one's business but our own." He paused. "Olivia, do you have regrets? Do you want to stop meeting?"

Her lips felt dry and her heart beat faster. She knew she should say yes, that they should stop. But she couldn't. When he looked at her, like he did now, she never wanted this to end.

"No."

It was little more than a whisper, but she might have shouted it. He moved his hand over hers, warm where hers was cold. They looked into each other's eyes, and it felt to her as though the oncoming storm was upon them. Flickers of heat raced through her blood from the touch of his hand, warming her, melting her bones. Around them, the sea oats rustled, their seedpods clicking like castanets, adding to her pensiveness. She leaned toward him, involuntarily or deliberately she didn't know, or even care. The wind grew still, as though holding its breath.

Their lips met, and it was heat lightning. In that electric instant, she saw everything clearly. She loved him. This felt right. True. As his arms tightened around her, she could feel his heart beat like thunder. She wrapped her arms around his neck and held him close as their breaths, tongues mingled. He buried his hands in her hair and his kiss deepened. When at last he tore his mouth from hers, he kissed her cheeks, her eyes, and with her head held in his trembling hands, he stopped and looked into her eyes.

"Olivia, I . . ."

"I . . ." she said concurrently, then stopped, alert. "Yes?"

"I love you."

She stared back into his eyes, hearing his confession, recognizing the dangers of this admission. Her body sank into his arms with surrender. "And I love you."

When he brought his mouth back to hers, her lips were wide in a grin. She was smiling, laughing, overcome with joy.

She pulled back and in his eyes she saw the truth of his feelings, and they mirrored her own. They both also recognized what dangers their love presented. As happy as she was, she had never been more afraid. The time of dreaming was over. Their love was a sin against their vows. She was willingly following Eve out of the Garden. And yet, she thought, holding him tight to her breast, *Oh, happy Fall.*

She reached up and loosened the constraints of her hair, then lay back on the wool blanket, letting her long hair spill around her. She met his gaze and called his name, "Russell," opening her arms in welcome.

Lovie lay with her head against Russell's chest as he played with her hair.

"I never want to leave our cocoon," she said, snuggling closer.

"My darling, we'll have to, unless you want to get drenched. That storm is moving in."

"I don't care. Let it blow. I'm not moving."

She heard his chuckle rumble in his chest. "Then I guess we'll stay and brave the storm together."

The double entendre felt ominous. She didn't intend to get serious so quickly. She wanted to treasure these few stolen moments, but reality already brought a chill with the oncoming storm.

"Russell, we do have to talk sometime. About what will happen when you leave? And us going back to our other lives."

His finger twirled a lock of her hair and held it still a moment. "I know." His voice sounded so distant. "I've been thinking of little else."

So that's what was troubling him, she thought. "Whatever happens, I want you to know that because of you, I'll never be the same person. Your love changed me. It's like we're two parts of one being." She pressed her face into his chest.

He released her hair and brought his arm up to his forehead, covering his eyes.

Lovie rose up on her elbows to look down at his face. "Russell, are *you* sorry we got involved? Tell me honestly. Do you regret it?"

He moved his arm and his eyes flashed with incredulousness. "What? No. No! Never. I meant what I said to you. I love you. I think I knew that I loved you the first moment I saw you, standing in the Exchange Club with your hair neatly braided, holding on to your folder like a prim teacher."

"Did you?" She relaxed, smiling shyly. "I thought it was only me."

His smile vanquished her fears, and she lay back down and put her head upon his shoulder. She played with the button on his shirt. "Sometimes, I wish," she began in a softer tone, "that we didn't fall in love. That we'd remained just colleagues."

His sigh rumbled in his chest. "Because we're married."

"Yes. What we're doing is wrong."

He didn't respond.

"Then why doesn't it feel wrong?" she cried. "How can loving you be wrong?"

He held her tighter. "Because we belong together. Neither of us asked for this; it just happened. I wrestled with this for many nights, determined not to show you how I felt. Yet here we are. And in my heart, I think I knew this was going to happen. I don't know that I could have stopped it. There's always been a certain inevitability about it."

"It has to be true. At the beginning I swore to myself that I was not in love with you. But I knew in my heart that wasn't true. From the moment I met you, it was like I'd known you all my life. I honestly think we were destined to be together. I even wondered if my passion for turtles was only God's design to bring us together. But Russell, if that's true, then *where were you?* I've been here all my life. Waiting for you. Why didn't you come to me before?"

"It's that timing thing again. I've been in all the wrong places." He paused. "Then again, I've spent my whole life searching for something. I've traveled the world." He lowered his chin to kiss the top of her head. "I know now I was searching for you."

She sighed and clutched his shirt. "Russell, *I* have no regrets. But where do we go from here? I can't go back to my old life."

"Olivia . . ."

He let the sentence drop, but he sounded so sad, even defeated. She felt the fear spring to life again.

He raised himself up on one elbow and looked at her. "Would you consider divorce?"

Lovie closed her eyes, remembering her conversation with Flo, and it felt like she was falling. She'd been wrestling with the question all day. Her mind swirled and her chest physically hurt, making it hard to breathe. This was the reality she didn't want to face. But it was always there, always lurking under the surface.

She thought of his wife, the woman he had described at dinner. Eleanor had a full life as Mrs. Bennett in their lavish home in Virginia. She no doubt competently entertained their friends, cared for their daughter, volunteered on countless committees.

She had all the prestige, the financial and social security that the name of Bennett afforded her. Even if they were not in love, there was that bond.

Lovie knew this situation and this connection all too well. What she was no longer sure of was whether the prestige of family and the bonds of a cordial marriage were enough to sustain her.

Divorce. Just thinking about the possibility made her stomach clench and her heart race. Her body rejected it; she actually wanted to throw up. A divorce was unthinkable for a woman in her family, in her circles. The scandal would be all-consuming.

Yet she knew that at a fundamental level she was not happy. Being with Russell, day after day, had showed her how unhappy she really was.

"I don't know," she murmured.

The wind gusted, spraying sand into her eyes, causing them to tear. She swiped at them, only making it worse. She choked back a cry.

Russell grabbed hold of her hands to still them. "I understand."

"Would you?" she asked him.

"Yes."

"Oh, Russell," she cried, feeling the burden of his reply, and buried her face against him.

"This is hard for both of us," he said. "I realize that. I just needed you to know how I felt. Olivia, I don't want to see you hurt."

"Or give me hope."

Russell squeezed her hands. "We always have hope."

She lifted her arm to wipe her eyes with her sleeve.

"Olivia, I will do whatever you decide."

"I don't know what to do! I've never been in this situation

before. I feel caught between the tides. I only know that I love you. There it is. I'm deeply, irrevocably, hopelessly in love with you."

He gathered her back in his arms while she rested her head against his shoulder. Another gust of cold wind blew in from the ocean.

"This should be a happy moment," she said, choking back a sob.

"Let's not decide tonight. Are you willing to take it day by day? To trust our instincts?"

"We have so little time."

"We have enough," he said against her head. "We'll know what to do when the time comes."

Would they? Lovie wondered.

"It's getting chilly," Russell said, rising. "We should leave or we'll get caught in this storm."

They gathered their things, and as they followed the narrow beam of his flashlight down the dune, she slanted her light to the small nest flag whipping in the wind. She blinked, disbelievingly, to see a small turtle scrambling resolutely toward the ocean.

"Russell!" she exclaimed, pointing by their feet. "Stop walking! It's a turtle!"

"Wha . . ."

They both stopped moving and scanned the sand with light. "There's only one," she said.

His red light illuminated the nest area, revealing a small crater where the concave dip had been. Several black flippers and tiny sandy turtle heads were wriggling their way to the surface.

"It's hatching!" Lovie cried out. She'd seen this many times before, but each time was like the first. She knelt beside him by the nest just as the sand heaved as though being pushed from a force below. On the second heave, the sand erupted and out bubbled hatchlings, scrambling over each other, tipping over and righting again, countless dark-shelled turtles determinedly seeking freedom.

Russell leaned over to kiss her softly, then helped her to her feet. "Talk about good timing. We got here at just the right moment. I think this is a good omen for us, don't you?"

She smiled, only slightly encouraged.

"Mind your step," he told her as they separated and went to opposite sides of the turtles as the group fanned out across the beach.

In the blue-black night, it was almost impossible to see the hatchlings as they raced down the slope. The bursts of lightning momentarily lit up the dark ocean, guiding the hatchlings to the sea.

Lovie stood on the beach and watched as one by one the hatchlings reached the threshold of the ocean and instinctively began to swim, disappearing into the black water. She wondered what it would be like to leave the warmth and security of the nest, to race doggedly across the unknown beach, to bravely dive beneath the surface and enter an entirely new world.

She saw Russell standing ankle-deep in the ocean. He raised his arm, beckoning her closer. As she drew near him, she felt the seductive warmth of the water swirl at her ankles and, reaching out, she took hold of his hand.

Out in the distance, the storm was building.

Seventeen

⚋

The dog days of summer were upon them. Sirius, the Dog Star, dominated the sky and was blamed for the seemingly endless spell of hot and humid days. Mosquitoes bit hard and flies died on windowsills. Panting dogs sprawled under porches. People poured onto the island, crowding the beaches. Tanned bodies lay on colorful towels like the brown dogs that in ancient days were sacrificed to appease Sirius.

Everyone was feeling the heat, complaining about how it was making them indolent, lazy, shade-seeking zombies. Heat lightning continued to illuminate the night skies while tempers flashed below. Flo teased Lovie that the heat could make a sinner out of a saint. Palmer whined that the ocean water was like a bathtub and the sun was too hot to surf. Miranda worried about hurricanes. Cara and Emmi moved with the sun from shade to shade to sip sweet tea and read. Lovie thought Sirius was the brightest, most beautiful star in the night sky. She loved it because when the sun set and darkness cloaked the earth, the Dog Star faithfully guided her to the dunes and Russell.

By mid-August, the mother turtles had swum off and the volunteers' work was done. All that remained of the season were the unhatched nests that would continue through October. But Dr. Bennett's Sea Turtle Project was effectively completed. All he had to do was write up the report and submit it to the development company. They'd agreed early on that Russell wouldn't be a frequent presence in the Rutledge house, but as it was the last week of August, Lovie had invited Russell for dinner so that they could go over the records for a final time. It would be a kind of farewell dinner. She'd invited Flo and Miranda, as well.

As she set the table with the Meissen china that she knew Russell liked, Lovie thought how hard it was to accept that this magical summer was over. And that the project was ending. Where did the time go? she wondered. It had flown by. She would give anything to stay in the beach house until the turtle season was truly complete with all the hatchlings off swimming in the Gulf Stream. Then she could sign off on the project, satisfied that the season was over, rather than leave before all the nests were hatched. She would give anything if that would allow her three more weeks with Russell.

She would give anything but her children's welfare, she amended. School began after Labor Day, calling them home to Charleston. Palmer was going back to Porter-Gaud School. Cara was enrolled in Ashley Hall. She had school supplies to buy, car pools to organize, and a million other details that circled around the school year. And Russell had to return to Florida after Labor Day as well to begin his classes at the university.

Lovie had no choice but to close up the beach house this week.

She felt tears prick at her eyes but sniffed and shook them away. There was no time for tears. She was resolved. Her intention was to keep so busy that she wouldn't slip into the vortex of grief over the end of their affair. Besides, she didn't want the children to wonder why she was so sad. They were morose enough just knowing they had to leave the beach. Palmer especially, she thought. He'd been positively sullen the last few days. He stayed in his room doing heaven only knew what and wouldn't so much as speak to her.

Tonight she'd planned an elaborate meal, sort of a farewell dinner with her children's favorite foods. She went to the butcher and purchased a fabulously lean leg of lamb. She slivered it with garlic and fetched fresh rosemary from Miranda's garden. It was in the oven now, sizzling and sending its mouthwatering aroma throughout the house. She made a Greek salad with tomatoes, cucumbers, and red onions from the farmers' market, snipped some oregano and mint, thank you again, Miranda, and dressed it with vinegar and oil. For dessert she had cold custard and berries from Johns Island. She was placing white cotton napkins beside the white china when Palmer emerged from his bedroom.

"Well, hello!" she called out. "The prodigal son has returned!"

He stood in the hall in wrinkled jeans and a T-shirt. His eyes were bloodshot, and if she didn't know better, she'd think he'd been drinking.

"Honey, are you feeling all right?"

Palmer ignored her question and let his gaze cross the room. "Why so fancy tonight?"

"We're having a guest for dinner."

"Who?"

"Dr. Bennett. I've invited him to—"

"I don't want him here!" he shouted.

Lovie froze, the napkin dangling from her hand. "Palmer . . ."

"I said he can't come here. Not in our house."

Lovie felt the blood drain from her face as she confronted Palmer's fury. It was so unlike him to shout at her. A horrid, blood-chilling suspicion crept in her mind, but she shook it off as paranoia.

The shouting brought Cara from her room. She hung back, leaning against the doorframe, her dark eyes watching.

"First of all, young man," Lovie said sharply, "don't you dare talk to your mother like that. Not ever, hear?" She was relieved to see that he appeared moderately contrite. "Second, Dr. Bennett is my colleague and I've invited him to dinner this one time before we leave. It's the decent thing to do."

Palmer snorted at that. "Does Daddy know?"

Alarms were going off in Lovie's mind, but she maintained her composure. "Of course your daddy doesn't know. He's in Europe."

"When's he coming home?"

"I don't know exactly."

"Uh-huh."

"What's that supposed to mean?"

"Just that Daddy's been gone for six weeks and you don't even know when he's coming home. Do you even care?"

Lovie reached out to place her hand on the table to steady herself.

"Palmer, honey," she said, gentling her voice, "of course I care. Your daddy was scheduled to come home this Friday night. But he wired to say he missed his flight and he was trying to get another. He didn't know when he'd be back. That's why *I* don't know when he'll be home. But it will be soon."

Palmer didn't respond. He stared at his feet, frowning.

"I've made your favorite dinner. Roast lamb. And custard."

"I'm not eating here. I'm going to Dick's."

"You most certainly are not. I've set a place for you at the table."

Palmer's mouth worked, but rather than speak he rammed his hands into his pockets and mulishly headed for the front door.

"Palmer Middleton Rutledge, you stop right where you are."

He stopped at the door but did not look back.

"I don't know what's going on in your head, but . . ."

Palmer spun on his heel. He still did not look at her, but he ground out, "I'm going to Dick's." Then he turned and went out the door.

Lovie ran after him, calling out as he ran down the porch stairs. "You come back here right now or your father will hear about this!"

Palmer turned and shouted back, "Oh, yeah? Good!"

Lovie's last view was the sight of her son's bright blond hair as he ran into the darkness.

The house went still. She could hear her heart beating in her chest, or it might have been the mantel clock ticking away the seconds as she stood staring into the night, wildly wondering what darkness in Palmer's mind had precipitated his outburst.

"Mama?"

Lovie spun around, surprised to find Cara at her side. "Cara!"

"What's up with him?" Cara asked with wide eyes.

"I'm not sure. I was going to ask you."

"He's been acting kind of weird this week. It might have something to with . . ." She abruptly stopped herself.

Lovie put her hand on Cara's shoulder. "With what?"

"Nothing," Cara replied cagily.

"Caretta, I've had enough secrecy for tonight. Tell me what you know."

Cara frowned and stuck her chin out stubbornly.

Lovie saw that her daughter was shaken by Palmer's flare-up and, more, that she knew something. Lovie guided Cara to the sofa and sat down beside her. She took a calming breath. "Cara, something's bothering Palmer. But I can't help him if I don't know what it is. If you know something, please tell me."

"Mama, I can't tattle."

"This wouldn't be tattling. I promise you, I won't get mad."

Cara looked at her hands tucked between her knees. "It's just some game he's been playing with the guys."

"Game? What game? Is he involved in that ding dong ditch game?" The neighborhood was getting upset with the antics of the boys ringing the bells and running off.

"No, ma'am."

Lovie was sure Cara knew what was bothering Palmer. "Then what game?" she prodded.

"Well," she began reluctantly, then in a gush, the story poured out. "It all started when we went to Fort Moultrie. The boys planned to walk through the fort. In the dark," she added, almost breathless at the thought of such a thing. "So they could try and see the ghost of Osceola. They had to go in one by one. Alone. It was Palmer's job to walk around the fort to make sure there were no devil worshippers or anything before we went in. He was gone a long time, and we all started to get kinda worried that something happened to him. When he got back he was acting all strange, kinda mad, and he said he was going home. The guys thought he saw devil worshippers, and when they asked him, he said he didn't but he was going home all the same. And he made me go home with him."

"That's all?" Lovie asked. "You came home?"

"Yes'm. Except that the boys all called him chicken and stuff like that."

Lovie sat back against the cushions and thought about the story. It was unlike Palmer to back down from the challenge. Something had spooked him when he walked around Fort Moultrie that night. Lovie felt the blood drain from her face.

"Cara," she said in an even voice, "did Palmer ever tell you what he saw that frightened him?"

She shook her head. "He wouldn't. Won't talk about that night." She looked at her mother. "Do you think he saw a ghost?"

"Hard to say," Lovie replied, her mind racing in a different direction from ghosts. "Did you or anyone else see anything? Or anyone?"

"Nope. Not even ol' Osceola."

"Cara, what night was it that y'all went to Fort Moultrie?"

Cara lifted her slim shoulders. "I don't know."

"Try and remember. Was it Sunday? Monday? Yesterday?"

Cara reached up and scratched her head. "I think it was Monday."

"You're sure?"

Cara nodded. "Yeah, because I was at Emmi's house on Sunday and her mom and dad were watching *The Smothers Brothers*. I remember because I was trying to talk Emmi into going to the fort with me but she wouldn't."

"Thank you, Cara. I don't think there's anything we need to worry about. Palmer's probably just upset about the teasing."

"That's what I thought," Cara said, reassured. "There's no such things as ghosts, are there." She made it sound like a statement, but Lovie heard the girl's need for reassurance.

"No, silly," she said, putting her arm around Cara's shoulders and giving them a gentle shake. "Now go on and finish setting the table. We're going to have a wonderful meal."

"Palmer will be sorry."

Lovie watched her daughter bolt off toward the kitchen, free of the burden of her secret. Lovie rose and immediately went to her desk and opened the turtle journal. She flipped through the pages, checking the dates. Her fingers stopped on Monday, August 19. She read the entry, then closed her eyes, placed her palms flat against the table, and leaned her weight against them.

She remembered that night well. On the evening of last Monday, she and Russell had walked the beach of Sullivan's Island to check the few nests there as an addendum to the final report. The moon and stars were particularly bright, they'd commented on it. There were only four nests, and when they were finished checking them they'd exited the beach and walked to the parking lot to their separate cars. Not seeing anyone, Russell had kissed her good-bye.

Lovie straightened and closed the journal, remembering the expression of her son's face when he turned to look at her at the bottom of the stairs. His blue eyes were roiling with the fire of resentment and the iciness of anger. She shivered and held the journal to her breast, thinking of the young boy she'd once held close to her heart and of the young man who had just turned his back on her.

She and Russell had parked their cars in the lot at Fort Moultrie.

Eighteen

~

It was Labor Day weekend, the farewell holiday of summer. For Lovie, September loomed with the same dread as the hurricane roiling somewhere out in the Atlantic. This final weekend at the beach house was a time for good-byes.

Stratton was due home from Europe on Monday and expected his family back on Tradd Street to greet him. Her beach house was packed up, ready to close tomorrow. She'd said her good-byes to friends. The turtle project's farewell party included promises to continue the project the following summer. Most of the volunteers had already left for points north. Tonight was her last night on the island this summer, and her hardest good-bye was the one she had to say to Russell Bennett.

Lovie lay in Russell's arms on the faithful red-and-black checked blanket that had served them well over the past weeks as they lay together on the dunes. Countless stars put on a dazzling display in the heavens. The beach felt otherworldly, bathed in the harvest moon's silvery light, revealing the untrammeled sand of low tide. Even the ocean had diminished its roar to serenely roll in and out, murmuring whispers of constancy along the shoreline. The air was still, as though the night were holding its breath, waiting, watching to see how the final moments of Lovie and Russell's summer would end.

Their lovemaking had been both tender and desperate. Now, in the aftermath, Lovie felt a calm that was born of resignation and acceptance. She had no more tears left. She didn't want to think of her life without him. She had a lifetime to endure that reality. Tonight Russell was here, in her arms. That was all she had, and it had to be enough.

This is how I'll always remember him, she thought. She closed her eyes. She would make a picture of this moment in her mind. She committed the sensation of his hand idly stroking her hair, his musky scent, the sound of his heart beating in his chest, to her mind so that on nights to come, after he was gone, she would have these memories to hold on to.

"It's getting late," he said.

Her heart stopped. "No, it's early yet."

"We should go."

She sighed and held him tighter. She heard the rattling of the tall, dry sea grasses stirring in the wind and the scuttling in the sand of a ghost crab. "I promised myself I wouldn't cry again."

He took his hand from her hair and played with her fingers on his chest. "My darling, I don't want you to cry. We knew this day was coming."

"That doesn't make it any easier."

"No."

"It's all so heartbreaking and frustrating," she said against his chest. "I feel helpless, and I don't like that feeling. I'm just going along with the plot as written, like some character in a tragic story of star-crossed lovers. We're no better off than Romeo and Juliet."

He brought her fingers to his lips, kissing them. "I don't think I like that example. They died, you know. Perhaps Lancelot and Guinevere?"

"You're trying to make me laugh. It won't work. Besides, I don't want to be a nun."

He pressed his lips to her palm. "Better than burned at the stake."

"Lancelot rescued her, you know." She clutched his shirt. "He came back for her."

His hand tightened around her hair as he pulled her head down so their foreheads touched. His whisper was tortured. "Don't you know leaving you is the hardest thing I'll ever have to do?"

"Then don't."

He kissed her then, and it sparked a violent passion. All reason and resolve was cast aside as they clung to each other with the final desperation. He kissed her face, her body, telling her he loved her, would love her always. When they made love a second time, Lovie held tight, reluctant to let go, knowing that she would never again find a love so true, so pure.

Russell rose up on his forearms to stare at her face as though memorizing each detail. He lifted his finger to wipe away the tears from her cheek.

"Olivia," he said in a husky voice, "I love you. I've never loved anyone the way I love you and I know I never will again. Come with me."

"Don't say that," Lovie said. "You know I can't. That you can't. We both knew that we'd have to end this at the end of the summer."

"I never promised that. We never said the words."

"But it was understood," she said, weakening.

"I'm asking you now. I'm saying the words. Come with me."

"Russell, how can I?"

"Move with me to Florida. Bring your children. We'll be a family."

"But Russell, we never intended to break up our families.

Think of the scandal. Not just for us, but for our families. How can we do that?"

He shook his head in dismay. "Olivia, I know it will be hard. But what else can we do? We can't continue like this. Neither of us. We have to decide. We either both leave our families and be together, or we say good-bye tonight."

Lovie clung to him, feeling the finality of the words. She couldn't let him go. Not tonight. It was too soon.

"Russell," she said, bringing her hand to his face. His breathing was heavy and he appeared stricken. She moved to sit upright on the blanket. "I have one idea."

He moved to join her, sitting cross-legged. His unbuttoned shirt hung open, exposing his finely muscled chest to the moonlight. "Tell me."

She reached out to take his hand. "I know we understood that we'd leave here tonight and never see each other again. We decided to do the right thing and go back to our families. Neither of us wants to see anyone hurt. But I keep asking myself: What if this love we have *is* our destiny? Do we have the right to deny it? And why do we have to? Are we willing to give up everything we possess, even our honor, to be together? To start a new life together?"

"Yes," he said.

"Wait." She brought her finger up to his lips. "Don't answer now. This decision is too big, it carries too much weight not only for us but for those we love to answer quickly." She paused, gathering her thoughts. "I propose we make a promise. We will wait six months. Time enough for us to return to our lives, to cool our heads, and to think through all the ramifications of our decisions. Carefully and deliberately. There must be no contact until the six months are over. None at all. No pressure of any kind."

Lovie counted on her fingers. "September, October, November, December, January, February, *March*. If in March—the Ides of March—if on March fifteenth either one of us chooses to leave our spouse, we will come back here to the beach house. If I come and you are not there—"

"No, that won't happen."

"Shhh . . . Or if you come and I am not there, there will be no recriminations, no anger, and no hatred." Her lips trembled. "Russell, don't let there ever be hatred between us."

"Never."

"If either of us chooses not to show up, then the other will never call again. We will abide by the decision, no matter how hard it may be to accept. Are we agreed? Oh, please say yes!"

"Yes," he replied, his eyes kindling with hope. "Absolutely."

Lovie felt her heart spring back to life. "And if we both decide to come that day to the beach house?"

He gave her a wistful smile and smoothed the hair from her face. "We may never know if our decisions were right or wrong. That is the uncertainty of every choice. If we both show up, it will be a new beginning. If one of us does not, it will be an end. Lovie, I can't predict what the future holds, but I can promise you this: Whatever decision you make, I will always love you."

Lovie felt like waltzing along the beach path as she made her way back to the beach house. She felt the moon's silvery light on her shoulders as her toes dug into the sand that was gloriously cool. She felt buoyant inside, her hope rising in her chest like helium, making her feel dizzy with joy.

She *knew* she would keep that date with Russell. It all seemed so easy now. She would return home to settle her affairs with Stratton. A divorce would cause a scandal in Charleston, her family and friends would never forgive her, but she was willing to risk that. She would take Palmer and Cara, and they'd live somewhere else with Russell. Florida, first. And if he traveled, they would go with him. Who knew where? What did it matter? Wouldn't the children love that? She would ask nothing from Stratton but her freedom. He could take the house, the furniture—he could have it all. That's all he wanted, anyway.

She felt so free. Her heart was aglow with light. Her hair flowed freely down her back. She lifted her arms and twirled in the sand, laughing, feeling the weight of her decision lift from her shoulders. She felt brave and confident, once again the young girl who had made it to the Point. The girl who bought her own car. The girl who kissed in the waves. Her path was clear, she thought, as she danced home.

She saw her pale yellow beach house perched prettily on the dune. The wild grass, yellow primroses, and gaillardia blanketed the earth and sand that rose and fell in an undulating pattern. She would miss her dear cottage, she thought with a tug of her heart. Perhaps someday she could return, after the scandal died down. She would return like the turtles, every few years, arriving under the cloak of the darkness. What changes the hatchlings must face when they return home to the beach of their birth after twenty-five or thirty years. What would Isle of Palms look like in ten years, twenty, thirty when the forest was gone and the resort was finished and more and more people moved in? Would it still be her quiet little island?

She couldn't worry about that now, she told herself as she walked up the porch stairs. She had enough changes to handle right now. The future would take care of itself. She had so much to do to leave the day after tomorrow. She wondered when Stratton would arrive home. How would she tell him that she was leaving him? She chewed her lip in thought as she set her canvas bag on the porch floor, then slipped off her sand-crusted sandals and shook some of the sand from her clothes. A mosquito hummed at her ear. She swatted at it, not wanting the pest to come inside. The door creaked as she swung it open.

Lovie's mouth froze open in a silent gasp when she saw Stratton sitting in the wide, cushioned chair with a glass of scotch. He stood and set the drink on the table when she entered the room.

His face was pale with restrained fury, and his eyes were dark. His shoulders were hunched, his meaty fists were clenched at his sides, and he was panting through his mouth, like a pierced bull about to charge. Lovie held tight to the doorframe, in part to steady herself from the shock of finding Stratton here at the house, tonight, and in part because she was a breath away from running.

That one second seemed to last minutes as a million thoughts raced through her mind. What was he doing here? Why was he so angry? Oh, my God, what time was it? Uppermost was relief that she'd come home alone. Russell had wanted to walk her back but she'd refused and said her good-bye at the beach. Surely he couldn't know about Russell, she thought in a breathless panic. How could he?

He knew.

It was the way he looked at her, his dark eyes narrowed and his teeth showing like one of his hunting dogs when it catches the scent. And it made her very afraid.

"Stratton! You're home."

"Where were you?" he ground out through thin, white lips.

She forced a look of innocent surprise on her face. "Why, I was at a turtle nest. I go out to check on them most nights."

"All alone? So late?"

"Of course. I do it all the time. It's quite safe." She feigned a relaxed attitude, but her voice sounded tinny and high. She brushed a bit of sand from her shorts as she moved into the house. "What a surprise to see you home at last! I'm sorry I wasn't here to greet you. I would have picked you up at the airport. Did you have a good flight?"

She was babbling. She had to stop herself. Flo's words came

back to haunt her, *You're a terrible liar.* Lovie raised her hands to pull back her wild hair. Her hands shook as she pulled the elastic from her wrist over her hand to make a sloppy bun. Bringing her hand down, she noticed that her Tiffany diamond and wedding band were off her finger. Her eyes darted to his, and in that second she saw that he'd noticed, too.

He lifted one brow as his gaze bored into hers. "Where's your ring?"

"Oh, I never wear that big ol' thing to the beach. It collects too much sand and I'm afraid I'd lose it when I dig . . ."

"Who is he?" His voice was low, like thunder, and his eyes flashed like lightning.

Lovie's heart hammered as she stared into the dark abyss of his eyes and instinctively knew this was a turning point. She had to trust Russell and their love enough for honesty. She had to find the courage. If she was going to tell him the truth, now was the moment. Come what may.

Her eyes darted around the room. It was just the way she'd left it a few hours earlier. Tidy, everything in its place. Too perfect. She had the numb feeling she often got right before a hurricane hit. It all could disappear in an instant. In a breath of time, all she loved and treasured could lie scattered and irreparably broken. She looked up again at Stratton's eyes. He took a step forward.

"Who is he?" he repeated. He spoke in a low voice, but it resonated in her body like thunder.

She took a breath, and in her mind, she ran.

"Who?" she replied. Even as she spoke, she knew she was damned.

It all happened so fast. He swooped down upon her like a hurricane.

"Who is he?" he roared, grabbing her shoulders and shaking her.

She felt her head whip back and forth, like a branch in the fierce storm's wind. Lovie was shaken, afraid, but still she refused to tell him. Some instinct told her never to mention the name.

Stratton released her with a disgusted shove. "Tell me, goddamn it!" he shouted, and swung his arm.

She felt the sharp sting of his hand against her cheek and fell back against the desk with a muffled grunt. She held up her arms protectively over her head. "Stop!" she begged him. "Stratton, no!" But her cries only seemed to urge him on. Her defiance was like oil on a flame. He screamed at her to tell him the name, hitting her each time. He asked her many times. Her wails rose up like the cry of a wounded animal and she tasted blood on her lips.

Her hair sprang loose from its hold. He grabbed a fistful and yanked her to her feet. The pain exploded in her head.

"Tell me his name, or by God I'll kill you," he shouted at her. His face was inches from her own, and she felt the heat of his breath and smelled the stink of drink. When she didn't speak, he bunched his fist, reared back his arm, and landed a punch against her face so hard her world exploded in white. She went sprawling over the desk, then tumbled in a heap to the floor. The desk, her papers, the lamp all came crashing down around her. She knew she was hurt, she could feel something was very wrong. Moaning, in a panic, she tried to crawl away from him, she needed to get away from the source of pain.

The door flew open, and from the corner of her eyes she saw Flo burst into the room. She ran to Lovie and stood in front of her, wide legged. All Lovie could see were the bottoms of her rose floral pajamas. Craning her neck, she saw that Flo was carrying a baseball bat.

"Don't you touch her!" Flo screamed at the top of her lungs. She stood glaring at Stratton, wielding the bat threateningly.

"Get out of my house," he shouted back at her.

"You're the one who's leaving. Now! Get the hell out before I call the police."

Stratton stood, breathing heavily, but reason slowly returned to his face. He looked at Lovie for a long moment, then again at Flo.

"You're her best friend," he said bitterly. "Suppose you tell me what's been going on this summer."

"I'm not telling you squat."

"You've just told me all I need to know." He teetered as he waved his hand in disgust. "And you're protecting her? I had a right to be angry."

"A right? You have no right to hit a woman like this. For *any* reason!" Flo shouted at him. She was so angry her chest heaved. "Now get out of here. Go on back across that bridge. You hate being here anyway. Go on! We don't want you here, you wife-beating son of a bitch."

Stratton staggered forward, Flo raised the bat, and Lovie cringed.

The door opened again and Miranda rushed in, her long pale orange hair flowing wildly down her scarlet Chinese silk robe. She stopped short when she saw the overturned furniture and Flo standing with a bat confronting Stratton before a huddled Lovie.

"What's going on here?" she said in her imperious voice. "I could hear the screams all the way to my bedroom."

"None of your business, Miranda," Stratton said. "Nor yours either," he said to Flo. "This is a family affair."

"Not any longer," she said to Stratton. "You should go. Right now. Or we will call the police."

Stratton worked his mouth, then lifted his arm and jabbed his index finger at Flo. "I'm going. Not because you told me to go. You're disgusting, do you know that? It's no wonder you're not married. Who'd have you? But *you*," he said, pointing to Lovie.

"You get things cleaned up here and bring my children home. I'll expect you back at the house by tomorrow. Not a day later, hear?"

He rolled his shoulders, salvaging his dignity, and went to the sofa to grab his jacket. Then picking up his bags, he strode to the door, turning once more to deliver a warning look to Lovie before he walked out.

Flo released a long sigh and lowered her arms. She turned and kneeled beside Lovie. Miranda hurried to their side, settling in a puddle of silk.

Lovie coughed and whimpered as she felt Miranda's fingers gently smooth the damp, bloodied hair from her face. Miranda gingerly lifted the arm that Lovie was cradling against her chest and tenderly moved probing fingers along the bones, stopping when Lovie yelped.

"I think your ribs could be broken," she said. "Oh, Lovie," Miranda said in a pitying tone. Then she turned her head and said to Flo, "We need to get her to a hospital."

"No hospital," Lovie said. "I'm fine."

"Oh, shut up," Flo said, though there was no anger in it. "I know why you're saying that. There's nothing to be ashamed of. Now honey, listen to me. You've got to see a doctor. I'll stay with you the whole time. Now come on, Lovie, try to stand," she said, firmly guiding Lovie to her feet. "Real easy now. Mama, grab her other arm and help her up."

Lovie could barely straighten and squelched her cry of pain as something sharp jabbed in her side. She found it easier to hold her breath while she rose. At last she was on her feet and found a wobbly balance. The women guided her to a chair.

Miranda hurried to the kitchen and returned with a cool damp cloth. With a mother's care, Miranda dabbed at the blood on her face. Lovie closed her eyes and caught the scent of Miranda's perfume.

"Flo, darling, get me some ice in a clean towel, would you?" When Flo left, Miranda asked, "Where are the children, dear?"

"At friends'," she said, realizing how extraordinarily fortunate they were not to be here to witness her shame.

"Thank heavens," Miranda said kindly. "You be a good girl now and go with Flo. And we'll clean up the house. Don't fret. We'll take care of you." She sniffed back a sob that caught in her throat. "Child, it's all going to be all right."

Nineteen

≈

Lovie had only been in a hospital three times in her life. Twice for the births of her children, then again for the death of her father. Life and death.

And now shame.

She brought her fingers to her face, letting the tips gently prod the bruised skin. How would she hide this from her children? She didn't want them to be afraid. And Russell . . . thank God they'd said good-bye. Russell was flying out tomorrow, she thought with relief. She didn't want to think what Russell might have done if he saw her and learned Stratton had hurt her. If only she'd gone away with him last night, she thought. Then Stratton would not have beaten her.

Beaten her . . . She closed her eyes tight, disbelieving the words. Her husband had beaten her. She'd heard of such things, but no one she knew had ever been abused. She felt such shame.

Lovie opened her eyes. Or, had they? What if she'd turned a blind eye to the troubles of her friends? No one wanted to peek behind the private curtains of a friend's home. Her mother taught her not to pry into someone else's marriage. It was too personal.

Lovie wouldn't dream of telling anyone what had happened

tonight, the shame of it was too great. When she went home to Charleston, she'd tell everyone the same story that she'd told the doctor: that coming home from turtle patrol in the dark, she'd fallen down the porch stairs. Lovie thought of her friend Lulu's bruises on her face. Lulu claimed they were from falling down the cellar stairs. How quick Lovie was to believe her. Now, she wasn't sure.

The green curtain that surrounded her cubicle noisily opened and the emergency room doctor walked in, carrying a clipboard. He was an older man with a shock of white hair and a pink, kindly face. She couldn't remember his name. The pain medicine made her a little groggy. She watched him study her chart and thought that he was a gentle man, someone's father and grandfather. She was relieved he wasn't some young intern all eager and shiny as a new penny, full of questions. This doctor looked up, and behind his heavy black glasses, his eyes shone with wisdom of experience and concern.

"Mrs. Rutledge, it's very late. I could keep you here for the night. Let you get some rest. Tomorrow you can make arrangements for help."

"No," she mumbled through swollen lips. "I'll be fine. My friend is outside. And I'll send for my maid."

He paused and looked at her chart. "Are you sure you feel safe going home?"

He looked at her again, and she knew what he was asking. He'd seen injuries like hers many times over the years of his practice and didn't believe for a minute that she'd fallen down the porch stairs in the dark. She considered whether to tell him the truth about her beating. But she felt too ashamed to utter the words.

Besides, what could he do? Other than offer her a night's stay, how could he help her? He'd mended her wounds and given her a prescription for pain medicine. If she wanted, he would file a police report. But of course Lovie could never do that. What happened between a husband and wife behind closed doors stayed behind closed doors.

"I'll be fine," she said again, resolute. "I have a safe place to go to," she told the doctor. "I have the beach house."

The inside of Flo's car was so dark Lovie saw her friend as a rigid silhouette beside her in the front seat. Florence Prescott had been her dearest friend since childhood, and Lovie knew that though she was calm and methodical with her patients, when it came to her loved ones she could be emotional—erupting in a fiery fury or sitting in an icy cold. In between those extremes, Flo was the soul of reason and good advice. Lovie knew Flo was stewing, holding back words. She was smoking, a bad habit she'd been trying to quit. The tip of the cigarette glowed red in the dark. They were all exhausted and the hour was late. They drove most of the way home from the city in silence, but when they began crossing the marsh from the mainland, Flo let the geyser spout.

"I can't believe you told him you fell off the goddamn porch!" Flo exclaimed, pounding the steering wheel for good measure. "Do you think he's a fool? Of course he knows you didn't tumble down any stairs. He's an ER doctor, for Christ's sake."

Miranda reached over from the backseat to tap Flo's shoulder. "We've had quite enough emotion for one night, don't you think?" she asked. "And don't take the Lord's name in vain. I don't want to tick Him off. I think we need all the help we can get right now."

Flo shook her head and sighed in frustration, but she cooled her tone of voice. "What are you going to tell your children? Your friends?" she asked Lovie.

Lovie had her head resting against the thick leather of Flo's big Lincoln. She moved her mouth slowly, maneuvering words through swollen lips. "I'm going to tell them I fell down the porch steps."

Flo cursed under her breath with a harsh shake of her head.

"And that is what *you* are going to tell people who ask," Lovie added. "Miranda, do you hear me back there?"

"I hear you," Miranda replied. "Don't you worry, Lovie dear. We'll do and say whatever you want. Won't we, Florence?"

Lovie relaxed, knowing Miranda had a strange power over her daughter. Lovie knew from childhood that if Miranda called her daughter Florence, she meant business.

"We'll come by tomorrow, too," Miranda said. "To clean up some and cook for the children."

"I've called Vivian," Lovie said. "She's coming tomorrow to help me pack up."

"Pack up?" asked Miranda. "You're not still going back to Charleston tomorrow?"

"Yes, ma'am."

"Because that bastard ordered you to go?" Flo asked, clearly angry.

Lovie put her fingertips to her temples and rubbed small circles. "No. Because I want to leave the island. I don't want a whisper of this to get back to Russell Bennett. Is that understood? He must leave as planned. And I want my children back home so they can start school on the first day." Her voice shook. "I will not have my children upset over this."

"Aw, hell. They're going to be upset anyway when they see you," Flo grumbled. "Do you think they'll believe your cockamamie story about falling off the porch? Lovie, you've got the balance of a mountain goat."

"They'll believe what I tell them. Besides, Flo, where else can I go? He won't let me stay at the beach house indefinitely."

"You could live with me," Miranda said.

"Thank you, dear, sweet Miranda," Lovie replied. "You are

the mother I never had and I love you for that. I would stay, but that would only be temporary. I don't have any skills. I've never held a job. I couldn't afford to get a place of my own. Even if I could, I won't lose custody of my children. I've thought this all through carefully. I really don't have a choice. I am going back."

"And what if he hits you again?"

Lovie's breath caught in her throat. Just hearing the words scared her. Of course she'd given this a lot of thought while sitting in the hospital, waiting and hurting. "I don't think he will."

"You don't *think* he will," Flo repeated. "Heaven help me, what does that mean? Has he hit you before?"

Lovie felt so vulnerable, so tired. "He's slapped me. Nothing serious."

"Lord help me," Miranda said softly from the back.

Flo took a long drag from her cigarette. "You can't go back. It's escalating, don't you see that?"

"No, I don't. Tonight was ugly. Terrifying . . . Flo, I gave him good reason."

"What!" Flo shouted out, swinging her head to glare at Lovie. The car swerved slightly before she corrected it. "There's never a good reason for a man to hit a woman. But to beat her up? Jesus Christ, Lovie!"

"Language!" Miranda called from the back.

"I'm sorry, Mama, but I get crazy when I hear talk like that."

"Don't you think I drove him to it?" Lovie cried. "I may not have broken his heart. But I did break my marriage vows."

"Lovie, did you forget I'm a social worker? I see abused women all the time, and so many of them believe he'll never do it again. Or they believe it's their fault. But then he does. These aren't all poor women I'm talking about, either. This kind of thing crosses all economic and class barriers. The poor have nowhere to go, and the rich hide the scandal. Women have to speak out against abuse if we're going to stop it."

"This is my life we're talking about. I'm not on some feminist crusade."

"Lovie," Flo argued, trying to calm her voice, "think about this life you're talking about. Do you really want to spend the rest of your life like this? Afraid of the next time that fist will fall?"

"I'll make changes. I'll—"

"Stop," Flo said. "You can't change it. We're talking about a pattern here, one that's been going on for years. Stratton is controlling. He has anger issues. It's not because of you he's behaving this way. You're his target. Something deeper inside of him makes him who he is. Long before Russell Bennett."

Lovie listened, let the words settle uncomfortably in her mind. "But the family . . . How can I break up my family?" Her voice broke.

"What if his anger finds new targets? What if he starts in on the children?"

"Don't you think I haven't gone over that possibility a million times in my mind? The only reason I'm going back is for my children."

"Your children can do well without him."

"But they can't do well without *me*."

"Oh, hell, Lovie! Is this life worth lying for?"

"I'm not lying," she replied, putting her forehead wearily in her palm. "I'm not saying anything."

"Not speaking up is still a lie."

"All right, then," Lovie said, dropping her palm and lifting her head. "It's a lie. One I'll have to live with. But I'm not telling anyone the truth about tonight. *I can't!* Now stop badgering me." Her voice shook. "And would you please get rid of that cigarette. It's making me sick!"

"Girls . . ." Miranda's voice rose up from the back, soothing the tension. "We're all tired and Lovie needs to rest. Let's settle down."

Flo tossed the butt of her cigarette out the window. "The truth always comes out eventually," she said in a calmer voice.

Lovie turned her head. "How did Stratton find out about me and Russell?"

Flo shifted in her seat and her hands tightened on the steering wheel. "There's been gossip. I told you that."

Lovie frowned and looked out the window. Bits of light from house windows pierced the blackness. She had to accept the possibility that malicious wagging tongues were the likely source. But she was terrified of her suspicion that the culprit was her son. "I wondered about . . . whether it was Palmer."

"Palmer? Why him?" Flo asked, shocked.

Lovie pictured her son's pale face and his angry eyes, overflowing with accusation. She told Flo about the outburst and Cara's story about Fort Moultrie. She told of how Russell and she had parked in that parking lot. "I'm worried that he saw us in the lot together . . . Russell kissed me good-bye."

"Oh, God," Flo said, shaking her head. "You have to talk to him," she said urgently. "Find out what he saw. He might not've seen a thing. But if he did see you together, he's going to wonder what really happened to you. Palmer is too old not to suspect the truth and too young to shoulder that burden."

Lovie put her hand to her mouth as tears welled up in her eyes. "I will," Lovie said, wondering how she'd ever find the courage to confront her son about such a sensitive matter, how she could look him in his eyes and face his anger again.

"But not tonight, dear," Miranda said from the back. They were pulling up at Lovie's beach house. "Tonight you just let the medicine do its work, dear, and get some sleep. Tomorrow will be here soon enough."

• • •

At ten o'clock the next morning, Vivian walked into the beach house, a bouquet of daisies in her hand. Miranda welcomed her like a long-lost cousin. As she ushered Vivian into the living room, the air was rent by a scream and Cara came bounding into the room, arms out, on a beeline for Vivian. She dropped her bag just in time to catch the girl in a tight embrace.

"Lord, Lord, child! What's got into you?"

Cara's face was buried against Vivian's breast. She was holding on tighter than an alligator with its prey. "I missed you."

From the bedroom, Lovie watched the exchange with bittersweet feelings. She knew Vivian loved this child more than she had a right to. Sometimes, Lovie was jealous of the bond they shared, especially this morning, when she'd told the white lie to Cara about her bruises.

"I've only been gone for the summer. But I'm here now, and I've come to help you pack up your things and bring you back home, where you belong."

"I belong here at the beach house," Cara replied.

In her room, Lovie smiled, ignoring the pain it took to do so.

"This won't be such a big job," Vivian said in a loud voice ringing with optimism. "I might even get time to walk down to the beach and take a peek at that ocean. Now, where's your mama?" she asked Cara.

"She's still in bed."

"Really?" Vivian asked with surprise. "I best go right to her, then."

"Let me get some water for those flowers," Miranda said.

"Is she awake?" Vivian asked.

"Yes, I believe she is," Miranda replied. "Uh, Vivian . . . Lovie's had an accident."

Cara said, "She's hurt pretty bad."

Vivian didn't reply and went directly to the bedroom.

"Miss Lovie? You awake?"

"Yes." Lovie lay on her back, propped up by pillows. Her cast lay against her belly.

"This room looks like a sickroom," Vivian exclaimed, going to the windows. "I always says that I like this room the most," she told Lovie as the first shade rattled up. She crossed the room, opening the blinds, chattering on. "It might not be as grand as your bedroom in town, but to me, this room looks so white and fresh, like a field of snow. Here we go." She pushed open the French doors to the porch, allowing the breeze to blow in from the blue ocean beyond. "Now, ain't this better?"

She turned toward the bed, and in the morning light Lovie could see her dark eyes widen as she stared at her. Vivian hurried to the bedside. "Miss Lovie, what happened to you? You look like you done gone ten rounds in a boxing match and lost. Is that a cast?"

"I broke my wrist. And a few ribs."

"Lord have mercy." Vivian stood beside the bed with her hands clasped around the daisies, shaking her head and studying Lovie's face with a frown.

"Thank you for coming on such short notice." Her words sounded slurred through her split lip.

"Why, Miss Lovie. Of course I'd come," Vivian said, and held out the flowers. "I came out in Mr. Stratton's big car to help you load up. And I brought these for you, to cheer you up. Looks like you need it, too."

"Daisies. So fresh. Thank you, Vivian."

"Miss Miranda went to fetch some water," she said, and set the flowers down on the bureau. "Miss Lovie, is that sun too much? You're blinking," Vivian said, moving to the windows.

"My eyes are a little sensitive."

Vivian went around the room, lowering the blinds.

"You can leave the porch doors open. The breeze is nice."

When Vivian returned to the bedside, her tight-lipped stare made Lovie self-conscious. She reached up with her good right hand and moved some of her hair over her face to conceal the bruises. "It's not as bad as it looks," she said with a soft laugh. "I really am so clumsy to fall down the stairs like that."

"Uh-huh." Vivian went to close the bedroom door. Then she came again beside Lovie, closer, so that she could speak softly. "Miss Lovie, there's no need for you to tell me that story. We both know you didn't fall down no stairs."

Lovie blanched.

"I understand why you have to make up a story like that," Vivian continued. "Your chil'ren, they don't need to know such things happen. They'd only be more scared than they already are. Cara came runnin' for me and wrapped her arms around my waist tight as a monkey. I ain't seen Palmer yet, but Cara is trying her best to act like nothing's happened. You know how she is."

"Yes."

Vivian looked at her hands. She held them together so tight they looked like knotted rope. "Miss Lovie, Cara is a fighter. She sometimes don't know when it's best to keep quiet. Who's to say the same won't happen to her someday?"

Lovie shuddered at the prospect. "Stratton would never lay a hand on her."

"Miss Lovie," Vivian said again, and she appeared uneasy. "How you think I got deaf in this left ear?"

"I don't know," Lovie replied haltingly, unsure of where this was going. "I guess I always assumed you were born that way, or maybe had a bad case of the mumps or some other illness when you were young."

Vivian shook her head. She took a breath and, looking off, began to speak. "I don't like to share my troubles, Miss Lovie. But I think it's fitting, given what's all going on, for me to share this story with you. You see, my daddy was a lot like your Mr. Stratton. He had a good job and worked hard, I'll give him that. Only that," she muttered to herself. "My mama worked, too, cleaning houses. Took in ironing at night to bring in something extra. I was the youngest of four but the only girl. I wasn't much older than Cara is now when it fell to me to do a lot of the cooking and the cleaning. I didn't mind. But my brothers were lazy good-for-nothings."

She glanced at Lovie and shrugged, as if to say none of that mattered anymore. Then she grew more serious. "Daddy's big failing was he liked the drink. He wasn't a happy drunk neither, like some folks I've known. The drink made him mean. When he come home nights, we knew when he was liquored up because he took off after my mama something awful. My brothers snuck out of the windows, knowing he'd come after them next. One night he got so mad, Lord, I don't even remember about what, he beat my mama bad and threw her out of the house. I stood up to him. I told him he had no right to throw my mama out of her own house."

She shrugged again and lifted her chin, her lips tight. Lovie could tell this was hard for Vivian to relive.

"That's when he beat me, too. He hit me till I couldn't remember no more. The next morning he was gone. Good riddance."

"Oh, Vivian . . ."

Vivian looked at her and it was clear she wasn't looking for sympathy. "Miss Lovie, what I'm trying to tell you is my mama tol' folks she *fell down the stairs*, too. Now, I saw her face. And your face looks like Mama's did. And the way mine did. That's how I know you didn't fall down no stairs."

Lovie looked down at the cast on her wrist and nodded in silent agreement.

"We both know Mr. Stratton gots trouble with the drink,

too. How sometimes he come home full of liquor and goes after you, like my daddy did. The chil'ren tells me what happens," she hurried to explain when she saw the shock in Lovie's eyes.

"He didn't beat me," Lovie said, dispelling that idea. "Not then," she said softly.

"They tol' me how he yells at you all the time and how afraid they are. That's *his* shame, Miss Lovie. Not yours."

Lovie felt tears welling up again and looked down, seeing her hand coming out from the cast.

"I got one more thing to say," Vivian said. "I loves Miss Cara, you know I do. But she's as stubborn and willful as I was as a child. Maybe that's why I try and stand up for her the way I do. Palmer's different. He'll sneak off, like my brothers. But one day, Cara is going to stand up to her daddy, and when she does . . ." She shook her head. "I'm afraid for that day."

Lovie's gaze shot back up and she and Vivian blinked together, equally sharing that fear. "I won't let him hit her," Lovie said vehemently. "Not ever. I'd rather die."

"Well, that's somethin'," Vivian said, but she sounded unconvinced. She let out a long breath. "Miss Lovie, you sure you want to go back to the big house? Why don't you stay here a spell? Think things through. I'll stay here with you."

"Thank you, Vivian," Lovie replied, deeply moved. Nonetheless, she'd made up her mind. "I appreciate your sharing your story. Truly. And I hear what you're telling me. But please don't worry. I must go back. I know what I'm doing."

"Well," Vivian said, slapping her palms on her thighs, "then I best not sit here yakking. There's work to be done. Have you had your breakfast? I think some nice soft eggs would be just the thing. And some juice, too. You could handle that, couldn't you?"

• • •

For the next several hours, Lovie lay in her bed and listened to the sounds of packing, doors slamming, and chatter in the beach house. Lying in bed and not taking charge felt like she was having an out-of-body experience. It was surreal and unpleasant. Her fingers tapped in agitation and the throbbing pain was relentless. She was feeling sorry for herself and depressed that her life had crumbled to this point.

Cara found excuses to come to her room. At first she was cagey, looking over when she thought Lovie wasn't looking, trying not to stare. Lovie knew the sight of her bruised face was frightening to her. As the day wore on, however, Cara grew accustomed to the injuries, and she'd come in and just plop against the bed to say hi. Each time the mattress jolted, Lovie felt a ricochet of pain but didn't say anything. The pain was worth a visit from her daughter. Miranda and Flo popped their heads in to ask questions about where she wanted things put. Vivian brought trays of food and iced tea, and made sure Lovie took her pain medicine on schedule.

The only one who did not make an appearance was Palmer. His absence made Lovie worry all the more. She heard his voice, so she knew when he was up. Later she'd heard from Vivian that he'd gone off to say good-bye to friends. They were planning on leaving by four o'clock, and her body felt wound up like a clock, counting the seconds until she heard his voice again. It was almost three when she saw a shadow at the door. She spotted Palmer looking in. She'd barely registered it was him when he hurried away.

"Palmer!" she called out as loudly as she could with broken ribs. She clutched the blanket and called again, "Palmer!"

She heard a shuffling of feet, and Palmer slunk forward at the door. His hair was longer now and fell over his eyes when he looked down, as he did now. "Come in," she said, and heard her eagerness in each syllable.

Palmer put his hands in the pockets of his shorts and walked in with reluctance. "Yeah?"

Lovie patted the bed, indicating he should come closer. Palmer walked over, dragging his feet like a condemned man.

"I wanted to talk to you."

His eyes were still on his feet. "About what?"

"Well, you were pretty angry the last time we spoke."

Palmer shrugged, his thin shoulders more muscular and fit after a summer of surfing. How tan he was. And he'd grown! She almost smiled, wondering if all that milk he drank had worked after all. How had she not noticed? Was she so self-absorbed with her own life this summer that she didn't notice the changes occurring in her own children? The answer stabbed her heart with remorse.

"I'm sorry we argued," she told him. *And for so much more.*

He didn't respond.

"Can I ask you what you were angry about?"

"I don't remember."

"Palmer," she said, "look at me, please."

Palmer dragged his eyes from the floor to her face and saw, really saw her bruised face in the full daylight. She saw the horror and despair reflected in his eyes as though they were clear blue pools. The water began to well up and he worked his mouth, trying to control his trembling lips.

"I'm sorry, Mama," he blurted out as his chest began to heave and the tears flowed down his cheeks. "I'm sorry."

Lovie's heart broke, and despite the pain she turned in the bed and reached out to her son. "Palmer, come here," she cried.

He fell to his knees by her bed and buried his head in his arms on the mattress as he wept. Lovie bent over him, mantling him like a mother bird would her young to keep it warm and safe from the elements. She kissed his head, smelling salt and sweat and tasting the tears on her own cheeks. She'd not seen her son cry in years. He'd been trying so hard to grow into his role as a man.

She heard a noise at the door and, looking up, saw Vivian. Lovie shook her head, and with a nod, Vivian quietly closed the bedroom door.

"Palmer, I know I haven't been around much this summer. I got caught up in the turtle project. I spent too much time away from home. I'm sorry for that."

Palmer raised his face, and she saw a flash of anger in his eyes that silenced her.

"I saw you," he said in a hoarse voice. "I saw you with *him*."

Lovie closed her eyes and shrank back, shamed by the accusation in his eyes, and the truth of it.

"You saw me with Dr. Bennett?" She had to be certain of what he saw.

"Yeah. I saw you walking with him. At Fort Moultrie."

Walking? she thought. "Where?"

"On the path by the beach. What does it matter? You were holding hands."

He spat the last out, again in accusation, but all she could think was that he didn't see Russell kiss her. She felt a heartbeat of relief and hope. That, at least, was something.

"Yes," she answered him levelly. "We've become close friends."

Palmer snorted with derision. It sounded like Stratton, and she cringed hearing it.

"Palmer, I'm sorry you saw that and it bothers you." Lovie took his hand in her one free hand. Her heart pounded, knowing what she had to ask, not so much for herself but for Palmer so that he could get it off his chest and not let guilt burrow a hole in his soul.

"I love you, Palmer. I'm your mother and nothing you could say can ever change that. But I need to ask you something and

you need to tell me. It's the only way I can help you feel better."
She squeezed his hand. "You said you were sorry. What are you
sorry for?"

He gave her a blank look.

"Palmer, it's okay to tell me. I think I already know."

He swung his head back and his control broke. "I'm sorry,
Mama. I didn't know he'd do this. I hate him! I hate him!"

Lovie heard the words and what they implied. They entered
her mind like poison, withering her heart. "You told Daddy what
you saw?"

"No!" he said, eyes round with shock. "I didn't tell him that!"

Lovie was confused and was sure her face showed it.

"Daddy came home early," Palmer told her. "I was just getting ready to leave. You don't know how much I wish I'd just
gotten the hell out before he came home. I was the only one
home and he was looking around, asking where everyone was. He
started drinking, and I could tell he was fueling up about something. Then he started in asking me about how much you were
at the beach." He sniffed. "And with who. I played dumb. I swear
I didn't tell Daddy that you were out with . . . him. I'm not so stupid I would fire him up like that."

Palmer's face looked haunted, and he ran his hand through
his hair. Lovie held her breath, listening.

"But you know him," Palmer said with a sneer. "It was like he
already knew. He kept after me, trying to get me to talk. I kept
trying to get out the door. I almost made it when he grabbed my
shoulder, angry-like. He asked me straight out if I knew Dr. Russell Bennett." Palmer's lips trembled and he wiped his nose with
his sleeve. "I had to tell him I knew who he was," Palmer said, his
eyes pleading for Lovie's understanding.

"I know, I know," Lovie reassured him.

"I told him you were just working with him, that's all. You
had to check the turtles. I swear, Mama, that's all I told him."

He wiped his eyes. "But he must've figured something from what I'd said. When I heard you were hurt . . . I knew it was him. I should've stayed home. I should've been there to protect you."

Lovie's heart sprang to life again. Flo had been right. This knowing had been a beast in him, eating him from the inside out. She felt the pain of her ribs clear to her heart as she leaned forward to place her hand on his head. "My poor boy," she said, gently stroking his hair. "I praise God you weren't there. I can take care of my own bruises"—she choked back a sob—"but I couldn't stand to see you hurt. My baby." She sniffed and tried to collect herself so that she could say the things she needed to tell him. "I'm okay. I'll heal. Now look at me, son. Look at me!"

Palmer dragged his gaze to his mother's. She read hope in his eyes now and the love she'd prayed to find there again. "I don't want you to take one lick of blame for what's happened, hear? This is between your father and me. Grown-up things that go way back. Darling, don't you know you did protect me? You didn't tell your daddy what you saw. We were just holding hands, but I can't imagine what he'd have done then."

"Mama, why were you holding his hands?" Palmer asked, and he looked her straight in the eyes.

She saw the man in him now, and yet he was still a boy. Looking at his tear-stained face, his shaggy blond hair, Lovie knew she was talking to the boy. She'd talk to him about this again someday . . . maybe. For now, however, she didn't think an untested thirteen-year-old could possibly understand the complications of her relationship with Russell, or his father, for that matter.

"Dr. Bennett and I are dear friends," she told him. "We were saying good-bye and you saw us at a tender moment. There's nothing wrong with sentiment. You'll understand that better when you get older."

Palmer narrowed his eyes slightly, considering her answer.

Then his face relaxed, and seeing this, Lovie felt her whole body uncoil with relief. He'd accepted her answer. It was enough for now.

"Okay," he said.

To her ears, he was eloquent. She ruffled his hair and leaned back against the pillows, trying not to moan with the sharp pain. Once she was settled, she closed her eyes, feeling her energy ebb. "You go on, now, and make sure you're all packed. We're going home soon. And Palmer?" She pried open an eye and turned her head to see him.

"Don't say anything to your father. Let me deal with him."

Palmer nodded, his relief palpable, and hurried out the door.

Vivian stepped into the room a moment later, her eyes roaming over Lovie's face.

"Everything okay in here?" she asked.

Lovie took a labored breath. "I could use a pain pill," she said softly. "Then I'm getting up. It's time to go."

Sea Turtle Journal

September 1, 1974

Final entry. 88 nests, 60 false crawls, 2 nest predations, 9 sea turtle strandings.

The Sea Turtle Project headed by Dr. Russell Bennett is completed. Dr. Bennett has delivered his final report and departed. Final nests on the island are in God's hands.

Twenty

⁓

That night, Lovie awoke with a start. She opened her eyes, momentarily stunned and confused, not sure where she was. She felt afraid. Blinking, she remembered she was sleeping in the yellow guest room of her house on Tradd Street. Yes, she thought with a breath. She'd been here three days. Yet she felt anxious, in danger. She turned her head on the pillow and gasped, clutching the blanket.

A lone figure stood at the side of the bed. It was Stratton. Instinctively she ducked her head and raised her arm in a protective gesture.

"Lovie, it's me," Stratton said quietly. "I won't hurt you."

Lovie lowered her arm but still clutched her blanket higher up her chest. Stratton was staring down at her, slump shouldered. Her eyes acclimated to the dim light, and she saw him raise his fingers to the bridge of his nose and his shoulders shake.

"I'm so sorry," he said in a broken voice. "I don't know what came over me. I was so angry. I just . . . lost control."

"I know," she murmured, not knowing what else to say. She was moved by his tears but felt no pity for him.

Stratton dropped to his knees by the bed. "Can you ever forgive me?"

"I don't know," she replied honestly.

He lowered his head. "I'll make it up to you. I swear, I will."

"All I want is your promise never to raise your hand to me again."

"You have my word."

"Your promise," she urged.

"You have my promise. I will never hit you again. I never could. Lovie, I never would have hit you in the first place if—"

"Stop, please. I can't talk about that now," she interrupted him. "Please, Stratton. I'm so tired and my brain is woozy from the medicine. We have to talk. But not now."

"All right," he agreed. "I just came in to . . . I don't know. To look at you. To see how bad it was. I'm so sorry."

She felt the mattress shift as he pressed his weight upon it and rose to a stand.

"Good night, Lovie. I love you."

She turned to her side and let the medicine do its work dousing the pain.

For ten days, Lovie slept in the guest room on the pretense that, injured as she was, she couldn't be jostled. Stratton knew the true reason she slept in a separate bedroom. And Vivian, of course. But Cara accepted the excuse without question, and Palmer remained aloof. Lovie was most troubled about her son's moodiness. She'd catch glimpses of him as he walked by, peeking in. When she called to him, he disappeared.

Thanks to the miracle of phone trees and car pools, Lovie was able to coordinate all the myriad details of sending her children off to begin a new school year like a wounded general at central command. Her bed was littered with schedules and memos and newsletters that had been sent to parents during the summer. In her usual competent manner, she'd ordered all the school uniforms before leaving for the summer and they were waiting for the children in boxes when they'd returned to Charleston. This year, however, she withdrew from all her committees, boards, and church groups. Her accident injuries made for a convenient excuse. In truth, she no longer had the heart.

Vivian temporarily moved into the maid's quarters to manage the house during Lovie's recuperation. There was a tacit understanding between the women that she was also there should Lovie need her, for whatever reason. Vivian helped the children get dressed for school, packed their lunches, and prepared dinners, though once word went out that Lovie had fallen and broken her ribs, food started arriving every hour from neighbors, church members, and friends.

Lovie had never felt so fragile. Most days she felt as though her life was spinning out of control and she was a passive observer. Ensconced in the yellow-trellised bedroom, Lovie felt like a guest in her own home. In the mornings she lay huddled under the covers as boisterous noises of a fresh day echoed up the stairwell. Listening to the high-pitched "good-byes" and slamming of the door as Palmer and Cara scurried out to their rides to Porter-Gaud and Ashley Hall, she rested her cheek against her pillow and smiled, filled with longing for them.

In contrast, when she heard the roar of Stratton's Mercedes as it took off down the street, she sighed with relief. *He's gone*, she'd think, and the tension in her body eased. At such moments Lovie realized how much she still feared him and his presence in the house. At night when she closed her eyes, sometimes she'd still see his fist coming toward her.

During the first two weeks, a loose pattern of lethargy developed, a far cry from the busy, organized schedule that was normal for her. From eight each morning until three in the afternoon, Lovie knew the only peace she had since leaving the beach house. During these few hours she'd let down her guard and let her mind wander to thoughts of Russell and the time they spent together. She visualized herself back on the beach with Russell at her side. She imagined the sound of the waves, the warmth of the sun, and the taste of his lips. With him, she'd been completely, totally happy.

Flo had been right. She had kept herself busy, satisfying the expectations of a good wife and a good mother. Lovie had set high standards for herself in this arena. But what about the expectations for *herself*? This past summer, she'd found respect in the eyes of the community. And in the eyes of Russell Bennett. She'd only ever found derision in Stratton's eyes. For the first time she was proud of her achievements, not as a wife and mother but as herself. Olivia Rutledge. Remembering, Lovie couldn't continue living again with the fear and oppression she felt now. God help her and her children, but she couldn't.

Thoughts of divorce had taken root that horrible night she'd sat alone in the hospital while the doctor tended her wounds. She'd wanted to talk to Russell about them, but she couldn't contact him. She couldn't call him on the phone, couldn't write him a letter. She had been the grand designer of the conditions of the promise and they'd sworn to abide by them. *There must be no contact until the six months are over. None at all. No pressure of any kind.* Lovie didn't know how she could wait that long.

Each day that passed, she felt a little stronger, a little surer of her decision. With time, the bruises on her face healed and she looked and felt more herself. She could dress herself using only her right hand as long as she didn't choose anything with lots of buttons and wore slip-on shoes. She began rising early in the mornings to help her children get off for school, discussed menus with Vivian, and managed important appointments.

In early October, Lovie was in the kitchen with Vivian

packing her children's lunches for tomorrow when Stratton strode into the kitchen. Lovie froze with her hand reaching for an apple.

Stratton cleared his throat nervously. "Lovie, if you don't mind. Will you join me in the library?" He turned and walked away, fully expecting her to join him.

Lovie and Vivian shared a commiserating glance. Lovie was calm as she untied the apron from around her waist and set it over the back of a chair. "I guess I can finish these later."

"Go on. Don't worry about these lunches. I'll finish them up and go on to my room. The children are in their rooms," Vivian added, assuring her of this salient fact.

Lovie nodded, nervously clasped her hands, and went to join her husband in the library. The handsome walnut-paneled room was a man's room. Old and rare books lined the shelves, and on the walls hung paintings of hunting scenes, both loves of Stratton's. This is where he retired to at the day's end to pay bills, read, or play solitaire for all she knew. He went into his office after dinner and closed the door, and she wouldn't see him for hours. Tonight, however, the door was wide open.

Stratton was sitting behind his large desk in his wide burgundy leather chair. His suit jacket and tie lay over a spare chair and he'd unbuttoned the constricting top buttons of his shirt. He'd gained weight in Europe, especially around his waist and neck. She thought his loud print shirt with its long pointed collar hideous but no doubt fashionable.

He waved her in when she paused at the entrance, her stomach clenching at the sight of the crystal highball glass filled with brown liquid in his hand. She stood in the doorway and hated the thought that she might want to run. No number of apologies or kindnesses would ever remove the memory of his beating from her mind.

"Care for a drink? I have sherry . . ."

"No, thank you."

He lifted his glass, took another sip, and then leaned back in his chair. "Come in, Lovie. Sit down."

Lovie was grateful for the new granny dresses with their long flowing lines, scooped necks, and flared sleeves. She'd ordered several, all made of soft floral fabric, so she could walk around the house without the constriction of waists, belts, or zippers against her slowly healing ribs. Sitting was still an accomplishment; rising from a chair more so with the help of only one hand. She slowly eased herself onto one of a pair of tapestry Belter chairs that had been in Stratton's family for more than one hundred years. She let her elbows rest on the elaborately carved arms and clasped her hands in her lap and looked at her husband.

He smiled. "It's great to see you up and around again. You look beautiful tonight."

"Thank you. I'm getting better. But I'm still quite tired."

"Are you still taking the pain medication?"

She shook her head, thinking how awkward this was, talking across a desk with her stomach in knots. They were speaking like strangers conducting a polite interview. "No. I'm just taking aspirin when I need it. Sometimes I find a nap and a cup of herbal tea do more for me than any pill." She looked at her hands. "I realize I spend a great deal of time resting in my room . . ."

"As long as you get well." He coughed and stood from the chair to walk around to the front of the desk. He leaned against it, half sitting. "You are feeling better? Your bones are healed?"

"Not quite."

"But your face is. You look good, beautiful. More yourself."

Lovie looked at her hands.

"I never meant to hurt you."

"You struck me." She said the words softly, still looking down.

"Yes, but I didn't realize how hard. You fell over the desk. That's what broke your bones. I'd never—"

"Okay. I know," she cut him off. She couldn't bear to listen to him rationalize away his guilt like this.

He stared at her, blank faced, and then drank from his glass. The chink of ice cubes made her skin crawl.

He cleared his throat again and looked at the ice he swirled in his glass. It was the Waterford pattern that she'd chosen before their wedding. "Lovie, it's been six weeks. We should start discussing when you are coming back to *our* room."

Lovie held her breath to conceal the shudder. "I'm still not healed."

"I'll be careful. Lovie, I miss you."

"Stratton . . ."

He came from the desk and took the seat beside her. Reaching out, he held her hand in his. She knew these hands so well, she thought, looking at them. The same hands that had caressed her and that had beaten her. She saw the gold band and thought, *In good times and bad*. Her throat constricted with the words she knew she had to say. She looked up at his face. He looked older, tired.

"Stratton, you know I care deeply for you," she began. She saw immediately the barely perceptible change in his expression, noting that she had substituted the word *care* for *love*. "You were my first love."

"And I still am. I love you," he interjected urgently.

She knew he expected, wanted her to say those same words to him. She had many times before. *I love you.* Words said so frequently—when he left in the morning, on the phone, before a trip—they held little meaning. But to say them now, those three words would carry so much weight. To say them now would mislead him. So she persevered.

"I think you love the idea of me," she said. "I'm your wife, the mother of your children. I keep your home, I organize our family schedule, I'm active in our church, I entertain your guests—

I know you love me as your wife. But I honestly don't feel that you love *me*. I'm not sure you even know me."

His face screwed up with confusion as he drew back, dropping her hands. "What the hell are you talking about? Of course I know you. We've been married for fifteen years! There's nothing I don't know about you. You make it sound as though my loving you for all those things you do for me and the family is somehow wrong."

"No, no, not at all," she countered. She wanted desperately for him to understand. "I know you're grateful and appreciate all I do for you, and for the family, as you said. Truly, Stratton." She held her breath, knowing she was about to light the powder keg. "That is a kind of love. But gratitude is what you feel for a secretary or a servant for a job well done. Vivian's been with us for as long as we've been married. I'm grateful to Vivian for staying here at the house and assuming my duties, and she does it remarkably well. I depend on her. But I'm not in love with her for doing that. Does that make sense?"

Stratton leaned back in the chair. The browns and golds of the tapestry blended with his hair. "Frankly, no," he said in a cold voice. "What you're saying is that you feel gratitude to me? That you are not in love with me."

He'd said the words aloud that she could not bring herself to utter. There it was. All she had to do was say yes.

"Yes."

His hand squeezed the glass so tightly she thought it would shatter. She saw his face mottle and his expression change from shock to anguish to settle on fury. Lovie's muscles tensed. In a sudden swoop, he threw the Waterford glass across the room. Lovie ducked against the chair and heard it crash against the wall.

"It's that guy," he roared. His hands grasped the arms of the chair until his knuckles whitened. "That Dr. Somebody."

"No, it's not him."

"So there is another man!" he shouted with a ring of triumph.

Lovie swallowed hard. "I didn't say that."

He rose to his feet and began to pace the room. Lovie clasped her hands so fiercely in her lap they felt numb.

"I knew it! When you didn't name him, I dared to hope I was wrong and that there really was no one else, that what I'd heard was just some nasty rumor. And to think I felt so horrible that I hit you. So guilty. I'll never be able to forget the sight of you on the floor, seeing what I'd done. But I believed that if I worked hard enough, groveled enough, begged for your forgiveness, that someday you would grant it to me and we'd move on. We could be a family. But now . . ."

He stopped and looked down at her, and his gaze cut her heart out with its scathing coldness. "Now I know you're no better than a whore."

Lovie's breath escaped her, and she hunched over as though physically hit in the solar plexus.

"Now the tables are turned!" he ground out. "I'm no longer the villain seeking forgiveness in this scenario." His shoulders drew back in righteousness as he paced. "I'm the wronged husband, the cuckolded fool. I was out working hard for my family, and you're vacationing with no thought but to your own pleasure." He stopped and pointed his finger as he bellowed, "It's you who needs forgiveness. Not me!"

Lovie cowered, each word a dagger.

Stratton stopped pacing and went to sit again in his chair behind the desk. He leaned far back and crossed his arms across his chest, trying hard to restrain his fury. Sweat beaded on his brow, and he panted like a horse after a long race. The emotions were so strong, the words spoken so colossal and irretrievable; they both retreated to their corners, exhausted.

Time cooled his rage and tempered Lovie's fear. She felt

spent but rallied her waning energy. That, she knew, was merely round two of this match.

Stratton rested his hand on some papers and thrummed his fingers deep in thought. Then he looked up. "God, Lovie, how did we get here?" He sighed and said with magnanimity, "I can try to forgive you."

Lovie, who was still hunched over her thighs in desolation, slowly raised herself to an upright position. She lifted her chin and spoke clearly though softly: "Thank you. Do you seek my forgiveness as well?"

He snorted in superior disbelief. "I think not."

"I see. And you see that beating as . . ."

"Deserved."

"Ah." She had to look off, not seeing the books or the paintings, only feeling the desperate squeezing of her heart. She'd been right. She mattered that little. Well, all right, then, she told herself. That made her decision that much easier. "I'm just curious," she said, facing him again. "What about *your* affairs? Do you think I should forgive you for those?"

He looked at his fingers on the desk, then again at her. "What affairs?"

She laughed a short, bitter sound. "I see."

He immediately changed his expression as the righteousness fled from his face, and in its place she saw a pained, pleading man. "Lovie, let's drop this entire pretense. I'm sick to death of fighting with you. I didn't call you in here to cast guilt or blame. Let's just say we're both guilty of some sin and let it go. There's no building from that. I want us to get back to where we were before."

She lowered her shoulders and felt curiously unafraid. She looked in his dark brown eyes, as rich and as hard as the walnut walls. "Stratton, try to understand. I don't want to go back where we were before. I can't. I'm not the woman I was. The woman who did your bidding without question, the woman you belittled, the woman you raged at when you were drunk. That woman doesn't exist anymore. Stratton, I can't be that wife."

"Can't? You *are* my wife."

She shook her head. "I want a divorce."

He stared at her for a long moment, his face implacable.

"Stratton, I'm sorry. I didn't mean to blurt it out like that. The last thing I want to do is hurt you. But you have to see there's no point in continuing our marriage. I'm not asking for anything from you. You can have the house, the furniture, the money, everything. I don't want anything from you. The children and I will just go someplace else to live. I won't make it difficult, I promise."

His brow rose in an inscrutable face. "The children? You think you can take my children from me?"

Lovie licked her lips as a new fear wormed into her heart. "Not take them, surely. We can work out a custody arrangement."

"No," he said gruffly, the word bubbling with fury and intent.

Lovie felt a wave of a cold. "What do you mean no?"

He stood up then, his hands on his desk, and leaned forward, eyes blazing. "I mean no! Do you think for a moment I'll hand over my children?"

"They're my children," Lovie cried. "I'm their mother! No court will take them from me."

"You're an unfit mother!" he shouted, pointing at her. "A whore who had an affair under the nose of her own children. Who do you think you are? This is my town. My name means something here. Divorce me and I swear I'll see to it that the children are taken away from you."

She pushed herself up from the chair, gasping at the pain of the sudden movement on her injured ribs. "I won't listen to this. You're too angry."

"Get back here."

She felt numb but kept moving, one foot in front of the other. She had to get out, away from him. She panted with the effort, but fear kept her moving. As she walked up the stairs, he came into the hall and bellowed after her.

"Try to divorce me and I'll crucify you to the cross!"

Twenty-one

◄━━

The offices of Robert Lee Davis were located on Broad Street near Meeting Street in the heart of Charleston. This intersection was known as the venerable Four Corners of Law, where the laws of God and man were said to meet. Charleston City Hall was located on the northeast corner; the Charleston County Courthouse on the northwest corner; the United States Federal Courthouse and Post Office on the southwest corner; and St. Michael's Church on the southeast corner.

Lovie passed the flower and sweetgrass basket ladies who sold their wares on the street corners as she made her way up the stairs of the white Federal-style building. She still couldn't drive with a broken wrist and she didn't want anyone to know where she was headed today. So she'd walked the six blocks along crumbling sidewalks on the unusually steamy October day. She wore panty hose, dress flats, and a loose-fitting A-line dress that was forgiving enough to let a little breeze flutter the hem. She hated the nylons that were de rigueur in the city and made her thighs sweat in the heat, but at least she could manipulate the new panty hose with one hand much better than she could the garters she remembered only too well.

As she walked, she thought women's fashions these days seemed to be anything goes. Hemlines were up and down, fabrics were neutral brown or gaudy colors, and hair was trailing down the back or cut short like a boy's. Women walked the streets dressed in outlandish outfits and wild prints she couldn't imagine when she was a young woman walking these same streets. But these brave women were few compared to the rest of the locals, who still wore their hair coiffed and attempted the new styles with a tad more decorum than Yankee girls up north. Although, with her broken ribs, the idea of going braless was appealing. She paused to catch her breath at the top of the stairs.

A gentleman opened the heavy brass door for her and she met a wall of deliciously air-conditioned coolness. Though the lobby was cold and formal with marble and brass, the third-floor law office waiting room was decorated traditionally with antiques and heavy silk drapes, making it appear more like someone's living room. A mature-looking secretary led her directly to Mr. Robert Davis's office and knocked gently on the door. They both heard, "Come in!"

"Go right in. Mr. Davis is expecting you." The secretary opened wide the door and stepped back, allowing her to pass.

Robert Lee Davis was small in stature compared to his impressive reputation. Small boned and slender, he sat behind an enormous partners' desk stacked high with papers. He was dwarfed by them. But his smile was gigantic, and he stood to walk directly to her side as the secretary discreetly closed the door behind her as she left.

"Olivia!" he said jovially. His red bow tie made his face appear cheerier.

"Bobby Lee," she responded, offering her hand. He took it and held it warmly. His owlish eyes scanned her face from behind wire-rim glasses. She smiled, but her toes curled in her shoes as she wondered if he could see any traces of the bruises under her makeup.

Bobby Lee Davis had been the Rutledge family lawyer for as long as she'd been married. He was a contemporary of Stratton's, but for reasons unknown to her, they didn't like each other. The Davis law firm had represented the Rutledge family for generations and so still managed their family issues and wealth distribution.

Lovie had always liked the diminutive man with the brilliant legal mind and his old-world manners. Like her, Bobby Lee was a nature buff, who took on pro bono cases to preserve and protect local wildlife and landscape. They'd formed a fast friendship over the years, and even though Stratton had moved his business matters to another law firm, Lovie always turned to Bobby Lee for her own legal advice.

"Take a seat, please," he said, ushering her to a celery-green velvet chair.

Lovie still had discomfort as she maneuvered herself into the chair. Bobby Lee rushed to assist her, his face troubled. Thankfully, he stayed on Lovie's side of the mountainous desk, which allowed them to talk in a more personal manner.

"I'd heard you were injured," he said, taking a Chippendale chair beside her and inching it closer. "Deborah sent you something, shrimp, I think it was."

"Yes, thank you. It was delicious. I hope she got my thank-you note."

Bobby Lee smiled and lifted his brows as though to say he didn't know but probably. "You fell down the stairs, is that it?"

The way that he said the words and the dubious look he cast her from over the rim of his glasses told her he didn't believe that sorry excuse. She was left to wonder how many other people in Charleston wondered.

"It could happen," she said with a slight laugh.

"It could. But your being here today makes me think that perhaps it didn't."

Lovie sighed and shook her head. "I'm speaking to you in confidence now."

His smile fell, and he assumed a professional expression. His owlish eyes grew hawkish. "Lawyer-client privilege."

Lovie launched into the long story of her summer, leaving out none of the details, not even those that embarrassed her. She had to be completely honest with Bobby Lee so that he could adequately advise her. She was grateful that he didn't shake his head or act surprised during the telling. He didn't speak save for a point of clarification. When she was finished, she told him why she had come.

"I want to go forward with a divorce."

"I see." He rubbed his jaw, then tilted his head, speculating. "Olivia . . . Lovie. You're sure about this? You don't want to go out and buy yourself some big, vulgar diamond instead?"

She smiled but shook her head.

Bobby Lee pursed his lips, then released a short, resigned sigh. "We're now at the day I always feared would come."

"What do you mean?"

"I've advised you for years to maintain some control of the money you gave to Stratton after you married. It was substantial."

"He's my husband. He invested it into our house and our business. It's *our* money."

"No, Lovie, it's not. It's *his* money. The deed of the house is in his name. The money that you"—he lifted his hands to make the classic quotation mark sign—"*gave* to his business is not likely recorded in your name. Other than a small trust fund and that cottage on the Isle of Palms, you may end up with little to nothing. Naturally your lawyer would fight for the money you brought to the marriage, the increased value of the house while you lived in it, and more. But there's no guarantee."

"I don't care about the money. I already told him that."

"You mustn't be naïve, Lovie. You've never *not* had money. It's tough out there in the real world without a cushion to fall back on. How will you raise the children? Do you have a job? Insurance? Do you even know what the minimum wage is these days?"

She licked her lips, feeling the first of flames of fear. "The only thing I care about is custody of my children. Stratton said he'd never let me take the children from him."

Bobby Lee's brows furrowed while his long, narrow fingers tapped his thigh. "Would he expose you?"

Lovie swallowed down the flush of shame. She had to be realistic and face all the questions a lawyer, and eventually a judge, would ask. "He said he would. He said no judge would award custody to an unfit mother."

"Can you plead recrimination? That is to say, do you have proof of adultery on his part?"

"He went to Europe with his secretary," she offered.

Bobby Lee offered a wan smile. "If traveling with a secretary were grounds for divorce, the divorce rate in this country would skyrocket. You'll need better proof than that."

Lovie's face turned scarlet as she admitted what she'd known in her heart for years. "He's been lying and cheating for years. He calls them late nights with the boys, and I believed him." She put her hand to her face. "That he could think I was so naïve, or he cared so little he tossed that pitiful excuse my way." She shook her head sadly. "Either way, what does that say about his feelings for me? I've had women calling the house asking for him. And every once in a while he wears a new tie, a pair of cuff links, things I'm sure he didn't buy for himself. I know he's been unfaithful. But I don't have proof."

Bobby Lee was silent a moment, his chin in his palm. "By the way, do you know if Stratton has proof?"

She sat wide-eyed and alert. She thought immediately of Palmer. But he'd said he only saw them holding hands and she believed him. She knew she was safe with Flo and Miranda. "He might argue that I told him I did."

"Did you?"

She shook her head. "No. He inferred it."

"Good." Bobby Lee steepled his fingers in thought. "Keep in mind that until 1949, divorce was illegal in this state. Now things have changed, of course. The way I see it, we have two grounds for divorce: adultery on his side and physical abuse on yours. We've discussed the adultery. We'll have to see what proof he has, if any. That is a major point. Without proof, he has nothing to fight you with.

"Now to your issue. To establish beating as grounds for divorce, the plaintiff must establish that a beating, or beatings, has taken place."

"Stratton has slapped me several times, but he's only beaten me once and he swears he never will again."

"Did you seek treatment?"

"I went to the hospital."

"Good. We have evidence of one serious beating."

Lovie nodded, silently thanking Miranda and Flo for insisting that she go.

"Assuming Stratton does have evidence of your infidelity and chooses to fight the divorce and seek full custody, you could be in for a battle. Stratton's lawyer will go after the adultery issue in a big way. You may have to be prepared to name your lover, if only to convince the judge that there was only one extramarital affair."

"No. I won't do that."

Bobby Lee went on, ignoring her outburst. "We would have

to establish your character to argue that this was a single event and that you are not, shall we say, wanton." He looked at her questioningly.

"No! Heavens, no. There was only one. And it wasn't an affair. Well, it was, but it wasn't casual. I'm trying to say . . ."

Bobby Lee reached out to tap her knee, shaking his head to silence her. "The law deals with facts, not emotion. You will also have to establish that though you broke your marriage vows once, that unfortunate slip is over now and that at the time you were very discreet." He looked again at her with question in his eyes.

"Yes," she replied quickly. "Very discreet."

"Good."

"Bobby Lee, do we have to go through all these sordid details? What about this no-fault divorce I've heard about?"

"Ah, yes. Well, it's a new pleading that began in California a few years back. South Carolina has adopted it. But if Stratton chooses to fight the divorce, then this is moot." He paused. "Lovie, I'm not going to speak to you as a lawyer now. I'm going to speak to you as a friend."

Lovie returned a wobbly smile.

"Attorneys will tell you that they will fight tooth and nail for everything they can get and how they'll need to do A, B, C, and D. All with the meter running. But I'm going to tell you now what the State of South Carolina will likely do. They'll grant you a divorce. You will lose your house. If I know Stratton as well as I think I do, he has already hidden all evidence of the money you've given him. With proof of adultery, they may not give you alimony, but they may give you child support until the children reach eighteen years of age. However, it is my opinion that there is a strong chance that given your inability to provide financially, your lack of a job or career, and your questionable character as revealed in the court, you could lose chief custody of your children. You may have to settle for visiting rights."

"No," she said, but it was little more than a whisper. Lovie sat rooted to the chair, numb with shock.

"As a man who has lived here all his life, a lawyer whose family has practiced law here for generations, and a friend who cares about your well-being, let me remind you of what should be obvious. It may be true that a lot of things are changing in this city, but the Rutledge name is, and always will be, revered here. John Rutledge is buried just down the block. I can't say I'm not worried that our jurisdiction will look with sympathy on their beloved son, Stratton Middleton Rutledge, should he seek to keep his children in a scandalous divorce brought on by his adulterous wife."

Lovie brought her hand to cover the cry that erupted from her mouth.

"Lovie, please," he said, putting his hand over hers in friendship. "That was harsh, but it is only a sampling of what you would have to face. And your children would have to face. Please, think long and hard about the repercussions of your decision should you decide to go through with this."

He rose and returned to stand behind his desk. He buzzed his secretary on the intercom. "Judy, could you get me Susan Raymond's phone number, please?" He idly moved a few papers on the desk, looking up when Judy entered the room, swiftly delivered a business card to Bobby Lee, then promptly left.

Bobby Lee walked back to the front of the desk and looked at Lovie with compassion in his eyes. "I'm a family lawyer, not a divorce lawyer. If you choose to go through with this—and I don't recommend you do—you may be left with nothing. You can damn well be sure Stratton will get the best and meanest pit bull of a lawyer money can buy." He handed her the business card. Lovie stared at the small ecru card through watery eyes.

"Call Susan," Bobby Lee told her. "She's better."

• • •

Lovie walked with frantic purpose, her head bent, arms pumping, disregarding the pain in her ribs. She walked the half mile from Bobby Lee's office to her mother's house on East Bay Street. As she paced, she felt as though the walls of the historic, pastel-colored houses on the narrow street were closing in on her. She couldn't catch her breath.

At last she reached the Battery and the coral stucco walls of her mother's home. The heavy black wrought-iron gate squeaked as she pushed it open and entered the cool shade of her garden. She stumbled across the cobblestone driveway to the rear elevator. It was a small rickety box with an accordion steel door, but it rumbled up to the third floor, letting her out at her mother's grand piazza. Lovie knocked on the door with her good hand, praying that her mother wasn't at some bridge or mah-jongg game or having cocktails with friends.

"Please, please, please be here," she murmured, then, with unutterable relief, heard the click of heels against wood flooring. She put a hand up to smooth her hair, then turned her face to the door as it swung open.

"Lovie!" Dee Dee cried as her mouth slipped open. She wore green-and-navy-striped pants and a navy cotton shirt with tiny gold buttons. A flash of gold at the ears and around her neck made her outfit complete. "You look exhausted. What are you doing here? I thought you were still recuperating at home."

"I was . . . am," she replied, breathless. "Mama, I need to talk with you." Her voice broke.

"Come in!" Dee Dee's face shifted from surprise to concern as she stepped back to let Lovie walk through.

Her mother had the entire top floor of what was once a single-family home. The East Battery had some of the most elegant and historic homes in the city, and finding this rare gem was a coup. The two-bedroom condo had high ceilings and tons of windows, and though the kitchen was small and almost useless, the huge porch with the expansive view of the harbor made it a must-have for a woman who never cared to cook again.

"Whatever is the matter?" Dee Dee crooned as she followed Lovie into the living room. She stood with her hands clasped in front of her. "Darling, do sit down. You're pacing like a bantam rooster and it's making me nervous."

Lovie tossed her purse onto the white sofa and carefully sat down beside it. She eased back into the down cushion. Once she was off her feet, her fatigue hit her like a brick. She brought her hands to her face, curled her legs up on the sofa, and began to cry.

Dee Dee hurried to a side table to grab tissues from a Chinese export porcelain box. "Here, your mascara is running. And if you must put your feet on the sofa, please take your shoes off. That's silk. Now tell me. What's this all about?"

Lovie sniffed and tore at her tissue. "Oh, Mama, I'm so confused. I don't know what to do."

"About what, honey? You have to go back to the beginning. Does this have something to do with Stratton?"

Lovie nodded as she wiped the tears from her face and blew her nose. The release of tears helped calm her after her panicked walk. She set the tissue on the sofa and took a deep breath. "I'm okay. Can I have some water, please?"

"Where are my manners? Of course. I was just so flustered seeing you in such a state. Now don't you move and I'll bring you some. Would you like anything a little stronger?"

"Just water, thanks."

Dee Dee picked up the used tissue between two fingers and went off to the kitchen.

Lovie slid her shoes off and stretched her legs out so her ankles rested on the glass and brass coffee table. Taking deep, cleansing breaths, she eased the pressure from her ribs and calmed her ragged nerves. Her meeting with Bobby Lee had unnerved her. She'd walked into his office fully expecting him to tell her not to worry, that Stratton could never take her children from her. The reality was quite different and it had scared her and shaken her to her core.

Dee Dee came back quickly, carrying a tray with a glass of ice water and two glasses of sherry. She delicately nudged Lovie's feet off the table, then set the tray down. Lovie adjusted her position, aware that her mother had no clue how uncomfortable this simple action still was for her.

Her mother sat beside Lovie and handed her a sherry. "You seem like you could use a little something—for medicinal purposes. Listen to your mama, now."

Lovie took a sip of the sherry. It was sweet and smooth and perfect. "Thank you, Mama."

"Now suppose you tell me what this is all about."

Lovie set the slim sherry glass on the table. "I went to see Bobby Lee. I just came from his office."

Dee Dee's attention sharpened. "You walked all the way here from Bobby Lee's? In your condition? No wonder you're flushed. You're supposed to be taking it easy. Whatever was so important that you had to see your lawyer today?"

Lovie's heart pounded. She had wondered on the way over whether to tell her mother. She'd always been so supportive of Stratton and proud to be his mother-in-law. Lovie had come because she had nowhere else to go. Where did a daughter go but to her mother when she was feeling lost?

"Mama, I went to see Bobby Lee because I want a divorce."

Dee Dee didn't reply right away. She appeared to be too stunned to speak.

Lovie rushed on. "I can't keep on in this marriage." Tears flooded her eyes. "Mama, he hit me."

"He *hit* you?"

Lovie looked at her, incredulous. "You didn't really think I fell down the stairs?"

Dee Dee appeared confused. "Why, yes. I did. That's what you told me."

Lovie's short laugh was laced with disbelief. Maybe her reputation was safe in Charleston, after all, she thought. It was all a matter of how closely one cared to look.

"Well, I didn't," Lovie told her. "The bruises on my face, my broken bones, they're from him."

Dee Dee's hand flew to her mouth and her fingers trembled. "No. He did that to you?"

Lovie nodded, reaching for another tissue. "A few weeks ago I came home from the beach and Stratton was there," she began, dabbing at her eyes. "I didn't even know he'd returned from Europe. He didn't call, wire . . ." She lifted her shoulders. "He'd been drinking." She looked at the cast on her wrist, and her lips began shaking. "He beat me, Mama. He beat me badly."

"Oh, my dear," Dee Dee cried, genuinely distressed. She opened her arms. Lovie leaned into them, resting her head on Dee Dee's shoulder as her mother wrapped her arms around her. Lovie couldn't remember the last time her mother had comforted her in this way. In the crook of her arm she smelled her mother's Chanel perfume and the faint sweet fragrance of her face powder. Scent held memories, and she knew why she'd come here directly from the lawyer. She cried for a while, comforted by these tears in her mother's arms.

When she felt more in control, she sat up and reached for another tissue. She wiped her face and blew her nose, feeling like she could talk now about the problem that brought her here for her mother's advice.

"Mama, Bobby Lee told me I could lose custody of the children."

"But that's preposterous," Dee Dee replied. "Everyone knows the mother gets the children."

"That's what I thought. But, there may be a problem

because . . ." She hesitated. She loved her mother, but their relationship always had ups and downs, usually correlating with her mother's moods. Dee Dee was always there to advise her on manners, fashion, flowers, and the arts. But she had never been Lovie's confidante. Her father was the one she couldn't keep a secret from, and she missed him terribly now.

Lovie realized in that moment that she couldn't, wouldn't, tell her mother about her relationship with Russell. Sadly, she knew Dee Dee couldn't be trusted with that secret. Bobby Lee's question flashed in her mind: *Does Stratton have proof of your infidelity?* Dee Dee was a social bee who buzzed about dipping into the nectar of gossip and moving on from flower to flower with it. Lovie could imagine her mother at a tête-à-tête with her friends, rolling her eyes in dramatic sympathy as she bravely told the sad tale of her daughter's *grande passion*, her *liaison amoureuse*.

"Because of what, dear?" Dee Dee asked again.

"Well," Lovie replied, scrambling in her mind for a suitable response. Fortunately, she found one in the truth. "Because of Stratton's influence in this town."

"Really?" Dee Dee sat straighter and her lip curled barely perceptibly. "It may be true the Rutledge name holds weight. But the Simmonses are a proud family, too." She plucked at the cuff of her sleeve. "Though we are in Charleston now. We're not in Aiken anymore. If Bobby Lee says so, I'd trust him. Oh, this is all so disturbing! Surely you can't mean to go through with this nonsense of a divorce. When I think of the scandal . . ."

"Mama!" Lovie exclaimed, pulling back. The two women were sitting knee to knee on the sofa. "You can't possibly think I should stay with him after he beat me?"

"Don't get all upset. Let's talk this through," she replied in a conciliatory tone. She bent over the table and gracefully lifted her sherry glass and took a dainty sip. "Is he sorry?"

"He says he is. But what difference does that make?"

"Never underestimate the power of an apology. Especially from a gentleman."

"How can I be sure he won't hit me again?"

"Oh, I can't imagine that he would."

No, you couldn't, Lovie thought. *You've never had to face a problem like this. Daddy would never have laid a hand on you. Or me.*

Dee Dee put her glass back on the table. "Darling, whatever did you do to provoke him like that?"

"You think it's *my* fault?"

"I didn't say that. But it seems so out of character for Stratton, that's all. He's a good husband and father. He has a bit of a temper, we all know that. But he's never laid a hand on you before. And never the children."

"You don't know what you're talking about. Stratton is a strict disciplinarian, especially with Palmer. That boy's received the belt plenty of times." She shuddered just to think of the sting of leather against skin. "But he never will again," she ground out.

"Boys need a firmer hand," Dee Dee said in a cajoling tone as she rose to walk across the room. She took a cigarette from a porcelain box on the side table and offered Lovie one.

Lovie shook her head, wondering how her mother didn't know she'd never smoked a cigarette in her life.

Dee Dee lit it and waved the match in the air, extinguishing the flame. She walked to the chair across from Lovie, exhaling a long plume of smoke. Lovie wondered how many times she'd watched that display. She waved her hand in front of her face, trying to get rid of the annoying trail of smoke.

"This conversation is so upsetting." Dee Dee went to one of the large windows and widened the opening. She returned to settle in her chair near Lovie, sighing heavily as though she was bearing the weight of the world on her shoulders. She leaned over to the ashtray in an agitated manner to tap the ash from her cigarette with a coral-tipped nail.

"Naturally I can't condone his hitting you. What mother could?" Dee Dee looked at her cigarette. "But I do believe that Stratton is a good man, deep down. Lovie, is there such a thing as a perfect man? Your father had his faults, bless his heart. If Stratton promises never to hit you again, and the two of you go get some help, talk to your minister or some therapist, I truly do believe you can work this whole"—she shook her hands like she was trying to get rid of something nasty that was sticking to them—"*mess* out." She glanced up, gauging Lovie's reaction.

Lovie kept her face still while inside, her heart was sinking. Taking her quiet as a positive sign, her mother continued. "Stratton travels a great deal, honey. Weeks at a time! And Lord knows he spends more on guns and fishing rods than any man I know, but those hobbies do keep a man out of the house a spell. And you go to the beach house in the summer. And," she added, brightening as a new thought entered her head, "don't you have separate bedrooms on account of your injuries? You could maintain those. Decorate yours all frilly, like you never could in a room you had to share with a man. Be extravagant, darling. Lots of fringe. He can afford it and you deserve it. Why, I know several friends whose marriages have lasted for decades under such arrangements. You wouldn't be the first. Or the last." She sat back again, confident she'd made her point.

Lovie let her face remain as smooth as glass as she studied her mother's face. Though it was artfully made up, the thick foundation meant to hide defects in fact revealed all the more clearly the deep lines of her mother's advancing age. The dewiness of youth that she'd had as a young bride in the thirties and forties had faded. Her parents' marriage had survived World War II and unspeakable tragedy. And yet, when her father had returned home, he'd found a world and social code not unlike that which had been firmly in place when he'd left. Michael Simmons had returned *home*. In the sixties, if her brother had lived, he might have been sent to Vietnam. Twenty years later, he, too, would have returned home to an unchanged world in Charleston. Lovie was brought up in this world; it was what she knew—and loved. It made up, she recognized, who she was.

Yet to hear her mother make light of what happened to her, to hear her mother send her back to a place that was a danger, to hear her mother making her terrible marriage sound like a slumber party—decorating with fringe—she could feel the sparks of anger licking at the glass. Inside, she felt ready to shatter.

"The other night," Lovie said in a low, shaky voice, "when I told him I wanted a divorce, he had that look in his eyes again. Like he wanted to hit me again. Mama, I . . . I'm afraid of him."

"You *told* him you wanted a divorce?" Dee Dee was appalled.

Lovie was flustered by the question. "Yes. Of course. That's why I went to see Bobby Lee."

"Oh, Lovie . . ." her mother moaned in distress.

"Stratton was horrible, Mama! He can be so mean and vindictive. You don't know that part of him. He called me terrible names and screamed at me that he'd take the children from me. They had to have heard him! I don't love him anymore. I just want to end this marriage. I'm only thirty-eight years old. I can start my life over again."

Dee Dee sat tensely with a straight back and gave her daughter a no-fooling come-to-Jesus glare. "Olivia Simmons Rutledge, you are no longer a child. You can't come running to your mama, boohooing and asking her to help you clean up the mess you made. You're an adult. A married woman with two children to take care of. You have to get hold of yourself and face your responsibilities. Do you think your father and I had nothing but roses and kisses all during our marriage? There were hard times. Times I wanted to pack my bag and go back to my mother. But I stayed and we made it work. Together. That's what married people do. They stick together and find a way to preserve the family. You put up with what you have to to make family work!"

She bent over the cocktail table to set her cigarette on the crystal ashtray, and when she sat back she raised her chin, obviously ready to make a pronouncement.

"Darling, I raised you better than this. Whether you're from Charleston or Aiken, or anywhere else south of the Mason Dixon Line, you hold inside of you the strength of Southern womanhood, handed down to you from me, your grandmothers, and beyond. You carry it in your genes. Listen to your mama, now. We women are the heart and soul of the family. The husband may be the trunk and our children the branches, but we are the sap that keeps it alive. Our family roots run deep. We do *not* rip them out. We cannot."

Then she reached over to take hold of Lovie's right hand. "I don't want to know any more of what's happened between you and Stratton. That's none of my business. But as your mother I'm advising you to run home and make peace with your husband. Do whatever you need to do to fix your marriage."

"Mama, I . . ." Lovie squeezed her mother's hand. "I came here for your help. Stratton has all my money. I've nowhere to go. Can I stay here? Please? Just until I figure things out?"

Dee Dee released Lovie's hand and turned to retrieve her cigarette. After she took a puff, she tilted her head and exhaled a plume of smoke.

"Absolutely not. I'm sorry, Olivia. I've said all I'm going to say on the matter. You made your bed, darling. Now you must lie in it."

Twenty-two

Lovie left her mother's house feeling worse than when she'd arrived. She was more confused than ever and needed the long walk to Tradd Street to clear her head. She wasn't completely sure whether it was her mother's words or the smoke from her cigarette that upset her stomach so much.

She often thought that parts of this golden peninsula where she lived, known as South of Broad, were like a painting come to life in pastel shades. Everywhere she looked there was history; she couldn't escape it. Charleston was a city out of a time long ago when wealthy rice planters built homes of grandeur along the Battery and so many churches with spiraling steeples that pierced the heavens that it became known as the Holy City. For three hundred years, this city was a model for all Southern women: she was beautiful, graceful—and a survivor. She withstood plagues, hurricanes, wars, poverty, fires, earthquakes, all with grace and a dignity born of never forgetting her proud heritage.

Lovie felt the heat of her tears as she walked along the cobbled streets. Each turn of her ankle in the crooked pavement brought a sharp pain, like the lash of punishment. She'd forgotten who she was and where she was from. This was her home.

There was no escaping, nowhere else for her to go. Even if she could leave, how would she support her children? She had no skills, no work experience. Bobby Lee and her mother had made her situation perfectly, painfully clear.

She felt unspeakable relief when she reached the white stucco walls surrounding her property. It was an impressive house, secure and strong, with a large black wooden gate at the entrance. She pushed open the heavy door and entered the cool of her garden. It was late; her children would already be home. God help her, she hoped her husband was not. She felt utterly spent.

"Miss Lovie, what's happened to you?" Vivian called out at seeing Lovie enter the kitchen door. She was standing at the sink, scrubbing potatoes. "You look like you're being chased by the devil."

Lovie almost smiled at how close to the truth that was. She set her purse on a chair and leaned against the back for support. "I went to see my mother."

Vivian frowned, silently expressing her opinion of Dee Dee Simmons. "I was getting worried at the hour. Ready to call out the guard!"

"I should have called," Lovie replied, wiping the perspiration from her brow. "I'm sorry you worried." She looked up at the wall clock. "You'll want to be going soon. I wanted to talk to you."

Vivian dried her hands on her apron and came closer, her eyes searching Lovie's face with concern. "You look ready to drop. Do you want some coffee?"

Lovie shook her head. "Vivian, I need to get away," she said. "Just for the night. It's terribly short notice, but can you possibly stay?"

"Yes'm, I can stay. But sit and let me get you some water before you faint."

Lovie didn't want to sit, yet she was exhausted from more exercise than she'd had in weeks. She slumped into the wood chair.

Vivian handed her a glass and, sipping, Lovie felt the cool water flow along her arid throat. She'd been holding her cry in for so long her throat felt raw.

"Are you all right?" Vivian asked, standing watch over her. Her tone was doubtful.

"Yes . . . no. I just need time to think. If you'll stay for the night, I'll pack a bag and leave right away. I won't be far. I just need a little time alone. I'll be back tomorrow morning."

Vivian eyed her suspiciously. "Where you going?"

"I'm going to the beach house."

A low voice thundered from the hall. "You're going *where?*"

Lovie and Vivian both swung their heads to the doorway to see Stratton standing there in his dark gray suit, his tie loosened at the neck. He still carried his briefcase.

Lovie set down the glass and swallowed the lump of fear that was rising in her throat.

Stratton stepped into the kitchen. "Did I hear you say you're going to the beach house?"

She swallowed again and almost coughed, her mouth was so dry. "Yes. I thought I'd go for the night. I need to get away. To think."

His eyes darkened. "Who is going with you?"

She knew what he was asking and she looked directly into his eyes. "No one. I swear on my children, I am going alone." When he didn't reply, she added, "There is no one else there, except of course Miranda. Everyone else has left."

She knew they were talking in code and that he understood she was telling him she was not going to meet her lover.

"Maybe I'll go with you," he said.

"You can," she replied evenly. "But I wish you wouldn't. I went to see Bobby Lee today." She saw his eyes widen slightly, enough to know that news had surprised him. "I also went to see my mother. I need time to think."

Stratton knew the truth when he heard it, and his shoulders lowered. She saw again a range of emotions flicker across his face, and she realized with a stab of regret that he was suffering, too.

Cara burst into the room. Her eyes were suspicious, leaving no doubt that she'd heard the tense words between her parents. She came to stand by her mother and leaned slightly against her chair.

"What's going on?" she asked, her eyes on her father.

"It's none of your business," Stratton told her.

"I thought I heard Mama say she was going to the beach house," she said.

"I might be, Cara," Lovie replied.

"Then I'm going, too," she exclaimed.

"Cara . . ." Lovie began to tell her she could not, but Stratton beat her to it.

"You're not going anywhere," he told her sharply. "And neither is your mother!"

Cara was lightning fast as she stepped in front of her father and boldly shouted, "She can go if she wants to. You're not the boss of her!"

It all happened in split-second timing. Stratton's face colored, and he raised his hand in the air. Cara took a step back, turning her shoulder in an instinctive protective move.

"Stratton!" Lovie shouted, jumping to her feet, knocking over her chair.

Stratton stilled his hand midair.

Vivian grabbed Cara's shoulders and pushed her along out of the room. Stratton dropped his hand to his side with an anguished sigh.

There was a long, pained silence between Stratton and Lovie as they struggled with what had almost happened.

Stratton spoke first. "I wouldn't have struck her. I swear it."

Lovie couldn't reply. She didn't believe him. That was the cold truth of it.

"What's happening to this family?" Stratton said with a cry in his voice. His face creased with anguish as he ran his shaky hand through his hair. "We need to fix this mess between us, Lovie. It's starting to affect our kids. My heart is breaking. I'm at the end of my tether. I raised my hand to my own daughter! Don't you know that's killing me? That's how far you're pushing me. But I didn't strike her. Thank the Lord, He held my hand back. I'm not an evil man, Lovie."

His voice broke and his eyes filled with tears. Lovie felt her heart twist in her chest.

"And Cara . . ." he continued. "Can't you see what's happening to our daughter? I tried to warn you about it, but you refuse to pay it any mind."

Lovie listened, hearing the frustration in his words, the hint of anger lurking. He was rationalizing again, blaming the incident on her.

"All I've been worried about is coming true," he expanded. "She's got a mouth on her and doesn't know her place." He shook his head, his lips a tight line. He took a breath, regaining his composure. Then his voice became pleading in tone, cajoling. "She needs her mother's guidance now more than ever. But how can she get that with you hiding up in that room all the time? The family needs you. I need you. We're falling apart, Lovie. Can't you see that? God help me, I don't know what to do." He raised his fingers to the bridge of his nose, holding back the tears pooling there.

Lovie could count on one hand the times she'd seen Stratton cry. The first was at the birth of Palmer. Then Cara. The third was at her bedside, when he'd witnessed what he'd done to her. And now this. Each time, she realized, she was the source of his tears.

Reaching out, she placed her palm on his chest and patted it as gently as she would her child. "I understand, Stratton," she said in a low voice. Her energy was waning. She felt her knees go watery at the weight of her decision. "I hear what you're telling me and I'm taking it to heart. I'm going to the beach house tonight, to ponder all you've just said, and all Bobby Lee and my mother said. And I have to listen to my heart as well. I can't do that here. There's too much noise. I need a little time to reflect so that when I return, we can talk again."

Stratton put his hand over hers and wrapped an arm around her, holding her close. "You go, then," he said with his lips against her hair. "Then you come home, where you belong. I love you. And I'm sorry."

Fall had come to the Isle of Palms. An early cold front brought a chill to the dawn air. Lovie wrapped a favorite patchwork wool and cashmere shawl of muted blues and creams around her shoulders, slipped her bare feet into sandals, and stepped off the rear porch of her beach house out into the still-gray morning. She lifted her nose and breathed in the heavy scent of pluff mud. It was strong this morning, and she smiled, feeling reassurance flow through her blood.

She was home.

She carefully made her way along the narrow beach path in the dim light. It was bordered by high walls of sand dunes that were crisscrossed with wildflower vines as thick as kudzu. September had brought two tropical storms that had wreaked havoc on the remaining sea turtle nests. But the heavy rains and the cool air had gifted the Lowcountry with brilliant color. The undulating dunes were blanketed with countless cheery heads of yellow primrose, gaillardia, and the tiny, sensual wild purple orchids she adored. She bent to inspect a primrose, her favorite, letting its soft buttery yellow blossom, damp with dew, rest in her fingertips.

These seemingly weak flowers had deep roots, she thought. Roots that went so deep they anchored even in the soft sand. Another lesson, she told herself, and left the blossom to the thousands of migrating birds and monarch butterflies that needed its sweetness to survive.

Her heels dug into the cool sand as she climbed the final, tall sand dune. She heard the roar of the ocean before she could see it. She reached the top and stopped as her breath escaped her. The vista of mighty ocean spread out to infinity to meet the heavens moved her to tears. She stood for a moment as the breath of the ocean washed over her, and tasted its salt. She breathed deep, feeling vulnerable and weak, never needing the ocean more.

"Hello, old friend," she said, near tears at seeing its breadth and power again. "I've missed you!"

She walked toward the sea, attuned to its temperament. The storms had ravaged the shoreline, cutting through the dunes and leaving a long line of wrack, a foot high in places. Shells of all kind and size—some magnificent—littered the wrack beside sponges and sea whip. Any other time she would have collected them, but her mind was preoccupied, roiling like the sea.

She had never seen a more beautiful morning on the beach, she thought with a sense of wonder. A fiercely pale blue sky was covered with a thin layer of pearly gray, wispy clouds, like lace over a gown. The turbulent ocean reflected the gray color, mysterious, even threatening. Yet in the distance, hints of pink fringed the horizon, promising dawn. The tide was going out, leaving a wide watery sheen on the sand that was aglow in brilliant rose reflection.

Lovie tugged the shawl tighter around her shoulders as she felt the dawning of hope pierce her dark despair. Despite the storms and incessant rain, another day dawned. The tides rolled in and out with the constancy of a metronome. The piercing cry of an osprey drew her attention toward Breach Inlet, where it circled, gliding, searching for a fish. A flock of pepper-and-salt sandpipers ran on skinny straight legs, poking their little black awls into the sand with an urgent hunger. Above, a laughing gull seemed to mock her pensive mood. She half smiled.

She'd spent the night curled in her bed, the lights out, the porch doors open, listening to the low roar of the ocean as the snore of a beloved. This morning she'd awakened at first light, having slept little but eager to rise, dress, and get to the ocean to see the sunrise.

The message of dawn was that life went on.

She looked over her shoulder back at the dune where she and Russell had made love during those glorious days of summer. The sea oats had been young and green then. Now it was fall and they were tall and amber, their long, dangling panicles catching the wind and sending tawny seeds out to colonize the dunes. Life, death, and rebirth, she thought. Beginnings and endings. Nothing remained the same.

She recalled Russell's words that they would take it day by day and trust that they would know what to do. This morning, Lovie knew what she had to do. The landscape might be changing around her, but what would never change was her responsibility to her children. Nothing mattered more to her than Palmer and Caretta.

Stratton didn't understand his daughter, but she did. Cara's challenging spirit defined her, and Lovie admired it, treasured it, and, perhaps unknowingly, fostered it. It was a quality Lovie knew she'd had once upon a time but had never nurtured. Russell recognized it. This past summer with him, she'd rediscovered glimpses of that adventurous, independent girl. It was as if part of her—the part she most wanted to be—was gaining strength with each success and each validation.

Stratton sensed this, he'd sniffed it out from the start, and it threatened him. By ordering Lovie to train her daughter in the social arts, he was reminding her not only of her obligations to her daughter but also of his expectations for his wife.

But Cara was not her! She wanted to channel her daughter's independence, not suppress it. If she did, Cara would grow up bitter and angry, a reflection of her father's worst qualities, as well as her own. Over and over during her troubled sleep she revisited the scene of Cara standing up to Stratton, defying him. She saw again the raised palm a breath away from a strike. That vision haunted her. What had flickered in Stratton's mind in that millisecond to still the hand? Was it Lovie's cry? Was it Cara's crouching in fear? Or was it the moral voice of his conscience?

Cara's defiance could be contained only so long. One day, Stratton would push her too far, and her natural rebelliousness would come bursting out in all its fury. Then, Lovie knew, she would have to be there to protect her. No matter what she wanted for herself, Lovie could not leave Cara to live alone with Stratton. After last night, she knew that one day, that hand would fall.

She had come to the beach house to quiet the noise and to listen, really listen, to the ageless wisdom she'd found here, on the beach, with her old friend. The myriad sounds of the waves, the hope of a new dawn, the castanet trembling of the grasses, the second spring of the wildflowers spoke to her. She understood the language of the changing seasons with the lessons of migrating birds and butterflies. Most of all, she heard the voice of the turtles in their constancy, their loyalty to instinct, their commitment to return.

Turtles had been a constant in her life. She'd forged a bond and made a vow to protect their nests. For nearly thirty years— from Cara's age until now—she'd protected the nests. She'd stood her ground with her brother. She'd gone toe-to-toe with mayors, councilmen, and now developers. She wouldn't back down to Russell with the raccoons, and she'd fought Stratton year after year to not sell the beach house. Protecting the nests is what she did. Her vocation defined her.

Lovie cast a wide, sweeping gaze around the beach and breathed deep with the certainty of decision. She knew who she was, where her history lay, and how deep were her roots. She would protect her nest. It was as simple and clear as that. Her role as a mother was bigger than her personal needs.

She would be there to raise her son and her daughter, to teach them their heritage, to reveal their Southern roots, to water and nourish and guide them to grow up and to scatter into the world as the adults they were meant to be. There could be no turning back from this commitment.

Lovie slunk to the dunes and brought her knees close to her chest, wrapping the shawl around herself. Her heart felt lifeless in her chest and tears streamed down her face. She stared out at the sea for a long time as her decision settled in her mind, heavy and somber. Out in the distant sky, the fringe of hopeful pink pushed back the gray clouds, allowing the brilliant blue to fill the sky. Lovie watched the dawn rise and felt none of the usual inspiration from the sight. She was cold, numb to its beauty. To her, today the sky appeared gray. This was, she knew, just the first of a long series of gray days she'd have to endure.

She rose and walked back across the beach, retracing her own long line of footprints in the sand. At the entrance to the path, she turned and looked once more across the shell-strewn beach that glittered now in the morning light.

"Good-bye, old friend," she whispered to the sea. "Good-bye, Russell."

Twenty-three

~≈~

The Ides of March blew in with a nor'easter. Bitter cold winds whipped the Lowcountry, spitting out icy drops that clung to trees and scattered the early azalea blossoms to the streets. South of Broad, windows were rattling. The sky had darkened so much that lights glowed in the windows at three in the afternoon. Inside the Rutledge house, yellow light spilled out on the floors from lamps but did little to brighten the mood.

Vivian carried a tray to the guest bedroom of Tradd Street, Lovie's room now. She knocked gently, then pushed the door open. Lovie was standing at the window, still as a statue in her blue flannel bathrobe and clutching a thick black woolen shawl around her shoulders. Her long blond hair hung loose and limp down her back.

"It sure is a day to stay indoors," Vivian said in a cheery voice. "I brought you some nice hot tea to take the chill off. And some of those pimento cheese sandwiches you're so fond of."

Lovie didn't respond.

Vivian frowned and shook her head, and set the tray on the table beside the upholstered chair. She wrung her hands in worry. The wind gusted again, shrieking through the windows like bad spirit. Vivian's dark eyes warily scanned the shadowy room as though she thought there was some voodoo in the air today.

"Miss Lovie, come away from that window and sit a spell. You've been standing there for hours. You gotta be tired." She walked closer and said, in a cajoling voice, "Please, Miss Lovie. Just some tea. It'll warm you up good."

Lovie brought her lips together. Just the thought of eating made her stomach clench. She knew Vivian was just trying to be helpful. She'd been bringing in all her favorite foods since morning, as though food might be the tonic for what ailed her. Lovie tightened her shawl around her and shook her head. "Just set it down, Vivian. Maybe later."

Lovie glanced over her shoulder to see Vivian poking at the logs in the fireplace, stirring up the sparks. There weren't enough logs in Charleston to warm her today, she thought, returning her gaze to the storm. The boughs of the live oak tree were shaking in the wind, scraping at her window like a ghost. Lovie shuddered and closed her eyes tight, feeling the howl of the ghost swirling in her chest.

The phone rang and Lovie let out a breath, welcoming the intrusion. She turned to Vivian, who stood unmoving, looking at the phone like a hunting dog pointing out the prey. Lovie had told her that she absolutely wasn't taking any calls today. Her lips pursed in annoyance as the phone continued to ring and ring. Vivian started wringing her hands again and looked to Lovie for instructions. Whoever it was just wasn't going to give up. With a sigh, she said, "Oh, go ahead and answer it. But take a message."

Vivian practically ran to the phone beside the bed. "Rutledge residence. Oh, Mrs. Simmons," she said, glancing to Lovie.

Lovie raised her hands and waved them in the universal signal that she wasn't here.

"Miss Lovie isn't feeling well, Mrs. Simmons. She's sleeping." There was a pause, and Vivian rolled her eyes. "The weather is so bad, you might not want to come out just now. I hear the streets might freeze. Yes'm." Vivian hung up the phone and glanced at Lovie.

"Mrs. Simmons says she'll call again later."

"Thank you," Lovie said with a slight smile.

The chime from the doorbell rang out. "Lord above," Vivian muttered. "There's no rest for the wicked. I'll be right back," she told Lovie. "See if you can have some tea while I'm gone."

Lovie held herself rigid, wondering who could be at the door. She wasn't even dressed. She'd deliberately not put on clothes so she wouldn't be able to run out of the house on a whim. Oh, go away, she thought bitterly. I don't want to see you, whoever you are. I don't want to see anyone. Except Russell . . .

Today had been the longest day of her life, and she knew tonight would be equally tragic. She'd prepared for today, not trusting that she'd have the strength to abide by her decision and not run wildly, crazy with joy, to the beach house to meet Russell on their assigned date. March 15 had been so long in coming. She'd been so strong, so committed these past months. When she'd returned from the beach house in October, she'd sat once more with Stratton in the walnut library and told him that she wanted to stay, to try to make their marriage work, for the sake of the children.

When she remained in the guest room, she'd expected him to rant and rail and demand that she return to their shared bedroom. But he did not. They never discussed the subject, and Lovie believed it was because he was content with their new sleeping arrangements, knowing that she had consented to so much more. Other than that, the family had fallen back into its normal routine. Lovie's injuries had healed and she was once again active in her home and community. Palmer was more engrossed than ever in his friends and sports but, sadly, not in studies. Cara complained daily about cotillion, but she'd found a few good friends in the drama and debate clubs at school.

Lovie had managed her days with grace and dedication. Her nights, however, were haunted by dreams of Russell and longing for what might have been. She'd sometimes awaken in the early hours of morning, sobbing, her pillow wet with tears.

So often she recalled her and Russell's last night together at their dune. It was an exquisite kind of torture. She'd lain in his arms and made him promise.

I propose we make a promise. We will wait six months. Time enough for us to return to our lives, to cool our heads, and to think through all the ramifications of our decisions. Carefully and deliberately. There must be no contact until the six months are over. None at all. No pressure of any kind. If on March fifteenth either one of us chooses to leave our spouse, we will come back here to the beach house. If either of us chooses not to show up, then the other will never call again. We will abide by the decision, no matter how hard it may be to accept. Are we agreed?

He had vowed to abide by the promise, as had she.

"Oh, stupid, hateful promise!" Lovie cried, clutching her robe at her heart. Why did she ever come up with such a Machiavellian scheme? They should have said their good-byes that night, as they had planned. To give each other hope was cruel. Instead she'd lived each day dreading the Ides of March. It had loomed before her like a death sentence in her self-constructed prison.

She began pacing the room, her thoughts running wild. What was he thinking now, she wondered? Where was he? Could he be on his way to the beach house at this very moment? Flying in this storm? What did he call himself? Lancelot to her Guinevere? *Where are you?* Lovie wondered, going to the window and looking out at the storm. She plastered her hands and cheek against the cold glass, feeling her heart splinter. "Russell, come back for me!"

Weeping, she sank to the floor and covered her face with her hands. She had to stop crying, she told herself, pulling herself to her feet. She had to hold herself together. She was strong enough to live through this night.

She looked out the window at the dark storm and shuddered at the sleet splattering at the window and the thin coating of ice forming on the branches. No, Russell, do not come tonight, she told him in her heart. It's too dangerous. And too late. She thought of the warm days they'd spent together in the summer and hoped that for him their love was a passing fancy, or at the very least a summer love he could forget once the winter's light made his commitments icy clear. She didn't want him to suffer as she did, to be overcome with regret.

The wind gusted and shook the windows, mocking her pain. And yet a part of her hoped he *did* suffer—bitterly and painfully—as she did. She clung to the belief that despite the pain, what they'd shared was real and not imagined. That regardless of whether they could be together, their love would endure in their hearts and minds for the rest of their lives.

She recalled his response to her on that fateful night:

We may never know if our decisions were right or wrong. That is the uncertainty of every choice. If we both show up, it will be a new beginning. If one of us does not, it will be an end. Lovie, I can't predict what the future holds. But I can promise you this. Whatever decision you make, I will always love you.

Lovie felt a shiver of anguish, even as she felt her strength of commitment return. As always, Russell's words sustained her.

From the stairwell, she heard Vivian talking to someone. Lovie remained at the window but cocked her ear, listening. For a wild moment, she wondered if Russell had come here, to her home. She felt her blood race.

"No, he ain't here," Vivian said. "Mr. Rutledge is eating out at the club tonight. And the chil'ren is gone, too. Having dinner with their grandmother, Mrs. Rutledge."

"Good. How is she?"

Lovie released her held breath, recognizing Flo's voice.

"She's just standing at the window, been like that for hours," Vivian told Flo. "She's not even dressed. She's not eating or talking, neither. She's not herself. I'm at my wit's end. I'm glad you're here, that's for true."

"We all knew today was going to be hard for her," Flo said. "You've been doing a great job here. No friend could do more. I'll spell you for a while. Get some rest yourself. In fact, maybe you should go home now. It's getting bad out there."

"No, ma'am. I already made plans to spend the night. Miss Lovie asked me to."

"She doesn't trust herself not to skip out in the dark," Flo said. "I swear, I do believe if she got one foot out the door, she'd run clear to the beach, damn the storm."

"It's a sad day all way round," Vivian said.

Lovie heard them enter and clutched her arms tightly around her, holding herself together.

"Lovie, it's me. Flo."

Lovie paused, wishing Flo would just go away. She looked over her shoulder. Flo was standing by the door dressed in a black A-line skirt, white blouse, and black jacket, her uniform for the clinic. Her face had lost its summer tan. Lovie thought she looked pale, tired, older. The summer's end had brought an end to her relationship with Bing as well. Flo never talked about it, but Lovie wondered if Russell had been right after all. She looked in her eyes, and Lovie saw compassion for a grief she didn't have to explain.

"Aw, Lovie," Flo said, shaking her head. "I'm so sorry to see you in such pain. What can I do to help you?"

At the sound of her friend's voice, Lovie's lips shook with loss of composure and she sharply turned her head away.

Flo rushed to her side and put her hands on her shoulders. "Let it go, sugar. There's no one here."

Lovie shook her head. "I can't," she choked out. "The only way I can get through this is to hold on tight. If I let go, I'll go screaming mad through that door straight for him, and you wouldn't be able to stop me."

"Wanna bet?" Flo teased with a wry grin.

Lovie didn't smile, but she felt her shoulders lower in her friend's grip. Flo dropped her hands and Lovie turned from the window to face her, wiping her face with her palms.

"Thanks. But Flo, I've known this day was coming and how hard it would be. I've prepared myself. Vivian's here like a watchdog. Stratton and the children are gone. I even had a lock put on the door and gave Vivian the key, just in case I go crazy." She laughed lightly and glanced at Flo's worried expression. "Don't worry. I don't think I'll get that bad. Drunk, maybe. But not crazy."

"I'll get drunk with you. Anytime. Want to start now?"

Lovie appreciated her friend's support. "Do you remember when we were children how we loved the myths of Odysseus? We used to act out the scenes," Lovie asked.

"Sure I do. I used to love to play Medusa. You were Perseus." She chuckled softly. "Lord, when I think of the aluminum foil snakes we made for my hair. I looked more like an alien than a Greek goddess."

It was Lovie's first smile that day. "For the record, Medusa wasn't a goddess. She was a monster. Why do you think I let you play the part?"

"I knew that." Flo grinned.

"Do you remember the story of Odysseus and the Sirens?"

"Vaguely." She cocked her head, perplexed. "That's kind of random. Where did that come from?"

"I've been thinking about it a lot today. About a lot of legends . . ." She shook her head and shrugged. "You think I'm nuts, don't you?"

"Of course not. Okay," said Flo, expelling a plume of air while she thought, "Odysseus, huh? It's been a long time. Let's see . . . If Odysseus and his crew heard the song of the Sirens they'd be led to their death. Something like that, right?"

"Yes. Circe warned him that hearing their call would fill their hearts with desire. The music would be so sweet they wouldn't be able to resist. So the shipmates filled their ears with wax."

Flo's face suddenly revealed that she understood what Lovie was telling her. "And Odysseus tied himself to the mast."

"Right. So he couldn't follow the Sirens' call. He suffered and cried out to be released, but of course the crew couldn't hear him. The ship gradually passed, and in time the song of the Sirens faded away. Odysseus lived to return home."

"So, my sweet friend, you're tying yourself to the mast."

"In a matter of speaking. I have come to terms with my decision to stay, but I don't trust myself not to hear the song of my heart. Even now, I want to run to the beach house. It's irrational, I know, I've made my decision." She shrugged. "But there it is."

They shared a look of understanding.

A knock sounded on the door, and Vivian walked in carrying a tray with a steaming pot of tea and two slices of cake. "I made you a coconut cake, Miss Lovie. It's your favorite. Come sit and have a piece with Miss Florence. Don't make me have to take away another pot of cold tea."

"I'd love a cup," Flo said, walking over to the piecrust table set beside the fireplace. A small fire burned, warming the room against the cold winds that seeped into the old house. She poked at the logs a bit with the fire iron and watched the red sparks jump and crackle before she took a seat on one of the slipper chairs beside the table.

"Lovie, come on, honey. Sit by the fire with me. It's toasty here, and it's the least you can do after I came all this way in this weather to see you. Oh, Vivian? You wouldn't have a little something stronger? Brandy, perhaps?" She acknowledged Vivian's wink of complicity before Vivian left the room.

Lovie reluctantly joined Flo at the table. She sat woodenly in her chair and stared disconsolately at the cake. Vivian's coconut cake was legendary. She'd learned it from her mother, who learned it from her mother. It was whispered that Vivian's mother had sold the recipe to a Charleston restaurateur and the restaurant had since become famous for it.

"She's been bringing me my favorite foods all day," Lovie said.

"What a dear, she is. If I had any money, I'd pay her the world to come cook for me. Don't you dare hurt her feelings. This cake is the devil to make. Eat some."

Flo poured two cups of the steaming fragrant orange spice tea. She put liberal amounts of milk and sugar in both and set one cup in front of Lovie along with a piece of cake.

"Eat," Flo ordered, and shoved her plate of cake toward her.

Lovie pushed the plate away. "I can't. I'll be sick."

"How long has it been since you've eaten?"

"My stomach is in knots." She sighed and said, as though it were a great concession, "I'll drink the tea."

"Lovie, you have to eat."

"Flo, stop pestering me. I'll eat later. I just can't." Her composure broke and she brought her hands to her face. "I'm dying inside. I just have to make it through this night. After this, the decision is sealed. I'll eat then. I'll go on, like I know I have to. But tonight, just let me be."

"Sure, honey," Flo said, and, dropping her fork, leaned back in her chair. "I admire your strength, Lovie. I know how deeply you loved Russell. I've never known a love like that and doubt I ever will. But watching you go through this hell, I think I might just hold myself lucky. You know, I admire your ability to be so rational."

"Rational?" Lovie cried. "If I'm doing the right thing, why does it still hurt so badly?"

"Oh, honey, it's going to hurt for a long, long time." Flo reached out across the table to take her friend's hand. "But I'll be here with you, every step of the way. I'll tie you to the mast and release you when the danger's past. I'm here. You're not alone."

Twenty-four

~~~

Memorial Day weekend arrived, and though the calendar said May, everyone knew that summer had come to the Lowcountry. The rains of March had fed the greening salt marshes. By April, flowers blanketed the landscape in pastels, and as May approached, the loggerheads were gathering in their tempestuous affairs offshore. Everywhere there were signs of renewal and rebirth.

Lovie got an early start to beat the holiday traffic, loaded food and children into her shiny new Dodge station wagon with its faux wood paneling, new-leather smell, and a radio that worked, and headed out of Charleston toward her beach house. It was a lovely car, but Lovie couldn't wait to get behind the wheel of the Gold Bug once she was back on the island. Vivian was meeting her there and Stratton was coming later. Lovie couldn't wait another minute to get to the beach. Her fingers danced on the steering wheel to the music of ABBA blaring from the radio as she said a prayer and crossed the ludicrously narrow two-lane Grace Bridge over the Cooper River. Once in Mount Pleasant, she looked in the rearview mirror and smiled to see Palmer and

Cara talking sleepily but amiably about their plans for the day. They were already in their swimsuits.

When she reached the Ben Sawyer Bridge, the swing bridge was fully open and a short line of cars waited in a queue. The man in the car in front of her was anxiously tapping the outside of his window, but Lovie put the car in neutral, rolled down her window, and took a moment to soak in the view of the tall white sailboat mast that leisurely sailed through the bridge. She was at the precipice of the islands, and at the sight of the mighty Intracoastal Waterway sparkling in the early morning sun, she felt the weight of the city begin to ease from her shoulders.

It took awhile for the boat to sail through, and though the kids in the back grumbled, Lovie was content to watch the bridge slowly swing closed and to follow the sailboat's unhurried journey along the waterway. When at last the bridge closed, she crossed onto Sullivan's Island, past the quaint cottages, some already festooned with fern palms and cheery red geraniums on their porches. It was still early, but already cars were parked in front, here for the weekend. At last she crossed the final bridge over Breach Inlet onto the Isle of Palms, and moments later, she was home.

The children bolted from the car, their towels flailing in the air behind them like brilliantly colored flags.

"Don't you bother about a thing," Vivian called to her as she climbed from the driver's seat of her sedan. "You go on and open up the house and let some of that nice breeze in." She sniffed the air and scrunched up her face. "I surely hope that sulfur smell don't last long."

Lovie laughed. It was a rare sound these days, and it bubbled from her throat with surprise. "Vivian, that's just the pluff mud! The perfume of the islands."

"Perfume? That what you call it?" Vivian smirked.

"Oh, Viv, it *is* good to be home."

Vivian looked at her face and smiled. "I can see you're going to do real good here. I'm going to cook up some shrimp and grits for dinner and maybe some banana pie for dessert. How does that sound?"

"Like heaven," Lovie replied.

The Isle of Palms was a kind of heaven for her. She felt her strength recharging by the minute. She needed that strength now, she thought, as she stood at the door, one hand resting on the warm metal of the knob, the other holding the key at the lock. She'd imagined this moment since March 15, feared what she might—or might not—discover when she entered the closed-up house. The question that had plagued her since the Ides of March hammered her brain now: *Had Russell come to the beach house on that fateful night? Would there be some letter, some sign to her that he'd waited for her?*

She unlocked the door and walked into the stale and steamy room. Her gaze swept across the dimly lit room. It was undisturbed and as quiet as the grave. Lovie went from window to window, opening the shutters in a seasonal ritual to the summer wind. Feeling the fresh air, she walked around the room, her sharp gaze scanning the pine floors and her fingers trailing over the cabbage rose chintz sofa and chairs, the wood coffee table, her pristine desk, the white mantel with its silver-framed photographs, the bookcase. She thought she might find a folded note propped up on the mantel or a shelf, or some small token that she'd recognize as his, some sign so she would know that he'd come for her.

She went into her bedroom and with more urgency searched the top of the bureaus, even the crisp matelassé spread on her bed. Nothing. In the kitchen, she searched the counters, the table, losing faith. She even went to Cara's and Palmer's rooms. She found nothing, not a piece of furniture moved or a pillow disturbed, no sign.

Then she stopped short with a new thought. But of course he wouldn't have left a note indoors! How silly of her to think he could get inside. With hope beating in her heart, she hurried to the French doors and pushed them open to the porch. She searched with an edge of desperation the wicker table and chairs and knelt before the straw baskets and her trusty red bucket and emptied out the dusty turtle team gear, sand-crusted sandals, and a thin layer of sand and dead bugs. As a last resort, she even checked the corners of the floor, thinking that a small scrap of paper could have been scattered by a strong wind.

She leaned against the porch railing, breathing out. She wished she could just be resigned. Lovie hadn't realized how much hope she'd been harboring that she would find a message from Russell. Even a briefly penned note that told her farewell would be something. She felt her disappointment as a heaviness on her chest. The air felt too thin, too warm. From inside she felt an anger bubbling, not only against Russell but also against herself. This was *her* beach house. *Her* refuge. Her teeth clenched in anger at the man who had stolen from her the joy that she used to feel when she stepped into this cottage.

"You okay, Miss Lovie?" Vivian called from the house.

Lovie pulled up and took a deep breath, and turned to face Vivian, her eyes flashing. "Just catching my breath."

"I found these in the mailbox," Vivian said, her eyes dark with concern. She handed Lovie a stack of mail.

"Thanks," she replied briskly, taking them in hand. She felt herself slipping into the vortex of self-pity again and needed to snap out of it. Quickly sifting through the pile, she saw the usual junk mail and advertising circulars. But the long white envelope caught her attention. The return address was the South Carolina Wildlife and Marine Resources Department. Curious, she set the other mail on the table and tore open the letter.

She gasped in surprise. Could it be, she wondered? Reading

quickly, she realized it truly was a letter granting approval for her to continue her project on the Isle of Palms and Sullivan's Island. She had to report all her findings and direct all questions to the new coordinator of marine turtles, Sally Hopkins. Lovie quickly looked at the second sheet. There was her formal permit, and one for Florence Prescott as well.

Lovie burst into a grin. Russell hadn't forgotten. He'd secured her permit, as he'd promised. She brought the papers to her chest. It may not have been the note she'd been looking for, but it was something.

"Good news?" Vivian asked.

"Yes," Lovie replied, grinning and feeling her energy rallying. "Surprising news." She felt the sun's warmth on her face, amazed at how quickly a day could switch from gloomy to bright. She was here at the beach house. There was work to be done to open the house and start the summer.

And the turtles were coming to lay their eggs. The first nests might already be on the beach. The possibility stirred her blood to action. "I'm fine!" Lovie said, turning with a smile on her face to face Vivian. "I'm home now. Let's unload the cars and get this day rolling."

Within three days, Lovie had marshaled together the volunteers for the turtle team. She didn't get the full forty, but twenty-seven on board were more than she'd ever had on her own before. All the summer residents wouldn't arrive for another week or so when schools in the north closed. At the meeting, the team decided they didn't have enough volunteers to cover Sullivan's Island, but they'd continue the northern end of Isle of Palms. Last summer they'd discovered there were too many nests up there to overlook. Lovie divvied up the island into sections to patrol, passed out schedules, and begged everyone to try to recruit more volunteers.

The first week of June, a tropical depression kept the coast cool and wet. Lovie was so proud of her volunteers as they donned slickers and made their rounds. The island's first three nests were located. The sun came back out, and with it came the tourists. By mid-June, the beaches exploded with colorful towels and umbrellas. The sea turtles kicked into high gear, too. Lovie and Flo were out checking the reported tracks most mornings now. By the summer solstice, there wasn't a stretch of beach that Lovie had not walked, and she'd faithfully recorded all her observations in her notebook.

The only spot she refused to go to was her and Russell's dune. She avoided so much as looking at it. When she had to walk past it, she deliberately kept her eyes on the ocean, turning her back to the memories sequestered behind the now soft green sea oats. She refused to surrender to her memories.

One morning in late June, Lovie was called out to check tracks near the Isle of Palms pier. It was a humid morning with thick cumulus clouds. With only one call, Lovie decided to walk the mile to the pier rather than drive. Sidestepping the large number of jellyfish scattering the beach, she walked briskly, enjoying the chance to stretch her legs. The pier jutted far out on high pilings into the ocean. Approaching, she saw Flo standing in the shade under the pilings, fanning herself with her hat.

During the summer months, especially on days the receding tide left tidal pools on the beach, this was a favorite place for children to run and play, toddlers splashing through the shallow pools with dogs barking at their heels and mothers close by. She remembered the days when Palmer and Cara were that young and tethered to their mother by some invisible string.

The turtle nest was below the tide line and too close to the motel. She and Flo were kneeling in front of a hole she'd dug in a dune and placing the turtle eggs into it when Lovie heard the low nasal buzz of an engine. Both she and Flo stopped what they were doing and looked at each other, frozen as they listened. They shared a knowing glance. They both heard the unmistakable sound of a small airplane. Memories washed over Lovie and, grabbing hold of her hat, she tilted her head to the sky. She could just make out a small single-engine plane coming in her direction. She rose as the thrum of the engine grew louder. Then she was running to the shoreline, eyes trained on the white airplane flying ever closer. She arched on tiptoe as it flew overhead, catching a fleeting glimpse of a dashing red-and-blue stripe. Her heart spontaneously leaped in her chest when the plane tipped its wing.

"Russell!" she cried out.

Questions whirled in her head and she didn't have answers for any of them. But she did have hope. Lots of airy, bubbling, spine-tickling, utterly irrational hope. Lovie lifted her hand over her eyes to block the sun as she watched the airplane disappear down the coast. Russell had come back!

"Lovie!" Flo called.

She twirled to face her, grinning wide. "Russell's back!"

"You don't know it was him," Flo said as she walked toward her.

"Of course it was!" Her heart was pounding in her chest.

"Lovie," Flo said in a censorious voice.

Lovie responded to the tone and, slowly, her arms fell to her sides. She stood for a moment, blinking in disbelief.

"What are you doing?" Flo asked her.

In her mind, Lovie saw herself twirling like a girl, just at the thought of seeing Russell again. She couldn't go back to those feelings. When would she learn? Yet even as her mind shouted the words, her heart pumped a heady, hopeful beat in her chest.

Flo came to stand in front of her. "Don't go back there," she told Lovie. "You've made your peace."

Lovie studied her friend's face, tan again, and her bright blue eyes filled with worry. She wanted to trust her with her feelings now, but couldn't. "I can't help my feelings," she said.

"If it is him, will you see him?"

Lovie brought her hands to her cheeks and held Flo's gaze, both shy and bold. She nodded.

"Then I hope it wasn't him," Flo snapped. "Come on, we've got to finish this nest."

Lovie spent the rest of the day hovering near the phone, pretending to read. The thought that Russell might show up knocking on her front door kept her on tenterhooks. By midafternoon those puffy white cumulus clouds had turned into thunderous cumulonimbus. That night, the predicted storm rolled over the island, bringing flashing light, clapping thunder, and sheets of rain. She usually enjoyed the pomp and circumstance of a good summer storm, but tonight the wind whistled like a banshee, knocking over the rocking chairs on her porch and sending her baskets scuttling. When the worst of it blew out to sea, the rain sounded as drum raps against the tin roof. In time, Lovie's lids grew heavy as she fell asleep to the tympanic beat.

Olivia.

Her name came on a breath of salt air.

I'm here.

His voice swirled around her, cool and moist like the mist that hovered over the sea. It was Russell. She recognized his scent, was overcome with sensations she recognized as her body's welcome to him and only him. Then he was with her and they were floating, her hair swirling around them, long and studded with pearls, a seductive Siren of the sea. Russell's long face was pale and unearthly, glowing in the phosphorescence. She was overcome with his scent, salt and sandalwood, when he pressed his cheek against hers. She felt the warmth of his breath on her face. As they floated like ethereal sea creatures in the blue, sun-kissed water, his beautiful long-fingered hands slid along her body like silk, from her calves, her inner thighs, her belly, and finally encircling her breasts. She clung to him in her dream, determined never to release him, crying, tasting salt water on her face as she arched up to meet him, his name on her lips.

When she awoke, she was covered in a sheen of perspiration and tears flowing down her cheeks. Feeling bewildered and like she was swimming in seaweed, she frantically pushed back the sheet and shoved her loose hair from her face and neck as though it were strangling her. She rose from the bed in a rush, then tee-tered, lurching for the bureau as her knees went watery and tiny black dots swam in front of her eyes. When her head cleared, she went directly out on the back porch. Dawn's rosy glow hovered over the pewter horizon. The world was silvery in the morning light, the decks were soaked with rain, and the herbs and flow-ers were standing tall, damp and perky. She wrapped her arms around herself, feeling unsure and vulnerable after the powerful dream. Waking slowly, she inhaled the freshness of the air that smelled intoxicatingly of green and an overpowering sweetness that came after a storm.

Lovie dressed quickly and made coffee. Opening the fridge, she groaned to see that again they were out of milk. While the children still slept, she drove to the Red & White grocery store. It was a breezy morning, still overcast with heavy clouds. She purchased milk, some local honey, and eggs Vivian wanted for a cake she planned to make. Walking back to her car, she waved at someone she knew but couldn't name, and stopped at the vil-lage bulletin board to scan for sales and announcements. Other than a multifamily "Spring Clean" garage sale on Forest Trail, it was slim pickings. Turning, she glanced at the metal box that held the *Charleston Courier*. A bold headline caught her attention. She froze.

FATAL AIRPLANE CRASH OFF MYRTLE BEACH

Lovie stood motionless, her purse hanging from her arm and groceries against her chest, as the blood drained from her face. She blinked, making sense of what she was seeing. She saw a bit of rust at the corner of the metal bin that was nearly full of papers. A Styrofoam cup lay in the dirt in the corner. Time moved slowly as she walked to the bin. She'd never remember how she found the dime to insert into the coin slot. She pulled open the box.

On the left of the front page was a large photograph of Russell Bennett. She dropped her grocery bag and pulled out a paper, her hands shaking as she brought it close. Her eyes greedily scanned the article, frantically grasping at words rather than complete sentences: *crashed, storm, died instantly.*

Lovie's hands squeezed, crumpling the paper to her chest. It felt like she was having a heart attack. She couldn't catch her breath, couldn't release the moan she felt trapped in her throat. Milk spilled over broken eggs across the sidewalk. Lovie slapped a palm to her mouth and ran to her car. She tore open the door and climbed in and spread out the newspaper across the wheel, tossing aside the rest of the pages. The article covered the entire third page. There was an insert in the corner showing a map of the coastline of South Carolina, and an arrow marked the location of the plane crash. She mouthed the words as she read, letting them sink into the great chasm forming in her chest. She read that his plane had crashed in the storm the afternoon before.

She reached up to trace the photograph of his face with her fingertip. It was a photo she'd seen before. Russell was standing by his plane, his hands on his hips. His face was deeply tanned.

A wind had caught his white-blond hair and ruffled it. His smile, so elegant, so refined, showed white teeth. It was a happy smile, spontaneous, like the one he'd showed her every time he opened a door to find her standing there or she met him on the beach. She let her hands drop and, leaning her head against the seat, closed her eyes, still in shock. Not quite believing. Russell Bennett was dead. He was not coming to see her—not today, not ever.

Olivia.

Lovie's eyes flew open and she looked around the car. It was Russell's voice. She sat clutching the steering wheel like a madwoman.

"Where are you?" she cried. When only silence reigned, she rammed the gear into first and drove fast the short distance to the pier. Slamming the door, she ran down the long stretch of wood to the end and clung to the railing, her hair whipping in the wind and her eyes wildly scanning the sea. The ocean was a tempest of whitetops and waves. A deep gray mist settled far out on the horizon like a pall, and from it she heard the sonorous bellow of a foghorn, over and over like the tolling of a funeral bell.

"Russell!" she cried out in anguish. "I'm here!"

Startled by her cry, the seagulls took flight from the pier. They dispersed in the air, then circled close, squawking for food.

She looked at the beach below the pier. She'd stood there just yesterday, she thought with grief. Saw his plane fly overhead yesterday. It *had* to have been his plane. He had to have seen her waving from below.

Now he was dead.

No! Not true, her brain screamed out. *Impossible!*

Olivia.

She startled, hearing again Russell's voice, as clear as if he were standing right beside her. She didn't believe in ghosts, but she couldn't doubt what she'd heard. Lovie stood very still, holding her breath, waiting to hear the voice again. Her body was going cold in the wind, and for one wild moment she thought of jumping into the water, to follow his voice. But the voice didn't return.

Lovie brought her fingers to her temples, wondering if despair could cause madness. But she wasn't crazy. She'd heard his voice, she was certain of it. She'd heard it in her dream last night. The paper had reported that his plane went down in the Atlantic off the South Carolina coast. His body had not been found.

Russell was out there, somewhere. Calling to her.

Miranda opened the door a crack. "Hello!" she crooned softly.

"I'm awake."

Miranda slipped into Lovie's bedroom and quietly closed the door behind her. Lovie was lying on her bed, her small hands tucked under her head. She smiled wanly in welcome as Miranda approached. Outside, the rain had returned and made tympanic sounds against the tin roof.

Miranda leaned over to place a kiss on her cheek. "You've been in here all day. How are you?"

"Fine."

"I can see how fine you are," Miranda replied. "I brought you some benne wafers to nibble on. And some praline cookies from Flo. She'll be here later."

"Thank you."

Miranda placed the box of the crisp sesame cookies on the bedside table. "We heard what happened. We're so sorry. Dr. Bennett was such a fine young man, with so much to offer. It's a shame. But we have to accept it was his time." She reached into her canvas bag and pulled out a worn black Bible and held it out to Lovie. "I brought you this, too. It's a special Bible to me. It's helped me through some difficult times. I'd like you to have it now."

Lovie didn't move to accept it. "I don't believe in God anymore."

"That's just your grief talking. It makes you angry. You're looking for someone to blame for all that's happened." She moved to sit on the bed and placed the Bible on the mattress between them. She took a deep breath. "Darling, that's the thing. There's no one to blame. It's just the way life is. Life and death. Joy and sadness. Good and bad."

Lovie turned her gaze away. She couldn't bear to hear the religious platitudes. "Please, Miranda. Not now. I'm tired. I just want to be alone for a while."

"Oh, child, you probably think I'm some dithering old woman, chatting away, with no idea of the pain you've been through. No one knows your pain, right?"

Lovie faced her again, shock and sadness across her face.

"Do you think I've never felt a loss like yours?"

"I'm sorry. I didn't mean to imply that."

"And so has your mother. Twice, including the loss of her son. She was devastated when Mickey died. As I know you were, too. But you both survived and continued on with your lives. Though Dee Dee doesn't come back to this house much, does she? Not that I can blame her. You, though, you're stronger than she is. You know that Mickey loved this house and the ocean. His spirit is here. It's what adds to the joy of this house. And so is Russell Bennett's spirit. I feel it lingering here," she said, looking around the room.

Lovie's eyes sharpened and she clutched her pillow, pushing herself closer. "You sense him here?"

"Oh, yes, dear. Quite clearly. Don't you?"

"Yes," Lovie said, her voice a harsh whisper. "I . . . I heard his voice calling me this morning. And in my dream."

"Did you?" Miranda's pale blue eyes sparked with interest. "That's very interesting."

"You don't think I'm crazy when I say that?"

"Crazy?" Miranda's laugh was like a peal of bells. "Good heavens, no. I hear voices all the time. Well, not all the time," she amended. "I'm not crazy, either. But sometimes old family houses are visited by spirits who feel a need to renew contact with us on earth. We all lead such busy lives we're usually unaware of their efforts to reach out to us with, say, a rap or a rush of feeling. So often they will contact us directly. If we are attuned and accepting of their presence, we can hear them. But all of us can hear them in our dreams. We let our guard down then. You said you dreamed of Russell?"

Lovie remembered the restless dream of the night before and, blushing, nodded. "It was so real. Not like a regular dream. It was like he was really there, but surreal. I felt him. Smelled him. And . . . I think I knew he was dead."

Miranda was excited. "Dream visitations are common. It's when the spirits just want to reassure us that they are safe and well on the other side and don't want us to worry about them anymore. But they aren't really dreams at all, are they? They're something more real."

"Yes. Exactly."

Miranda tilted her head in thought. "But to hear his voice this morning . . ." Her finger tapped her lips. "That's significant. I wonder . . . Do you have unfinished business between you?"

Lovie's eyes widened. This was too private to share with Miranda. She slipped deeper under the blanket and shook her head.

"Lovie, you may not believe it now, but someday—quicker than you know—you'll be in your sixties like me and be able to look back at all this heartache and know it was all part of God's plan. Now, don't give me that look. I swanny, you and Flo are two peas in a pod. For now, you just have to take my word for it, honey."

Lovie didn't speak.

"Tell you what," Miranda said in an encouraging tone. "I'm not going to sit here and preach at you. I'll spare you that. You sit there and relax and I'm just going to read to you a bit. Okay?"

Miranda opened the worn leather Bible, turning to where she'd marked the spot with a silken gold bookmark. She cleared her throat and then began reading. She'd selected Psalm 30, which spoke about rising from anguish and despair. She read in her melodious voice only those few passages that had held the message that had sustained her at her husband's passing.

When she finished, Miranda closed the Bible and left it on the mattress, inches away from Lovie's hand. Lovie's eyes were closed, but when Miranda left, Lovie's fingertips inched over to the Bible.

Later that afternoon, Lovie spotted Cara swinging her legs dejectedly on a long, low-lying limb of the old live oak tree in the back. The proud tree was at least two hundred years old and perfect for climbing, with branches that curled and twisted low like a herd of elephants' trunks. It was Cara's favorite place to read. Lovie often caught her daughter lying on the low branch, miles away on some adventure in a book.

Lovie came walking from her bedroom porch in a slow gait. She stopped in front of the tree. "What are you doing sitting up in that tree like a cat?"

"I'm just thinking," Cara replied dully, moving to sit up.

"What's the matter, precious?" Lovie asked. "Is everything okay between you and Emmi?"

"Oh, she's fine, I reckon," Cara replied with a sigh. "She's hanging out with Tom Peterson."

"Is he that new boy who moved here last summer?"

Cara nodded. "Emmi's got a crush on him."

"I thought you did, too."

Cara shrugged, but her face was pink and scowling. "Maybe before. Not now. It's all stupid. Emmi's stupid. She's acting all weird and googly-eyed around him. I can't stand it."

"Ah, I see."

Cara's scowl deepened. "It doesn't matter anymore."

"Oh? Why is that?"

"On accounta I'm never getting married."

"Oh." Lovie brushed a mosquito away, wondering if her marriage troubles were having a bad influence on Cara. She'd been trying so hard not to let the children feel the underlying tension. Kids were so perceptive; it was the parents who were fooled. "Why do you say that, Cara?"

"It's like Emmi's not Emmi anymore. She's this other person or somethin' when he's around, and I don't like her. Is that what happens when you fall in love?"

Lovie tried not to laugh and forced a serious face. "Yes, it is. When you're in love you act goofy. All googly-eyed. And it feels wonderful. Like nothing else in the world. It's not Emmi's fault. She's happy, Cara. Someday it will happen to you."

She shook her head definitively. "Ick," she replied, not liking that answer at all.

"But the goofy part only lasts for a little while," Lovie went on to explain. "Then it settles down into something different. Better."

Cara looked up at Lovie with skepticism. "Uh-huh," she said, but her tone said she didn't believe her.

Lovie eyed her child and thought her sullenness went too deep for boy trouble. "What else is troubling you, Caretta? Come on, you can tell me."

Cara dangled her legs and stared at the cookies awhile. "Then why're you so sad all the time?"

Lovie breathed deep. Yes, she thought to herself. This is the thorn that needs pulling. "Because my friend died."

"I know," she said, dangling her legs. "In a plane crash."

"Yes. Do you remember him? Dr. Russell Bennett? He was the man who helped me with the turtle project last summer."

Cara looked at Lovie, squinting like she was trying to remember him.

"He took you to the nest hatching . . ."

"Oh, yeah," Cara answered.

Lovie thought it was sad that Russell could already be forgotten, then thinking further, she was relieved that he didn't make a big impression.

"Is it hard when a friend dies?" asked Cara. "I mean, it's not like a brother or your daddy or like that."

Lovie moved to sit on the limb beside Cara. "Yes, it's hard," she answered in a soft voice. She leaned close to Cara and lay her cheek on the top of her head, feeling comfort from the closeness. "It can be very hard, if you cared for your friend a great deal."

She raised her eyebrows. "Like if Emmi died?"

"Yes," Lovie replied, "like if Emmi died. There's an empty space in your heart."

"But you have other friends," Cara said, trying to make sense of it. "And you have me and Palmer and Daddy. And Vivian."

"I know. And having you means so much to me. But that doesn't make losing a friend less sad. It's like some part of you is missing, and it hurts."

Cara thought about that, her face scrunched up in thought. "Mama, what do you call it when someone loses a leg but it still hurts?"

"Do you mean ghost pains?"

"Yeah, that's it," she said. "Is that what you're feeling now? Ghost pains?"

Lovie turned to kiss Cara's head, marveling at a child's perspicacity.

"Yes, dear. Mama's having ghost pains."

●　●　●

For three days Lovie remained in her room, hiding her grief. She'd rather her children think she was sick than in mourning. Hers was a private grief, not one to show in public. Flo took over for her on the turtle team, telling everyone Lovie wasn't feeling well. Whether they believed the excuse or not, Lovie didn't care. She was beyond the reach of gossip.

Only at night did she come out, like the lifeless vampire, a walking-dead thing. She sneaked out her bedroom porch to the beach and walked for hours, crying openly, cursing the stars and staring out at the sea.

Some people believed that the sea was a living, breathing beast. Seductive one moment, vindictive the next. Throughout history, sailors spoke to her lovingly, sensitive to her mercurial moods. Lovie knew it was true, and there were moments when she looked into the blackness of the ocean, as dark and fathomless as a spectral eye, and heard its voice calling to her, a voice that sounded like Russell's, luring her to the mysteries and peace of its depths. On those infinite nights, Lovie didn't know from where she found the strength to find her way home.

As the Fourth of July weekend approached, Lovie eschewed the crowds. She couldn't leave her cocoon, even while recognizing that she was being self-indulgent with her grief, thanks to Vivian's support. She was in her room, curled in an armchair, trying to read while listening to Joan Baez, when she heard Stratton's voice in the living room. She set down Archie Carr's book and turned off the phonograph. Perched on the edge of the chair, she listened to any words she could catch outside her door.

"Where's your mama?" Stratton asked.

"She's sleeping," Palmer answered.

"Sleeping, huh?" Stratton said with a slur. "We'll see about that."

Lovie tensed and slunk back in her chair. She heard Stratton's heavy footsteps approach, then a scurry of more steps stopping at her door.

"What's the matter with you, boy?" Stratton said. His voice sounded weary and annoyed.

"She's sleeping," Palmer said again, his voice shaky yet gruff.

"I heard you the first time and I don't care, hear? Now, git."

"No, sir. I'm . . . I'm going to stay right here." He cleared his throat. "I'm going to make sure Mama doesn't fall down the stairs again."

Lovie's breath caught and she brought her hand to her mouth.

She clutched the arms of her chair, ready to leap, imagining father and son staring at one another. She couldn't imagine what Stratton was thinking but felt sure his hand would rise and fall, smacking her son's face for his impudence.

"Aw, son," Stratton said in a miserable voice. "You shame me. And I deserve it. I know it. I'm not going to hurt your mama. I promise you. I'll never hurt her again. You have my word."

A moment later Stratton entered her room and closed the door. He stood at the foot of the bed dressed in his tan suit, his tie loose at the neck. His shoulders drooped in defeat.

"You're here early," Lovie said. "I didn't expect you until the weekend."

"I canceled my appointments and flew home early. I, uh, I heard about Bennett's plane crash."

Lovie brought her knees up and plucked at some unseen lint on the chair. "Yes. It's all very tragic. We were all stunned."

"I thought as much. I wanted to get home and see how you were. You didn't answer my calls."

She sighed and shook her head. "I'm sorry. I haven't been feeling well."

Stratton removed his jacket and tossed it on the bed. Then he sat on the mattress with a heavy sigh.

"Was it him?" he asked.

Lovie brought her fingers to her face and pinched her nose by her eyes. "Stop it."

Stratton stared at the floor. Then he brought his hands to his face as his shoulders shook.

Lovie felt a sudden surge of pity. "Stratton . . ."

"What more do you want me to do?" he asked in a broken moan. "I've done all a man can do," he said, shaking his head. He lifted his head to face her, his dark eyes pulsing with resentment. "I stuck to the marriage when you broke the vows. That's more than most men would do, I can tell you. By all accounts I should have divorced you long ago, but I didn't. I stayed by you. I tried, Lovie, I tried."

"Why didn't you let me go?" she cried, her own anguish breaking through at last. "I didn't ask you to hold on. I didn't *want* you to. I asked you for a divorce but you wouldn't let me go. Why didn't you let me go?" she cried again.

"I was saving our family!"

"No. You were saving your pride!"

"You left me with precious little of it!" he roared back.

"And you left me none at all!"

They stared at each other, breathing hard, each feeling excruciating pain.

Lovie rose and walked to the French doors, opening them wide. She felt the cool evening air blow in, smelled its sweetness, and gradually her heart rate lowered. What was the use of fighting? she thought as the malaise of depression returned. Lovie knew there would be no winner in this fight. Both of them would bear scars that would never completely heal.

"All this pain could have been avoided," she said. Lovie skipped a beat to let the tension defuse. She turned to face him again. "Even now . . . This was your moment. You could have shown compassion, shared as an equal in the pain of this failure we call a marriage. You could have asked me for my forgiveness and let me ask for yours.

"But you stand there in your pride and arrogance to once again remind me of all my failures and faults. How I betrayed our vows. How you were the rock while I floundered. How, against your better judgment, against your very nature, you have lowered yourself to save our marriage, to save our family."

"I did all I could," he replied, stunned and confused by her outburst. "I *am* the rock of this family. Are you denying that we were fine until you had your affair with Russell Bennett?"

Hearing him speak Russell's name aloud took her aback. She sucked in her breath and looked directly at him.

"The trouble in our marriage began long before last summer. Russell was not the first affair in our marriage. We both know it, even if you don't admit it."

Stratton averted his gaze, but there was agreement in the faint nod of his head. It spoke volumes to Lovie.

"This is not what either of us signed up for. Stratton, I loved you when I married you. But I didn't know what real love was. I was following the life that was laid out for me by my mother, and her mother. It was what was expected of me. I dare say that was the same for you. We are not the same young, naïve, guileless people we were then. Why do you still want to go on?" she asked him. "Do you think we can? After all this?"

"Yes," he replied firmly, with typical bravado. "You're still my wife. We're still a family. I won't let it all go. I can't."

Lovie looked at her husband, listened to his words, and understood all. *I won't let go.*

Every man had his breaking point. For some, it would have come with the admission of an affair. The loss of face would have been all it took for a vain man to boot a woman out of the house. For others, the loss of something that was *his*, or worse, having someone else take something he treasured from him, was an act that a controlling man could never allow. Stratton fell into the latter category. If she looked at the situation through his eyes, it was simple. She was his. The children were his. He claimed everything, and his ego couldn't conceive of admitting defeat.

To be fair, she knew this about him when she'd married him. She'd relied on his strength and determination to build her home. He was her sole support. She depended on him.

She looked at her husband's face and saw the years they'd shared in the lines that coursed down his face and gathered at his eyes and in the gray hairs that blended with the brown. She had her gray hairs, too, she thought. Lord help them, there was no villain in this marriage. There was blame enough to share. They'd married so young. They hadn't yet realized that they were not the best match. Lovie approached her husband and reached out for his hand.

"It won't be the same," she warned him. "We have to set new boundaries. We can never go back to where we were."

He sighed and looked at his hands splayed across his thighs. She instinctively knew he looked at his wedding band. "So," he said, his voice low with defeat, "what are these new boundaries you need?"

Lovie returned to her chair and crossed her legs Indian style, her mind racing. She wasn't prepared for this discussion. Not yet. She ran her hands through her hair, pushing it back from her face, and looked at her husband.

"I don't know all the answers," she began. "But I do know what I need. And that's my summers at the beach house. My work with the sea turtles is nonnegotiable. It's important to me, and more, it's important to the turtles. I must be here early May. And I will stay until the last nest emerges. I'll manage with the children's school schedule somehow."

"I won't see you for months."

"You'll be traveling during this time anyway, Stratton. This schedule works for us."

He pursed his lips and met her gaze, measuring her resolve. This was a man known for his power of negotiation. She stared back at him, unbroken. She had come too far to retreat now. He must have seen her determination because he nodded in agreement.

"Will you be returning to our bedroom?" he asked pointedly.

Lovie's whole body stiffened at the thought of sharing his bed. "It's too soon to make that decision, Stratton." Then, remembering another discussion at another time, she added, "Let's take it day by day and see where we end up."

Stratton's shoulders drew back and he looked out for a long while at the sea. Lovie didn't press him but waited as tense as a cat curled on the chair.

"All right," he replied at length. "I can start with that."

Lovie's muscles uncoiled, and she moved one step closer to truce. "Those are the conditions that I need, Stratton. But I ask only one thing."

He didn't scowl or get angry, as she thought he might. Rather, his face was open, willing to hear her. She took heart.

"Stratton, we need counseling. I'd like us to talk more and to really hear what we're saying."

He shook his head obstinately. "I won't go to therapy."

"It's marriage counseling," she clarified. She pressed her hands together and spoke calmly and deliberately. "Stratton, I'm afraid of your anger. I can't live in the same house with you, afraid you'll strike out at me, or our children."

"It kills me to hear you say that. I'm so sorry I struck you, Lovie. I'll never strike you again. I swear," Stratton said with urgency.

"If I didn't believe you, I couldn't go back. But my fear is still there and it will take time. And there are other issues," she said, choosing not to throw his drinking and infidelity in his face now. "I know you have your issues, too. Please, Stratton."

He reached far forward across the distance between them to take her hand, so small in his. Then he patted it. "If it brings your forgiveness, we can try." He half smiled. "And see where we end up."

She returned his smile. "Yes, Stratton. We can try."

He placed his other hand over hers and held them tight, his thick gold band catching the last of the day's light. He bent to kiss her forehead, sealing their pact. Then he released her hands, rose, and went to the door. Opening it, she caught a glimpse of Palmer's and Cara's faces peering in before they quickly darted back. Stratton looked over his broad shoulder and offered her a ghost of a smile.

After he left, Lovie walked across the room and leaned on the doorjamb, peering out. She saw Stratton sitting on the front porch with Palmer and Cara on either side of him, talking. She rested her cheek against her hand, breathing in the sight. She watched him leave, her heart beating as softly in her chest as the wings of a dove.

"I'm going to take a walk," she told Vivian, then ventured a tired smile. "I need to think. Don't wait dinner for me. I'll be late."

Twenty-five

L ovie walked the beach and wrapped her patchwork shawl closer around her shoulders. In the distance, a lone cargo ship cruised toward a port far across the ocean, its line of red lights bobbing like lightning bugs. At her feet, a ghost crab skittered across her path. Breach Inlet was a tempest tonight, white-capped waves churning in the dangerous currents.

She approached the turnoff for the path to the cottage. To the left was the small dune. She had not had the strength to return to it, nor the desire. She stood at the foot of the dune, as a summer full of memories flitted through her mind, one more vivid than the next.

Their last night together had been a night very much like this one. Sultry, with a full moon that spread its silvery light across the sand. The stars ahead were dazzling, the air so still it had felt otherworldly.

Olivia.

Lovie went still. She heard Russell's voice in her head, calling her name. She felt the hair on her neck tingling and felt suddenly afraid. Was she losing her mind? Was her grief so desperate? But it had sounded so real . . . She waited another moment, listening intently, but heard only the gentle roar of the surf.

She shook her head, clearing it. She was tired, she thought. Imagining things.

"Enough," she said to herself. No more fears. Tonight was a night for decisions and reconciliation. She had to claim her life back, not only for her own welfare but also for that of her family.

Putting one foot before the other, she began to climb the dune. It was such a small dune to hold so many memories, she thought as her heels dug into the cold sand. It was wreathed with green vines and dotted with clumps of strong, unyielding sea oats, the roots of which went deep, holding the dune firm. This was where she and Russell had spread out the red-and-black checkered blanket and held each other while listening to the roar of the surf and the sea oats rustling and the beat of each other's heart.

She reached the top of the dune, awash in memories. Every year the dunes altered in configuration with the ravaging wind of winter storms. But her little dune persevered, she thought, letting her gaze cross the gentle contours of sand.

Her attention was caught by a small red flag sticking out from the sand. It was the same kind of flag that she and Russell had used to mark the false crawls during the project. Curious that the flag was way up here, she walked closer. A nest had never been laid here. It didn't make sense for a flag to have been planted on this dune. Who would have put it here?

As quickly as she had the thought, she knew the answer. Lovie's deadened heart felt a spark of life. Russell would be just this clever. She dropped to her knees and began to dig, like a dog on the scent. Every fiber in her being was on alert as she probed deeper, faster, the tiny shells in the sand scraping her tender skin and the sand pushing under her nails. When her fingers hit metal, she wasn't shocked.

Lovie pulled a small tin box from the hole and brushed away the sand. With a twinge in her heart, she recognized it. The box was decorated with perforations in the metal. It once had held shells on her back porch. Her heart beat harder in her chest as the realization of what this all meant bloomed in her thoughts. With trembling fingers, she opened the box with reverence.

There was a letter. The paper was fine and slightly yellowed from age and the elements. She opened it. A breeze caught the edges as she tilted the paper in the moonlight to read. She immediately recognized Russell's slanted, elegant penmanship.

March 15, 1975

My darling Olivia,

I don't blame you in the least for not coming to meet me. I know better than most the complicated bonds that tie us to our responsibilities. Yes, I confess I had hoped that you would come. I waited at the beach house all night, masked by the dark like the thief that I was, hoping against hope to steal you away.

I don't doubt for a moment that you loved me. Love me still. But you have made your decision. As promised, I will respect it.

But if you should ever change your mind, or if circumstances occur where you ever find your life untenable, I want you to have the freedom to leave—even if you do not choose to come to me.

You carry my love within you. A day will never dawn nor a sunset slip into the horizon when I will not think of you. I accept that the mind often dictates the heart. Yet I believe that the heart is the truer guide.

So, if in the course of time, you should want to come to me, do not hesitate. Know that I will be waiting for you. You will always have my heart—my love.

Always,
Russell

Lovie folded the letter slowly, then pressed the paper to her heart. "Russell!" She said his name aloud, knowing she was heard.

She understood all now. Russell had come to the beach house on March 15. He'd sat in the dark on her back porch, waiting for her. When she didn't come, he'd written this letter. But where could he leave it? She could imagine him thinking this situation through in his organized manner. He'd paced the porch, searching for possibilities. He knew he couldn't slip the letter under the door, or leave it propped on the porch table for fear that someone else might discover it and read it. He must have exhausted a litany of possibilities before he settled on his plan. When he'd found this tin box on her porch, when he devised his plan, he must have smiled with the memory of the Point. He would have emptied the shells from the box and placed his letter inside to protect it. Then he would have taken one of the flags from the red bucket and climbed to their dune. There, at a place that held precious memories for them both, he had buried his letter, marking the spot with the flag in such a way that only she would understand. His intent was for her—and only her—to find the treasure.

And at last, she had.

Lovie felt the tight string that she'd held herself together with for so many months begin to loosen. She took great, heaving breaths, and at last, the knot was released and she let loose all the anguish and disappointment and heartbreak that had been locked inside her. Lovie howled at the moon, not caring who heard her. She sobbed loud and freely, stretching out on the sand, belly to the earth, clutching his letter to her heart.

Lovie lay on her and Russell's dune, her sanctuary, and felt her tears flow as freely as a welcoming rain, nourishing her soul, bringing it back to life. Her heart grew roots to this hallowed ground. Closing her eyes, she heard again Russell's voice on the surf. *Olivia*. Smiling, she fell asleep, and in her dreams, he returned to her.

When she awoke, the night was chilled and intensely quiet. Stars shone cold overhead. She was curled on her side, her knees up, shivering, with Russell's letter still clutched at her chest. She pulled herself up to sit on the dune, the damp cool of morning waking her further. She saw the letter in her hand and, kissing it, tucked it into her pants pocket. The spark of her self-confidence had been reignited. It glowed as a small ember now, but she would continue to feed it until she felt it blazing inside her.

She shook the sand from her hair and rubbed her face with her palms. What time it was, she couldn't guess, but the softening of the darkness told her that dawn was near.

Looking out at the sea, she stiffened when she caught sight of a hulking, shadowy creature in the surf. It sat at the edge of the beach where water met sand, a great prehistoric beast sniffing the air. It was a loggerhead!

Her senses went on alert and she crouched lower on the dunes. She'd seen sea turtles on the beach many times before, but never had she witnessed one emerging from the sea. This female turtle had heard the call of her ancestors and journeyed through spirals of swift water and a living broth of plankton and invertebrates. She ignored the hunger in her belly to push on past schools of great fish and solitary sharks, following instincts that had guided mothers of her kind for more than two hundred million years. When at last she reached her home shores, she mingled with the other turtles in the swells. Mating was a tempestuous contest of wills. Then she left the male, to swim alone on her voyage of continuity. Inside her body, she carried the hope of the next generation of sea turtles.

Now she'd arrived at this border between water and land. This was her moment of reckoning. She would have to leave all she knew, all that was safe, to face the dangers of the unknown. To climb across the vast and dangerous distance to the dunes and nest.

Yet this powerful female waited. What instincts were coming to play at this moment? Lovie wondered. Did she sense the stealthy movement of a predator in the shadows? Perhaps she sensed Lovie's presence on the dune.

"You're safe, mother," Lovie whispered to her, tears welling up. "I won't hurt you."

The great turtle slowly turned at the shoreline and lumbered back into the sea. Lovie knew a fierce disappointment, but her breath caught at the sight of a large chunk missing from the turtle's rear shell. It had to be a shark bite. Poor mother! Magnificent beast, it's no wonder you are wary. She'd been wounded, but here she was, resilient and determined to continue her destiny. Her return to the sea was not a retreat. She would try again. Perhaps later today at a different beach. Perhaps tomorrow at this same location. The decision she made would be hers alone, guided by her instinct and experience.

The first pink rays of dawn broke through the darkness and slowly stretched across the horizon to usher in a new day. Lovie felt her soul expand with light to become part of something so much bigger than her mere self. She felt at peace knowing that at the end of her time here on earth, her name would be written not in this sand but in heaven.

Sea Turtle Journal

July 3, 1975

Saw a sea turtle emerge from the sea at 3rd Avenue. She sat in the shallow water of the shoreline for a while, then returned to the sea. What prompted her decision not to come ashore? Must look for nest tomorrow, or the following day.

This magnificent, wounded sea turtle taught me that life is a series of decisions. My challenge is to endure the consequences of my decisions—come what may. What good was it to sit and mope over what might have been? I am alive and must face another decision today. And yet another the next day. And so on, and so on, stroke after stroke in this crazy current we call life. Like the loggerhead, though bitten by predators, I must persevere. She is a solitary swimmer.

Aren't we all in the end? We enter and exit this life alone.

Twenty-six

~

Present Day

L ovie rocked in her chair on the porch in the hush of twilight, the chill of the night seeping into her tired bones. She
reached up to tug her shawl a little closer, but even this effort was
too much. The past felt closer to her than the present. When she
closed her eyes, she saw the faces of those who had already made
the journey to the other side. They clustered around her, pressing close—Stratton, who had died quickly from a massive heart
attack at his club; her brother Mickey; her father; her mother.
And, of course, Russell. She felt his presence strongly now, much
closer than the rest. She listened for his voice. But only the rise
and fall of the cicadas and the occasional cry of a night bird disturbed the deep silence.

Across from her, the calico cat was curled on a cushion in a
deep sleep. How Lovie longed to sleep like that! Since the cancer
had spread to conquer her frail body, the pain awakened her frequently during the night, so she never felt rested. What would it
be like to close her eyes and sleep as she did when she was young,
without aches and pains, without tossing and turning? And to
dream! Oh, that would be heaven.

On the table, the candle in the lantern was sputtering. Yet

its pale flicker valiantly glowed like the pale moon beginning its ascent in the sky. She remembered a night way back when she identified with the moon on its solitary path across the night sky. That night, so very long ago, shone brighter in her memory tonight.

Those were sad days, but she no longer felt the painful stabs of the past. Time had mellowed her to a complacent acceptance. She had consented to life, discovered new joys, welcomed grandchildren, and in the end had discovered there was great contentment in the balance.

She turned her gaze from the ocean to her daughter sitting in the chair beside her. She smiled wistfully. Now, here was the swing of the pendulum to balance, she thought. Her own sweet Caretta . . . After so many years apart, they sat here again, mother and daughter, on the porch of their beloved beach house. She studied Cara's face, the proud straight nose and dark shining eyes inherited from her father. Her long neck, her full lips so striking now. She smiled. The awkward, brainy duckling had grown up to be a swan. Lovie's gaze shifted to see their hands entwined. Though they didn't speak, this bond spoke eloquently of the deep love they shared.

She felt again the heavy weight of memories on her heart. Love, yes. Love was always there between them. But sadly, there had been discord, too. Disagreement. Distance. Too many years of misunderstandings and cold silences.

Lovie looked out over the beach and recalled simpler days when she was a young mother and Palmer and Cara were children playing tag with the waves. Everything seemed so much easier then. She gave an order to her children and it was obeyed. She was the source of all that mattered to them—food, shelter and, of course, love. What she needed most in those early days was endurance and physical strength. But she *had* paid attention to her children. She'd watched them with a keen eye, relishing their achievements, helping them through difficult moments, monitoring their progress with more focus than she'd ever offered the sea turtles. Even so young, they'd given her clues as to who they were going to grow up to become.

She closed her eyes and chuckled at the memory. Cara and Palmer, the rogue and the rascal.

"Mama? It's getting chilly. Would you like to go in?"

Lovie turned her head. Cara's eyes were shining with worry. In the spring, her prayer had been for God to send her daughter back home. Cara had come, and stayed, and cared for her. Now the summer was over and winter beckoned. Cara being here now was the answer to her prayer.

"Caretta?" she began in a raspy voice. There was so much she wanted to say to her, to explain. She felt the minutes of her life slipping away like sand between her fingers.

"Yes, Mama?"

Lovie looked into Cara's eyes, felt her hand in hers. "You're a good girl."

Cara's smile trembled. "Thank you, Mama. There's nothing more I ever wanted to hear from you." She bent to kiss her mother's cheek. "Lord, you're as cold as ice. Are you sure you won't come inside?"

Lovie gently shook her head and squeezed Cara's hand. The effort was monumental, but Cara understood.

"I'll just go get you a blanket. I'll be right back."

Lovie began a hacking coughing spell that shook her body like a rag doll and left her gasping for breath. It felt like she was drowning in her own body. She felt her heart flutter in a panic like a bird trapped in her chest. She looked out at the ocean, her old friend, seeking comfort while her breathing slowly settled.

Soon, she heard from the sea.

When she could, she leaned back in her rocker, breathing heavily. Her gaze fell to the wicker porch table where she and Flo and Miranda had shared so many evenings. On top, her sea turtle journal lay open beside her pen. She had been writing her entry, as she had for so many years. The breeze fluttered the pages, skimming through a lifetime of days and nights in an instant.

It seemed to her that her life had sped by as quickly. And throughout, the sea turtles had been her constant. They'd been her lifelong source of inspiration and comfort. Russell had understood that about her. Didn't every woman need a creative source that reflected her alone, and not her husband or her children?

Over the span of fifty years, Lovie's simple sea turtle protection efforts had grown from being a local Turtle Lady to being part of a statewide program under the direction of the South Carolina Department of Natural Resources. Other programs now existed in Florida, Georgia, and North Carolina, as well as hospitals for sea turtle rehabilitation. Lovie had proudly held many permits—since that first one had arrived at such a serendipitous moment in 1975. Now when she watched the mother sea turtles return to nest, she gained great satisfaction knowing that these females were hatchlings that she had helped survive the journey from the nest to the sea so long ago.

It was October, and another nesting season, her last, was over. Her beloved sea turtles had swum off to forage in warmer waters. She missed them already. Each of the many times she had followed a sea turtle as it crawled back into the ocean, Lovie waited until that final moment when the turtle lifted her large head to take a final breath, then slipped under the dark veil of the water. Lovie had always been transfixed by the sight of those powerful flippers propelling her forward into a mysterious world as she jubilantly swam home.

She sighed heavily. Now her life had come full circle. The season was over. Her children were grown and self-sufficient. Her marriage vows fulfilled. Her duties and responsibilities were finished at last. She had done her best. She could finally let go.

Olivia!

She smiled. Russell was calling to her, more impatiently. He was coming for her—and she was ready.

I'm here, her heart called to him. *At the beach house, as I once promised you I would be, so long ago. I'm free to go with you, my love. Come for me!*

Lovie's hand moved to open the worn black leather Bible on her lap. Miranda's gift to her had been such a comfort all these years. She pulled out a sheet of paper, as thin and soft with age as spun silk. Russell's letter. She couldn't read it in the dim light, but she didn't need to. Each word was written on her heart.

Olivia!

He was closer now; his voice was louder, filling her head. She looked out to the sea and saw a mist rolling in, soft and pearlescent. A foghorn bellowed in a melancholy toll.

Olivia!

She clutched the letter to her heart as the first pain struck. It stabbed like a knife, cutting deep. Her breath stilled in her chest as the earthly bonds were severed. At last, she was free to go to him.

"Russell!" she released on a final breath, and in a sudden burst of light, she was swimming under the waves.